MISCHANCE CREEK

GARRY DISHER

First published in Great Britain in 2026 by Viper,
an imprint of Profile Books Ltd
29 Cloth Fair
London
EC1A 7JQ

www.viperbooks.co.uk

First published in Australia in 2025 by The Text Publishing Company

Copyright © Garry Disher, 2025

1 3 5 7 9 10 8 6 4 2

Typeset in Freight Text by MacGuru Ltd
Printed and bound in Great Britain by
CPI Group (UK) Ltd, Croydon CR0 4YY

The moral right of the author has been asserted.

All rights reserved. Without limiting the rights under copyright reserved above, no part of this publication may be reproduced, stored or introduced into a retrieval system, or transmitted, in any form or by any means (electronic, mechanical, photocopying, recording or otherwise), without the prior written permission of both the copyright owner and the publisher of this book.

A CIP catalogue record for this book is available from the British Library.

Our product safety representative in the EU is BGC Sustainability & Compliance, 7 avenue du Général Leclerc, Paris, 75014, France. https://baldwinglobalconsulting.com

ISBN 978 1 80522 601 7
eISBN 978 1 80522 602 4

PRAISE FOR GARRY DISHER

'Garry Disher is one of Australia's most admired novelists ... A superb chronicler of cop culture'
Sunday Times

'A terrific plot, nuanced characters and solid procedures, served up on refreshing new turf. Done with smooth, assured mastery'
The New York Times

'Disher keeps the various narrative plates spinning with the dexterity of a master storyteller for an engrossing tale of characters who range from morally ambiguous to wholly indefensible'
Guardian

'Only a writer at the top of his game like Garry Disher could control such a colourful cast and complex plot while maintaining an atmosphere of paranoid suspense'
The Times

'Disher's ability to create atmosphere and threat in the wide open spaces of South Australia rivals James Lee Burke's in the bayous of Louisiana, and that is no small feat ... Here, Disher underlines his exceptional talent'
Daily Mail

'[The] characterisation is every bit as acutely realised as one expects from this award-winning writer'
Financial Times

ALSO BY GARRY DISHER AND AVAILABLE FROM VIPER

The Way It Is Now
Sanctuary
Under the Cold Bright Lights

THE PAUL HIRSCH MYSTERIES
Bitter Wash Road
Peace
Consolation
Day's End
Mischance Creek

THE HAL CHALLIS INVESTIGATIONS
The Dragon Man
Kittyhawk Down
Snapshot
Chain of Evidence
Blood Moon
Whispering Death
Signal Loss

For Carmel Shute, Karina Kilmore and Robert Gott

1

A Thursday morning in mid-November, and Senior Constable Paul Hirschhausen was getting through a firearms audit. He could only snatch two hours here, a day there for it, checking gun safes and ammunition storage out in the dry back country halfway between Adelaide and the Flinders Ranges. Next on today's list: Mark Button, a Lee Enfield .303 rifle.

Button lived on a small sheep property behind the Razorback. To reach it, Hirsch left the Barrier Highway south of Tiverton and made a slow loop east, juddering over corrugations and stone eruptions before slowing for a buckled stock ramp at the entrance to a short driveway. He turned in and parked his SA Police HiLux outside a house with stone walls and a rusting corrugated iron roof – a converted shearers' quarters, remnant of a past when the big sheep properties boasted housing for overseers, cooks, shearers and station hands. Fran Button's old station wagon was missing but Mark's battered Jeep sat in the carport, with a faded sticker in the rear window reading: *If You Don't Know, Vote No*. Another remnant, this one from the recent referendum. Hirsch had seen hundreds of similar declarations back then, on cars, fences, shop windows. If You Don't Know, Find Out, he always thought sourly.

He stiffened: a rifle shot, sharp, full-throated. He drew his pistol. Another shot, then a third. They came regularly after that: heavy cracks, evenly spaced, that repeated from echoey hillslope to limestone reef to farm shed and out along the road behind him. Understanding what it meant now, he reholstered the Glock and crossed Button's yard. Reached a tired fence beyond the implement shed, slipped despondently between the wires rather than chance the top barbed strand, and headed through star thistles to a killing field.

A scene familiar to him, these past two or three months. Skeletal sheep in a stockyard pen, a farmer morosely watching, and a professional shooter leaning over a top rail to fire straight into one skull after another. Hirsch watched for a while, unwilling to break in. Mark Button was standing clear, rubbing his right thumb anxiously, repetitively, against his forefinger. The shooter was a local professional named Brad Ullmer. He was smooth and efficient, and each old ewe – already drooping, panting and barely alive – dropped like a stone.

Time passed; the shooting paused. Button crossed wearily to rejoin Ullmer. They had both spotted Hirsch by now, and looked across at him as they conferred, then Button beckoned. As Hirsch approached, Ullmer peeled away to a dusty white twin-cab ute parked in the shade of a ghost gum. A gunrack inside the rear window. A towbar, dust, dents; a cracked brake light. Hirsch saw him lean in, back out with a thermos and a food container and flop in the dirt, his spine against one wheel.

Hirsch turned to Button and held out his hand. 'Sorry to interrupt, Mark.'

Button, about fifty, small, wiry, badly shaven, was regretful. 'Won't shake hands with ya: been dragging carcasses since dawn.'

Hirsch glanced instinctively at Button's hand, then across the stony ground to a recently dug pit. A flatbed truck and a large yellow excavator were parked nearby, casting a bit of shade for the driver, who waved tepidly. Hirsch knew he'd been digging similar pits all over the Mid North.

'How're things?' Hirsch asked, knowing it was a pointless question.

'Well, as you can see, I'm still alive,' Button said, standing side-on to Hirsch in that self-conscious way of men. 'Rather have my feet up in front of the TV, though. This is your patrol day?'

'Not this time. The firearms audit has rolled around again.'

Button sighed, pushed back his hat, checked his watch. 'Can't Fran do it when she gets back? She's shopping.'

Hirsch shook his head. 'Afraid not.'

Button was the registered owner. His wife wasn't supposed to know where he kept the gun-safe key.

'Well, can you give us half an hour or so? Time's money.'

'Sure,' Hirsch said.

'I just need to drag this batch to the pit and move the next batch in, and it'll soon be over.'

'Go for it.'

A pause, an embarrassed wince. 'It's, you know ...' A rush of words: 'I'd do the shooting myself, but I won't lie, it'd break my heart. Just watching's bad enough.'

Hirsch clasped Button's shoulder briefly. 'Take your time.'

Alone again, Hirsch turned and headed to where Ullmer was having his smoko. The shooter stood as he drew near: a tall, gaunt man in his late forties. Heavy work pants, a thick khaki shirt, battered boots, blurred tatts on each forearm. Stubble and nicotine-yellow teeth. His gaze met Hirsch's then flicked away. A man whose occupation – like that of septic-tank cleaner, another local job – was necessary but unpalatable.

'Brad.'

'Paul,' Ullmer said, tossing the dregs of his tea in the dust and pulling his rolling tobacco from his top pocket. A quick, shy glance: 'Patrol day?'

'Firearms audit.'

Ullmer nodded towards his rifle, resting stock down against the side panel of his ute. 'You already checked me out.'

As a registered shooter, Ullmer was licensed to cull kangaroos and feral dogs, goats and pigs. In leaner times he took tourists on hunting trips and did a bit of handyman work. His permits had always been in order and his guns legally secured. 'You're good, just wanted to say hello,' Hirsch said.

'Hell of a thing,' Ullmer said, jerking his head towards the stockyard before rolling, licking and lighting his cigarette.

'Sad is what it is,' Hirsch said.

'Weeks, I been doing this. Weeks and weeks.'

'Must get you down.'

Ullmer shrugged. 'Someone has to do it.'

He drew deeply on his cigarette – already a damp, bedraggled-looking thing – as if it might save his life. Jetted smoke away from Hirsch, examined the butt, dropped it in the dirt, ground it out with the toe of one boot. 'Filthy habit,' he muttered.

It was Hirsch's turn to shrug: each to his own.

'Better get back to it,' Ullmer said.

Hirsch watched him return to the stockyard and help Button finish running sheep from the main pen to the killing pen. Only a small number, he noticed. To cut down on panic and distress? Then, giving Ullmer an over-to-you gesture, Button joined Hirsch and together they watched the shooter load his rifle, swing the barrel neatly over the top rail, start firing again.

'How many?' asked Hirsch eventually.

Button shook his head in weary disgust. 'Got a permit for two hundred – old, unproductive stock, quote unquote.'

'Out of how many?'

'Twelve hundred,' Button said. He'd been losing ten ewes a day to hunger and thirst, he said. He'd long run out of hay – so had the nation, pretty much – and starving kangaroos had stripped what pasture he had left. Grain was expensive; he was nearly broke. 'Don't know what I'm going to do if the bank comes calling.'

Hirsch said nothing. He was sorry. He was powerless.

'This time last year,' Button went on, gesturing at Ullmer and the miserable ewes, 'sheep were worth over a hundred bucks a head. Now they're worth nothing. Can't even give them away. None of the abattoirs will take them, and even if they did, they'd pay bugger all and the transport costs would cripple me. Breaks my heart, doing this, but it's worse to let them starve or die of thirst.'

He was being paid a small sum per head from the national flock reduction scheme. 'Just a few bucks, I hasten to add.' He glared, as if Hirsch had accused him of ingratitude. 'A drop in the ocean if you consider that I've already spent a shitload of money on feed this year. For nothing.'

Unexpectedly then, Button cocked his head at Hirsch and said, half-humorously, 'The whole thing's brought out the leftie in me.'

'Really,' said Hirsch flatly.

Button was no leftie. He came from a sturdy man-on-the-land tradition and had been vocal during the Indigenous Voice referendum campaign. He'd be voting 'no', he stated, because he was 'sick of saying sorry to the Abos' and feared a yes vote would mean he'd have to give his land back to the local Ngadjuri people. He wasn't alone in saying these things, and Hirsch had sometimes felt surrounded by men and women trying to hold on for dear life. Suddenly their options were dwindling and their tenancy felt insecure.

Even more insecure now, of course, given the drought. With the Mid North changing around them in bewildering and undesirable ways, the locals felt pushed closer to dispossession. What an irony.

'Yep,' Button said. 'Take the big supermarkets. Fucking us over, parasitic bloody, price-gouging cunts ... All we want is a fair price for what we produce.'

'Maybe you could diversify,' Hirsch suggested. 'Drought-resistant crops. Give up grazing altogether.'

Button looked at Hirsch as if he were mad, then together they watched as Ullmer fired another headshot, and another, before removing the cartridge clip. Seeing him glance across at them, faintly irritated, Button sighed again. 'Better get back to it.'

'Sure.'

Hirsch stayed until the end, watching the last ewe tumble into the pit and the excavator nudge soil over the mass grave before crawling on its tracks to the rear of the truck, where it was soon loaded and Button was counting hundred-dollar notes into the driver's hand, then Ullmer's. So that Hirsch felt he was adding insult to injury later when he dutifully examined the man's gun safe, drank the man's tea.

2

Drank the man's tea ...

Hirsch was awash with tea, always, on the days he patrolled, audited firearms or simply popped in to say hello. The ritual was unvarying. The lonely people of the back country – a struggling farmer, a retired shearer, a newly married oldest son, a widow with a schizophrenic daughter – would check that he'd had the good sense to park out of the molten sun, then invite him into a hot, dim kitchen for a cuppa and maybe a rock bun or stale shortbread from the Tiverton general store. Always stale – they were kept in a tin for best, for visitors. Not that anyone dropped in these days: the endless heat, the cost of fuel, the general despondency. Then, seated at a scratched and chipped wooden or Formica table, Hirsch, the bringer of news, would be grilled. Had he popped in on Pete Jarvis yet? His windmill broke and he's had to cart water. Is it true Shirley Reid's kids are back living at home? Couldn't make a go of it in the city, apparently. And Trina Gould's baby must be due soon.

And Hirsch would grill his hosts gently in return. Did you get your bedroom fan fixed? Have you got enough food to be going on with? Anything you want popped in the post? Or he might replace a fuse. Inflate a back tyre with the HiLux's cigarette-lighter pump. Fetch down a box of Christmas decorations from the top cupboard.

And the drought. They'd say, 'Sure is dry.' And he'd respond, 'Sure is.' And someone, a joker, might add, 'Been watching that cloud since January.' And Hirsch would laugh, just as he'd laughed last week, or at the last place, and would again this afternoon and next week, knowing there was no cloud in the sky above him. This drought was worse than 1967, according to the old-timers whose fathers had almost walked off the land back then, or 2008 or 2024, according to later generations, who were thinking of pulling their kids out of boarding school in Adelaide and sending them to Redruth High. Maybe climate change would be mentioned – slyly humorous eyes expecting Hirsch to side with science rather than, as the locals considered far more likely, the immutable cycling of the seasons. After all, he wasn't from the land: his mindset was different. And he wore a uniform, which kind of lumped him in with those big-city types who closed down rural banks, post offices and clinics, amalgamated primary schools and expected you to do everything online.

And so he laughed, even though he didn't often feel up to it these days, knowing that the rituals of talk and tea and buns and laughter kept him in the fold. They stood for 'How're you doing?' out in a land of isolated homesteads crouched along dusty, rarely travelled back roads.

Next stop, Alastair Stanyer, who owned two rifles – a Remington .243 and a Lithgow .303 – and a Barathrum Arms shotgun. Hirsch texted his destination to his boss at the Redruth police station, then rattled along bad roads for ninety minutes to a region south-east of the Mischance Creek ruins and turned in at a narrow, bullet-holed sign: *A Stanyer*.

Stanyer was an old name in the district, dating back to the 1850s discovery of copper, further south near Redruth. The first Stanyer had made his pile in the usual way: not from digging holes in the ground but selling buckets, shovels, pickaxes, boots, dungarees and shirts to those who did. And dresses, tablecloths, napkins, canned food and pianos to their wives. When the copper played out, the Stanyers switched to making fortunes from cereal crops and fine merino wool. Now only two Stanyers remained: Mitchell – prosperous, married to the mayor – and Alastair, his black-sheep younger brother.

Funny how two brothers could take such diverse paths after sharing the same shitty childhood. According to the gossip Hirsch picked up in the pub, the shop, at Saturday tennis, the Stanyer brothers and their mother had been victims of a pious, churchgoing prick of a man. The stories were graphic enough for Hirsch to visualise the atmosphere in the Stanyer house: heavy footsteps approaching; the boys and their mother freezing as a shadow falls through a doorway. But where Mitchell had later flourished, Alastair had pursued his interest in booze, drugs and student politics, and was punished for it. When both parents died in a light-plane crash, Mitch inherited the big house and most of the sprawling Stanyer acreage. Alastair got a few blighted paddocks out in rain-shadow country.

And he hadn't even held on to that. After a decade of binge-drinking, risky investments and mounting debts he was eventually bailed out by Mitch, and now owned nothing but an old Land Rover, three firearms and the clothes on his back. He lived rent-free in an old mustering outstation on the land that had once been his. He was pretty much a recluse because, the locals said, Mitch's wife Clarissa – the mayor – didn't want her husband to have anything to do with him.

Hirsch rumbled over a stock ramp and followed a track at a walking pace, over and around stone reefs for four kilometres, flinching each time the chassis of the Toyota bottomed out. Finally, chased by a dust cloud, he saw the outstation come into view and pulled into the meagre shade thrown by a stand of pepper trees. He got out and made a circle of Alastair's Land Rover. It was a classic Series II, a short-wheelbase two-seater with a canvas-topped tray. Sad-looking now: a big dent in the rear bumper, old grime on the side panels, a tear in the tonneau cover and the tyres needed air. It hadn't been driven since the last time he was here, a month earlier.

He crossed a yard pocked by little anthills. Eyed the shack – local stone, logs and rusty corrugated iron – for signs of life. Nothing apart from a generator chugging somewhere at the rear. A crooked chimney and a listing front porch. A side sleepout of sun-blasted fibro sheeting. A TV antenna on a tower fifteen metres high. Drawn curtains: well, nothing odd about that, out in this country. Parsley dying in one terracotta pot, a geranium thriving in another.

At that moment the buckled front door was tugged inwards, the bottom edge catching on worn linoleum, and Stanyer appeared with a Jack Russell at his heels. Hirsch needn't have driven all this way, he said. 'Could've just phoned.'

It wasn't an unusual response. People didn't want to be a nuisance; they were fine; their situations didn't warrant the long drive on inhospitable roads. Or they were shy, unused to conversation, or found human company a strain.

Or they had something to hide.

'I needed to call in anyway, Al,' Hirsch said, bending to pat the dog. 'It's the annual firearms audit. Gun safe, ammo, access – you know the drill.'

It might have been a last straw for Alastair Stanyer. He sagged, shook his head, stepped back to let Hirsch enter. 'Seems like you only just done it,' he muttered.

'This time last year, Al, believe it or not.'

Stanyer shook his head, a man who looked old but was barely into his forties. Thin, wiry, with the dark, permanently burdened expression of one who believed life would always deliver disappointment. But edgier today, and he was holding himself stiffly. A bruised forearm and a cut lip.

'Been in the wars?'

'Fell off a ladder,' Stanyer said, turning away and speaking over his shoulder. 'Well, let's get it over with.'

'Let's,' agreed Hirsch. The little house was stifling, stale, and he wasn't likely to be offered tea and a biscuit.

The entryway opened on to a living area with a fireplace at the far end, a sink, fridge and stove in the near corner and two fraying armchairs on a faded carpet in between. A boxy old TV and DVD player on two shelves; DVDs at a lean on a third. Hirsch glanced at the titles as he passed: *Nowhere to Hide*, *Million Dollar Murders* and other true crime shows, Bourne and James Bond thrillers, *Mama Mia*, outback ute musters and Michael McIntyre. The air, more stifling now, was stirred by a clacking portable fan.

Placing his broad-brimmed summer-uniform hat on the dining table, Hirsch followed Stanyer through to a corridor with doors opening onto a bedroom, a bathroom and laundry, and finally a room fitted with a desk, an ancient computer, a grimy bare mattress propped against one wall and a gun safe. They went in. Perspiration was breaking out on every centimetre of Hirsch's body, responding to the heat of an unmediated sun beating down on roofing iron.

'Thusly,' Stanyer said, gesturing.

The gun safe was steel, purpose-built, bolted to the wall. Hirsch tugged on the door. Locked.

'Key?'

'I know the rules. I keep it separate. And my paperwork's up to date.'

Hirsch nodded. 'I know, I checked. If you could show me the guns themselves?'

It was as if Hirsch were being deeply trying, but Alastair Stanyer left the room, his trailing bootlaces snapping at the worn floor, a hole in his shorts showing a wink of white flesh, and returned with a key on a haybale twine. Old sweat gusted as he approached with the key.

'Thanks, but I'd like you to open it, please.'

'Whatever you like,' Stanyer said, further put-upon.

Hirsch tensed – habit and Stanyer's mood – with his gun hand near the butt of his holstered Glock. But Stanyer merely opened the safe and stepped aside, saying 'Thusly,' again.

Hirsch peered in, then compared the contents with the clipboard list. Lithgow .303, Remington .243 fitted with a scope, and a Barathrum Arms shotgun. All were worn, clean, well cared for. 'If you could open each weapon, please.'

'They're not weapons. I use them to hunt.'

'Al, I need to check they're not loaded.'

Stanyer shrugged, removed each firearm and showed the empty clips and chambers.

'Ammunition.'

Stanyer almost rolled his eyes as he eased himself down onto one knee with a grunt of pain. He lifted a corner of the carpet and stabbed at the keypad of a little floor safe. 'Stored separate, like I'm supposed to.'

Hirsch cast a quick look into the safe, saw loose shotgun shells and packeted cartridges and said, 'Thanks, all good. Same time next year.'

'Yeah, but it's not as if I won't see you in the meantime. You're round here every month.'

'True,' admitted Hirsch. 'Part of the job.'

Following Stanyer back to the main room, he paused before collecting his hat from the table. 'You doing all right?'

'Fine.'

'Anything you need, next time I'm passing through?'

'She's right,' Alastair Stanyer said. He wouldn't look at Hirsch. Kept plucking at a shirt button that was already loose.

Then, unexpectedly: 'You in a rush?'

Lonely, Hirsch thought. Unmarried, out of luck, mostly ignored by his luckier older brother. Not old yet, but who'd look after him when he was?

Sadness crept over Hirsch as he thought of his own situation; his mother. How could he help her properly when he was stuck up here, three hours to the north? Wearing himself out investigating diesel theft and checking firearms. Running long-range patrols that covered areas the size of a small nation. Sinking litres of tar-black tea and stale biscuits every single fucking day. He checked his watch. At this rate he wouldn't be back at the little one-room Tiverton police station until mid-afternoon, with paperwork to be done as soon as he got there.

But he was a country cop, and the job was as much welfare counselling as catching villains. 'No rush.'

'Cuppa?'

'Sure. Actually, just a glass of water.'

Poured from a plastic jug in the fridge. Hirsch sipped: the water was tinged with the flavours of plastic and the minerally earth. Bore water, he thought. Boiled to death. No one had water in their household tanks after this long without rain.

They sat at the table, Alastair Stanyer still plucking at his button until – Hirsch was unkindly pleased to see – it finally slipped its moorings.

'Damn thing,' Stanyer said, embarrassed, turning to place it on the bench behind him. Now he began to run his thumb and forefinger up and down the barrel of his water glass. Shot Hirsch a quick, shy glance. 'These firearm checks – you ever had to fine anyone?'

Hirsch's thought: he's got another gun somewhere. Bouncing around in the back of his Land Rover or propped up against the wall of his toolshed or under his bed.

Or he's just trying to make conversation. Hirsch sipped from his glass. 'Sometimes. The odd bloke who keeps his twenty-two loaded on the back seat. Last year I had a five-year-old show me exactly where daddy kept the key to the gun safe.'

That amused Stanyer. His eyes creased. Then lost focus, his hollow cheeks and recessed eyes darkening in the kitchen's dim light. Hirsch took a final glance around the place. On a shelf above the little refrigerator was a *Women's Weekly* cookbook, a target-shooting trophy and a framed photograph: school cadets, the boys holding rifles.

'Boarding school?'

'Westbury,' Alastair said. 'Me and Mitch both went there.'

He elaborated, Hirsch reading between the lines of what he didn't reveal. School of the Air until the brothers were twelve, and then, in what probably amounted to a permanent rupture in the bonds of family life, they'd been shipped down to the Westbury School. Five years in a crowded dormitory. Misery, according to an exposé on 7.30 last year.

The first-week induction – fists, boots, waterboarding and anal insertions – had gone on through to Year 12 for some of the boys. Also freezing classrooms, crap food, muddy cadet camps and spit-screaming masters.

Nan Washburn, who raised miniature ponies in Tiverton, once told Hirsch that she'd been removed from her mother's hugs and her father's boisterous love just when she'd needed them most. She'd coped afterwards, making the most of life, but some of her boarding-school peers had struggled in adult life. But then, as she'd told Hirsch, there were plenty who thrived afterwards, making use of school connections that encouraged good fortune to fall into their laps. 'Like Mitchell Stanyer,' she said. 'Born-to-rule. Like his wife.'

Hirsch drained his glass now, stood and said, 'Well, miles to go before I sleep.'

'You know Frost?' Stanyer said.

Hirsch looked at him blankly.

'Robert Frost. It's from a poem.'

'Oh, right,' Hirsch said. 'No, just something my old man used to say.'

And suddenly his father's face was in his head, the timbre of his father's voice was in his ears and a rush of feelings swept across him. He grabbed his hat and was about to step off the veranda when the diesel generator cut out.

'Ah, fuck,' Stanyer said, slumping against the doorjamb. 'Last of the fuel. I was sure I had another day or two left.'

Hirsch hesitated, then said, 'I've got ten litres I can let you have.'

Stanyer screwed up his face. 'Can't pay ya. Bit short this week.'

'On the house,' Hirsch said. He crossed to the HiLux, leaned in and returned with a full jerrycan, the weight of the diesel leaning him over. 'Show me the way.'

The generator was in a small wooden enclosure at the rear of the house. Dead weeds in a garden box, a ladder against the wall. And a shooting range, Hirsch realised. A long stretch of dirt leading to an empty tomato tin on an old tree stump and a few shot-up tins lying in the dirt on either side of it. Closer to, a dozen ejected .22 cartridges.

Hirsch gave a jerk of his chin as he poured the diesel. 'Keeping your eye in?'

Alastair Stanyer shuffled his feet. 'I'm allowed.'

Hirsch wasn't going to arrest him for taking potshots at tin cans, or even check the regulations. Out in the middle of nowhere, and not a house in sight.

A glug and the last stream of fuel ran into the tank. 'That should do you.'

'Thanks. I'll order a tanker tomorrow.'

'Good-oh,' Hirsch said, waving goodbye.

3

Hirsch brooded as he headed back the way he'd come. He could've stayed longer with the guy. What a life: far from the nearest town, shitty internet, bugger-all mobile phone reception. No bus at the end of anyone's driveway out here, let alone a bank, doctor or dentist less than an hour away. If someone like Alastair Stanyer fell off a ladder or suffered from some other chronic painful or life-threatening condition, he might wait eight or twelve weeks to get an appointment.

Next on the list, Trina and Pete Gould: Mossberg 802 rifle. Heading north and east now, Hirsch eyed the dusty emptiness on either side. An emptiness more apparent than real, he knew that now. Busy ants, sometimes an emu, an echidna or a snake. Dark smudges of mulga scrub that broke up the reddish-tan stretches of denuded soil; skeletal sheep huddled in the shade of heat-stunned gumtrees; bleached roofs squatting behind cypress hedges far off the road. And on every horizon a thin, blue-grey line of hills dividing the dirt from the sky.

With fifteen minutes to go before he reached the Goulds' house, he tapped a number in his contacts. Seconds passed. The ringtone played out, replaced by his mother's voice on the answering machine – the old chirpy version, which only served to complicate his sadness. He left a message, and ten minutes later was parking under a straggly gum beside the Goulds' transportable cabin. No sign of Pete's Pajero, but Trina's little Corolla was there, and she let him in, saying, 'Hot enough for you?'

Through to the kitchen, where he was offered tea but said, 'First things first: I need to check Pete's gun safe and rifle.'

Trina, a big-boned, red-haired, take-charge woman, currently pregnant, said, 'Ha! Wasted trip! I told him, with a kid in the house and hopefully more to come, no guns allowed. He sold it to his brother in Port Lincoln a while ago. Tea?'

Hirsch grinned. They settled at the table and chatted for a while: how life would change for Trina once the baby was born, how she wished she had easy access to a mothers' group, how Pete, a fencing contractor, was reduced to part-time parcel delivery-driving these days.

'With fuel the price it is!'

Hirsch nodded along, commiserating. Life had shrunk for many locals, work drying up for fencing contractors, dam diggers, shearers, shed hands, crop sprayers. He was finishing his tea, getting up to go, when she asked if he'd mind cleaning the filter between the underground water tank and the hot water service. 'My belly gets in the way!'

And so he was on his knees, scraping debris from the filter

with an old toothbrush, when Trina rested her palm on the crown of his head. 'Paul, are you okay?'

Not a hundred per cent, he might have said. But he looked around and up at her, risked a smile and said, 'Just a long day.'

She didn't believe him. 'See you next patrol?' she asked as he was leaving.

He knew that at one level she was desperate for it. 'Sure.'

Eyes prickling, he waved as he headed back out to the road. Trina returned the wave, rubbing her belly distractedly.

Not a hundred per cent. He tried calling his mother again. This time she answered. Told him, with a gust of rueful laughter close to tears, how she was coping. 'I've started talking to the damn cat. "There's already food in your bowl," or "Please don't bring me any more mice."'

Hirsch pictured the cat, a slinky black thing named Cynthia. She'd always been more his father's cat than his mother's, but she was stuck with her now. And Cynthia was the kind of cat you spoke to. Weren't all cats? Unlikely, but Hirsch had certainly spoken to that damn cat when he visited. Usually telling her to get off his lap.

He was about to reassure his mother that it was normal, she wasn't going crazy, when she said, bewildered, embarrassed: 'I even speak to your dad.'

'Understandable.'

'Is it?' Eva Hirschhausen said. 'Understandable that I also see and hear him? I think I must be going mad.'

'You're—'

'Yesterday I was contemplating the big garden box near the compost, and it was like he was right there, telling me I always put in too many tomato plants, they choke themselves.'

Hirsch could hear his father saying that. 'Mum, it's normal. It's a well-known phenomenon. It happened to Wendy when her husband died.'

'How is she? Give her my love.'

'Will do.'

'Anyway, I see your dad out of the corner of my eye ten times a day, and sometimes I distinctly hear him say, "Eva?" like he's going to ask me if I've seen his reading glasses anywhere. I open the wardrobe and smell him.'

'Mum—'

'You're still coming on Saturday?'

'Yep, all arranged. I'll get there in time for lunch.'

She said, on a note of apology, 'You can't stay two nights?'

Hirsch's past few weeks of firearms auditing had put him behind. 'No, sorry. I'm having dinner with Wendy and Kate Friday night, and I need an early start on Monday. But I'll spend most of the weekend with you.'

'That's lovely,' Eva Hirschhausen said, and her wistfulness compounded Hirsch's own mess of feelings. Guilt, sadness, helplessness ...

His parents had always been vigorous in retirement. Both of them fit and active. Curious. Lawn bowls, travel, gardening, volunteering for the Red Cross. He'd imagined them being hard at it until their nineties. Who knew that a disease could rob a man of his wits and personality so quickly? Transform him into someone who'd walk out the back door when his wife wasn't looking and set off to find the lost places of his life – down the hill to Junction Road, where the traffic teemed.

Hirsch was passing Alastair Stanyer's driveway entrance on the return journey when his drifting mind began to join dots. The guy's bruises. The ladder leaning against his back wall. Had Al been cleaning the gutters? Drunk in charge of a ladder?

The more Hirsch thought about it, the more convinced he was that Stanyer had been beaten up, not fallen headfirst into the dirt. Hirsch saw that dirt again, the spent cartridges …

Spent cartridges. *For a twenty-two*. He braked, threw the police Toyota into a U-turn and sped back. He was prepared to give Stanyer some wriggle room – maybe a friend had come by with a .22 calibre rifle or target pistol, or he'd recently acquired such a gun and hadn't got around to registering it – but he needed to check.

But when he pulled into the yard a few minutes later, there was no old Land Rover listing in the shade. No answer when he knocked on the locked front door. No chugging generator noise. And no cartridges in the backyard, let alone shot-up soup tins.

But there were fresh scuff-marks in the dirt – as if Alastair, scouting around for glimpses of brass, had been in a panic. As if he knew that Hirsch would twig, turn around, come back.

As I did, Hirsch thought – if a bit slow on the uptake.

But what was the crime here? Ownership of an unregistered firearm so underpowered it was useless for much more than plinking at tin cans? That was worth a rap over the knuckles, a fine at worst – and that's if I went all-out cop on him. More likely I'd've given him time to fix the paperwork.

So, why run? *Where* run?

Hirsch walked downhill, past the house and a rickety shed. Stopped to read the dirt. Here were fresh vehicle tracks leading into and across a washaway, then up the other side. Looked like a poor excuse for an escape route ... maybe it led out to the road, or deeper into the back country. No point chasing the guy. Call by later in the hope he comes back.

But the behaviour bothered Hirsch: an overreaction. Something to do with the gun itself? Not just unregistered but stolen? Or used in a crime.

4

He called Sergeant Brandl on his way back. 'I'm not sure what to make of it,' he told her. 'The gun's stolen? He can't afford to register it? Can't afford a fine?'

But his boss merely grunted, then said, 'Stanyer? Any connection to the mayor?'

'His brother's married to her.'

Silence. Humming between them the fact that Clarissa Stanyer, newly elected, had recently demanded a police presence at the next council meeting. To deal, she said, with the unruly elements who'd disrupted last month's meeting.

Eventually Hirsch said, 'I'll drop in on him from time to time. He's bound to come back.'

'What do you know about him?'

'Keeps to himself. A bit of a sad case.'

'A sad case whose brother's married to the mayor. Suicidal?'

'No idea. Didn't seem to be.'

'Mental health issues?'

Hirsch had no idea about that either. He said so, and signed off.

Half an hour later, tired of bouncing over the back roads of the Mid North, he was braking for the Barrier Highway intersection. A signpost there pointed north to Tiverton (pop. 235), and south to Penhale (pop. 114) and Redruth (pop. 922), the latter boasting a hospital, a high school, shops, businesses and Hirsch's boss. But Hirsch was heading north.

The blessed relief of bitumen – no more bone-shaking – and by 3.45 he was slowing for the southern outskirts of Tiverton.

The grain silos appeared first, then a few little blinds-drawn houses, Ed Tennant's general store, the Mechanics Institute and the Methodist manse. There'd once been a handful of other commercial buildings along the highway, but they were boarded up now, and the old Adelaide Bank building was only opened on Fridays, for Dr Pillai's clinic. Otherwise, there was a grain business down one of the side streets, owned by Al Stanyer's brother Mitchell, and more little houses ducking their heads from the sun.

And finally, the primary school opposite the small brick house that doubled as the police station and his residence. School had finished for the day and parents' cars were stretching both ways along the highway and cramming the little access road. It had been like that ever since the amalgamation of Penhale and Muncowie primary schools with Tiverton's. The unintended and unanticipated effects were a year of parking hassles, traffic congestion, parents complaining about greater petrol costs and driving times, and kids defending their tribal roots to the death in the new environment.

All the irritations and abrasions of too many people in too small a space, Hirsch was thinking as he pulled into the police station driveway, and he wasn't surprised to see Vikki Bastian charging across the highway as he got out. She taught the juniors and was referred to as an ice queen – tall, blonde, snootily good-looking – by those who didn't know her.

Just now, though, her shirt was untucked, her ponytail loose and her face reddened by panic under a sheen of perspiration.

'Thank God you're back.'

'Problem?'

'I need you. There's a situation out the front and it's getting ugly.'

Hirsch reluctantly settled his uniform hat back on his head. 'What's it about?'

'Don't know, but I'm scared someone's going to throw a punch.'

'Well, who?' Hirsch asked, following Vikki back down the driveway.

'Two of the Penhale parents – Trent McRae and Lily Dayman.'

Hirsch didn't know either name. It was possible that McRae and Dayman were airing some ongoing Penhale grievance, but the tussle was more likely rooted in parking hassles and school-parent politics. Last December he'd calmed a Tiverton mother furious because the school wouldn't create a speaking role for her daughter in the end-of-year play, and two weeks ago his colleagues in Redruth had faced a machete-wielding father whose son's unfinished crayon drawing wasn't hung in the classroom. Adelaide cop friends had told him similar stories. It was as if the nation's schools were boiling over: teachers receiving abusive emails and late-night phone calls; parents trespassing onto playgrounds to hunt down their kids' rivals; fathers beating up principals.

Hirsch sent a quick advisory text to his colleagues in Redruth, then paused with Vikki on the footpath, letting a road train and a Telstra van pass. When the highway cleared, he trotted across with Vikki panting alongside him, labouring in flimsy sandals. He shot her a quick glance: 'What can you tell me about them?'

'Her? Not much ... she's married to the new Penhale mail driver. But I've had dealings with Trent. He came storming into my classroom a while back because a note got sent home, his daughter had nits. She's not even in my class!'

Hirsch shot Vikki another glance. McRae tackled you because you're young and a woman, he thought.

'Every day it's the same,' she went on, puffing, scowling, as they trotted down the little access street that divided the school oval from the old Methodist manse. 'Parents turn up early and just sit there doing their nails or checking their socials, and if we're *really* lucky, they come in for a chat about their little darlings – leaving their cars parked at an angle so other cars can't get by and you end up with parking rage – aimed at us. As if it's *our* fault.'

Trailed by ragged, ironical cheering from some of the open car windows, Hirsch headed towards the turning circle at the end. Only a handful of these waiting parents would be suffering a relationship breakdown, financial woes, the loss of a job, an addiction or mental health issues – and only a tiny fraction would consider taking these things out on a schoolteacher. Still, if he were asked, he'd say there was a growing disregard for the police, nurses, teachers and medics these days. Occupations and roles once trusted and respected.

He could hear shouting now, and activated his bodycam. A hotted-up silver V8 Holden ute sat beside a white Hyundai SUV, and a man was remonstrating with a woman. The altercation effectively blocked access to the turning circle that took vehicles around to the school gates, where Hirsch could see the principal, another teacher, the school receptionist and a huddle of expectant children.

His phone buzzed. He checked the screen. 'Sergeant?'

Brandl's voice was a rasp in his ear. 'Trent McRae,' she said. 'I arrested him last year, high as a kite and surrounded by blister packs in the ceiling of the chemist's. Divorced, lives with his mother in Penhale. Not always given to clear thinking.'

'Okay.'

'Look, he's a project, all right?'

Ah. For a year or two now, Hirsch's sergeant had been taking the odd ratbag under her wing for informal counselling, chats and welfare visits. 'I'll go easy, Sarge,' he said.

'That's all I ask. But if he loses it ...'

'I understand.'

Hirsch set off again, glancing briefly at Vikki Bastian, gesturing to her to keep back. A moment of hesitation, and then she was hurrying across to join her colleagues at the school gates.

Good.

He reached the Holden ute, examining it as he passed along its flank: mag wheels, lowered suspension, a fitted tray canopy and a customised air scoop. The Hyundai was demure in comparison. Even the vehicles told him what to expect: dickhead parent, respectable parent.

And then he was stepping between the drivers, his fingers nimbly straight-arming one, then the other, barely touching their shoulders. 'Before we sort this out,' he said mildly, 'let's get both vehicles onto the verge so the other parents can drive through and collect their kids?'

'Yeah, well she—'

'Trent, not now, all right? Sergeant Brandl says hi, by the way. Let's get both vehicles off to the side.'

Hirsch had only half-expected it, but they complied, the ute pulling ahead, the SUV coming in close behind. With access to the turning circle now clear, he stood on the verge and began to wave the waiting cars through. Some horn toots, a couple of gesturing fists, a couple of shouts.

'Fuck you,' McRae responded, making as if to chase one car on foot.

'Trent,' Hirsch warned.

Trent McRae was of the species *Boofheadus australiensis*.

Solid, round-faced, the beginnings of a mullet, mirrored sunglasses resting on the bill of a baseball cap. A cocksure expression – which only he was likely to read as quickness and shrewdness. He said, still cocksure, 'Yeah, well, like I said, this bitch started it.'

'Keep it polite, Trent, okay?'

McRae unravelled rapidly. His fleshy face was red as he spat out, 'Fuck that, the bitch started it.'

Hirsch was firm. 'Let's just keep our voices down.'

Perhaps that was a mistake. 'What a good idea,' the woman said, with a kind of studied decorum that barely concealed her contempt.

Lily Dayman was in her late twenties, dressed in Nike runners, a cotton skirt, a T-shirt. Mild-looking, but there was a glint in her eyes, and her voice was modulated to goad.

'Please,' Hirsch said, shooting her a warning look.

She touched the flat of her hand to her sternum. 'I didn't start anything. Mr McRae, on the other hand, was sitting here with his engine running for a good twenty minutes. I'm supposed to breathe in his pollution?'

'For the *air-con*,' stormed McRae. 'Maybe you've heard of it?'

Hirsch shook his head. Cars edged past him; the kids at the gate dwindled in number. He wanted to drag both parents back to read the three signposts at the entrance to the turning circle, each one displaying a silhouetted kid with a backpack and, variously, the words *Kiss & Go* and *Stay with your car* and *2-minute limit*.

Dayman was saying, 'It poisons the air, running an engine unnecessarily.'

'Junk science,' McRae said.

'Oh, you're on top of the science, are you?'

'Please Mrs Dayman,' Hirsch said.

'We're in a heatwave,' stormed McRae. 'Thirty-five degrees, or hadn't you noticed?'

'Well, fan your face with your *Boy Racer* magazine or whatever the fuck it is you read. Can you read?'

McRae was galvanised. 'You stupid fucking entitled stuck-up—'

Hirsch got between them again and tried a tactic that usually worked. Smiling broadly, he stuck out his hand to McRae, then Dayman, told them his name, gestured at the police station in the distance, and saw them respond automatically: two dampish handshakes, two muttered names, some of the tension leaking away.

'Look,' he continued, 'I know the school amalgamations have made it hard on everyone, and the Education Department's looking to upgrade the traffic flow, but the signage is clear. Everyone needs to drop off and pick up as quickly as possible.'

McRae was disgusted. 'Yeah, well, what if for some reason we get here early? We supposed to park out on the highway and get totalled by a road train?'

Unlikely, and McRae knew it. But Hirsch didn't want to argue. He pointed to the children still waiting at the gate: fewer of them now, and two were watching anxiously. 'How about we leave it at that. Apologise if you can, and then collect your kids. And please, in future try not to get here too early.'

'Don't you want to know what else happened?' Dayman demanded.

Hirsch groaned inwardly. Breathed out. 'And what was that?'

'He called me an Abo.'

McRae seemed momentarily confused. 'Your husband, your *husband*, not you.'

Dayman gave him an opaque smile. 'My husband's an Abo? Actually, what do you mean by that?'

'You know what I mean. I should've got that mail job. I'm from around here. Experienced.'

The Redruth-to-Penhale mail driving job, guessed Hirsch. He'd heard it had gone to an Indigenous man – whose mob had been here long before Trent McRae's, but no point telling him that. No point telling him it was unlikely he'd have been offered the job in the first place.

'My husband was hired fair and square,' Dayman said.

'Yeah, well, your jurisdiction's not my jurisdiction.'

Hirsch felt a great sapping of his energy: he'd heard the expression too often, post-Covid. The first thing he did was glance at McRae's rear number plate. Sure enough, it bore a passing resemblance to a state-issued plate, but was homemade, with seven, not six, random numbers and letters. He had a fair idea of how it would go now: McRae would claim to be a sovereign citizen, beyond the reach of mainstream society's laws, regulations and expectations. The situation had reached a point, nationwide, in which any coalface officer like Hirsch could expect a run-in with a sovereign citizen sooner or later.

The official line was mixed: on the one hand, men and women like McRae were usually young, poorly educated and not doing so well in the fishpond of life. They blamed their setbacks on mainstream society, of which the police were a part, and looked to internet crazies for answers. From there it was a short step into a rabbit hole of conspiracies that explained everything.

The advice was: go easy on them. No big deal.

On the other hand, if they broke the law, they should be penalised. It was illegal to drive around in a car not fitted with official plates. And in Hirsch's experience, other offences flowed from something like that. He fully expected to learn that Trent McRae's ute was unregistered and his driver's licence invalid. If he'd broken into the Redruth pharmacy last year, God knows what he'd been up to this year.

He sighed, turned to Dayman. 'Mrs Dayman, do you wish to make—'

She backed away, shook her head, washed her hands together. 'Nup, I'm done, don't want the hassle,' and a moment later was swinging her Hyundai around the turning circle.

McRae, watching her collect a small boy at the school gate, said, 'Look at that. Knows she hasn't got a leg to stand on.'

Hirsch said, 'Trent, your number plate.'

'Don't have to explain anything to you.'

'It's fake,' said Hirsch reproachfully.

'*You're* the fake. And you are *this close* to being tried for fraud, genocide and crimes against humanity.'

Patiently Hirsch said, 'You need proper South Australian plates.'

'I am a resident of Terra Australis. There is no such thing as South Australia.'

'Then perhaps you can show me your licence?'

McRae puffed up with importance. 'I'm not under your jurisdiction of government; your laws don't apply. I am a citizen of a parallel community.'

'Please, quit the bullshit. I need to see your licence – and the rego papers, if you have them.'

'I don't need either to drive on the roads of Terra Australis.'

'Well, any idiot can get behind the wheel of a car,' Hirsch said testily. 'Look, if you put the original plates back on right away, and show me a valid licence and registration, I'm prepared to overlook this.' He gestured at the number plate. 'Otherwise, I can't let you drive anywhere. If you have an accident and hurt someone, hurt your own kid, it's going to be a million times worse, legally. Is there anyone who can come and pick you both up?'

'As a sovereign citizen of a parallel community, I don't have to listen to anything you tell me to do.'

'Okay.' Hirsch shook his head in frustration. 'It's my intention to issue you with two infringements: not displaying plates registered to this vehicle, and refusal to obey a police directive, namely—'

'And I now read you *your* rights. You have the right to remain silent, the right not to do anything, the right to bugger off to wherever you came from.'

'Sweet,' said Hirsch.

Which earned him a pistoning fist to the stomach. He doubled over, seared with pain. Easing onto one hip in the dirt, he placed one hand over his midriff and swallowed a lungful of poorly tuned V8 exhaust as McRae piled neatly into his ute, fired it up and whisked around the turning circle. Pausing to gather a fretting pony-tailed child, McRae snarled down to the highway intersection. A flare of one brake light, then father and daughter were howling south.

Maybe home to Penhale. Or maybe into the wild blue yonder if there was a custody dispute, Hirsch thought, knowing a fair bit by now about the debris that flowed through the bloodstreams of young men like Trent McRae.

He climbed to his feet, shrugged off offers of help, and trudged, half-bent over, back to the police station. Got behind the wheel and called Sergeant Brandl as he set out sedately after yet another of the pissant small-town outlaws that were the bane of his existence.

5

'There's no custody dispute to worry about,' the sergeant told him. 'If I know Trent, he'll head home. But let's meet in the pub carpark first,' she added, closing the call.

She doesn't want me to arrest him, thought Hirsch sourly. He checked the HiLux's onboard display terminal as he drove. Trent McRae, one arrest – the pharmacy break-in. Current licence, no restrictions. Hirsch dug deeper, flicking his gaze back and forth between the screen and the road ahead. The ute, registration up to date, was owned by McRae's mother. No surprise. It was how indulgent parents got around the rule that banned young L- and P-plate drivers from driving the powerful vehicles they wanted.

So why the false plate? Was McRae transitioning: on his way to becoming a rebel? Or was he torn between obeying mainstream authority figures and the numbskulls in his parallel community?

And it bothered Hirsch, Brandl's blithe claim that there were no child custody issues. Sovereign citizens had been known to argue before the courts that children were property.

Hirsch switched his full attention to the highway, accelerating past the grain silos and down a shallow valley with dry paddocks and distant bald hills on either side. A glint of reflected light halfway up a treeless slope materialised as a farm ute, winding downhill, raising dust. Crows rose and settled from roadkill and smaller birds dotted the phone and powerlines as the police HiLux ate up the kilometres. Oncoming drivers lifted a finger from the steering wheel; Hirsch responded. It was what you did out here. It said hello, respected the other's right to be on the road and acknowledged the commonality of their task – getting from A to B in the heat of the day, along a sun-softened stripe of tar, under a dome of bleached sky. What would you call that colour? Not blue. Hirsch fumbled for his sunglasses. And as a gust eddied out on the red, thistly topsoil, a dust wraith leaned, twirled and vanished.

Finally, a smudge in the distance clarified as the township of Penhale with its huddle of faded rooftops and gumtree canopies. Fences and yards. A kit home with a sandpit, a line pegged with nappies and jumpsuits, a drooping horse sheltered beneath a she-oak struggling for nourishment in a half-hectare of dirt. Then the disused railway station and the pub and beyond them, huddled behind hedges and oleanders, a dwindling row of little stone houses just like Tiverton's. Blinds and awnings shutting out the heat and all signs of the greater world.

Sergeant Brandl's police Kia was parked in the grudging

shade of the pub's side wall. She climbed out as Hirsch pulled in behind her. Waited, arms folded across her wiry frame, as he locked up. Jerking her head, she said, 'Quick drink first,' and began walking around to the pub's front steps until Hirsch called, 'Boss, are you sure we've got time?'

Brandl said, over her shoulder, 'I phoned on the way here. He's at home. His daughter's with him.'

Hirsch followed reluctantly up the steps, to a table in the filtered shade of the vine-hung front veranda.

They were on duty, so it was a lemon squash and a Coke in tall glasses beaded with condensation. The barman was mute and unsurprised, as if he had uniformed police drinking at his establishment every day. No other voices nearby. No sense of people moving about. Hirsch and Brandl were in a bubble, with only a passing truck or car every now and then.

'Cheers,' Hirsch said.

His sergeant echoed it. Hilary Brandl always seemed to quiver in a raw-boned way, as if gearing up to run a marathon. Hirsch liked her: a friend, a good boss. And now she said, 'I'm sorry Trent hit you – he's an idiot, and there need to be consequences – but I'd rather not go in flat-footed or heavy-handed.'

She paused. Hirsch wanted to protest; he'd been punched in the guts – a crime – but eventually shrugged a reluctant 'Okay.'

'To fill you in on a few things. First, it's just your typical country-town story. He grew up here in Penhale and he's never lived anywhere else. Ordinary childhood, no abuse that I know of, but not much money and his dad died last year after a long illness – so that might be considered a trigger.'

Hirsch sipped his Coke.

'A stoner all through high school,' Brandl went on. 'A few police warnings that didn't make it to the official record. The usual.'

Hirsch nodded. Trent McRae was the kind of minor dirtbag who makes things tougher for everyone. Rude, belligerent, light-fingered, lazy, with a taste for pub brawls, binge drinking and ice. Not particularly good at any of it.

'Anyway, long story short, he got a local girl pregnant and married her, she divorced him when their daughter was a toddler, and now he lives with his mother. But the pair of them fight all the time, and he can't hold down a job. Spends all his time on the internet.'

No surprise, thought Hirsch.

Brandl went on: 'Remember that fixated threat assessment workshop I went to early in the year?'

Hirsch remembered. Brandl rarely attended seminars, conferences or training sessions; didn't like being away from the coalface. And he remembered because having to oversee law and order throughout the entire region while she was away was enough to make him question his intention to take the sergeant's exam one day. When she got back, she filled him in on what she'd learned. Strategies for recognising, then derailing or circumscribing, the kinds of fixations that might lead someone to commit a violent crime against an individual – a 'wronged' father putting a bullet into a Family Court judge – or institution – a bullied kid burning down his high school.

Brandl waited for a truck to rattle past then said defensively, 'So, after what happened last year, you can't blame me for keeping tabs on guys like Trent.'

Hirsch nodded. Last year a posse of young local Trent-lookalikes had been recruited by far-right militia nutters. 'Fair enough.'

'He was spiralling when I arrested him for the chemist break-in,' Brandl said. 'His dad had died, he couldn't hold down a job, he hated living with his mother. So rather than charge him I got him to apologise and help with the clean-up – something to break the pattern, right? And I liked him, he seemed genuine. No sulking, no malingering, just a kid who'd made a wrong turn and wanted to get back on track.'

The sergeant finished her drink. She looked uncomfortable. 'I was surprised to hear about him acting out earlier. How bad was it?'

'Boss, if we forget for the moment that he punched me, he was spouting sovereign citizen garbage.'

The sergeant picked up her empty glass, looked around for service, put it down again. 'Disappointing.'

'He could be working up to something.'

Brandl said eventually, 'Look, let's just have a quiet word and see what's going on with him. Personally, I think if he got a decent job he'd settle down.'

Hirsch told her about the mail delivery job.

'Shit,' she said. 'Still, at least he's looking for work.'

They were awkward with each other. Hirsch said, 'What about psych support?'

The sergeant was disgusted. 'One mental health nurse

in the entire district? He can't get in to see her until next March.'

'But you talk to him, though. Does it help?'

'Remains to be seen,' Brandl said. Pausing, she fished in her uniform's breast pocket. 'I had this psych eval done. Quote: *Mr McRae shows evidence of grievances, hatred, bias and perceived injustices, which at the current time is personalised and idiosyncratic rather than indicative of a desire to embrace a group ideology.* Unquote.'

'Someone did a short course in psychobabble.'

'But not me, Senior Constable Hirschhausen. You said Trent seemed pretty cranked up about not getting the mail delivery job?'

'Yes.'

'Like I said, I've been trying to "disrupt his pathways"' – she made quote marks with her fingers – 'by taking an interest in his life, offering friendly advice, calling in occasionally. Which is why I don't want to go in heavy now. A kind word. Get him to apologise for hitting you.'

Hirsch sighed. 'Okay, I'll give it a go.'

'Thank you. I appreciate it. And it would be good if we can get his mother and his ex-wife more involved. So far, they seem to think it's entirely my responsibility.'

The mother and the ex-wife have tried, thought Hirsch, and it hasn't worked. Or they're not convinced a grown man with a grudge is their responsibility. 'Tell me about his ex.'

'Name's Erica Woodhead. She's a nurse. She has custody but she works eight till four, so Trent's mother usually handles the school run. Why Trent did it today I don't know.'

6

An intervention, thought Hirsch as they stepped out into the heat again. He'd run a few over the years. Perhaps most police did. Also doctors, lawyers, social workers and even best friends. It was instinctive. If someone was being an idiot, not making good choices, you didn't just leave them to it. You offered a bit of tough love: advice, practical help, a friendly warning. And hoped it worked.

But you needed some kind of connection with the person you wanted to help: some kind of sympathy or fellow feeling. Trent McRae tweaked that in the sergeant somehow.

They drove separately to a squat 1970s house of tan brick that had probably seemed stylish and desirable at the time but was now just tired. It sat in a buckled expanse of concrete dimpled here and there with holes for stick-like roses and underdone shrubs; one drooping bottlebrush. A place of shortcuts, with a sun-faded Commodore in the driveway and a sign on the front gate advertising hairstyling and beauty treatments.

'Ah, bugger,' Brandl said: no sign of Trent McRae's V8 ute.

Hirsch trailed her through the front gate. He could see past the bottlebrush now to a strange weatherboard lean-to against a side wall. Jerry-built, with a narrow door and window and a skillion roof from which a downpipe led to a small plastic rainwater tank fitted with a tap.

Noticing his gaze, Brandl said, 'Trent's man-cave. He and his mother rub each other up the wrong way. Let's get out of this damn sun.'

Up onto the paltry shade of the front porch. The doorbell produced a faint, tinkling response, but time passed before they heard the main door open. A small child looked at them through the screen door.

'Thank God,' murmured Brandl, relieved. She leaned in. 'Hello, Josie.'

A picture of tortured shyness. 'Hello.'

Brandl straightened, indicated Hirsch. 'This is Paul.'

'Hello, Josie. Is your dad here?'

The child didn't answer, just stared at him blankly. Then a shift in her small face: 'You were at my school.'

'Yes.'

'Are you going to put Daddy in jail?'

'No, no,' Brandl said. 'He's not in any trouble.'

Josie McRae looked sceptical. She swung on the edge of the main door.

'Is your grandma in?'

'She's sick.'

'Sick as a dog,' a voice said, over the slap of bare feet approaching from the gloom.

Audrey McRae was in her careworn late forties and wore baggy pyjama pants and a loose T-shirt. Pale, sweaty, with bony feet and legs, she seemed to drive all of her home's stored heat ahead of her as she shoved open the screen door with one hand and absently touched her granddaughter's tangled plait with the other.

'If you want Trent, he's not here. When you called and I told him it was you on the phone, he just took off.'

'Do you know where—'

McRae slumped abruptly, her hip striking the wall. One hand grabbed the doorframe for support, the other shaded her eyes briefly. 'Sorry, end stages of a migraine,' she murmured. She sounded as if she wanted to curl into a ball.

'Sorry to trouble you, Mrs McRae,' Hirsch said. 'If you could just tell us where Trent went, we'll be on our way.'

After a quick, irritated glance at Hirsch, Brandl said, 'Why don't you go back to bed, Audrey. Do you want us to fetch Erica for you?' A quick check of her watch. 'She'd be home by now?'

Audrey McRae ignored her. Clammy with illness and distrust, trying to focus through her pain, she said, 'What's he done now?'

Then she seemed to recall her granddaughter. Pressing the blonde head against her thigh as if to hide hard truths, she continued, with a pervasive sense of futility, 'Is he in trouble? I dunno where he went.'

Brandl removed her cap and swiped at her damp forehead. 'I won't lie, he's in a bit of strife. Got into an argument over parking, a scuffle with my colleague here, and he hasn't got proper plates on his ute. All we want is a word.'

Audrey McRae began shaking her head as if finally undone by the unfairness of it all. She took her granddaughter to school every morning and picked her up every afternoon – it was just what a decent person did. And on the one occasion she asks her son to pull his weight, look what happens. 'The bloody school amalgamation,' she said. 'Josie used to be able to walk there and back.' She gestured towards a distant rooftop and huddled peppertrees. 'Hundred and fifty metres.'

She made a half-suppressed whimper. Brandl turned to Hirsch. 'I'll get her back to bed. You go and fetch Josie's mum. Erica Woodhead, Mawson Street, last house on the left.'

Mawson Street boasted ten houses, five of which backed onto a dustbowl cemetery bordered by gumtrees. The last house on the left was an older model kit home set on stilts, with a struggling lawn up to the front steps. A little Polo in the driveway. No customised V8 ute.

Hirsch parked, trotted to the veranda and knocked. The Polo ticked: it had been driven recently.

No answer, and Hirsch was wondering if he should just barge in – maybe Trent had been and gone, leaving his ex-wife lying on the kitchen floor in a pool of blood – when a woman appeared from the side yard. Still in her nurses' scrubs, carrying a watering can, faintly alarmed. 'Is something wrong?'

Hirsch stepped down off the veranda and introduced himself. 'Are you Erica Woodhead, Josie's mother?'

A hand went to her throat. 'Yes. Is she all right?'

'She's fine,' Hirsch said, going on to explain.

'Poor Audrey. I'll go around there right away.'

'If I could have just a minute?' Hirsch asked. 'Sergeant Brandl's helping her, everything's fine.'

Woodhead looked at him levelly. 'You want to talk about Trent.'

'Yes.'

'Come in out of the heat,' Woodhead said, stepping onto the veranda.

Hirsch sent Brandl a quick text – *All good here, no Trent, see you in five* – and followed Woodhead into the house, down a hallway to the kitchen. She seemed smiling and competent, the same age as her ex-husband but much older in all the ways that mattered. Solid build; short dark hair; a fine gold chain around her neck. The kitchen was dimly lit until she released the blind above the sink. Light flooded in, she said 'Whoa!' shading her eyes comically, then tugged the blind halfway down again. 'Drink? Water, beer …'

'Water.'

A bottle of sparkling from the fridge, two glasses from the freezer, and all the while she was assessing Hirsch. He didn't feel a buzz of attraction or speculation from her: she was a clever woman assessing the angles and working out how she'd deal with them. 'I really do need to check on Audrey,' she said, joining him at the table.

'I'll be quick. How often does Trent do the school run?'

'Never. He's sort of not interested, and usually sleeps in anyway. Audrey's happy to do it.'

'Today he got into an argument with another parent, who criticised him for letting his engine run for the aircon.'

Erica Woodhead shrugged, as if knowing there was more. 'And?'

'He's got a set of false plates on his car. When I asked about that, he said the police have no jurisdiction over him.' Pause. 'And he punched me.'

The warm alertness vanished. 'Sorry. But you do know he's got issues, right?'

Hirsch was non-committal. 'Issues.'

'Did he tell you about his parallel community?'

'Yes.'

Woodhead looked at her watch again. 'Yeah, well, he can go on living in it, waiting for the great reset to happen, but meanwhile I'm a full-time nurse and mother, trying to make ends meet.'

A woman with a pragmatic kernel, Hirsch thought. Saving herself. 'The great reset?'

'Garbage he reads on the internet. He's not drinking or on drugs like before – there's no way I'd let him near Josie if he was – but his head's full of stuff. Some big change coming.'

It's how lone-wolf shooters and bombmakers are formed, thought Hirsch. 'What about his friends?'

She shrugged. 'Wouldn't know. There's no one around anyway. No jobs.'

Then she stirred, banging her glass onto the table, getting ready to leave. 'Look, we're not close, all right? We should never have married, not at that age. I grew up, and he didn't. But I want Josie to be in his life.'

'Okay.'

She grabbed her keys. 'And his mum adores her.'

Hirsch grabbed his cap, ready to follow. 'Do you know where he might have gone?'

'No idea.'

'He didn't stop here?'

'No.'

'Okay, thanks. But if he calls or visits, please let us know.'

Woodhead stalked down the hallway, Hirsch trailing. She said, over her shoulder, 'He's not wrong about everything, you know. Waste, corruption ... And the rates I pay on this place: outrageous. Council needs to pay for their private roads and CCTV cameras, somehow, right? Have to keep their eye on us plebs.'

Uh huh, thought Hirsch.

Then she was locking the house and about to unlock her car. Hirsch, watching from across the roof of the HiLux, saw her pause and frown; a sense of making up her mind.

Staring right at him, she said, 'There was a shotgun.'

Hirsch went still. 'Okay ...'

'It belonged to Trent's dad, he's dead now, but I made him get rid of it when Josie started spending more time there. I think he did. He got sick and died after that.'

Penhale was in Hirsch's patrol area. According to his files, there was only one registered gun owner in the town: the publican, who owned one of the nation's ubiquitous .22 rifles.

Hirsch followed Erica Woodhead back to her mother-in-law's house, learned that Audrey McRae knew nothing about any shotgun, said goodbye to Sergeant Brandl and returned to Tiverton feeling crabbed and carping, full of gaps and absences.

7

Entering through the back door, Hirsch stripped off his sweaty uniform and padded naked to the bathroom, his mobile phone to one ear. 'Only me,' he said.

'Only you,' Wendy Street said.

'Just got home after a slightly hellish day. We still on for dinner tomorrow night?'

'Yep. It's been so hot, I thought we'd just have cold meat and a salad.'

'Sounds good,' Hirsch said. 'Want me to bring anything?'

'All good, Aitch,' she said breezily and Hirsch, released, turned on the taps full blast.

A two-minute shower, owing to the town's water restrictions, and then he was pulling on shorts and T-shirt and opening the fridge.

Nothing to excite him. He checked the time: five minutes before the shop closed.

Ed Tennant's store carried groceries, limp fruit and vegetables – the distance, the heat – and hardware ranging from gumboots and shovels to stepladders and nails. The place was also a licensed post office, a branch of the Mid North Library Service and a second-hand bookshop.

Heading down an aisle between racks of shelving – not one of them sitting true on the creaking floorboards – he came to a poky office in the back wall. Ed was counting the day's takings into a grubby Commonwealth Bank satchel, ready for deposit in Redruth the next morning. He was not alone in doing that. Whole bush districts stirred with the physical transfer of cash on Friday mornings. The country copper in Hirsch feared an armed holdup one day: a small-town grocer like Ed Tennant ambushed on a lonely bend of the Barrier Highway by someone armed with a farm .22.

He tapped on the door. Tennant, a slight, disgruntled-looking man in his sixties, held up a warning hand, scribbled a figure on a pad, then turned. 'Paul.'

'Hi, Ed. Sorry to interrupt.'

'Do you for?'

'Tonight's dinner, mainly, but do you know who Al Stanyer hangs out with?'

Tennant shook his head. 'No idea.'

'You ever see him with anyone?'

'His brother, years ago. I have no idea what he's up to these days.'

Hirsch thanked him and headed for the freezers. He sized up the depressing iced-over pickings and wandered to the trays of vegetables. He grabbed an onion, a garlic head, a leek and a wrinkly capsicum; a pat of mince from the fridge, and headed to the cash register.

*

After a kind of stir-fry, he watched half an episode of *The Crown*, asked himself why, switched off, wandered restlessly out into the hallway and stared at the walls, which were still in want of a paint job. Almost six years now. Into the kitchen for a reckless moment of dishwashing. But when that was over, the evening hours still stretched, untenanted, ahead.

He could always answer his emails.

He stepped through the connecting door to the police station – the front room of the little house – and fired up the PC. But he'd only got as far as the SA Police logo when he heard the squeak and clunk of an old vehicle pulling up outside. He waited. There was a timid knock, and the street door opened to reveal a thin, bony woman in a shapeless dress and dusty sandals.

Dorrie Alkawaro. He'd seen her shopping, delivering her grandson to Saturday morning tennis and once, in Redruth, using the photocopier in the Indigenous drop-in centre. 'Mrs Alkawaro. Come in.'

Dorrie Alkawaro slid half-hunched into the room as if reluctant to make an impression on the air. As if not to let heat in, as if not to be a nuisance. 'Sorry it's so late.'

'We never close,' Hirsch joked, unfolding gingerly from his office chair, knowing how it always scooted back on its wheels as if eager to be rid of him.

He reached the front counter just as she did; just as his chair smacked against the filing cabinet. She looked stiff with fright.

'Is anything wrong?'

She examined the countertop. Ran her thin fingers over it, the old woodgrain surface scuffed here and there, then caught herself and took a step back apologetically. One of her eyes was filmy. 'I was just coming back from town.'

Hirsch had learned in his first week in the Mid North that 'town' meant Adelaide, almost three hours south. 'Okay.'

'Someone run me off the road.'

The story came out. She'd been almost home, between Penhale and Tiverton, when a car tailgated her for several kilometres before overtaking, drawing well ahead, U-turning and coming right at her. 'Playing chicken. Run me off the road.'

Hirsch made notes. 'Any damage?'

'Almost hit a tree.'

'Are you hurt?'

'Coulda been.'

'Can you describe the other vehicle?'

'Maybe silver? It was dark, and I was trying not to hit anything.'

'Car? Ute?'

'Maybe a ute?'

'Can you describe the driver?'

Dorrie struggled. 'I think he was kind of young with long hair at the back, but he come out of nowhere ...'

By now Hirsch was thinking: Trent McRae. There had been other cases over the months. Up around Muncowie, and along the stretches north and south of Tiverton. Solo burnouts and donuts in addition to tailgating and playing chicken. Usually at night, meaning that descriptions were scant and contradictory.

Then he saw that Dorrie was trembling. 'Hey, hey,' he said, guiding her to the police station's 'waiting room' – an op-shop sofa in the far corner.

'Tea? Cold drink?'

She looked up at him in a quivering funk, as if imploring him to explain the world to her. 'That'd be good. Just water, thanks.'

He had a little bar fridge under the main counter. Fetched out two bottles of spring water and two chilled glasses and rolled his desk chair across the floor until he was seated almost knee to knee with her. She wouldn't look at him. He rolled back a couple of metres and that worked, and they drank in silence until Dorrie said, 'It's not right what they do to the Aboriginal people.'

'You think you were targeted?'

But she answered a different question. 'And Banjo.'

Banjo was her son, killed when his Kawasaki skidded in gravel out on Tiverton Hills Road. 'You think Banjo was targeted?'

Her mouth opened as if the notion hadn't occurred to her. *She's talking about something else*, Hirsch thought. He was about to ask when she said, 'Won't let me leave flowers and that.'

She'd erected a roadside memorial at the crash site, a simple white cross and flowers every week. It occurred to Hirsch that he hadn't seen it lately. 'Who won't?'

'Council. Said enough time's gone by and it's an eyesore.'

'Sorry,' Hirsch said inadequately.

'Them people,' Dorrie Alkawaro said.

He wrote it up when she was gone, and had barely started on his emails when Vikki Bastian knocked on the street door. Poked her head in and said, 'You busy, Paul? Tell me if you are.'

He never did. She didn't abuse the privilege – called in no more than once a fortnight – and he knew she was lonely and shy, and considered him a friend. 'It's fine.'

Still in the doorway she said, 'I just wanted to thank you for today.'

He waved a hand and said, 'Just doing my job, ma'am.'

It was a game they played, movie-dialogue clichés, but this one didn't register. She seemed preoccupied, and she'd never popped in this late before: 8:20. The reason became apparent when she tripped comically on the stretch of carpet between the door and the front counter, and again when he took her through the connecting door to his little suite of kitchen, bedroom, bathroom and sitting room. She collapsed onto the sofa, slightly flushed and disorganised, and admitted that she'd dined at the pub. 'Parmi. Big mistake.'

Hirsch shuddered. 'Brave woman,' he said, eyeing her carefully. Presumably she'd eaten alone – and presumably that had made her feel more out of place and time than she usually felt. 'Coffee?'

She shook her head violently. 'I'd never get to sleep. Peppermint tea?'

Hirsch stepped through the archway into the kitchen nook, fetched a pair of mugs and boiled the kettle. She'd once told him he was a good listener, a voice of reason, to which he'd shrugged and said, 'On my good days.' His antenna for such things was probably underdeveloped and certainly sometimes wrong, but he'd never sensed a hidden motive in her. Born in the district – her mother had died when she was eight; her father bred stud merinos down near Redruth – she'd been shunted off to boarding school when she was twelve. Returned to the Mid North to take up a teaching job at Tiverton Primary and was disappointed to find that she no longer belonged. Her old primary school friends were married with kids, working in the Redruth IGA, or styling people's hair in a remodelled spare bedroom. 'We don't have anything in common anymore,' she'd told him. Not that she wanted to go back to the city: 'Don't have anything to talk about with them, either.' A country girl, she said, who didn't fit into the country. Probably a victim of her looks, that ice-queen thing – as if she understood the world and nothing surprised her. But Hirsch knew that people and the things they did to each other bewildered her. And the disdainful face softened when she was with him; became more mobile and showed her passion for the kids she taught, the locals who were doing it tough.

When he returned with the tea he found her on her feet, staring at his print of *Christina's World* on the wall above the sofa.

'That is a seriously creepy painting.'

Hirsch liked it. He'd been carting it from share houses to one-bedroom flats to rental digs for years. 'Oh?'

Vikki turned. 'It depresses me.'

'In what way?' he asked, placing the mugs on the coffee

table and settling into an armchair so that she would also sit.

It worked. She flopped onto the sofa again, recovered, reached for her tea. 'You know, the way things are these days.'

He sensed that she wasn't talking about herself. 'I know,' he said, not quite truthfully.

'The drought and everything,' she said, with a half-glance over her shoulder at the painting.

Did Hirsch see drought in *Christina's World*? No. The scene was rural, with a grassy slope more summery-dry than drought-stricken, and a farmhouse, a barn and outbuildings along the skyline. Christina lay on one hip in the foreground, caught by the painter in the act of dragging herself uphill. Hirsch thought it a hopeful painting.

'Okay ...'

'She's vulnerable,' Vikki said. 'She's lost something, or it's out of reach.'

Hirsch knew he'd feel troubled now, whenever he looked at the painting. He'd walk through his sitting room and plonk himself down to watch TV and Christina would be there behind him, searching alone. 'Who was at the pub?' he asked, for something to say.

She answered elliptically. 'Everything's affecting me lately.'

Something other than today's parking rage, thought Hirsch. 'Oh?'

'Especially the kids.'

'The school amalgamation?'

'Well, yeah; class sizes have practically doubled. But what I mean is, the kids are so anxious now. There's nothing sadder than an anxious child. They say things like, "The bank's going to take the farm away from us."'

Hirsch thought of Mark Button this morning, shooting his sheep, worrying about the bank.

Meanwhile Vikki was smoothing her skirt as if to dry her palms. 'Kids are like antennas,' she said. 'Barometers. They pick things up. You can just hear the conversations around the dinner table. And some are quite jumpy. Mum and Dad yelling all the time, I suppose.' She paused, looked at Hirsch, her mouth a grim slash. 'Or worse, they're depressed, some of them. Six and seven years old.'

She was helpless and so was he, and she leaned against him briefly later, when he walked her to her car in the moonlight.

8

Friday, early, and there was already a foretaste of heat when Hirsch walked the town. The air was still and galahs called from the gumtrees: he thought of it as the siren song of summer in the bush. Apart from playing tennis for the town, walking around it was his only exercise. He needed it, with the amount of time he spent at his desk or at the wheel of the HiLux. Very rarely was he called on to scale cliffs, forge rivers, snatch drivers from burning wrecks or track suspects across the vast outback terrain. And dawn was the coolest part of the day just now. Peaceful, as the shadows of night receded. Calming, apart from the guard dog tearing along the cyclone fence surrounding Mitch Stanyer's seed business. And no one about this morning except for Mr Cromer watering his roses, Mrs Lidstrom walking her fox terrier – a nasty little brick with fangs – and, at the edge of town, Nan Washburn pouring a line of oats into a cement trough for her miniature ponies.

He made a final loop to check on the town paddock,

which was divided by a stand of gumtrees from the tennis courts and the oval on the northern edge of the town. A twenty-five-acre strip of land sandwiched between the highway and Mitch Stanyer's lucerne property, the paddock was a remnant of the colonial era when the highway had been a stock route wide enough for bullock teams and the droving and overnight penning of sheep and cattle. Now it was farmed by local volunteers, its harvest income generally enough to keep the community in tennis nets and playground equipment. But not this year. Only a sparse and unavailing strip of dead wheat stalks this year, the shrivelled heads not worth reaping, and the air of hopelessness had prompted some of the less town-proud locals to start using it as a tip.

Hirsch froze. A few garbage bags and tin cans was one thing: here was a mountain of new rubbish. With one eye open for snakes, he slipped through the fence and approached. A fridge, mattresses, the cabinetry guts of an old kitchen, and a massive pile of bricks and soil. You didn't sneak in rubble like that via a cardboard box on the back seat of your car. He toed a brick, a few chips of asbestos sheeting. Given that he walked around the town every morning, he had a pretty good idea of who was doing what in Tiverton – painting the front room; putting up a granny flat – but no one was remodelling, to his knowledge. Maybe outsiders had somehow got wind of the town paddock tip; spotted it from the highway. A passing builder or rubbish removalist?

Fishing out his phone, he snapped half-a-dozen photos.

*

He was at his desk by eight. The leaflets in their wire racks, the police posters (drink and drug driving), the general store calendar (the September wildflowers along the base of the Tiverton Hills, photographed the year before the drought), his holstered Glock in the bottom drawer and his hat at a grabbable distance on an old wooden coatrack beside his desk.

His head filled with matters messily unresolved, he fired off yet another email to the district council's public works manager. A more urgent request for rubbish clean-up this time, photos attached.

Then he scrolled through emails. Too many of them, and too many SAPOL messages that appeared to be generic or repetitious but which might contain a sting in the tail – some small-print, final-paragraph demand that would land him with a sharp 'please explain' in a few weeks if he missed it.

It soured his mood so that he attacked the keyboard more as a release of aggression than a means of communication, and so the morning passed. He barely registered the highway traffic: the occasional semi-trailer passing through to Peterborough, Hawker or Broken Hill, the occasional minibus on its way to the Flinders Ranges; a salesman or two; a few local farm utes and family station wagons.

His mobile pinged: a text from his mother. Warm anticipation and hesitance in equal measure, as if she were granting him a last-minute police emergency or a better offer. She didn't play games, there was no hint of emotional blackmail, but life had dealt her a hard blow and she expected more of the same. She was floundering; Hirsch supposed her recovery would take a long time. So would his. And it would never be complete: that forever ache at the back of your soul.

He sighed; texted back: *See you tomorrow, can't wait.*

Meanwhile the heat was building. He switched on the air conditioner, which rattled as it began to stir the air. Then he checked the town and district WTF Facebook page. Mostly it was posts of stupefying triviality – trees down, haystack thefts and missing sheepdogs; typical social-media grievances – but occasionally some fuckwit would post video of himself spray-painting an ejaculating penis on a shop wall and be astounded when the police knocked on his door. Otherwise, the page was a barometer of the district's mood. Hirsch had noted more – and more desperate-sounding – *for sale* posts on Marketplace. More pleas for rental properties. And more blame. Yes, the drought was bad, and the Mid North, like most places, had always been subject to decisions made over the horizon somewhere – Adelaide, Canberra, Wall Street – but now there were rumblings about forces closer to home. Hirsch recalled a post from last week, Mark Button ranting about a $250 district council fine for failing to remove fire risks on his property. *Fire risks? There's nothing left to burn!* Two weeks earlier, Kev Henry the publican remarked that the local council hadn't needed to bring in a consultant on $3,000 a month: *Hell, I'll do it for three bucks*. And now a new post, from Russ Fanning out near Desolation Hill: *Wish the council would sign off on a flash new road to my place.*

Hirsch paused. Was it his imagination, or were people getting stuck into the local council more often lately?

Back to the job: tackling abusive and legally problematic posts, bantering with a few of the ratbags, skimming the rest. The Best Christmas Lights competition was on again this year, first prize a dinner for two at the Dugout in Redruth, to which someone had added predictably that second prize was *two* dinners for two. A Penhale woman asking if anyone was interested in setting up a shopping ride-share to Clare every Monday. And another reminder from Rosie Llewellyn about her Peterborough exhibition, opening in seven days' time.

That jogged his memory: he needed to check Llewellyn's .22 rifle. Maybe a quick run out to her place after lunch?

Next he updated his own segment, *Plod POV*. Beware of haybale scams: never pay the full amount upfront; verify that the hay exists and the seller is legitimate before paying a deposit. Those with acreage, please remember to slash long grass and clear all fire hazards (or the council will fine you, he wanted to add), and avoid mowing, slashing and outdoor angle-grinding on high-fire-danger days. Please report instances of rubbish-dumping on the town paddock. And be alert for drivers playing chicken and tailgating on the highway: *Anyone with dashcam footage or further information please get in touch*.

He waited. Eventually, a handful of replies trickled in. The offending vehicle had been a white ute; a silver ute; silver, yes, but a station wagon. Plates obscured. And: *He came up close behind me and wouldn't pass and I was scared to pull over in case he stopped too. Eventually he overtook but it was too dark to get a good look.*

Dorrie Alkawaro? She didn't strike him as the type to use Facebook, or certainly not after she'd made a police report. He replied to each message: *Please get in touch*, and waited. The cursor winked. Nothing more.

He finished the morning by reviewing his keeping-tabs list. Husbands or partners on intervention orders; newcomers with a prison record; a handful of names on the Sex Offenders Register; upcoming court cases. Only one item of interest: Jerry Poulakis, facing trial on domestic violence offences, had, that morning, jumped from a Northern Expressway flyover into 110 km/h traffic.

Hirsch twisted himself into a familiar knot. His heart didn't bleed for the guy: Poulakis had caused a lot of misery. But he must've been in utter despair, at the limit of his endurance, and a part of Hirsch could get close to imagining that. At least there were no kids in the mix. No kids for Poulakis to annihilate along with himself.

He added Trent McRae to the keeping-tabs list and reached for the desk phone to call the house in Penhale. Audrey answered. No, Trent hadn't come home. He hadn't contacted her. She wasn't worried. She just wanted to be left alone.

He called the ex-wife: voicemail. She'd be at work.

Lunch, then he hit the road.

Rosie Llewellyn – .22 Ruger rifle – rented the renovated overseer's cottage of a working sheep station that moonlighted as tourist accommodation. A signpost in her front yard read *Rosie Llewellyn Photography* but Hirsch suspected that her real home was the caravan parked in the carport beside her LandCruiser. She spent several months a year in it, touring around the Mid North, the Flinders Ranges and central Australia, photographing hills, gumtrees, stone ruins, rock art and contemporary outback life. A woman travelling alone – snakes, human and animal – it made sense that she'd travel with a rifle.

She answered his knock, a stringy, sundried woman of sixty-five. 'Come in out of the heat. Is this a patrol visit? I don't have much time.'

'Off on another jaunt?'

She shook her head, blew a strand of hair away from her left eye. 'Sorting photos for the exhibition.'

Hirsch nodded. 'Right: I saw your Facebook post.'

Lewellyn put her hands on her hips. Almost impatient.

Hirsch said hastily, 'Firearms audit, Rosie. If I could have a quick look at your twenty-two?'

Almost a sigh this time. 'Sure.'

She took him to the rear of the LandCruiser and showed him the Ruger locked in a purpose-built safe in the rear compartment. It was unloaded.

'Ammunition?'

'Glove box. I keep it locked.'

'Thanks. All good,' Hirsch said.

She cocked her head at him. 'If I recall correctly, didn't you buy a couple of photos from me last year?'

Hirsch nodded. 'Your Clare show.'

'Would you like a preview of the new show?'

'Sure,' said Hirsch, smiling inwardly. The locals had a

saying: don't step inside Rosie's place or you'll find yourself opening your wallet.

Then he thought: Mum. Take her something other than flowers tomorrow.

Rosie was crossing the yard in her determined way, expecting Hirsch to follow. Onto the veranda, through the door and straight down the hallway to her studio, a roomy expanse lined with benches and laced with the scent of chemicals, presumably from the darkroom in the far corner. Hirsch took a moment to glance around at the walls. Men, women and children at work and play in arid landscapes. A man wearing his Akubra tipped back, his lower face brown, his brow starkly white. Two solemn children, just their heads and shoulders and a lonely range of hills behind them. A laughing woman, gleamingly half-naked, soap in one hand, caught mid-shock as water streamed over her from a perforated bucket hanging from a tree.

And a gaunt-faced woman of the inland, devoid of expectations but suspicious of the camera. Head and shoulders, a pinched, sharecropper face, a hint of pepper trees and a tank stand in the background.

'Where was this taken?'

'Those aren't for sale,' Rosie said impatiently.

'I recognise her.'

'Really?' said Rosie, barely interested. 'I did a series on schools. Kids, parents, grandparents.'

Hirsch nodded. Trent McRae's mother, photographed in the grounds of the Penhale Primary School – back when it was viable.

He followed Rosie to a workbench, where she began removing unmounted photographs from plastic sleeves and arranging them on a bench. He gazed along and down, and one photo caught his attention: a scowling little girl staggering under the weight of a huge black cat. Furthermore, she was standing in the doorway of a falling-down barn where a black 1950s Mark V Jaguar was mouldering. A rich grazier's folly: the roof of the old sedan had been cut off and a tray mounted to the rear half to convert it into a ute, and it had been left there – possibly since the 1950s – piled high with haybales.

'This one.'

'Good choice.'

Another photo caught his eye. Two juxtaposed vehicles, the old and the new. In the foreground an ancient, rusted-through tractor and, on the road beyond it, a man staring into the guts of a broken-down Isuzu truck loaded with fuel drums.

Recalling that he'd been seeing similar trucks for a while now, he asked, 'Where was this taken?'

'Up near End Point Park.'

'Recently?'

Rosie shook her head; puffed at the errant strand of hair again. 'God, ages ago. Two, three years?'

Hirsch shrugged. Fuel and other goods were always being delivered to the sheep properties of the Mid North. He folded Rosie's invoice into his pocket, said goodbye and was halfway down the driveway when his phone rang. Sergeant Brandl, wanting him to attend to a distressed motorist, name of Annika Nordrum, out near Anna Gorge.

9

'Everyone's tied up,' she said. 'Me, emergency services, Redruth Motors, the CFA ...'

'Yeah, yeah,' Hirsch said.

'That's the spirit,' Brandl said cheerfully. 'I've sent you the coordinates.'

And so Hirsch checked the onboard display terminal mounted to his dash and headed north for the hard-baked country beyond the Mischance Creek ruins, taking one of the many long runs of corrugations and potholes that passed as roads out there. The sun was high and hot.

He drove for over an hour until finally he breasted a low rise in a juddering swoop and almost collided with a woman, a border collie and an old maroon Mazda ute strung out across the road.

'Trust me, not Google Maps,' he was saying a minute later, scratching the dog behind the ears.

Annika Nordrum stood with him in glum contemplation

of her ute. Fitted with a camper shell, it sat crosswise to the road, nose down in the ditch as if trying to steer under the farmgate set in the fence just there.

'Yeah, well, I put my trust in that sign,' she said disgustedly, pointing to *Anna Gorge* hand-painted on a strip of tin nailed to the gate, the words barely visible behind dust, bird shit and bullet holes.

'Anna Gorge *the sheep station*,' Hirsch said. 'Now abandoned. The actual gorge is a thirty-minute drive that way,' he added, gesturing to the north-east.

She screwed up her face. 'Two cheers for technology.'

'Yep. I could spend a month putting up signs and arrows around the district, saying ABC is fifty ks that way, and XYZ is twenty that way.'

Nordrum continued to stare gloomily at the Mazda. 'I tried reversing and the tyres just kept spinning.'

'Good thing you've got a sat phone,' Hirsch said, thinking also that a more experienced person would have kept to the crown of the road, noticed that the gate hadn't been opened for decades and checked the ditch first. And done all of the above in a four-wheel-drive vehicle.

But who was he to be critical? When he was busted down to uniform and posted up here six years ago, he'd arrived without an ounce of bush sense. The Mid North had been a mystery; the distances and emptiness overwhelming. Not so mysterious nowadays. Richer and more complex. But he'd always be considered a newcomer.

Now Nordrum, a slight twenty-something figure in hiking boots, knee-length cargo shorts and a sleeveless khaki work shirt, stared at the track beyond the gate. It was no more than a scribble, fading to nothing across baked red soil. 'Maybe,' she said, pointing, 'the property backs onto the gorge?'

Hirsch shook his head. 'Not that I'm aware of. And I don't know who owns it these days.' He grinned. 'Maybe someone with a shotgun who doesn't like trespassers?'

She rolled her eyes at him, then contemplated the winch on the front of the police Toyota. 'Any chance you can pull me out?'

'Give it a go,' Hirsch said, hoping that her steering, sump and brake lines hadn't been damaged. If so, it would mean a breakdown truck. He wasn't keen on towing her the seventy kilometres to Tiverton.

This wasn't the first time and wouldn't be the last that he'd pulled out careless and unlucky motorists – himself included – deceived by the apparent dryness of creek crossings and claypans.

'Let's have a look,' he said, crouching to peer under the Mazda's cocked-up rear bumper for somewhere to hook on.

When he got to his feet again, he saw that Nordrum had begun to spool out his winch cable, dragging it across the dirt, passing it to him wordlessly. He scooted under the bumper, connected the winch hook and backed out again, feeling flushed. Brushing off the dust and grit, he said, 'In neutral and handbrake off,' as he climbed behind the wheel of the HiLux.

She gave a little nod and hand gesture to say that she understood, waved okay from the Mazda's driver's seat and Hirsch started the winch. With the dog barking encouragement, the cable tautened, and amid creaks from both vehicles and the crush of rolling tyres, the little camper jerked free of the ditch. 'Whoa,' Hirsch shouted.

The brake lights winked on and the Mazda rocked gently as Nordrum got out. 'Thank you.'

'Don't thank me yet,' Hirsch said, crouching to peer at the front underside of her ute. He got to his feet again. 'Now you can thank me. Things look okay, but keep an eye on your brakes, steering and gauges. Meanwhile, let's get both vehicles onto the side of the road, just in case.'

In case there was traffic. A farmer passing sometime in the next few days ...

That done, Nordrum said, 'I'm stoked. You're a lifesaver.'

'Someone would have been along eventually,' Hirsch said.

He paused: Annika Nordrum had a satellite phone but how well prepared was she otherwise? And why was she heading for Anna Gorge? No one ever went there. The roads were shocking. 'Have you got emergency gear? Plenty of food and water?'

Nordrum nodded. Her brown hair had mostly escaped a short ponytail and was pasted damply to her forehead and neck. She had a narrow, faintly lived-in face, as if she'd had her share of setbacks. 'Plenty of everything,' she said, 'including locator beacons.'

'More than most tourists travel with,' Hirsch said.

'I'm not a tourist,' she said simply. 'I'm looking for my mother's body.'

10

'But your father's body wasn't found at the gorge,' observed Hirsch a couple of minutes later.

They were drinking tea and sharing Nordrum's Anzac biscuits in the thin shade of the police Toyota – which was more fun, as far as Hirsch was concerned, than checking emails or auditing firearms.

'He was found at Breadbox Plain.'

Hirsch nodded. 'I remember now.'

A big story at the time, almost seven years ago, just before he'd arrived in the Mid North. A couple from Adelaide on a fossicking trip. The husband found dead at the bottom of a mineshaft at Breadbox Plain, a godforsaken expanse of red dirt dotted with quartz reefs, dry creek beds, mulga scrub and treacherous, long-abandoned holes in the ground. The wife never found. No subsequent credit card or mobile phone activity.

'But Breadbox is an hour from here,' he continued, 'so why are you searching Anna Gorge?'

'It's where Mum and Dad *said* they were going. They didn't say anything about Breadbox Plain.'

'Maybe they wanted to fossick there too, and it was more efficient to split up?'

Frustration made Nordrum impatient. 'I don't know. I have no way of knowing. All I know is, Dad called me when they arrived, all excited. Anna Gorge had "untapped potential", quote, unquote.'

Ben and Heather Nordrum had owned a little gem shop in North Adelaide, selling jewellery made by Heather and vials of gold dust and trays of nuggets, polished stones and crystals graded by Ben. Otherwise, they liked to go fossicking three or four times a year, poking around the outback for gold, opals and semi-precious stones.

'Or,' said Hirsch, 'maybe the gorge turned out to be not such a good place. Hence Breadbox Plain.'

'Maybe,' Nordrum muttered, dampening a finger, rubbing at a dust smear on her knee.

The border collie had been leaning, panting, against Hirsch's shoulder. Now she licked his salty neck. He laughed and ducked away. 'She likes me.'

'Ah, Bella's quite undiscriminating,' Nordrum said, leaning to peer past him at her dog.

'You're intending to camp at the gorge? How long for?'

'As long as it takes.'

'Did you take over your parents' business?'

Nordrum snorted. 'That's a story in itself. Short answer, I just recently sold it. Getting probate was a nightmare: Dad dead, Mum missing. But I was never interested to begin with.

Uni, teaching, travel, the usual. At the same time, nothing's ever felt quite right, if you know what I mean. As if I can't settle until I know what happened.'

'Makes sense. Did anyone see your parents at the gorge, or the gold diggings?'

Nordrum shook her head. 'According to the inquest, they stopped for a pub lunch in Muncowie, and that was it, last sighting.'

Hirsch knew Muncowie, a defeated huddle of tin roofs on the Barrier Highway about an hour west of where they were standing. Just red dirt and patches of mulga in between. And he knew the pub, the publican and the bleary old geezers who daily propped up the bar. No way would he eat a Muncowie Arms pub lunch or even drink the beer. But all he said was, 'Okay.'

Annika Nordrum took a mouthful of tea; swiped at a fly supping at the moisture in her left eye; flapped her shirt-front to cool her chest. 'I wasn't that surprised when I didn't hear from them again. They were experienced. Always well prepared. Then one day there's a knock on my door. The police. Sorry to inform you, et cetera, et cetera. They said someone found Bella wandering down the middle of the road, hungry and dehydrated, had a look around, spotted the ute, and you know the rest.'

Hirsch gestured at the Mazda. 'This same ute?'

'Yes.'

'And it was at Breadbox Plain?'

'Yes.'

There was a pause, and Hirsch said, 'Your dad's death was ruled an accident?'

'Yes. Broken neck, and "other injuries consistent with a fall", quote, unquote.'

She's read the official findings a million times, Hirsch thought. 'I'm sorry.'

'Thank you.'

'Were doubts raised? Do *you* have doubts?'

'About how he died? Not really. It's just ... Why did he go to Breadbox Plain in the first place? Why didn't Mum go with him? And if she did, why wasn't she found? There was a big search – eventually. Even a helicopter.'

'You think she might have stayed on at Anna Gorge?'

'Yes.'

Hirsch tried to put it delicately. 'Is there any reason why they'd split up?'

Nordrum swayed away as if to see his face clearly. 'I'll say this right now, they were boringly happy with each other.'

'What I mean is, would they split up to fossick in two places at once?'

'Nice save,' Nordrum said. She slumped again. 'Even if they did split up, how was my mother supposed to survive? Everything was found with Dad: the ute, their food, their equipment, Bella ... So, I'm working on the theory they had spares of everything. A tent, Esky, cooker ...'

'But nothing was found at the time.'

That fired Nordrum up. 'They didn't even search Anna Gorge. No matter how hard I argued.'

Hirsch visualised the next few days for Nordrum, ranging along the base and around the rim of the gorge. The disappointment if she found nothing. The eeriness if she did – even if it was only an abandoned tent.

She tossed the dregs of her tea. 'Sorry to keep you.'

Hirsch shrugged and they continued to sit. Nordrum reached down into her boot and scratched her ankle. Came upright again, brushing Hirsch's shoulder unconsciously. Strangely, Hirsch felt as if they'd known each other forever. They were friends sitting side-by-side, something they'd always done. They were not playing helpful policeman and motorist in distress.

'Did the inquest come up with any theories?'

Nordrum snorted again. 'Yes, and so did the media, the police and so-called friends. Mum was with Dad, saw him fall in and wandered off to get help.'

'But why wouldn't she take the ute?'

'That's the strange thing. It wouldn't start. It was quite driveable, but it turns out one of the battery leads had come off, and the thinking was, rough roads had loosened it. But wouldn't it have just conked out randomly in the middle of nowhere in that case?' Another shrug. 'It was neatly parked beside the mineshaft.'

Hirsch had no explanation for that. 'Okay.'

'Another theory was, she wandered off to do some fossicking of her own and got disorientated, bitten by a snake, even fell into another mineshaft. Not to mention that she wandered off because she and Dad had a fight, and got lost – and meanwhile Dad committed suicide. Or that she had a lover who bumped Dad off and whisked her away. So on and so forth.'

'But you think she wasn't even there.'

'There was a lot to *indicate* she was there. Her backpack and purse et cetera. But it was all contained in one place, in or around the ute. My mother could be messy, setting up a new camp spot. And the first thing she always did was arrange a shade cloth to cook and eat under.'

'No tracks, shoeprints …?'

'Who knows? Whoever got there first would've trampled over everything, unaware Dad might not have been alone. And it was another full day before they tracked me down, and when I asked them where Mum was, they had no idea what I was talking about. I mean, her stuff was there, a woman's stuff, so why hadn't they twigged? They didn't exactly fill me with confidence.'

Hirsch thought of Sergeant Kropp, his first boss in the Mid North, who would've handled the search and subsequent investigation at the time. Now retired – in disgrace – and living near Clare. He'd been a lazy bugger, his two constables had been lazy bullies, and Breadbox Plain was a long drive from the Redruth police station. It was likely that by the time Kropp and his gang got there, the place was flooded with search volunteers, and no one to warn them not to disturb vehicle tracks or shoeprints.

For that matter, would anyone have been alert or meticulous enough to view it as a possible crime scene and done the business with fingerprints and DNA? Unlikely. Ruled a misadventure from the start.

'Do you happen to know if crime-scene people attended?'

'No. Look, I'm clutching at straws,' Annika Nordrum said.

'If Mum's not at Breadbox Plain, she's at Anna Gorge. Ran out of food and water when Dad didn't come back. She might have tried walking to the main road and got lost. Anything could have happened. It's worth a look, that's all.'

'True,' Hirsch said.

He pictured the Tiverton police station. It was possible that some of the initial paperwork was stored in the dented filing cabinet behind his desk. Or moth-eaten in the filing cabinet that was rusting in what used to be the lockup attached to the back of the house and was now storage for his garden tools. Or it was all stored in the main district police station down in Redruth.

Meanwhile the bushflies had found his eyes. He felt hot and clammy; time to go home. A cold shower, a bit more office work and dinner with Wendy and Kate at the end of the day. He stood, regret on his face. 'I'm afraid I need to get back.'

Nordrum stood too; stretched her spine, patted dust from the seat of her pants. 'Sorry to bend your ear like that, and thanks for all the help.'

'That's what I'm here for,' Hirsch said. 'But could you call me every day or two?' He gave her his card. 'Especially if you move location. It's pretty harsh out here. Lonely. Just so I know you're okay.'

11

He was halfway back to Tiverton when the sergeant called.

'Did you find her okay?'

'All good,' Hirsch said. 'Pulled her out of a ditch. No damage. But there's an interesting story,' he added, going on to relate it briefly.

When he'd finished, Brandl said, 'Vaguely remember it.'

'I wouldn't mind reading the file,' Hirsch said. 'But I don't know if I have it or you do.'

'No idea,' Brandl said. 'I'll have a look. The main thing is, how switched-on is she? We're not going to find *her* bones out in the middle of nowhere?'

'She seemed well equipped and promised to stay in touch.'

'Let's hope she does.'

Hirsch bought a bottle of Clare riesling at the pub and was passing the shop on his way back when he saw Ed Tennant unpinning ads and flyers from his veranda noticeboard. He parked outside the police station and hurried across the highway, calling, 'Ed? Got a minute?'

Tennant scowled. He was more put-upon by life than anyone Hirsch knew. 'Only a minute.'

'Do you remember the Nordrum case a few years back? Husband found in a mineshaft, wife—'

'I remember,' Tennant said, ripping away a Blyth Cinema flyer in a kind of fury.

'Just wondering what you can tell me about it.'

A distracted shrug. 'Can't tell you anything about it, except that when the search party got going, I had my best-ever week of trading.'

Hirsch visualised the influx of police and emergency services personnel. 'I met the daughter this afternoon.'

Tennant stared thoughtfully at the cobwebs clinging to the tops of his veranda posts. 'Late twenties, driving an old Mazda ute?'

'That's her.'

'She was in here first thing. Instant coffee, matches and tissues.'

'You talk to her?'

'Nup.'

Hirsch went into the shop, selected a dozen halfway decent yellow roses from a bucket, took them to Ed's wife at the cash register, and returned to the police station, restless now. He wasn't due at Wendy's until six. Rather than read his inexhaustible emails he banged out through the back door and around to the old lockup. Thick-walled, with a door to withstand a battering ram, it was always dark and cool inside. Shapes and shadows flared when he flicked on the light. His gardening stuff. A broken chair. The battered filing cabinet. Otherwise there was only one narrow patch of dusty sunlight leaking in from the barred window set high in the far wall. Had that window snatched hope away from the wife-beaters, rowdy shearers and Indigenous men who'd been incarcerated here? Some of them had scratched their despair into the walls: *fuck all coppers* and *Kropp is a cunt* and *If you find this I am dead*.

He began searching the filing cabinet, starting at the top. Musty copies of expense sheets going back years, submitted by Constables A. Antic and S. Christou and droves of other men he'd never heard of. No women had ever served in Tiverton. Accident reports. A hayshed hanging, ruled a suicide by Constable B. Squire. The theft of fuel, chainsaws, toolboxes, sheep and sheepdogs – same old same old, Hirsch thought. A truck fire report – to which Senior Constable T. Bleasdale had appended a note: *insurance job?* He found the Nordrum file towards the back of the second drawer.

Settled at his desk, he began with a quick run-through, pausing at the photographs: a broad patch of red soil, mulga scrub in the background and the Mazda camper in the foreground – with the driver's door open. Why? A backpack in the dirt, near the back tyre – why not stowed in the ute? A large plastic crate crammed with food tins and packets – also just sitting in the sun. Leaning against the ute, a pick and a shovel, with a bucket, a sieve and an empty tub nearby. Again, why? To do a wet-sieve of creek sand? What creek? With what water?

Next, several interior shots of the ute, showing the keys

in the ignition, a satellite phone in the centre console and two sleeping bags on a foam mattress in the back, along with a foldup chair, dogfood packets and a feeding bowl. A calico sack, photographed with the top open to reveal the contents: a muddle of dull and dusty pebbles – gemstones in their unpolished state? A handbag, then the handbag sitting beside its contents: a purse, a mobile phone, tissues, a ballpoint pen, keys and receipts. The contents of the purse: a few dollars and a driver's licence, Medicare card, library card and two credit cards, all in the name of Heather Nordrum. A separate wallet with Ben Nordrum's cash and cards.

Hirsch found himself staring at the wall. According to Annika, her father had called to say that Anna Gorge looked promising. Presumably he'd used the satellite phone. Did his wife have one, too?

He returned to the photographs and a shot of Bella the border collie grinning up at the camera. So who found the dog and where?

Hirsch leafed through the initial reports. Frustratingly – and typically – the answer was vague: 'A local farmer' and 'in the middle of the road'. Hirsch didn't want to have anything to do with his old sergeant again but added a note to his to-do list: *Contact Kropp re dog*.

Next, a bundle of shots of the mineshaft entrance: a square of old logs and railway sleepers partially concealed by dry grass and a scrap of roofing iron. He knew that some of the Breadbox shafts went down twelve metres and were a hundred years old. Among these photographs were others that puzzled him: sets of animal bones, rifle and shotgun shells, a threepenny coin, an empty corned-beef tin. He checked the reverse of each photo: *found vicinity mineshaft*. The tin was ninety years old. These items related to the place's gold era, not the Nordrums.

Finally, a packet of photographs of Annika Nordrum's father: establishing shots of his body twisted at the bottom of the shaft, and closeups of his face and hands. Wearing jeans, boots and a long-sleeved shirt, he lay partly on one hip, chest down, head turned aside and chin extended at an unnatural angle. Sunglasses and an Adelaide Crows cap nearby.

Catastrophic head injuries, according to the pathologist's report. Consistent with a fall.

He hadn't spotted the mineshaft opening because he'd been wearing sunglasses?

Unlikely.

Hirsch was reaching for a packet of autopsy photos when his phone buzzed, set to remind him that he had thirty minutes to shower, change and pack a bag for the weekend.

12

At 6 p.m., hair damp from his shower, Hirsch headed south along the Barrier Highway, the weekender bag in the boot of his off-duty old Nissan, the wine and the roses on the passenger seat. Apart from a handful of farm utes heading for the Tiverton pub, the highway was quiet, as if waiting for something to happen. Birds watched him from the powerlines and the sun, a few degrees above the horizon, turned the hilltops a vivid tan.

Five kilometres later, the Bitter Wash Road turnoff took him towards other hills. Dirt, gravel and potholes, and his narrow-tyred little car didn't like it. Twitched its tail, lost traction, juddered. Dust roiled and stones pinged as Hirsch kept to the crown of the road, relying on oncoming-vehicle dust as an advance warning as he steered into blind corners. But he met no one as the road wound around undulating hillocks, deeper into harder country. Over a rise and on his left was a strip of intact stone wall dating from the 1880s, a time of pastoral dreams – dreams that amounted to dust whenever there was a drought. Possession, thought Hirsch, and dispossession. The folly of reproducing English ways where they didn't belong.

The past persisted; the place was imprinted with it. In addition to the colonial past there was the recent past – ten-year-old wind-farm turbines strung along a nearby ridgeline – and a long Indigenous past – Ngadjuri rock art, if you knew where to look for it. Hirsch's own past, too. As he came sweeping up and over another rise, there was the Tin Hut Corner where, only three weeks after his posting to the Mid North, he'd found the body of a farmer's wife – a murder staged as a suicide.

Two kilometres later, Wendy Street's driveway. Hirsch turned in past a line of pepper trees and shrubs then parked beside the veranda of a small, red-roofed house. As always, he scoped the place: mother and daughter were alone out here. Then again, so was anyone who didn't live in a town. Wendy's Golf in the carport, the gardening shed with the door that needed repairing, the new satellite dish on the roof and Kate in the veranda hammock, reading, rocking absently, one thin leg bent, tensing for leverage on the warped old floorboards. He remembered powerfully the day he'd first met her. Six years ago and she was eleven years old, reading *To Kill a Mockingbird* in the hammock. She was still a reader. Still thin and small-boned, still wary, contained and unblinkingly solemn.

She'd accepted him into her life with her mother readily enough back then, but she was older now, she had reservations. Last year she'd needed to remind him that he wasn't her father; her father had been killed in a car crash when she was eight. This year she seemed to find him too cop, too male, too politically unsound.

'Don't worry, Aitch, she thinks I'm a lost cause, too,' Wendy assured him one night.

Sometimes he wondered if there was an ick factor in Kate's reservations: Hirsch in her mother's bed, Hirsch sharing the bathroom. 'Give it time,' Wendy told him. 'She's going through a stage.'

Going through a stage was right: there was no constancy. Sometimes the old bantering Kate returned. Like now: as he mounted the veranda steps, bearing the wilted roses and the riesling, he heard her say, 'It is a truth universally acknowledged that a single man, trapped in an outdated mindset, will bring his sweetie wine and roses.'

Hirsch snapped his fingers: 'Isn't that the famous opening sentence of *Mutant Chainsawing Zombie Chicks*?'

'Close,' Kate said, still reading, still rocking – but with some faint creasing around her eyes and mouth.

Hirsch clocked the cover of her book – Jane Austen – before opening the screen door and walking down the hallway to the kitchen. Wendy, a slight, intense woman with some grey in her hair these days, tilted her cheek for a kiss as she continued to whip a salad spinner around. They exchanged their news, poured wine, clinked glasses, set the table and called the brat for dinner. It was familiar and comforting.

Later, forks at rest on emptied plates, Wendy said, 'Vikki's right, kids do pick up on their parents' anxieties. The other day a boy in my Year Ten maths said, "We're going to lose the farm."'

Kate said, 'Don't forget Tracy Mackey's dad.' She turned to Hirsch and explained: a Farrell Flat farmer; a shotgun suicide.

Hirsch saw Wendy flinch. She's visualising me, he thought, first on the scene if any Tiverton farmer should blow his head off. She's worried what it'll do to me on top of everything: my father; that business with the baby and the dog last year.

To signal that he was all right, he reached a hand to hers and tried a contented smile. It worked. Briefly then, they all three reached hands to each other.

Hirsch recovered first, deflecting to jokiness in his usual way. 'Meanwhile in other news, yesterday I had a guy tell me he didn't need proper number plates because he's a citizen of a parallel community.'

Mother and daughter lit up. Said, '*Strawman*,' in unison.

'Strawman?'

'This boy in Mum's Year Eleven maths.'

'His name's Drew Sampson,' Wendy said, 'and he never does homework, never does class work, spends all his time looking at his phone or walking around the classroom or up and down the corridors. When I first tackled him about it, he said we're all born with two personas. One's the real you, flesh-and-blood, the other's your strawman. Your strawman's legally responsible for everything, not the real you. So he doesn't have to do homework or even attend school.'

Hirsch nodded: Trent McRae in a nutshell.

'No one likes him,' Kate said.

'But some of the other kids are starting to listen,' said Wendy, sounding fed up.

After dinner they settled in front of the TV, Wendy tucked against Hirsch on the sofa, Kate stretched face-down on a beanbag. He tried to concentrate but his head was too full, drawn more to the room than the screen. The furniture. The photos lit by flickering pulses of TV colour, particularly the two Rosie Llewellyn shots that he'd given as presents last Christmas. For Wendy, a kelpie and a little boy, lost in his father's rubber boots, staring down a stroppy ram. For Kate, a sweaty, exhausted jillaroo resting her cheek against the jawline of a black horse. Otherwise, the walls and mantel held photographs from a period before Hirsch: Kate pushing a teddy bear in a little wooden trolley, the brim of a knitted pom-pom beanie falling over her eyes and nose. Alan Street. Alan Street with Wendy, with Kate, with both. Alan and Wendy on their wedding day.

Their full lives long before he met them.

But at bedtime, as he was placing his watch on Wendy's chest of drawers, Hirsch saw a new photo. She was watching him. 'Like it?'

She'd sneaked a shot of Hirsch on a chair beside the hammock a few weeks ago, a biology textbook open on his lap, Kate rocking, caught in the moment of realising that he'd just fired a joke test question at her. Beginning to smile, which was better than one of her scowls.

That had been a good day. He glanced at Wendy. 'Yeah,' he said. 'Really like it.'

13

That delight was still in him when he rose at dawn on Saturday, walked three or four kilometres each way along Wendy's road, showered and made coffee and toast. He let the others sleep. They'd curse him if he woke them.

Then, at 8 a.m., trying to push away the thought that he'd be disappointing his mother again, he decided to cram in a bit of police work before driving to her place. How often had he done that, cancelled a visit, cut a weekend short, arrived at 3.30 for a noon lunch?

But he was more or less in the vicinity of Alastair Stanyer's shack. Only half an hour away. Stupid not to check. And so he bounced and shuddered out along Bitter Wash Road and then north onto Mischance Creek Road and finally at a crawl along Stanyer's driveway.

He found no indication that Al had been back. In fact, the cabin and the outbuildings looked as if they'd slid further down to dust in the meantime, with not even a visiting boot or tyre print to suggest human intervention.

He'd lost an hour, and could still make it to the Adelaide Hills for a late lunch, but Mitchell Stanyer and his wife lived close to where Bitter Wash Road met the Barrier Highway. Stupid not to see if they knew where Alastair was.

He'd started retracing his route when an oncoming vehicle braked as it was about to pass. He recognised the driver – Auntie Steph at the wheel of a Honda Odyssey people mover – just as she recognised him. They both stopped, reversed, drew level and settled in for a catch-up, open window to open window in the middle of the road.

Eyeing the dusty Nissan, Steph cocked an eyebrow. 'Undercover work?'

'Off to spend the weekend with my mother,' Hirsch said. He stuck his head out the better to examine her car. 'New wheels?'

She banged her palms on the steering wheel. 'Piece of crap.'

Muted shouts, giggles and faces pressed against the rear windows. She had kids on board. 'Where're you going?'

'To collect bush tucker,' Steph said.

Stephanie Ingram was a comfortable-looking woman in her mid-sixties, with grey-streaked hair and dangly earrings. Manager of a Redruth drop-in centre known as the Wurlie, for years she'd been taking Ngadjuri and white children into the back country to gather nardoo seeds and other Indigenous foods, and to see rock and cave art.

'I guess by now you know where all the good stuff is.'

'Sure do.' Then, putting on her wry stirrer's face, Ingram added: 'Despite what a hundred and seventy years of whitefella hooves and ploughs have done to blackfella country.' She threw up her hands. 'And still you people persist.'

Hirsch, recalling his conversation with Mark Button, grinned and took the bait. 'Actually, I've been spreading the word among my people: why not try new crops and farming methods.'

'Better still,' Steph twinkled, 'give it all back to us.' She glanced at the kids again. 'We'll also check out the birthing tree – if it's still standing.'

The birthing tree, sacred to the Ngadjuri people, was a grand old ghost gum at the corner of Mischance Creek Road and a rough track leading to the disused End Point Park sheep station. When Steph had heard that the district council wanted to chop it down to widen and improve the track, she'd sought an injunction – which, to Hirsch's relief, was granted. He'd thought he might have to deal with cowboys coming in with chainsaws, chippers and graders in the middle of the night, or Steph and her mob chaining themselves to the trunk and dying of heatstroke in the middle of the day.

'Any sign of roadworks yet?'

Steph shook her head. 'But I saw a fuel truck go up there a few days ago. Maybe they've started grading at the other end.'

'Beats me why they want to improve that road to begin with. It's never used, no one lives along it, and there are plenty of others in worse condition.'

Steph shrugged. 'Beats me, too. The council, in its infinite wisdom.' She cocked her head at Hirsch. 'Speaking of which: know what her ladyship calls me?'

'Her ladyship?'

'The mayor.'

Deciding that discretion mattered here, Hirsch didn't let on that he was on his way to the mayor's house. 'No.'

'She calls me Mrs Every-weed-is-sacred. Or Mrs Hands-off-that-patch-of-dirt-there's-artifacts-on-it.'

Hirsch said, 'Nice.'

'Yeah, nice.'

Passing Wendy's place twenty minutes later, he was soon at the Barrier Highway intersection. No traffic, so he accelerated across and up Mawson Road. It was marginally better country here, despite the drought. Better fences, better road surfaces, and he could see the old homestead overlooking the Tiverton to Penhale valley. Sprawling, imposing, with garden trees and lawns green all year round, it sat at the end of a grand curving driveway, recently graded.

He was hoping for Mitchell Stanyer, whom he'd met once before: Beretta pump-action shotgun. But when he mounted the broad veranda, knocked on the front door and stood waiting in air screened from the heat by the dense weave of a grapevine, it was Clarissa Stanyer who answered. She informed him promptly and coolly that she had not seen her brother-in-law and nor did she expect to. She added wearily, 'What's he done now?'

The mayor was in her late forties and wore a blue-grey skirt to her knees, a sleeveless grey top and no jewellery apart from a sleek Apple watch. She was a still, contained figure, hard to read, and seemed to regard Hirsch along the slope of a long, fine nose – an effect offset by the pair of curious spaniels panting up at him from either side of her tanned bare feet.

Feeling clumsy, Hirsch dissembled. 'I dropped in on him just now – I like to keep tabs, if you know what I mean. He wasn't home and I was wondering if you or your husband had seen him recently.'

She wasn't interested. 'I'm actually glad you called by, Constable Hirschhausen. You've seen the rubbish, I take it?'

Hirsch was on the back foot. 'Rubbish?'

'On the town paddock. My husband saw it yesterday morning when he checked his lucerne irrigators. He then called me, and I cancelled an important meeting to see for myself.'

Hirsch nodded. 'I am aware of it. I emailed Nathan Bull about it, in fact.'

Clarissa's face said she had a poor opinion of the council's public works manager. 'Fridges, mattresses, bricks, asbestos ... It looks like a whole house has been dumped there. To quote my husband, an absolute eyesore.'

As if the rubbish was an affront to the Stanyer name. Clarissa was fairly new in the role of mayor. Hirsch had never spoken to her and his only contact so far had been as a member of the audience when she opened the Redruth Show back in September. Now that he thought about it, she'd deployed the words 'my husband' with a certain tone then, too. My husband, the landowner. My husband, whose family has been here for generations.

'It must've been dumped two or three nights ago,' he said weakly. His dawn walk of the town didn't always include the town paddock.

The mayor regarded Hirsch as if he were not only a mere public servant, but also in serious breach of her notions of correct behaviour. 'I hope you won't pass the buck, Constable Hirschhausen. What matters is, who dumped it in the first place? According to my husband, people have been dumping small amounts for some time now.'

Hirsch rolled his shoulders uncomfortably. 'As I remarked in my email to Mr Bull, I'm hoping the council can send a clean-up truck.'

A sniff, a small puff of disdain as she eyed first his old car, then his casual weekend gear. 'And I'm hoping the Tiverton policeman can do his job.'

Hirsch blinked. Then he saw a glint in her eyes and realised that at some level Clarissa Stanyer was stirring for the sake of it. He suddenly saw someone unprincipled, unapologetic and indifferent to how people saw her – which must give her a lot of freedom and power.

He didn't want to get into the issue of rubbish-dumping with her. A greyish area, legally. When did simple littering become the criminal disposal of rubbish? Hirsch knew he had the power to arrest and charge, and magistrates the power to issue fines, but the district council also had powers and responsibilities – at least for rubbish clean-up, he thought, whether or not the culprit was arrested.

Intending neither to cede his authority nor seem clumsy or overemphatic, he laced his voice with a touch of grit: 'There's only me, Mrs Stanyer. I work twelve-hour days sometimes, seven days a week. Perhaps the council could install CCTV cameras? Other councils do. I'll happily monitor the video footage,' he added, immediately regretting the words.

Clarissa Stanyer looked at him. Barely moving the muscles of her face (Botox?) she said, 'Be sure, Mr Hirschhausen, that I shall raise the matter at our council meeting next week – at which you will be present, if I'm not mistaken.'

Hirsch was momentarily confused. Was he expected to attend because she'd be raising the matter of CCTV installation, or the standard of his policing?

Then she continued: 'Matters got very rowdy at last month's meeting, and we've been receiving death threats ever since.'

Oh, God. Hirsch didn't want to work after hours and doubted anyone would pay for it. 'Getting back to the matter of your brother-in-law, Mrs Stanyer. Is Mr Stanyer here? Perhaps he knows where Alastair might've gone?'

'I very much doubt that. He's been out east since yesterday morning – we have a property there – and I can't imagine he'd call in on Alastair.' The name was sour in her mouth, and she turned away as if to re-enter the house. 'They don't get along,' she said, over her shoulder.

As clear a bugger-off as Hirsch had ever received. 'Out east ...?'

Clarissa turned to face him again. A woman who hated obduracy. '*Way* out east.'

'Okay.'

They were interrupted by a dust-dulled black Range Rover

sweeping up the driveway, the driver glancing at the little Nissan before steering around to the rear of the property. Clarissa Stanyer smiled coolly at Hirsch, a woman who'd never doubted her place in the world. 'Your good fortune,' she said, eyes half-lidded. 'My husband's back early.'

Then Mitchell Stanyer appeared below them, wearing the pastoralists' uniform of moleskin pants, khaki shirt and R. M. Williams boots. He was older than his wife, solid, greying and slightly crumpled and whiskery. Wherever he's been, Hirsch thought, he camped out last night. And now Stanyer came boomingly up the veranda steps and across the boards, hand outstretched. 'Senior Constable Hirschhausen.'

At least *he* knows my correct rank, Hirsch thought sourly. Everything about Stanyer was rural-manly – the manner, the hand grip. Hirsch glanced at that hand. The knuckles were clean: they probably hadn't been landing blows on his younger brother recently.

'How can we help?' Stanyer asked, just as his wife hooked her arm around his in a conjoined display of satisfaction and said, 'I'd been telling Constable Hirschhausen that you were tending to matters at the Park.'

Hirsch said, 'The Park?'

'End Point Park Station,' Clarissa Stanyer said, and her husband's eyes went flat and distant briefly. He wants her to shut up, Hirsch thought.

His bad angel stirred. 'I'd always wondered who owned it.'

'Bought it years ago,' said Mitchell Stanyer stiffly.

'I heard about the road-widening issue. Ran into Steph Ingram earlier.'

Clarissa Stanyer, sticking up for her husband: 'For your information, that road is gazetted, on all the survey maps.'

'I see.'

'We certainly hope you do, Mr Hirschhausen. Mrs Ingram doesn't. But we acceded to her damn birthing tree injunction and will simply grade the road, now that we cannot widen it.'

Hirsch was curious. He looked from husband to wife and back again. 'Are you intending to develop the place?'

'Any development in the current climate would surely be welcome?' Clarissa said.

In campaign mode, thought Hirsch. He turned to Mitchell. 'I actually called in to ask about Alastair, Mr Stanyer. As I was telling your wife, I'm concerned for him. Did you see him yesterday? This morning?'

'Nope. Not for months.'

Hirsch hedged. 'Last time I saw him he looked like he'd been in the wars – cuts and bruises.'

Stanyer gave him a use-your-brains look. 'Falling down drunk, perhaps?'

'Do you know who his friends are?'

'Not a clue.'

'Okay, not important. Just a welfare check.'

'Welfare check.' To think that a Stanyer should require welfare ... Mitchell Stanyer's distaste was there and gone again, on a face with deep-set eyes bracketed by seamed and sun-aged skin.

And Clarissa said, 'I'll tell you what kind of check Alastair needs: a check on how he treats other people's property.

My husband's trailer, for example. His chainsaw. His good ladder. When and if you do see him, kindly prompt him to return everything. In good order.'

'Been a year,' Mitchell added.

They're half-serious, realised Hirsch. They see me as their tame cop. He said, 'A civil suit might sort him out,' thanked them and left.

14

Back onto the highway and down through Penhale – where Hirsch told himself he could spare a moment to check if Trent McRae had returned.

But there was no V8 ute parked outside his mother's house or his ex-wife's, and both women seemed distracted: they were taking Josie to swimming lessons. And no, they'd not seen or heard from Trent, a fact that didn't seem to bother them: the idiot had made his bed and could lie in it.

Hirsch returned to the highway and headed down through Redruth and Riverton to Tarlee, where he turned off for Eudunda, his thoughts returning to the Stanyer brothers' dynamics. The no-hoper and the anointed first-born. It was always possible that nature had played a role – Hirsch had seen great discrepancies between the children of even the mildest, most loving parents: a daughter who joined the Greens while her brother supported a vicious little Christian Nationalist party – but more likely that Mitchell's ambition and Alastair's haplessness had been forged by their father.

Mitchell had also been given a head start. He'd inherited the best slice of the old man's land and parlayed the income from it into acquiring the seed business in Tiverton, the lucerne property abutting the town paddock and – as Hirsch now knew – End Point Park Station. Then he'd married well, meeting Clarissa after many years as a bachelor farmer. According to local gossip she was a businesswoman from Adelaide in search of a sea change, and they'd met when bidding against each other at a farm auction.

The kilometres unfurled. Wendy had taken Hirsch to a Gillian Welch concert last year, and he played the latest album now, to mark an end to the morning. The natural world looked faintly more abundant – less droughty, at least – and noticeably greener as he drove through the Barossa Valley, with its well-irrigated winery slopes, driveways and tasting-room lawns. That was a nice marker to end the morning with, too.

Then out the other end and onto a back way into the Adelaide Hills. Dry country again. Nothing to anchor the topsoil on the bald, brown-grey hills, one of them blackened by a recent bushfire. He drove up into the network of small towns and connecting roads until he reached Balhannah. At the base of Iverson Street, a gentle upslope from the main road, grief swamped him. He felt as if he were sullying the ground where his father had been voyaging home. Except that, no: Karl Hirschhausen had been walking away from the house at the top of Iverson Street, towards some other home. The one where he'd grown up? The Tonsley house, where Hirsch was raised? 'Walking to some hazy-memory home, anyway,' Hirsch's mother had said. 'In the middle of the road. In the middle of the day. I'd chase after him and guide him back home and he'd get upset, and the next day we'd do it all again ...'

Until that one day, a few weeks earlier, when her back was turned for too long.

Hirsch had seen enough car crashes. He could almost hear the slap-flip of the impact, and he blinked as he steered uphill and pulled hard against the kerb outside 12 Iverson Street. A triple-fronted brick veneer, bought by his parents in retirement, back when Hirsch was still a probationary constable. A weedy paddock on the left, an elderly couple on the right, a plant nursery beyond the back fence.

He got out, grabbed his bag and Rosie Llewellyn's photo, and edged past his mother's burgundy Magna. It sat in the sun because his father's project, a racing-green Austin-Healey Sprite, was nestled half-restored in the carport. Hirsch had told his mother she should sell it, and she'd said, almost impatiently, 'Darling, the last thing on my mind.'

But it's probably worth a bit, he'd wanted to say. Money you could do with.

He ducked into the shade of the carport and viewed the little soft-top sportscar glumly. Cracked leather, fretting rubber seals, scuffed and faded carpets, a non-original gearstick knob. His father's mild rumble was in his head: 'All that can wait. I need to sort out the wiring loom first.'

The rats had not only feasted on the wiring loom; they'd also nested in the cramped space behind the dash, and Hirsch, visualising his father's hands at work, almost staggered. The image of the old man's squat, square-ended fingers. The dents, scrapes, scars and arthritic knuckles left by a lifetime of carpentry. Keeping active in retirement and exercising his brain should have saved Karl Hirschhausen from dementia, but it hadn't. He'd become a not-so-old, slightly stooped man tottering down the middle of the road.

Hirsch edged around the Sprite's chrome front bumper and in through the side entrance of the house to the airconditioned chill of the kitchen. His mother looked up in faint alarm. Seated at the table with a cryptic crossword book, glasses hooked on the tip of her nose, she was on her feet at once, wreathed in smiles. Rangy and tall – like her late husband, like her son. A bit absent-minded. Loving in a practical, distracted way.

'Darling,' she said, coming around the table to hug him – a clutch and release that finished with a step back to examine him. 'So lovely to see you.'

'Sorry I'm late.'

She waved that off. Her face and the kitchen and all the old smells and Cynthia winding around his shins threatened to do Hirsch in again. He did what he did when emotions threatened: he undercut them. 'Thought I'd find you busily stewing fruit or something.'

She hated cooking of any kind, and gave him a hand flip. 'There's a salad for you in the fridge.' Then spotting the wrapped photograph, she said, 'What's that?'

Hirsch waggled it at her. 'Expensive gift.'

She gave him a greedy little grin, took it from his hands and unwrapped it carefully. She'd recycle the paper.

'Oh,' she said.

The cross little girl with the cat that resembled Cynthia; the classic British car converted to a ute. 'It made me think of Dad,' Hirsch said.

'I can see that,' his mother said, emotions working across her face. Sad, loving, looking back along the years. Her husband and his hobby. Her husband who would've got a kick from this photograph. She turned on her heel and Hirsch followed her along the hallway. The entire house was dimly lit, the hot sun barred by blinds and curtains. An older-era house, with a floral carpet, dated furniture and pale blue walls. Hirsch found himself drawing it all in as if for the last time. As if he'd been away for a lifetime.

Into the end room, called the den, and here the digital age had made a mark. A Bluetooth sound system, headphones, a MacBook, a printer and shelves for books and CDs. Puzzle books, car manuals, novels, biographies.

'Here, I think,' his mother said, removing a framed poster from the wall. Almost art deco in style, it advertised an Austin-Healey Sprite.

'Perfect,' Hirsch said, thinking this was a good sign: remove the image first, then the actual car.

And after that she might take her late husband's clothes and vehicle memorabilia to the Salvos. Not the spanners, screwdrivers, sockets: his mother was a practical woman. And not the CDs, which they'd bought together. Popular classics, '60s and '70s rock, Fairport Convention, Leonard Cohen, k.d. lang, some early blues; some edgier folk and country.

He dutifully ate the salad, then they talked. Later a drive to the pub for dinner. A bit of crap TV before bed, Cynthia immediately claiming Hirsch's lap. Then a walk on Sunday morning before the heat set in. Siesta and a late-afternoon swim in the local pool. An early dinner of fish and chips, and Hirsch kissed his mother goodbye and headed back to the Mid North, thinking of her, and the week that stretched ahead of her.

When last he'd visited, he'd heard her on the phone to Centrelink, repeating patiently, 'The recipient is not available to sign those forms, the recipient – my husband – recently died, which is why I am talking to you,' and, 'My husband is unable to come to the phone, my husband has died,' and, 'The recipient is unable to call back later, the recipient – my husband – is dead.' Bureaucratic nightmares were going to be a part of her life now.

But mostly Hirsch thought of their day-and-a-half together, the things they'd said but mostly not said, and he knew that somehow, for both of them, it was enough to be going on with.

15

Dawn on Monday, Hirsch walking his town. As he was cutting down a side street, he encountered Bob Muir strapping a ladder to the roof of his Mercedes van, *Tiverton Electrics* scrolled on the driver's door. 'Another hot one.'

'Another hot one,' Hirsch agreed. It was what you said, along with 'Sure is dry.'

He added: 'Got a minute?'

Muir wiped his hands on his work shorts. He was older than Hirsch, solid, slow-moving, darkly watchful, almost morose. A friend now, after a rocky start, after it was clear that Hirsch was a patient, listening kind of cop, not a lazy, violent kind. And, crucially, Hirsch had joined the tennis club. 'Sure.'

'A husband and wife fossicking out east, a year before I was stationed here. The husband found dead, ruled an accident, the wife never found.'

Muir nodded. 'Breadbox Plain. I helped with the search.'

'Anything strike you at the time?'

Muir stared at Hirsch for a time. 'You're re-opening it?'

Hirsch shook his head. 'I met their daughter out near Anna Gorge. She says she's looking for her mother.'

Muir's mind worked, and he said, 'She reckons they split up?'

'She thinks it's a possibility.'

Muir pondered that. 'But the husband had the tent, the food ...'

'I know,' Hirsch said, bidding his friend a good day.

Next, Sergeant Brandl's Monday briefing.

Listening to Radio National, Hirsch reached the outskirts of Redruth at 7.45, reducing speed as he trundled through the town, passing the old copper mine that had kept the colony of South Australia profitable for many years, then down a shallow slope to the centre, a mix of colonial-era and modern shops skirting the town square – which, in these days of drought, was a small, triangular patch of dead grass sporting a faded green rotunda at one end and a statue to the war dead at the other. Then he was accelerating out past Redruth Toyota and the old ANZ bank, now a craft gallery.

He turned into a side street and parked in the shade of a massive gumtree opposite the Redruth police station – a purpose-built structure, not the front room of some old house on the highway. Brick, with a suite of rooms behind a civilian-staffed front desk and a spacious yard at the rear, with a lockable garage for the station's fleet of one sedan and two SUVs.

With a wave to Mr Pickett, the civilian clerk stationed at

the front desk, Hirsch entered a keycode into the security pad and stepped into a corridor lined with rooms: Sergeant Brandl's office, interview room, briefing room, unisex bathroom, tearoom, storage and lockup. The time was 7.55 now and the sergeant was seated at the briefing room table fiddling with a laptop connected wirelessly to the large wall monitor behind her.

She gestured a distracted hello to Hirsch and by the time he'd taken his seat the screen had flickered to life: the SA Police logo and a list of agenda items. Also behind her was a grimy whiteboard mounted on wheels; some charts and maps on the other walls. Queen Elizabeth II continued to preside over the proceedings from the end wall, frumpishly benign, slightly dusty, slightly skewed.

A plate of Redruth Bakery pastries sat in the middle of the table, connected by a trail of powdered sugar to Tim Medlin on one side of the table and croissant flakes to Jean Landy on the other. Hirsch said, 'People,' and reached for an apricot Danish.

Landy, mid-chew, thin and nervily capable, waved her croissant at him. Medlin said, 'Morning,' and ducked his head as if he'd committed a faux pas. Prematurely balding, with the look of a young priest, he showed a naive inability to understand wickedness that suited him more for office work than day-to-day policing.

Brandl finished her fiddling. 'Let's get started. Two general things. First, I'm getting pressure from above, parliamentarians getting hate mail postmarked Clare, Redruth, Spalding and Tiverton. I don't know how we're supposed to deal with it or even work out who's responsible, but at least keep your eyes and ears open. Second, we all know there's more ice around. A contact in the Drug Squad thinks it's being cooked locally, not imported, so, again, keep your eyes and ears open.' She turned to Landy. 'Now ... other news. Jean, you first.'

They met every Monday morning, if possible, to discuss local crimes, incidents, actions and results. Sometimes the pooling of information and the filling of gaps helped one or all of them solve a crime or discern a pattern, but mostly it boiled down to reporting a driving offence here, a shoplifting there.

Today Landy related that someone had taken advantage of a recent power outage – caused by a grassfire out on the Goyder Highway – to jemmy open the hospital's drug safe. 'Hence no CCTV, but we're tracking down anyone who was at the hospital that day, working, visiting a patient, et cetera.'

'Sounds spur of the moment,' Brandl commented.

'Agree. But while we're on the topic of the hospital, Dr Pillai had a strange experience last Thursday.'

The Redruth doctor sometimes made house calls on the elderly and ill, and had almost reached home from calming a panicky asthmatic in Booborowie when she overtook a Pajero crawling along in the middle of the Barrier Highway, just north of Redruth.

'The driver was on her mobile, so the doc gave a warning toot as she passed. Big mistake. Next thing she knows, the Pajero's alongside her and the passenger – possibly the husband or partner – is throwing dim sims at her.' She paused. 'Death by takeaway.'

They almost laughed – dim sims! – but nothing much surprised them anymore. Hirsch himself had attended at a recent road fatality in which the driver's mates had grieved by performing donuts and burnouts that blocked emergency-vehicle access to a hotted-up Impreza wrapped around a gum tree. By the time the body had been extracted and loaded, a glovebox torch and a first-aid kit had been swiped from Hirsch's HiLux, drugs from the ambulance, and hi-vis jackets, radios and a GPS unit from the Emergency Services van.

'Did she get a plate number?'

Landy shook her head. 'White Nissan four-wheel drive; older model. She saw it swerve and sideswipe a guardrail before it continued on its merry way. At least we didn't have to do a death knock.'

Hirsch had made a death knock after the Impreza incident. They'd all made death knocks at some time. Waited for a front door to open before informing a parent, partner or close friend that a loved one had been killed. Sometimes you had the urge to point out that the loved one was a fuckwit who'd brought it on themselves – through meth, booze, speeding, hooning or throwing dim sims at another driver – but you generally stopped yourself in time.

'Moving right along,' the sergeant said. 'Tim?'

Medlin, who usually worked alongside Landy, said: 'Not much more to add. A bloke broke his back falling off his bike mustering sheep. A petrol driveaway on Thursday night. Caught on CCTV but the plates were bogus.'

Hirsch went still. Exchanged a glance with Brandl. 'Where? Here?'

Medlin gestured towards Redruth's main street. 'The Caltex place.'

'Hotted-up Holden ute?'

'Yeah, how d'you know?'

With another glance at Brandl, Hirsch said, 'The sergeant and I caught an incident the same afternoon. If it's the same guy, his name's Trent McRae, from Penhale. Considers himself a sovereign citizen.'

General eye-rolling: enough said.

'If any of you spot him,' Brandl said, 'let me know. I don't want him arrested yet' – here she shot Hirsch an embarrassed look – 'but it'd be good if we got him in for an interview. Cuff him if he's being an active threat to himself or someone else, of course. That it?'

'Final thing,' Medlin said. 'Me and Jean had a quiet word with the bar staff at the Cornish.'

The Cornish was the worst of Redruth's three pubs, maybe owing to its location: off the main street near the defunct railway station; within cooee of the saleyards. 'What about?'

'Offering beer discounted according to bra size.'

'This place,' Brandl said, shaking her head. 'Paul? Your turn.'

Taking his cue from her – keep quiet about the punch in the guts – Hirsch described the incident at the Tiverton primary school briefly, then related the Annika Nordrum story, concluding: 'It all happened before our time and the paperwork's on the slim side, but if you're out east this week and see her poking around in an old red Mazda ute, you'll know what it's about.'

He took a swig of coffee before telling them about the

Tiverton town paddock. 'Huge pile of rubbish, probably from a house demolition, and the mayor gave me a hard time. If you hear of old buildings being pulled down and the rubble disappearing overnight, let me know.'

Another swig. The Alastair Stanyer story. 'The mayor's brother-in-law, as it happens. He seems more pathetic than dangerous, and for all I know he's fishing up on the Murray, but if you spot an old green Land Rover with this rego, let me know.'

He pointed to the screen: the sergeant had posted the plate number.

'Next, that domestic violence be-on-the-lookout I mentioned last month: Jerry Poulakis. He offed himself a few days ago.'

No one objected to his tone or language. A useful, neutral shorthand.

'Finally,' he said, 'another bit of road hooning.'

He related Dorrie Alkawaro's experience, then glanced at Jean Landy. 'A long shot, but could it be linked to what happened to Dr Pillai?'

'Different vehicle,' she said, and paused. 'You're thinking it's racial?'

'Worth looking at.'

They both turned to the sergeant. 'Sarge?'

Brandl nodded. 'Anything's possible. There've been similar complaints all year, so maybe it's time for a proper follow-up. Tim, go back six months and cross-check for racial overrepresentation. Paul, before you head back today, pop in and see if Auntie Steph can add anything.'

Then she glanced around at them, her face troubled. 'Finally, the council meeting Thursday night. As you know, the mayor's asked us to attend in case things get as rowdy as they did last month.'

Dutiful groans and Brandl grinned and said, 'I know, right? You'd think it never got more heated than a point of order regarding the potholes in Tiver Street.'

But Landy didn't grin. 'People are doing it tough these days. Fertile ground for My Place nutters.'

That wrapped it up for another week.

16

It was still only 9 a.m. Hirsch called Steph Ingram as he left, ensured that she was at the Wurlie and told her, 'See you in five.'

Making a U-turn outside the police station, he returned to the intersection and paused to check for cross-traffic. He glanced across at a dusty white Subaru Outback outside Redruth Toyota and felt his skin tingle. A quality of intense stillness in the driver – male, youngish, heavy around the neck and shoulders – staring down the side street at the police station. Only snipers, sentries and surveillance cops have that level of focus: most people's heads are restless most of the time. Continually altering position, even if subtly. Hirsch made the turn onto the main street and gradually accelerated, watching his mirrors all the while. He saw the Outback pull away from the kerb and come in close behind him.

He had a clearer view of the driver now, the guy steering with his forearms, his hands busy with a phone. Not making a call, Hirsch realised: taking photos.

His own phone was mounted in a dash cradle. A moment later he was saying, 'I'm just approaching the rotunda and I've got Trent McRae on my arse, driving a white Subaru SUV.'

'On it,' Sergeant Brandl said.

The Subaru tailed Hirsch as he turned slightly uphill between the shops and the town square and parked outside a cluster of stately stone buildings: a church, the town hall and adjunct municipal offices. Set back from the road and sandwiched between them was Steph Ingram's Ngadjuri drop-in centre, with a sign above the front door reading *The Wurlie* in the red, yellow and black colours of the Indigenous flag. He got out just as McRae braked hard alongside him, passenger-side window down.

'Trent? What're you doing?'

'I like to know who and what I'm dealing with,' McRae said, firing off more photos before slipping the phone into his shirt pocket and reaching for a little spiral notebook on the dash. His expression of cunning was almost comical as he waved it at Hirsch and began writing.

'Happy to help,' said Hirsch. 'How about you pull over and—'

'How about I don't listen to you because I don't have to,' McRae said. He hadn't shaved; his eyes buzzed. Looked past Hirsch at the Wurlie and said, 'You going in there?'

'Is that a problem?'

McRae was checking his mirrors. 'Knew you'd call backup.' He smirked as though he'd scored a point, and took off with a squeal of rubber.

Hirsch looked back along the street to his sergeant at the wheel of the Redruth Kia. He waved her on but she pulled in. 'What did he want?'

Why wasn't she chasing him? 'Checking me out.'

'New wheels. Did you get his plates?'

'Obscured this time.'

'Okay, I'd better get after him,' Brandl said.

'I'll help.'

'No. You check with Steph,' the sergeant said, losing vital seconds as she pulled out and immediately braked for a road train blasting its horn.

Nothing Hirsch could do about it. He grabbed his phone, locked up and crossed to the Wurlie, aka the Redruth and District First People's Art, Cultural Heritage, Education and Welfare Centre. According to Auntie Steph, the 'First People's' designation had been imposed on her mob by a po-faced state government mob. 'The rest of the name's bearable. Just.'

As he neared the front wall, Hirsch could see where spray-painted graffiti had been sandblasted away. *Boong Central* and *First Nation=Stone Age Nation*, things like that. The entry door had been propped open with a cracked green plastic outdoor chair, so he walked in and down a short corridor, his progress monitored by wall-mounted wooden shields and woomeras, dot paintings, Namatjira-inspired watercolours and headshots of Indigenous elders.

Hirsch knocked on the door marked manager, heard, 'It's open,' and walked in.

Steph Ingram was working at an old laptop. She gestured

at a straight-backed wooden chair and said, 'Pull up a pew, be with you in a sec.'

The office was hot from all the days and weeks. The air and the flyers and a small Indigenous flag pinned to a corkboard were being stirred sluggishly by a ceiling fan. 'I'd aircon the whole place if I could,' she'd told him once, 'but the council's halved our funding. It's like we're trespassers in our own land.'

Right now she looked hot, wrung out, her temples moist, damp patches on her T-shirt. He watched her finish typing, close the laptop and lean back in her chair – just as a drawing pin pinged onto the floor and the corkboard flag folded limply in on itself. 'Damn thing,' she said, glancing briefly, turning to Hirsch again. 'Keeps happening.'

'You didn't have it up last time I was here.'

Ingram laughed without humour. 'I bought it for the council chambers but you-know-who said no thanks. Just like she said no thanks to a Progress Pride flag earlier in the year. And she's been wondering aloud whether a welcome to country was strictly necessary at council meetings anymore.'

Hirsch imagined the confrontation between Steph Ingram and Clarissa Stanyer: fire and ice. Steph said, 'You wanted to see me?'

Hirsch related Dorrie Alkawaro's experience. 'I was wondering if the same thing's happened to anyone else in your mob.'

Ingram stared at the wall and thought. 'Doug said he was tailgated a few weeks ago. I'll ask around. You think it was a targeted thing?'

Hirsch shrugged. 'Could be. Could also be random.'

'There's targeting and there's targeting,' Steph said, and she looked at Hirsch, as if wanting him to tease the meaning out of her.

'The graffiti?'

'Well, sure. But around the time I was applying to protect the birthing tree I learned they were putting pressure on some of the less, shall we say, politically astute elders, like Doug. You know the kind of thing: persuade me to withdraw the injunction and the Wurlie would get more funding and Doug a slab of beer.'

Uncle Doug was the Wurlie's uncomplicated all-round handyman. 'Who put the pressure on? The mayor?'

'Too canny for that. Not her husband, either. Maybe one of his station managers?'

Hirsch made a mental note: get a description from Uncle Doug. 'Amounts to bribery,' he said.

Ingram nodded. 'Anyway, Doug didn't bite. Told me all about it.' She paused. 'And while we're on the subject of targeting, there's something I'd like you to see.'

She took him through to the backyard, first crossing a big meeting room where six women were addressing envelopes. They looked up, saw a cop and looked down again after shooting hard-to-read looks at Steph. She smiled at them, waved reassuringly and then was ushering Hirsch out to a cobbled courtyard and the Honda people mover he'd seen her driving on Saturday morning. It was still dusty from its trip out east.

Hirsch said, 'Sugar in the fuel tank again?'

Ingram shook her head. 'No, thank God. These days we keep it locked up when we're not using it. But it broke down on me the other day.'

'And you haven't the funding to repair it.'

Steph sighed. 'The thing is, it was dodgy to begin with.' She shook her head wearily. 'I made the mistake of letting Doug buy it.' She gestured. 'How many ks do you think it's done? It's a 2012 model.'

Hirsch shrugged. 'Three hundred thousand? More?'

'Exactly. Not the sixty-nine thousand showing on the clock.' Steph paused. 'Bloody Doug. Too trusting.'

'Of who?'

'You know Nick Sampson?'

'Certainly do.'

Nicholas Sampson ran a business in motor repairs and used car and farm machinery out on the road to Morgan, along a stretch of mean, falling-down dwellings more rust than iron, more dust than stone, always with weedy front yards and stripped cars and skeletal horses out the back. Sampson often featured in Sergeant Brandl's Monday briefings, suspected of stripping, recycling and rebirthing stolen cars. The image she pasted to her wall-monitor was of a man as dented, grimy and questionable as his vehicles and VIN numbers.

Now the Sampson name rang another bell. The strawman kid in Wendy's Year 11 maths class.

Meanwhile Steph was saying, 'I know, I know, you get what you pay for, but, look, I love Uncle Doug, we all do, the Wurlie would be lost without him, but Nick Sampson saw him coming, just like he sees kids coming – Indigenous and white – with their first nine hundred and ninety-nine dollars, wanting to buy their first car. Can't you throw a scare into him?' Auntie Steph, who always seemed wryly competent and unimpressed, looked earnest and a little lost.

'I'll see what I can do,' Hirsch said.

'Get him to buy the car back for what we paid and we'll leave it at that.'

She might be able to leave it at that, but Hirsch couldn't. Not if a crime had been committed.

17

Head full of complications, he returned to his Toyota, just as Sergeant Brandl was pulling up on the other side of the road. Checking for traffic, he trotted across. 'No luck?'

'Lost him.'

Hirsch looked back the way she'd come. Trent McRae had gone up a side street, he thought, or even managed to leave the town and was out along a dirt track.

He returned his attention to the sergeant. 'Fancy dropping in on Nick Sampson?'

'What's he done now?'

Hirsch explained. 'Hard to prove, but maybe lean on him a bit?'

'Half the job, leaning,' Sergeant Brandl said. She checked her watch. 'It'll have to be brief.'

She followed him out along the Morgan road and, just as they parked, Nicholas Sampson emerged from an old shed, distributing the filth on his hands with a filthier rag. He could have been Trent McRae's father, Aussie boofhead in his fifties. If you had any life smarts, his face would have told you not to buy one of his used vehicles or trust that he hadn't used sawdust to silence the clunks in your transmission. If you were young, poor, naive or in a hurry, you might find yourself lining his pockets.

'Do you for?' A smoker's rasp.

His overalls were mostly oil and grease. A patina of oil, grease and fuel emissions on everything in fact, realised Hirsch as he stared in at the dimly lit hoist and workbenches. But there was a cleaner item in Sampson's workshop: a white Nissan Patrol 4WD with a dented left-hand side panel. Idly wondering if he'd find a paper bag that smelled of dim sims in the footwell, Hirsch gave Sergeant Brandl a little head-tilt and wandered over to check. And Brandl, picking up on what he was doing, fixed Sampson with one of her patented unimpressed looks and said: 'Morning, Nicholas.'

Sampson was torn, his head swivelling between Hirsch and Brandl, meaning Hirsch had to be quick with his phone: shots of the Nissan, side, front and rear, and of Sampson himself. Pocketing the phone again, he rejoined the sergeant, who was saying, 'There's a matter you can help us with.'

'Yeah? What would that be?'

Responding to a nod from Brandl, Hirsch said, 'You sold a people mover to the Wurlie.'

Sampson turned to him lazily. 'Didn't *sell* it, as such. No hard word was applied. Bloke came in and *chose* it, fair and square.'

'Not fair and square,' Brandl said. 'You fiddled with the odometer – and not for the first time, as we all know.'

Sampson was cool and contained. 'That is a lie. You

cannot prove it. That Honda had legit low mileage and I have the paperwork to prove it.'

'Really.'

'Bought it fair and square at Harbour Auctions in Port Adelaide. I get a lot of my stuff from them.'

Hirsch shook his head. 'A ringing endorsement.' It was likely that Harbour Auctions was as crooked as the dealers who bought their stock.

Sampson hooded his eyes. There was no warmth in the smile he directed at Hirsch. 'I'm yet to receive any complaints about the Golf I sold your lady friend – Wendy, is that her name? Wendy Street?'

In the seconds he took to digest this, Hirsch understood many things. That Nicholas Sampson stored information. That he connected it to other information. That he used information to drive a wedge, to prise and unsettle. And if that caused pain? Bonus. Like now, somehow insinuating there was something off about Wendy, and Hirsch, and their relationship. How come she hadn't bought from a reputable dealer, like Redruth Toyota? How could Hirsch have let that happen? What else was she up to? Didn't he have any control over his little woman?

Hirsch kept it pleasant. Even smiled and said, 'Yeah, it is a good car.'

'And everyone accuses me of selling crap.'

'A shame,' Hirsch said. 'Incidentally,' he added, 'I think Mrs Street teaches your son? Drew? Year Eleven maths?'

It didn't work. Sampson's return look said: *You need to take a better shot than that.*

Brandl cut in. 'Getting back to the Honda: Mrs Ingram's wondering if you might buy it back. It keeps breaking down.'

This was business and Sampson was on firm territory. 'Tell you what, I won't buy it back, but as it's still covered by the two-month, three-thousand-kilometre warranty, I'll give it a thorough going-over for her.'

The sergeant was unimpressed. 'We hate to see people being ripped off, Mr Sampson. And we hate to see them driving dodgy vehicles. You don't have to clean up afterwards; we do.'

Sampson shrugged. 'You can go through my files if you like. You can have a test drive of every vehicle on the lot if you like.'

Hirsch was amused. 'You mean now? Without a warrant?'

'You can't go through my paperwork now, no. I'd like my accountant present, and my lawyer. But if you want to have a squiz at anything out on the lot, go your hardest.'

'The lot' was a sloping half-hectare of stony dirt and dead grass, crammed with rusty augers on fretting tyres next to twenty-year-old Falcon station wagons; elderly Bedford trucks next to 6x4 trailers; grey Massey Fergusons next to Cox ride-on mowers. And lounging between a World War II Blitz Buggy and a tiny cobwebbed Mini Cooper was Trent McRae's V8 ute – minus its sovereign citizen plates.

'He traded it,' Sampson told them a moment later – on his knees now, tugging at the Patrol's cracked passenger-side headlight.

'Trent did? His mother's the registered owner.'

'Trent. But she okayed it, all on the up and up.'

'And down and sideways,' Sergeant Brandl said. 'Traded it in for an old Subaru Outback, correct?'

'If you know that, why are you asking me?' Sampson said as the headlight came free. He unhooked the wiring, got to his feet and tossed it with a clang into a large fuel drum that served as a rubbish bin. Came back to them, hands wide, asking for reason to prevail. 'None of my business what my customers think or do.'

Hirsch asked, 'What kind of deal was it?'

'You mean, what money changed hands? That's police business, is it? If you must know, both vehicles were close in value. Subarus are good cars and the ute was well looked after. But who can afford to run a V8 these days? So the ute plus a thousand got him the Subaru.'

'He got rid of the ute because of the running costs?'

'Makes sense,' Sampson said.

Always answers a slightly different question, Hirsch thought. A man who's sat on the other side of an interview-room table a few times. 'When was this?'

'Friday.'

Held on to it long enough to tailgate Dorrie Alkawaro on Thursday night – if it was him. But his mother was the registered owner, so why hadn't she said anything about a sale when Hirsch spoke to her on Saturday morning?

'The Subaru's registration details please, Mr Sampson.'

'Sure,' Sampson said, crossing to a wire basket of invoices, receipts and unopened business envelopes on a bench next to a grimy grey landline handset and a metal pipe in the jaws of a vice.

He returned with the sale documents. Photographing them with his phone, Hirsch said, 'Did he give any indication of where he was going?'

'Not to me. Why would he?'

'You're not friends, similar interests?' persisted Hirsch.

'What are you on about?'

'Just wondering.'

Sampson's mouth twisted. 'Yeah, well, go and wonder somewhere else.'

18

They went and wondered out on the road, leaning their rumps against Sampson's shit-brown Falcon station wagon. Brandl, checking Hirsch's photographs of the Nissan Patrol, said, 'Swiped a guardrail?'

'Looks like it.'

'Show Doctor Pillai?'

'Good idea.'

Failing to find Sandali Pillai in her surgery overlooking the town square, they tried the hospital, where she often performed minor surgeries or patched up, prescribed, smiled and patted forearms. She was poking at a keyboard in her office, a slight, intense woman wearing hoop earrings. Brandl, resting an arm against her doorjamb, said, 'Quick word, Sandy?'

She smiled around at them. 'How can I help?'

They stepped in. Hirsch said, 'We're here about the dim sim attack. Would you mind looking at a few photos?'

He swiped at his phone, found the damaged Nissan in

Nicholas Sampson's garage, and showed her the screen. 'Have you seen this vehicle before? There's more than one photo.'

'It could be the one,' she said. She began swiping, pausing at a shot of the Patrol's rear door. 'Yeah, I remember that bumper sticker.'

If you don't know, vote no. She swiped again: Nicholas Sampson, half-turned to the camera.

'Is that the man who threw dim sims at you?'

Pillai shook her head. 'I know who that is: Nick Sampson. The man who threw the dim sims at me was a lot younger and had a mullet.'

'Thanks,' Hirsch said, pocketing the phone.

Sergeant Brandl cocked her head. 'Just wondering, Sandy: is there anyone around here you *haven't* treated?'

An opaque smile. 'Nice seeing you both.'

Outside in the car park, Brandl said, 'Let's check the rego.'

They used the VDU mounted to the dash of her Kia. The registered owner of the Patrol in Nicholas Sampson's garage was Debra Goldfinch aged seventy-one in Redruth North.

'I need to get back to the station,' Brandl said. 'Maybe you could see if she's home before you leave?'

Hirsch gave the sergeant a salute and climbed behind the wheel again. He had one errand to run before he knocked on Debra Goldfinch's door, and a couple of minutes later had trundled down to the Sikh-run Caltex petrol station and was peering into the bain-maries steaming between a pile of tyres on special and a stand of fuel additives. Last Monday he'd bought butter chicken. Today, samosas, fried rice and chicken korma.

With the takeaways scenting the cab of the HiLux, he headed north out of town, to Owen-Smyth Street, near the saleyards. When he knocked on the front door of a tired-looking 1970s brick veneer, it was answered by a woman as tired as the house – but stroppy with it. Bulky, mid-thirties, riven by grievances and disappointment. The driver Dr Pillai had tooted at? She had the look of someone who'd not take kindly to implied criticism from anyone – let alone someone with dark skin.

'Yeah?'

'I'm looking for a Debra Goldfinch.'

'She's my mum. She's not here.'

'Do you know when she'll be back?'

'Like, never? She's in a nursing home.'

'Penny! The fuck you talking to?' a voice said and the man who came in behind her could have been her twin. Burly, sour, with an oily mullet and good dim-sim-throwing musculature. 'Police? Whatcha want?'

'May I have your name, sir?'

'Why?'

Hirsch gestured towards the distant stockyards. 'We're investigating the theft of a prize ram in the early hours of last Friday, before the auction. We were wondering if you heard anything? Saw anything?'

'The name's Ty Moloney and the answer's no.'

'Mrs Moloney?'

'We're not married. And like Ty said, no.'

Not that we'd tell you anyway.

Wondering if the pair had stripped Mrs Goldfinch of all her assets, Hirsch filled Sergeant Brandl in by phone as he headed north to Tiverton.

He made one last stop: Audrey McRae. 'Don't know nothing about Trent buying a Subaru,' she said.

'Audrey, the ute he traded in was registered in *your* name.'

That seemed to baffle her. 'Me? I thought it was all sorted.'

'You don't remember paying the rego for the last few years?'

'Bills come in; they get paid. I don't keep track.'

'Has Trent been back here, Mrs McRae? Driving the Subaru or anything else?'

'Nup. Haven't seen him.'

'Please let us know when you do. Get him to call us.'

'You keep saying that.'

A broken record. That pretty much sums up police work, Hirsch thought, hitting the road again. He checked the time: lunch. Wendy would be in the high school staffroom.

He had her on speed dial and a moment later she was saying, scorn in her voice: 'Nick Sampson's playing games with you. He didn't sell me the car, his wife did. It was her car. And I didn't go to his crummy yard, she put an ad in the school newsletter.'

19

Tuesday, dawn, Hirsch on his walk around the town. Coming to the final stretch, he waved to the delivery guy dropping bundled copies of the *Advertiser* on the shop veranda, thumped his knuckles for reassurance on the bonnet of the police Toyota as he entered the police-station driveway, and went in via his back door. Then, breakfasted, showered and shaved, he packed lunch and a flask of tea, pinned his mobile number to the front door and headed north out of town, into the slanting sun.

Traffic was light, nothing of concern until a road train came rocketing towards him halfway to Muncowie. Drifting over the dividing line; snaking a little as the driver braked, wide-eyed to see a cop car. Hirsch gave him a little finger wag and kept going, watching the twitchy rear trailer in his mirrors briefly, then concentrating on the road again. Mirages; skinny sheep fleeing from the fence line on either side; a sparrowhawk banking above a patch of dead grass; and the rising sun striping the world with long, hot shadows.

Twenty minutes later he reached Muncowie and the Breadbox Plain turn-off. No traffic at all, just a neglected gravel road with rattling corrugations and thumping potholes. Eventually he came to a sagging wire fence protecting a stretch of ochre soil swept clean by the winds of the seasons. Winds that erased tyre impressions and foot-, hoof- and paw-prints in the crusty surface. Until the next traveller came along. Until the next erasing wind.

Hirsch hadn't expected to encounter anyone but there were fresh vehicle tracks beyond the main entrance to the old goldfield with its sad, bent, signposted cyclone gate – *Danger Deep Mine Shafts* and *Danger Unmarked Holes* and *Keep Out Open Mine Shafts*, each illustrated with stick figures advising visitors not to run or trip. He got out, lifted the glovebox binoculars to his eyes. There, just above a slight rise, was the faded maroon roof of Annika Nordrum's Mazda ute.

Great minds, he thought.

He turned in, shut the gate behind him and followed her tracks across the dirt. Past a claypan, up the little rise. He glimpsed shadow scoops in the soil here and there – probably the spore of kangaroos, emus, wild dogs or wild goats. And he was proceeding slowly enough to see fairy rings, too, half-circles brushed on the surface by bent-over grass stalks stirred by the wind.

He slowed for stone reefs. They were like pimples and scales along the spines of large sightless creatures floating just under the surface. Now he was over the rise and crossing a broader, flatter expanse to a parking spot beside the Mazda.

Annika Nordrum was a few metres away, staring down. She glanced around at him briefly, waved, and resumed her vigil – if that's what it was. All she said when he joined her was, 'This is the one.'

Hirsch recognised the mineshaft opening from the file photos. A square of sunken, sun-weathered logs around the rim, partly concealed by dead grass and barely distinguishable from the dusty earth all around it. A hundred years old; twelve metres deep. If you were careless, you'd easily topple in. 'I think you're right.'

'I've started searching at Anna Gorge, but I had to see this again.'

'Makes sense,' Hirsch said, thinking also that the site of her father's death was a tangible thing for her. Searching for her mother's bones wasn't.

They chatted, shared her flask of tea, and when he told her he'd found the police file on her father's death, she said, 'Any chance I could look through it?'

Hirsch mused on that. There was nothing top secret there. 'I'm in the office tomorrow. Lunch? Samosas and salad.'

'Samosas?'

He told her about the Sikh-run service station. 'And if you have any useful documents, bring them with you.'

'Will do.'

Hirsch lingered a while after she'd left, peering into the shaft, strolling for a few hundred metres in each direction. He was mindful of other shafts in the tricky terrain. The crust of undisturbed soil, the saltbush and the bluebush, the tips of stone beneath his feet, and the bleached old mallee trunks and dead grass. Nothing benign about any of those things today.

Then he set out on a long swing further south and east of Breadbox Plain, knocking on doors. The first visit was uneventful: a safely secured .303 rifle followed by a mug of tea, news and gossip – an uncle's bank foreclosure, the cost of fuel, the abattoir declining to buy drought-scrawny sheep.

The second was slightly more dramatic, Hirsch warning an old geezer not to stow his loaded .22 Ruger on the back seat of his station wagon: 'Next time, Steve, I'll have to fine you.' At the third property, where he braked to allow a truckload of hay to heave its way between a set of stone pillars marked *Melrose Park Merino Stud*, he was reminded again that some of the properties in his patrol area were not doing it tough. Three rifles, two shotguns, all secure.

By now it was 3.30. He checked the other names on his list. A toss-up between finishing at a decent time or getting back well after dark, and he decided on the former.

It gave him time to check the birthing tree along the way. Tucked into the corner of a paddock where Mischance Creek Road and the track up to End Point Park sheep station intersected, the tree was broad, lofty, beautifully formed, its colours mottled grey, white and tan. It was lucky to have survived in a land that barely sustained stubby mallee, he thought.

He glanced up End Point Road, then down at his watch. Did he really want to drive up there just to see a couple of graders at work?

Time to go home. But as he was about to turn onto the long final stretch a few minutes later, he was forced to brake for two vehicles taking up most of the road: Brad Ullmer's Great Wall ute, and a dusty white Isuzu truck cocked up on a jack. He got out and approached, stating the obvious: 'Flat tyre?'

Ullmer was on his knees in the dirt, finger-tightening wheel nuts while the Isuzu driver looked on. A wheel brace and the dud tyre lay nearby. 'You could say that,' he said, glancing briefly at Hirsch. He got to his feet, fitted the wheel brace and heaved down on it, his powerful shoulders, forearms and legs flexing with the strain.

'Can I help?'

'All good.'

Hirsch turned to the other man and stuck out his hand. 'Paul Hirschhausen. Tiverton police station.'

The driver seemed to glance at Ullmer for permission before accepting the shake. 'Shane,' he said. Pause. 'Shane Arnold.'

Arnold was about thirty. A shaved head, shorts, a T-shirt. *Sandals*, Hirsch noticed, thinking: idiot. Reluctant to meet Hirsch's gaze, but if Hirsch had a dollar for every innocent person who wouldn't look at him …

'Good tyre-wrecking roads out here,' he said conversationally.

After another pause, Arnold said, 'Yeah.'

They watched Brad Ullmer tighten another wheel nut. The sun beat down, there was no shade, the air was still. The bottom of the spare barely cleared the ground, and the jack, nestling ever deeper in the powdery dirt, looked too flimsy to support a loaded truck.

Maybe they were using Ullmer's own jack? The Isuzu driver didn't inspire confidence. Would he have a jack on board, or even know how to use it? Was this the truck Steph Ingram had seen recently? Keeping it casual, Hirsch strolled across to the tray and rapped a drum with his knuckles. It boomed emptily.

'Lucky you weren't fully loaded,' he said, joining Arnold again.

'Yeah.'

'And lucky *you* came along, Brad.'

Ullmer threw his strength into another nut-tightening. 'Was on another cull.'

Hirsch turned to Arnold to explain. 'Brad here's a professional shooter. The drought's meant a lot of the farmers have had to cull stock they can't feed.'

He was making banal conversation to give himself time to read the truck driver. According to a sign on the open door, Arnold drove for an Adelaide firm, Thrupp's All-Over Logistics of Thebarton. On the passenger seat was a paper bag, possibly containing a snack. Between the seats, a puny 300 mL bottle of water. And the sandals. And his mouth hung open as if he didn't know what a professional shooter or even a sheep was.

'Oh. Right.'

'On your way home?'

The question seemed to stump him. 'Yeah.'

'Been delivering fuel to End Point Park?'

'Er, yeah.'

'I heard they're improving the road up there.'

'I just deliver,' Arnold said, looking for guidance again but not getting it. Ullmer had finished with the wheel nuts and was winding the jack down. The truck groaned in relief.

'Much in the way of heavy equipment?' Hirsch said. 'Graders?'

An agonising silence. 'One or two.'

Hirsch wanted to say, 'You don't know for sure?' but decided to help Ullmer hoist the old tyre into a cradle beneath the tray of the Isuzu.

'Thanks,' Ullmer muttered, brushing dust from his hands.

'He's a bit hopeless,' Hirsch murmured. 'Lucky you came along. Where were you shooting?'

Ullmer gestured vaguely to the north. 'Just on my way home,' he said.

Acknowledging Ullmer's austere sense of client confidentiality, Hirsch changed direction. 'Been up End Point Road lately?'

'Not for years.'

'I heard they want to widen it.'

'Not sure why.'

'Exactly,' Hirsch said, but by then Ullmer was wandering towards Arnold, who was pissing on a fencepost.

'Good to go, mate.'

Arnold finished, adjusted himself, wouldn't look at Hirsch or Ullmer, and said, 'Thanks.'

'You better buy another spare as soon as you can. Don't wait till you get to the city: stop at the tyre place in Redruth.'

This seemed to stretch Arnold's capabilities. 'Er, okay.' Pause. 'Sounds like a plan.'

20

There was no fresh rubbish on the home paddock when Hirsch made his dawn patrol on Wednesday, but the old pile was still there. He found himself imagining the burden of monitoring the overnight CCTV feed – should the council ever get around to installing cameras. He tried, but failed, to see it as a new skill, a new crime-fighting toy. Hours of watching chronic rubbish dumpers spot the cameras, have second thoughts and drive on. Nothing to charge them with.

Aware that Annika Nordrum was coming for lunch, he cleaned the kitchen, raced through his emails, threw most of the snail mail into a winery carton for recycling, fielded phone calls and tried Alastair Stanyer's landline: no reply. He signed a stat dec. Gave a road-condition report to a minibus of botanists heading for the Mischance Creek Nature Reserve, and directions to the Desolation Hill lookout to a family of Americans wearing Akubra hats hung with corks.

No one wrapped their car around a tree, bashed a loved one or reported their leaf blower missing.

He checked the Facebook page from time to time. Increasingly, as the year wore on, he'd been struck by how flat everyone seemed. It was as if the district's helplessness had flatlined. Christmas and the New Year quivered faintly on the horizon, that's all: Siegert Road Poultry was advising everyone to get in early with their turkey orders, Ed Tennant had ordered thirty Christmas trees, and don't forget the New Year's Eve Ball at the Institute. The ball was an annual headache for Hirsch. He would've liked to take a turn around the dancefloor with Wendy, but instead he was expected to monitor the drunks – who sometimes did wrap themselves around trees.

At noon, when he slipped across the road to buy bottled water, he spotted Annika Nordrum's red ute angle-parked outside the general store. Bella was tethered to a veranda post, and he found Annika staring morosely at the crates of vegetables, a shopping basket in the crook of one arm. A dust smear on one calf, one sock at half mast, the other crumpled around the top of a dusty lace-up boot. A creased, damp sleeveless shirt. Tendrils of hair adhering limply to the back of her neck.

'Caught me shopping.' She looked down at her feet. 'I did get semi spruced up for lunch.'

'No one stays spruced up for long around here,' Hirsch said. 'As for Ed's vegetables ...'

'I know. Maybe tinned would be better.'

Hirsch guided her to a creaky aisle, selected tinned tomatoes for himself and waited for her at the cash register. Grabbing Bella's lead and stowing her purchases in an Esky later, she said, 'Never guess what I found in the glovebox,' and leaned into the Mazda again, emerging with a tattered, buff-coloured business envelope. 'The rego papers and a little notebook and a map. Dad's writing.'

'As if they were hidden?'

'Don't think so. Just tucked inside the owner's manual.'

Hirsch shook his head. The slapdash nature of the original investigation. 'Great, we'll throw it into the mix.'

She handed him the envelope. 'Okay. Lead on. Samosas.'

'I also have some leftover korma.'

'Indian food in the outback. The world's shrinking.'

Fracturing, in Hirsch's view. He said nothing and led the way across the street, knowing that small-town tongues would wag. He was newish and he was the cop: those factors were enough in themselves. The assessing and speculating had probably been ongoing since day one. What's he like? Will he try to fit in? Does he do the right thing by people? Does he play tennis, by any chance? Any experience as a club treasurer?

Aware of all this, Hirsch had been doing his best. He'd taken a couple of teens with a manic-depressive mother under his wing, for example. He'd joined the tennis club. He'd twice taken a turn in the Santa suit for the town and farm kids on Christmas Eve. Shopped locally. More inclined to hand out a warning than a fine. And he'd been seeing Wendy Street for a while now. A lovely woman; taught many of the local kids at Redruth High. So what was he doing with a woman who wasn't Wendy Street? A youngish woman; good looking. Ushering her into the cop shop on a work day.

With dishes rinsed, glasses of water at their elbows and the aircon rattling, they made a few dedicated piles of Nordrum paperwork on the kitchen table: case notes and photographs from the old station lockup, and the material Annika had found in her ute.

But before they could begin, Hirsch inadvertently knocked one of the piles, revealing a close-up photo of Ben Nordrum dead at the base of the mineshaft. Too late, he dragged a manila folder across it.

Fingers clamped his forearm. 'I want to see.'

'It's not pretty.'

'It's also been a few years since it happened. And I had to identify his body at the time.'

Hirsch withdrew the folder. 'Okay.'

'Not going to dwell,' she told him.

He watched her flick through the photos, barely pausing at those of her father. The shaft itself seemed to interest her more. 'I noticed the other day how someone could fall in if they weren't careful.'

Hirsch nodded. The erosion of the decades – beating winds, sun, rain and arid dryness – had almost blurred all distinctions between the mineshaft entrance and the wider area.

Reaching for the remaining photographs now, Nordrum seemed to go into a troubled trance before saying, 'It all looks so ... *ordinary*, like they just rocked up and started unpacking.'

'But if you spot any anomalies, anything at all ...'

She sighed, shrugged, leaned over the spread of photos.

Straightened her back a moment later and said, 'Okay, for a start, why's the driver's door open?'

'Good.'

'It's like Dad jumped out and went straight to the hole and fell in. Yet he'd also unpacked a few things – or he and Mum had.' She threw up her hands. 'Who knows?'

Then she seemed to hunch her shoulders. 'Or he threw himself in for some reason.'

Because he'd done something to his wife and was racked with guilt? Or had learnt something that drove him to suicide? Hirsch read these speculations in her face, and silence spread. The aircon was intrusive suddenly: loud, giving one of its perilous clicks and hesitations before rattling their nerves again.

'Anything else strike you?'

'Apart from the fact food's been left out in the sun and no one's put up a shade cloth? There's only one chair.'

'Yes.'

'No one's put out any food or water for Bella.'

'How did they usually cook?'

'In winter, maybe over an open fire. In dry country, in summer, a little two-burner gas cooker on bare dirt. They were super careful.'

Hirsch checked the list of items found at the scene. A gas cooker and spare cylinders, still in a plastic crate in the Mazda. He showed the list to Annika, who said distractedly, 'If they did decide to split up and search different areas, how was Mum supposed to cook? If Dad was making a racing visit to the diggings and didn't intend to stay, why cart all that stuff around with him? And if he was going to stay overnight or even a couple of nights, why wouldn't he leave Bella with Mum? For protection, if nothing else.'

Her expression turned rueful. 'I seem to be talking myself into the fact they didn't split up, don't I? They were together.'

'But the area was searched.'

'Yeah, but how thorough was it? And we both know how hard it is to spot some of those shafts.'

'Whatever happened, it can't have been long after arrival,' Hirsch said. 'Barely any unpacking.'

With an air of clutching at straws, Annika Nordrum said, 'What if it was staged?'

Hirsch had to be careful. The inquest had ruled her father's death an accident, and he himself could come up with innocent reasons for every anomaly.

He tried to explain his reasoning, but she cut in: 'Can they tell if others were there? Like if Dad was moved from somewhere else? Or killed on the surface and thrown in?'

'Perhaps not after all this time, and back then it seems no one saw any reason to conduct a forensic examination of the site.'

'Do they know how long Dad had been dead before he was found?'

Hirsch checked the file. 'Rigor mortis ... been and gone. But there's factors that would've affected the rate of decomposition. He wasn't lying out in the sun, for example. It'd be cooler at the bottom of the shaft.' He paused. 'There were blowflies, but that happens quite quickly.'

'I was wondering about Bella. How thirsty or hungry she was. If she could smell that Dad was nearby, wouldn't she hang around rather than head off down the road?'

'I don't know enough about dog behaviour.'

'Nor do I. Who found her?'

'According to the file, a local farmer. It's something I intend to follow up.'

'Okay, thank you.'

'When your dad called you, he used a satellite phone?'

'Yes. Not much mobile reception out there.'

'The phone was among his things.'

'The one I've been using,' Nordrum said. Then she cocked her head. 'Huh. You're saying it would've been stolen if ...?'

Hirsch shrugged and they fell silent again. Bella groaned in her sleep.

Hirsch broke in. 'Let's have a look at the stuff you found in the ute.'

'Sure,' Annika said, reaching for the envelope and removing a Moleskine notebook. She blew on it, swiped it with the palm of her hand, wiped her hand on her shorts. 'Still a bit gritty.'

'The dust gets into everything,' Hirsch said, topping up their water glasses. The aircon note changed again as Annika flipped through the pages.

'Thought you might be interested in this,' she said, 'but how it fits in with everything else, I don't know.'

She'd cracked open the spine on a hand-drawn mud map. A careless ballpoint circle around the words *A Gorge*; boldly scratched parallel lines that maybe depicted the roads south and east of the gorge; a huddle of tiny squares, with a dotted track north and east of them ending in a jaunty question mark, also circled. Unlikely that any of it was to scale.

'Typical of my dad,' Nordrum said. 'Slapdash.'

She was teary. Blinked the tears away. 'Hard to work out where this is, or what it means, or how to get there. I mean, is that dotted line a hundred metres or a hundred kilometres?'

'These little blocks could be the Mischance Creek ruins,' offered Hirsch, 'but they could also be a station homestead, a collection of rocks or your dad's shorthand for diamonds, who knows?'

'It's not diamond country but you're right. All a bit hopeless.' A shrug. 'Maybe they finished at the gorge. Or the gorge was the start of a long seam of gold or sapphires? The thing is, Dad's line of crosses goes in one direction and where he was found was a long way in the opposite direction.'

They were finished by two o'clock. Waving Annika and her dog goodbye, Hirsch took a mug of green tea through to his desk and sorted the Nordrum material into separate manila folders: incident reports, photocopies of Annika's diary and 'map', photographs, coroner's report, path report, investigative timeline and witness statements – including those given by the Muncowie Arms publican and Annika herself, six years earlier. One last flick through revealed no mention of, or statement from, the farmer who'd found the Nordrums' dog wandering down the middle of the road. The phone rang occasionally; emails dropped into the in-box; he signed another stat dec.

21

Thursday, dawn.

Hirsch began his foot patrol with a check of the town paddock. The council still hadn't cleaned away the mattresses, garbage bags or building rubble, but a warning sign had mysteriously appeared: ANY PERSON DUMPING RUBBISH IN THIS AREA WILL BE PROSECUTED. Well, it was a start.

Continuing his walk of the town, he came upon Bob Muir loading his van again. 'Just been to the town paddock—'

Muir was shaking his head before he'd finished. 'A shitty business.'

Hirsch weighed up what to say next, knowing that his friend had a greater loyalty to the town and its residents than to the policeman who'd blown in only six years ago. 'I was wondering if you saw ... if you know ...'

Muir shook his head emphatically. 'All that demolition material? Wouldn't have a clue. Not local, I don't think. The smaller stuff? Could be anyone.'

Expecting another reserved answer, but needing to ask, Hirsch said, 'How well do you know Al Stanyer?'

'Not well. Keeps to himself. Why?'

'Welfare check,' Hirsch said, hating to lie to his friend. 'He hasn't been at home for a few days.'

'Have you tried his brother?'

'No luck.'

'Well, that's about it for me,' Muir said. 'He used to drink up at the Muncowie pub, but whether or not he still does, couldn't tell you.'

Hirsch was at his desk by 7.30. Reports, emails, phone calls. Again, no reply when he called Alastair Stanyer's landline. The Muncowie publican confirmed that Stanyer used to prop up his bar but hadn't been in for weeks – 'The cost of fuel the way it is.' Then a chat with his mother, another at morning recess with Wendy Street – who asked airily, 'Who're you having lunch with today?' – and finally with Annika Nordrum, who said she'd already roamed over a good three-quarters of Anna Gorge and was thinking of searching further afield, using her father's map.

'Map of what, that's the question,' Hirsch said.

'I know.'

'Good luck, be careful, keep me informed,' Hirsch said.

By late morning his office was stifling, his back stiff, and auditing firearms seemed infinitely more appealing than desk work. So, after an early lunch, he pinned his mobile number to the front door, climbed behind the wheel of his stifling SA Police Toyota and was soon bumping over the outback again.

The residents of Tiverton Hills Road this time. Brett Ralph: a Remington 12-gauge. Shotgun and shells were securely and separately locked up. Then Megan Schultz, a little .22 rifle. But her cat happened to be missing: Hirsch found it by the stench of its carcass. He jump-started Chris Inglis' station wagon and Bryn Jones expected him to hold a couple of wires, bare-fingered, while he traced an electrical fault in his tractor. And Lyn Deval was asleep, drunk, on a sofa in her screened-in front porch.

All of their firearms were in order. Hirsch made no arrests, issued no warnings, received a couple of matey slaps on the back.

Bloated with tea and biscuits, he reached Pandowie Station, south-east of Mischance Creek, by mid-afternoon. Two shotguns, three rifles. The place was a working sheep property that had been tarted up to include tourist accommodation and a range of 'unique outback experiences'. Not right now, though. Too hot, too dry, for mustering, shearing, horse-riding or creek-bed fossicking.

Confirming that the firearms were properly secured, he headed out through the stately front gates again, and decided to call in on Trina Gould. He found her alone, slow-moving, holding one hand to the small of her back. She smiled tiredly and said, 'I didn't hear about your dad until recently. So sorry, Paul.'

Hirsch blinked. 'Thanks. How're you?'

'A waiting game.'

'And Pete?'

She closed down a little. 'Fine. Not here at the moment.'

They were talking over cups of tea when his mobile buzzed. Sergeant Brandl: he needed to get his arse over to Jack Minack's farm. Something about bank officials, a barricade, a stand-off.

Trina, who was listening in, grew distressed. Put a hand to her throat when he'd ended the call and said, 'You'll find Pete there. Please, please, please don't arrest him. Just tell him to come home.'

The story came out. Trina's husband and a few other locals had been getting together occasionally to spout ideas about government action and inaction. Sometimes it was too much government – taxes and levies – and sometimes too little – no protection for primary producers. 'It's getting worse,' Trina said. 'Pete gets really worked up and, you know, with the baby coming and everything ...'

With the baby coming and everything, Trina Gould couldn't care less about the economy or big or little government, she wanted a loving and attentive husband at her side.

Given all that, Hirsch was only slightly surprised to see Trent McRae among the ragtag group of fifteen men and women gathered behind a pair of locked front gates when he pulled up at the Minack farm, a few kilometres northeast of Penhale, forty minutes later. He recognised most of them. Trina's husband; struggling small-scale farmers like Mark and Fran Button; a Redruth carpenter and a Tiverton builder for whom work had dried up; a Booborowie giftshop owner, bankrupted in May.

Nicholas Sampson.

And Jack Minack.

Minack had long been a pain in the butt to Hirsch, often at closing time in the Tiverton pub – so much so that seeing him now brought on a sense memory: the stench of vomit. Minack was one of those guys who spreads into early middle age without the benefit of dignity, and he liked to stake a belligerent claim on his barstool at closing time. His wife had reliably collected him in the old days, pre-Hirsch, but she was long gone, taking the kids with her. These days the turfing out and the confiscation of car keys was Hirsch's job.

Which often meant sluicing vomit from his shoes and cuffs, or the rear seats and footwells of the HiLux.

Minack wasn't drunk, puking or even clutching a pint today, but he was emotional, there on the other side of his front gates. Shouting, waving a fist, at three men in suits clustered near a white Lexus sedan. The bankers, presumably. Or sheriffs? Bailiffs?

Still seated in the HiLux, Hirsch swung his gaze over the equally ragtag vehicles ranged inside Minack's front fence. Utes, family sedans and a white Subaru Outback, all parked as if to repel invaders.

Then he realised that one of the suits was gesturing at him. The gesture meant: 'Well? Are you going to get out and help?'

Instead, Hirsch phoned Sergeant Brandl. 'Just spotted Trent, boss, with his Subaru. You want me to have a word with him? Bring him in?'

She sounded harried. 'See what you can do, but it's action

stations here, a truck rollover outside Farrell Flat, a hundred sheep, bodies up and down the road.'

'Fair enough,' Hirsch said, stepping out into the heat.

The same suit gestured again – about time! – and settled his rump against the bonnet of the Lexus. The second stood with his jacket hooked over his shoulder while he worked his phone one-handedly. The third, holding a briefcase, seemed to be looking for strength as he trudged through the dirt to Jack Minack's gate. As if this was his tenth stand-off of the day.

Hoping to seem neutral, amiable, Hirsch removed his uniform hat, left it on the driver's seat and strolled towards the gates, swigging from a bottle of spring water. It didn't particularly fool anyone – he was still a cop – but he hoped the locals knew him to be a fair man. The suits merely glanced. Only Jack Minack reacted, shouting at the man with the briefcase: 'Piss-weak. You can't deal with me man-to-man; you have to bring in the cops.'

He swung on Hirsch. 'How much they paying you?'

'Easy, Jack.'

'Don't fucking Jack me. You don't get to use my first name like I'm just anyone.'

Okay, I'll side with the suits, thought Hirsch. Approaching the man with the briefcase, he said, 'Paul Hirschhausen,' and stuck out his hand.

The guy actually looked down at it first. Recovered – but not before he was jeered at – and shook. 'William Hammond, thanks for coming.'

'My sergeant said you're serving a foreclosure notice?'

'Already have. Needless to say, Mr Minack tore it up, but I have time-stamped photographic evidence not only of our fastening the notice to his front entrance, but also of its destruction at his hands.'

He sounds like one of my SAPOL emails, thought Hirsch.

Minack shouted, 'Fuck you and your evidence. You can't just take my place away from me.'

'We can and we will,' Hammond said. He was the tidiest man Hirsch had seen in months. Had managed to walk from the Lexus to Jack Minack's front gates without getting dust on his polished shoes.

Minack was unimpressed. 'You and whose army?'

'A bailiff, the sheriff, the police or maybe all three.'

'*Then I'll have you for trespassing*,' screamed Minack, arousing another sense-memory in Hirsch: the prick at closing time, spit flying as he shouted, '*Get your fucking hands off me.*'

Nicholas Sampson muscled in now, almost jostling Minack aside as he snarled, 'Whose laws you operating under, eh? Whose laws?'

Hammond ignored him. 'We've bent over backwards for you, Mr Minack. Loans, grace periods, repayment plans ... Going back months. Since late last year, in fact.'

That wound Minack up even further. '*There's a fucking drought on – or haven't you noticed in your cosy office?*'

Mark Button's turn: '*Doing the bidding of others.*'

Again Hirsch recalled what Vikki Bastian's pupils had told her: 'We might lose the farm.' He left Hammond and approached the gates, trying to screw a bemused and amiable expression onto his face. Wished he was wearing his hat as he shaded his eyes and said, 'Jack, maybe we could go up to the house and sort this out? And the rest of you go home? You've made your point. Too hot for this.'

It might have been another closing-time. Minack jutted his whiskery chin and soft, straining belly at Hirsch. 'You here at whose bidding? The bank? The government? The fucking crooked mayor?'

'Easy, mate.'

'You're not my mate.'

Mark Button again: 'Take a man's livelihood away from him.'

Behind Hirsch, Hammond put on a reasonable voice. 'We don't *want* to take Mr Minack's livelihood away from him. You think we need another property like this on our books, drought-stricken and farmed to death?'

Hirsch winced: Don't insult a tradesman or his trade. Minack made a grab for Hammond over the gates, screaming, '*Greedy fucking money-grubbing prick.*'

Hammond stepped back and Hirsch stepped in. 'Leave it, Jack. You don't want an assault charge on top of everything else.'

'Fuck you,' Minack said, but subsided when Nick Sampson put an arm around his shoulders and murmured in his ear.

Hirsch said, 'Maybe take Jack back to the house, Mr Sampson?'

Instead, Sampson shouted past Hirsch: 'Do Australians own Australia anymore? Do you even know who you're acting for?'

'I've had enough of this,' Hammond said, retreating further.

He turned to Hirsch. 'Look, thanks for your help, but we're leaving. We came here in good faith to serve papers on Mr Minack, and now that that's done, it's time we went home.' Glancing around as if great peril awaited – the heat, the vast emptiness, the hostile men and women ranged against him – he added, 'Arguing has got us nowhere, we're outnumbered and, frankly, I've got better things to do than listen to these nutjobs.'

He stalked off to the Lexus. They're not nuts, Hirsch thought, they're frightened. He gazed at the mix of sensible hats, work-damaged bodies, sun-damaged faces and worn, faded, everyday clothes on the other side of the twin gates. Hammond represented all that was wrong in their lives and now they were bellowing it at him, snatches and fragments of hate and discord: the interest rates, the banks, the unfairness. All things that Hirsch – and probably Hammond – had heard before.

And then Trent McRae came waltzing up to the fence and had his say: Hirsch was serving the faceless Jews and Satanists who pulled the strings of business and politics.

'Trent—'

McRae smirked and melted away.

Hirsch heard the Lexus fire up, swung his head and saw it wheel off in a display of contempt and dust. He turned back to Jack Minack's little gang. This could be a Trump rally, he thought, taking in faces everlastingly stunned, angry, fearful, unsophisticated, bewildered and suspicious of the mainstream. Not part of a movement yet, but if enough of them cast themselves as a powerless, persecuted minority, they were headed in that direction.

He reached a hand to one of the gates and shook it gently in emphasis. 'They're gone, Jack. How about we call it a day?'

Minack seemed deflated. He'd given good defiance but hadn't won anything. The Buttons sidled up, and Fran gave him a hug. 'We need to get home Jack, okay? So sorry. I'll bring around a casserole soon.'

'Yeah, right, thanks,' Minack said, sorting through the keys hanging from his belt. He opened both gates. People drifted to their cars.

But Hirsch was watching the white Subaru. He watched Trent McRae get in, start it, U-turn and speed down the driveway towards the house. A back way out? He couldn't give chase: tempers were still high.

Pete Gould was simmering. 'The drought's *our* fault, is that what those pricks are saying?'

Hirsch said immediately, 'How's Trina doing? She must be due soon.'

Meaning: why aren't you with her? Gould went red; looked awkward and lost. 'Yeah, good. A waiting game,' he said, turning away.

Jack Minack also seemed lost. 'What happens now?'

Hirsch stepped away, giving room as the first car rumbled out onto the road, the driver nodding goodbye. 'Have you talked to a lawyer?'

'What?'

Another car left, then another. Hirsch, slipping through

the gates and ushering Minack to one side, said, 'Those men are going to be back pretty soon, Jack. It might not be too late to work something out with the bank. I suggest you get legal advice.'

'No money.'

'Legal Aid,' Hirsch said.

He felt tetchy with Minack's anxiety and bewilderment, even though he thought he understood it. A lawyer – educated, well-dressed, working in an office full of filing cabinets, enormous books and sleek equipment – represented all that Minack wasn't. How could he begin to talk to someone like that, in a room like that? What would he say? His words would tangle; he'd sound dumb to himself. What would they think of him? Would they even care? He was just a bloke who knew how to run a few sheep and sow a crop of wheat – and not very skilfully, either.

'Legal Aid's free,' Hirsch added.

But Minack turned hard again. 'Nothing's free in this country.'

He looked about for support but the sun was going down, dinners had to be cooked, evening TV beckoned. Soon only Nicholas Sampson remained. He stood off to one side, smoking a cigarette with the air of a man keeping opinions close to his chest as Hirsch asked, 'You going to be okay, now, Jack?'

Jack Minack: .22 Squires Bingham bolt-action rifle. All safely secured when Hirsch had checked last week.

But a week can be a long time. 'Would you like me to come down to the house for a bit, talk things over?'

Minack gestured bitterly. 'Ah, bloody sick of the lot of you.'

Now Sampson wandered up. 'He'll be fine, won't you, Jack?'

'Yep.'

'I'll look after him.'

'That's good of you,' Hirsch said.

22

Realising that he had time to swing by Al Stanyer's shack, Hirsch headed further east, then north, but was still some distance away when he spotted a late afternoon sun-flash on glass, out on the scrubby plain that had once been the old Mischance Creek merino stud but was now a designated nature reserve. He pulled onto the powdery verge and, motor idling, scanned the area with his binoculars.

Annika Nordrum's little Mazda pitching about like a rowboat in heaving seas, throwing up dust as she steered beside a sheep pad. In the next instant, Hirsch thought: *Jesus, the fissure.*

He switched off, shot out and stood at the fence, waving his arms madly. She sailed on: hadn't spotted him. Now he was through the fence and charging downslope at an oblique angle, leaping over rocks, depressions, weathered animal bones, hoping to get slightly ahead of her, hoping she'd glimpse him in her peripheral vision. Waving his arms; yelling. He could see the fissure – an ancient geological fault that had been known to swallow kangaroos, sheep and careless mustering trailbikes – because his position was elevated, but she was at ground level and heading straight for it. She wouldn't necessarily die if she took a nosedive, but she'd certainly wreck the Mazda and injure herself and Bella, whose snout was in the open passenger-side window, snatching bites of air.

He was thinking these things when he saw her brake sharply, kicking up more dust. Now she was waving at him, but still inching forwards. Holding his palm up warningly, he continued skittering down the slope, dust coating his shoes, the Mid North's last grass seeds catching in his socks.

Halting when he reached the edge of the fissure, he jabbed a pointed forefinger at the ground: *look out*.

She gaped at him and then, thank God, switched off and got out. Began approaching him, unconcerned, on the opposite side. She looked faintly puzzled. 'What are you – oh, wow,' she said, freezing, taking a step back. 'That was close,' she said, a hand over her heart. 'Thank you.'

'It's called Pattenden's Fissure,' called Hirsch, projecting his words a little, as if the Grand Canyon separated them.

'Lucky.'

'Lucky,' Hirsch agreed.

He looked down. In its six-kilometre run, the fissure varied in depth from two to five metres and in width from three to eight, and doubled as a creek in heavy rains: Hirsch could see sand, driftwood and smooth, water-tumbled stones in the bottom. Powdery edges, too: he stepped back smartly as a wedge of soil slid away, centimetres from his toes.

'Careful,' Annika said, also stepping back.

'What're you doing here?'

'Trying to make sense of Dad's map. Remember that line of dots and squiggles? It could be this ... this ... ravine.'

'Gulch,' said Hirsch. 'Abyss. Gorge. Crevasse.'

'Trench, wadi, chasm, fissure.'

'Fissure it is.'

Just then Bella hopped out of the Mazda. She sniffed the tyres, the dirt; then, reaching Annika, dropped to her belly and crept forward.

Panicked, Annika crouched and grabbed her collar. 'No, you don't.' Glanced at Hirsch again and said, 'Have you been driving around all day?'

He told her about the ongoing firearms audit as she nodded, barely listening. 'Anyway, I was getting nowhere at the gorge and decided to follow Dad's map.' Shrugged and added: 'Not as if he ever drew anything to scale.'

'Annika, this is government land, a nature reserve.'

'I know, I checked. I'm not trespassing.'

'But you do need permission,' Hirsch said. 'It's mostly scientists who visit. They're trying to regenerate with the sorts of trees and grasses found pre-European settlement.' He pointed. 'It stops being a reserve a few kilometres that way, where it meets End Point Road. Beyond that it's private land.'

She slumped. 'Yeah, sure, okay.'

'I need to get home,' Hirsch said, waving goodbye, toiling back up the slope to his superheated Toyota.

*

He reached Tiverton late afternoon and after a shower he poured a beer and called Wendy. She could only spare five minutes: 'Staff meeting.'

He called his mother, who cried, 'Darling!' joyfully, as if he didn't call her every day, but was otherwise distracted, as though she'd misplaced her glasses. Their conversation was predictable: what they'd been doing, who they'd seen. And when he asked if she'd given any thought to driving up to see him soon, she prevaricated. She'd become a great prevaricator, and great at not wanting to be a bother to anyone. 'I don't know, dear. It's such a long way, and there's the garden to think of, and you all lead such busy lives.'

'You don't have to stay with Wendy and Kate, if that's what's bothering you. There's a good Airbnb in town, or the Woolman pub in Redruth.'

'I don't know, dear. Maybe. I'll think about it.'

He checked his watch: not yet 6 p.m. and the district council meeting started at 8. Still bothered by the incident at Jack Minack's gates that afternoon, he decided to do a bit of research.

23

He started by googling a string of linked terms: *local council, shire council, corruption, disruption, My Place* ...

Most of the results were a grab-bag of news stories reporting council ineptitude, greed, corruption and minor criminality – a mayor trading planning favours for cocaine, for example; councillors who never attended meetings; developers offering and paying bribes; financial mismanagement – and ratepayer frustration volatile enough to involve the police. In several cases, state governments had stepped in, dismantling councils and installing administrators.

Was it Hirsch's imagination? Were there more local-government corruption and mismanagement stories than there used to be? Perhaps fewer controls were in place, or standards were slipping.

Plenty of well-run local councils, of course.

But some had had the misfortune to be targeted by My Place agitators, particularly in Victoria and New South

Wales. Hirsch scanned the news stories: meetings behind closed doors; a police presence; security guards ...

It wasn't easy to determine what My Place stood for. At a simple level it seemed to be about Covid-era anti-lockdown, anti-vaccination and freedom of movement ideas, but mostly it argued that local councils were corporate entities set on undermining property rights. Therefore, council rates, taxes and fines were invalid. The installation of CCTV cameras was citizen surveillance, not protection. And local government efforts to keep key services close to everyone was a plot to keep people contained.

The answer? Create parallel communities divorced from the mainstream until one day a great reset occurred, a great awakening.

Through what mechanism? Hirsch thought. Probably violence.

He rolled his chair back from the monitor and stared into space, trying to link Trent McRae's sovereign-citizen ideas with the localised and ongoing grumbling on social media and the mood at Jack Minack's farmgate. If you were a small-town dickhead, you'd start small: storm a local council meeting before working your way up to Parliament House.

He rolled the chair back to his PC and read some of the My Place social media chatter. It ranged from ill-informed hot air to alarming anger. Mostly, though, sympathisers couldn't seem to make up their minds whether Jewish bankers or Moslem ideologues were to blame for everything.

*

At 7 p.m. Hirsch pinned his phone number to the front door and reached the Redruth police station in time for the sergeant's short briefing. 'Stand around and look serious. Defuse rather than wind people up: they're stressed enough already. Make allowances, in other words.' She glanced at Medlin. 'We need someone to hold the fort here, Tim, just in case. Call if you need us.'

'Sergeant.'

It made sense to Hirsch that Landy rather than Medlin should attend. Tim was tall and bulky but Jean would be more useful. Always up for a bit of joyful snarling and baton-wielding.

The council meetings were held monthly in a large room at the rear of the town hall. It boasted a high pressed-tin ceiling and photographs around the walls. Colonial-era Redruth and the copper mine; a sprinkling of past mayors; prize-winning merino rams in full fleece. A massive clock crept towards the 8 p.m. mark.

The mayor and her ward councillors sat at a long wooden table on a low stage at the far end, overlooking several rows of lightweight stackable chairs separated by a centre aisle. Hirsch stood, arms folded, against one side wall, Jean Landy against the other. His back ached after days of bouncing around over rough roads, so he moved slightly and often, seeking and failing to find comfort. Landy was restless too – more through tension though, Hirsch thought, watching her constant hip-bumping and head swivelling. As for the sergeant, she sat behind and to one side of the mayor and the councillors, a hard expression on her face.

Between them, they had most of the room covered.

Hirsch watched Clarissa Stanyer, curious to see how her demeanour translated to council business. He couldn't see her as a warm and cuddly figure in any situation, and right now she was tapping loose pages together, leaning in to confer with the man on her left, the woman on her right, sometimes casting cool smiles at the audience – the ratepayers, the curious, the windbags, the potential hecklers. Under it she seemed to be quivering with energy, ready for a fight. A woman able to read and handle a room. Able to seduce, coax, browbeat, flatter, demolish.

A minute to go. Hirsch switched his attention to the audience. A mix of shorts and T-shirts alongside casual and best shirts, trousers and skirts. It was as if no one was sure how to dress: this wasn't the footy, the Blyth cinema, the Dugout bistro or church, where the conventions were clearer. The feeling of the crowd varied, too. Disarray, stunned senses and possibly confusing allegiances; also shyness, awkwardness. Dotted among the many people he didn't know, he recognised the pharmacist, a mechanic from Redruth Motors and the woman in charge of the aged-care centre attached to the hospital. Also Auntie Steph, and Ed Tennant, Nan Washburn and a couple of others from Tiverton. A fair-sized crowd, it seemed to him. Over a hundred – surely a greater number than you would normally get at a small-town council meeting? If so, perhaps it was because times were bad, change was needed. Or it was the cumulative effect of this council's planning decisions and punitive fines and bylaws.

Some of the audience glanced at him curiously, others indifferently. But a few frowned – because they thought the mayor had the police in her pocket? Because a police presence smacked of a police state? Because they feared being silenced?

Or because they were My Place agitators? But what did those people even look like?

Unable to see the rear rows clearly, Hirsch began to sidle along the wall – just as Clarissa Stanyer banged her gavel and called the meeting to order. The audience stirred; a few coughed; conversations trailed away.

After a brief opening statement and welcome, Stanyer listed the agenda items. The minutes of the prior meeting were adopted. And then she said that the first item of business concerned helicopter flights above the town and the old copper mine. No acknowledgment of country, Hirsch noted, staring at the back of Auntie Steph's head. She, sensing it, turned around and eyed him flatly.

'At the peak of the tourist season,' Stanyer was saying, 'we think we can run to at least four flights a day. At all other times, a few times a week. This should not only cope with demand – it's not as if we're the Eiffel Tower – but also not cause undue noise issues.'

An abrupt movement caught Hirsch's attention – but it was only an elderly woman fanning her face against the mounting, closed-in heat. He glanced up. The ceiling fans barely chopped at the air.

Meanwhile the mayor was introducing Don Beadel, the district's arts and tourism manager. A man with a shiny face and startled hair, he wore a short-sleeved shirt with a red tie. He wasn't actually sporting pens in a pocket protector, but he had that look. To Hirsch's knowledge, he'd delivered no arts of any kind to the Mid North – but he had beavered away diligently on behalf of tourist operators for many years.

Beadel rose, blushing, from his front-row seat and faced the locals, most of whom looked on blankly as he began to speak. The existing mine buildings would not be disturbed in any way, he said. The helipad would be situated on a vacant block of land half a kilometre away and the company whose tender they'd accepted would use only experienced pilots and a quiet machine, with flight paths still to be determined but certainly far from populated areas.

A woman got to her feet. Hirsch recognised Lorraine Whistler, who managed the high-school tuckshop. 'You've already accepted a tender?'

'Why, yes. We—'

'Without running it past the community? Who's going to pay for all this? Us?'

'Well, the helicopter will be leased and—'

Another woman stood. Hirsch recognised the stocky figure of Peta Renshaw, who owned a smallholding between Penhale and Tiverton. She cocked her head at Beadel, very sure of herself. 'What do you mean, no flights over populated areas? Plenty of people live around the mine. Have you asked them what they think?'

'We've sought expert opinion and I'm assured—'

Whistler pitched in again. 'Isn't it true, Mr Beadel, that you have a conflict of interest?'

Beadel, floundering, looked to Clarissa Stanyer for help.

The mayor stood, scowling. 'If you'd let Mr Beadel finish,' she said, her voice dangerously even, 'you'll understand that all of this is merely at the proposal stage. Nothing is set in stone—'

'Sounds like it is!'

'—and so, if you could all kindly wait until the matter is up for public discussion before—'

'Already decided!'

Hirsch couldn't see who was interjecting; he saw Landy swivelling her head, too.

Whistler shouted, 'Isn't it true the helipad site is on land your brother-in-law owns?'

Another interjector: 'The same guy you've been paying a consultancy fee? Three thousand bucks a month, isn't it? Proposal stage my arse.'

Beadel looked lost now, the victim of a baffling and unfair attack, not getting the mayoral support he thought he was owed. Clarissa Stanyer slashed her hand at him and he dropped like a stone into his seat.

Now she turned a meaningful look onto Brandl. The sergeant, to her credit, responded with a minute shrug. Voices had been raised, but no one had acted violently; Whistler and Renshaw hardly looked dangerous. And if the mayor and her councillors couldn't run an orderly meeting, that wasn't in any way a police matter.

Well, well, thought Hirsch. Maybe the nutters have had it right all along. Within five minutes we've had allegations of cronyism and conflicts of interest.

The muttering got louder, and the mayor, full of controlled fury, snarled at Lorraine Whistler: 'Are you even a ratepayer?'

The hall erupted, people yelling, getting to their feet, waving their fists. Hirsch checked with the sergeant. She was standing now, watching, arms folded, while the mayor banged her gavel. *'Clear the gallery.* This meeting will now continue in camera.'

A signal for Steph Ingram to stand. 'While we're on the subject of consultancy fees,' she said in a calm voice that somehow managed to penetrate the din, 'how much did you pay the thug who tried to pressure us into letting you cut down the birthing tree? To benefit your husband, I might add?'

Hirsch was not surprised to see some muted derision from the crowd. Maybe they thought her people were getting uppity, now they had a drop-in centre …

Most were nodding, though. Looking for a reaction from the mayor.

She didn't disappoint. 'You people,' she steamed. 'Someone with forward-thinking ideas chooses to develop a bit of unused land or a creek and suddenly it's sacred?'

That galvanised the Truro councillor. Craig Tetsworth leapt to his feet and stood shoulder-to-shoulder with the mayor. He cupped both hands around his plump, moist lips and shouted, 'Exactly. You don't know what you're talking about. Like the miners' dugouts – they're not Abo, they're *European*. Do your homework.'

A crowd divided along old lines, Hirsch thought. His gaze was restless now. He saw Sergeant Brandl weaving towards him. Jean Landy had stepped away from the wall, one hand hovering at her baton, her gaze fixed on the seats at the rear. He craned to see what had caught her interest. Began to pace her as she edged along the wall towards the main doors.

Among the semi-obscured figures back there, he thought he recognised Trent McRae and Nicholas Sampson. Perhaps his bodycam would confirm that – not that the pair had said or done anything. Perhaps they hadn't expected a police presence? He tried wading through the throng of people now streaming out of their seats, heading for the doors. But then the shouting behind him got more heated and he paused to check. Clarissa Stanyer was remonstrating with Steph Ingram, Nan Buchanan and Peta Renshaw. He drew nearer. Steph was demanding a part-time healthcare nurse, Peta Renshaw a forensic examination of the council's books, and Nan Buchanan that councillors read their briefing papers for a change. It was fiery, but not about to erupt into a fistfight, so he hurriedly returned to the melee at the rear until, shoulder-to-shoulder with Jean Landy, he was pushing out onto the street. Suddenly Redruth was just another small town again. Peaceful, mostly empty, air temperature a tad cooler thanks to the clouds.

24

Friday, 7 a.m.

Hirsch, barely out of the shower, answered a pounding on his front door. 'We were told to check in with you first,' said the older of the two men on the doorstep.

His name was Adam Powick and he wore clean overalls with the words Powick and RDC stitched across the bib beneath the Redruth and District Council's wattle logo. Looking as if he'd pulled an all-nighter at the pub, he was about fifty, bleary, with combed-over baldness and a hit-and-miss morning shave. 'About the rubbish clean-up?'

Hirsch gathered himself. 'Oh, right.'

'They didn't tell you?'

'They didn't tell me.'

'That sounds about right,' Powick said. 'This is Kev.'

Kev's surname was Tetsworth, according to his overalls. Younger than Powick, overalls filthy, boots oil-stained and a grin on his face that any normal person might want to wipe off.

Behind both men, parked on the highway across from the police station, was a small council tip truck.

Hirsch was about to inform them that a larger tipper was needed when Tetsworth said, 'If you could show us the way?'

'Tea, coffee?' Hirsch said. 'I was just about to have breakfast.'

'Mate, we're on the clock.'

And so Hirsch found himself crammed into the cab of their truck for the short drive around to the access road and the town paddock gate. Powick eyed the rubbish gloomily over the steering wheel, said, 'Should've come with the Volvo.'

'Yeah, and the bobcat.'

Assuming they meant a larger truck and a machine to scoop up the rubbish, Hirsch said, 'Well, I did tell your boss.'

That set off dark mutterings, and then Powick was parking the truck alongside a pair of mattresses and they all got out. 'Keep an eye out for snakes,' Hirsch said.

Tetsworth gave him a look. Either no pissy snake was going to spoil his day, or Hirsch had stated the obvious.

Feeling weary already, and the day barely started, Hirsch said, 'I'll leave you to it.'

Tetsworth pulled another face. He was full of faces, and this one said that he had no time for a man who didn't pull his weight. He expects me to pitch in and help, Hirsch realised.

Powick, too? Hirsch checked: Powick, pulling on thick leather gloves, gave Hirsch the tiniest of headshakes. A kind of permission to leave.

Hirsch gave the tiniest of smiles in return. 'Where will you take all this stuff?'

'Redruth tip.'

Hirsch gazed doubtfully at the mound of demolition rubble: bricks, timber, roofing iron, cracked fibro-cement. 'There could be asbestos among that lot.'

'You an expert?' asked Tetsworth, grabbing a mattress by one corner. Already dismissing Hirsch, he said, 'Come on, Powie, give us a hand.'

Powick smiled bleakly at Hirsch, muttered, 'You get what you pay for,' and turned to help the younger man.

'I was thinking hazmat gear,' Hirsch called after him.

That earned him a casual wave, so he skirted around the pile, checking for identifiers in the newest material – a name and address on a convenient envelope – but the cracked plastic bucket, empty paint tin and garbage bag leaking disposable nappies were anonymous.

As he was about to leave, he spotted a set of spindly black metal folding legs topped by something that looked like a white umbrella, tautly stretched but torn. He kicked at it. A photographer's lighting kit, he realised. Next to it, a handheld reflector. He toed that, too, revealing an old camera. Vintage, black, with knobs on the side and one big lens above another. A Rolleiflex. Worth hundreds of dollars – if not thousands. Dumped because it was irreparable? More likely dumped because it looked old.

Glimpsing the corner of a photo in a clear plastic sleeve, and ignoring Tetsworth's yell of, 'You making more work for us?' Hirsch switched his attention to the lighting kit again.

Nudging it to one side revealed dozens of photos in plastic sleeves.

He sifted through them. Desolation Hill at sunset – in real life just a desolate hill but Rosie Llewellyn had captured some aura of timeless might. Then Uluru, glowing. A massive road train snarling towards the lens. Some tricky shadows striping the Mischance Creek ruins.

Telling Powick, 'Leave this stuff, please, it's stolen,' he trotted back to the police station.

Returned with the HiLux, photographed and then loaded the camera, lighting kit and photographs, and called Rosie Llewellyn. No answer. Had a coffee, called again. Still no answer. That made him nervous.

He checked the local FB page. The usual Marketplace listings and missing sheepdogs, bogus roof repairer warnings and advice about Sampson Motors in Redruth: *Get your own pre-purchase report, not one supplied by this rip-off merchant*.

And, yesterday evening, Rosie had posted that some bastard had stolen her caravan. A furious heading, a professional publicity photo of the caravan against the backdrop of Arkaroo Rock, then a run of angry caps:

MY WHITE 2021 JAYCO JOURNEY 17 FOOT CARAVAN WAS STOLEN FROM THE REAR OF MID NORTH ARTS IN PETERBOROUGH AROUND 10.06 THIS MORNING. I'M STILL CHASING DOWN CCTV FOOTAGE BUT IT WAS DRIVEN AT SPEED SOUTH ALONG THE HIGHWAY SO IF ANYONE IN MUNCOWIE, TIVERTON, PENHALE, REDRUTH OR ANYONE ELSE SAW ANYTHING, LET ME

KNOW ASAP. IT WAS TOWED OFF BY A WHITE SUV, UNCLEAR WHAT MAKE. THANK YOU EVERYONE FOR YOUR MESSAGES, SHARES, LIKES AND KIND WORDS. MY WHOLE LIFE IS IN THAT VAN, SO PLEASE SHARE THE HELL OUT OF THIS POST. THANK YOU, ROSIE LLEWELLYN C/- TIVERTON POST OFFICE SOUTH AUSTRALIA.

why hadn't she called him?

Hirsch checked the recent crime and incident logs. She'd reported the theft to Peterborough police. That made sense. He contacted them, learned nothing new, tried Rosie again.

This time she answered and was astonished that he was interested. 'I reported it to the Peterborough police,' she said.

A strange woman, he thought, neither fully connected to nor disengaged from the world. Maybe she saw everything in two dimensions.

But she was happy for Hirsch to drop in on her.

He was there by 10.30. Alerted by his arrival, she hurried off her veranda and across the yard and was peering through his side windows before he could unfasten his seatbelt. 'I thought you found my stuff?'

Hirsch shut the driver's door and pulled out his phone. 'Sorry, Rosie, it's evidence. I can probably let you have it all back once we've checked for prints and DNA.' He proffered his phone. 'This is what I found.'

She peered at and swiped through the photos he'd taken that morning. 'My Rollei! I don't care so much about the rest, I have copies of all the photos and the gear's easy to replace, but that camera's priceless.'

'I thought it might be. My theory is, it didn't look valuable, it looked old.'

'Unlike my Canon and Nikon, which I notice you haven't recovered,' Llewellyn said glumly. 'Or various lenses, the MacBook. Stuff I'll never see again?'

'We're working on it,' said Hirsch, hedging the truth. 'You said you'd been looking for CCTV footage?'

'I'll show you what I've got.'

She took Hirsch through to her studio, where he roamed again, examining the photos on her walls while she fired up an old Dell. He stopped again at her shot of the Isuzu truck laden with fuel drums and the underfed dustbowl face of Audrey McRae.

'You ready?' Llewellyn said. 'Here. It's not much, but it's a start. Footage overlooking the gallery's backyard, and laneway footage where it passes the carwash at the rear of the BP on the highway.'

'You've been busy. Have the Peterborough police seen it?'

'I gave them copies.'

'Can you give me a copy?' Hirsch asked, as the video began to play.

'Sure.'

As Rosie plugged in a memory stick, Hirsch watched the screen. It flickered, clarified. A stretch of backyard fence palings, rubbish bins, an outside toilet, flattened cardboard secured by a house brick. And an uncoupled caravan taking up most of the image field.

'Watch.'

The caravan rocked gently. A towbar was hooking on, barely visible. 'Where did you park your LandCruiser?'

'Out the front where it wouldn't block the laneway.'

'You hadn't got around to unloading?'

'No. I was barely there five minutes. Unhitched, parked, went in to say hello,' Llewellyn said. 'The plan was to start hanging photos for the opening tonight.'

'What will you do now?"

Llewellyn snorted. 'Keep going; just start a week late, that's all. But I'll have to reprint, remount and reframe, which is going to eat into my profits. Bastard.'

'You think it's one person?'

'See for yourself.'

Hirsch watched the screen image shift to a sign on a brick wall, *Peterborough Self-Serve Carwash*, briefly obscured as the top halves of a white SUV followed by a caravan slid past. One head on board: Trent McRae. Presumably at the wheel of the Subaru from Sampson Motors. According to the time stamp, McRae had stolen the caravan at 10.06 a.m. the previous day.

And possibly towed it to Jack Minack's place in time to join the foreclosure protest?

'Looks like he towed it down the laneway,' Rosie was saying, 'then out past the carwash and onto the highway. I'm still looking for other video footage, but I hope that's enough for people to be going on with.'

She removed the memory stick, passing it to Hirsch as he tried to make sense of what she'd just said. 'What do you mean, "people to be going on with"?'

She seemed puzzled. Fiddled with her laptop and said, 'Facebook.'

He peered at the screen and groaned. In the time it had taken for him to drive here, she'd updated her post with the carwash video, asking: *Anyone recognise the prick driving?*

'Rosie, you need to be careful. It probably *is* your caravan in the act of being nicked, but what if it isn't? What if, coincidentally, someone else drove past towing a caravan at around the same time? You could find yourself being sued.'

What he didn't say was, Trent McRae might now go deeper to ground, or retaliate, or even find himself being targeted by vigilantes.

'You want me to take it down?'

'Just the video for now,' Hirsch said, meaning forever. He sweetened the pill. 'But I can tell you that I recognise the driver.'

'Who? I'll rip his balls off.'

'Rosie ...'

'Bloody useless, that's all I can say.' But she began taking down the carwash clip.

Pocketing the memory stick, Hirsch said goodbye and stepped out into the heat again. Half blinded, shading his eyes, he got behind the wheel and cranked up the aircon.

Sergeant Brandl answered on the first ring. 'And you have no doubt?'

'It's clearly him.'

'Don't recall seeing it near the town hall last night.'

'Stashed it somewhere,' Hirsch said, 'possibly on Jack

Minack's property. It means Trent has a home base now, somewhere to sleep. The freedom to move around.'

'The freedom to do what, though?'

'Something's keeping him here, Sergeant. Political stirring among other things. Stealing caravans.'

And punching me in the stomach ...

Brandl sounded world-weary. 'No more slaps on the wrist.'

'Exactly. We arrest him,' Hirsch said.

A sigh. 'Okay. Where are you now?'

'Still out east.'

'Check with Audrey on your way home.'

'For all the good that will do,' Hirsch said.

'I'll check with Minack,' promised the sergeant.

Hirsch drove a short distance down the road and pulled into the shade of a few gumtrees clustered in the corner of a stony paddock. Breakfast had been hours ago. He sipped half a mug of sweetened black tea from his vacuum flask, nibbled a rock bun Wendy had made, fired up the HiLux and lumbered on again.

'Why can't you just leave me alone,' said Audrey McRae half an hour later. 'I haven't seen Trent, haven't heard from him.'

'We think he stole a caravan, Mrs McRae.'

'Yeah, well, so you say. Don't know what it's got to do with me.'

'How close is he to Nicholas Sampson, down in Redruth?'

'How the hell would I know?'

'What about Jack Minack?'

'Don't even know who that is.'

Frustrated, Hirsch turned to go, and then he found himself making a leap that felt exactly right. 'A professional photographer named Rosie Llewellyn took your photo a year or two ago.'

'Yeah, so?'

'How did that come about?'

'School sports day. Back when the school was still open.'

'Was Ms Llewellyn there officially?'

Audrey McRae shook her head. 'Just, you know, taking photos of people.'

Photos of rural life in all its forms, thought Hirsch. A school sports day: a few skinny, scrappy kids running around. Pepper trees and tank stands. Parents and grandparents. 'It's a very good photo,' he said. 'Artistic. I think she showed it in one of her exhibitions?'

A pantomime of expressions passed across McRae's face: embarrassed pride, bafflement; objection; shyness. 'Yeah, well ...'

'What did Trent think?'

'He said I looked ugly, but also I should've been paid for it.'

25

Later, eating an early lunch at his desk, Hirsch ran both Tetsworth's and Powick's names. A couple of speeding fines for Powick; a drug misdemeanour charge for Tetsworth.

But it was worth noting that Tetsworth was the nephew of the wet-lipped Truro Ward councillor.

By 1 p.m. Hirsch had cleared a backlog of emails, handled a working with children application and taken a stolen chainsaw report. He called Alastair Stanyer's landline. No reply.

A one-step-forward-and-a-hundred-back kind of life, being a country copper.

Bored, he wandered around to the town paddock. Most of the rubbish had been cleared away. Only Powick was at work. Protected by a dust mask and goggles, he was tossing the last half-bricks, rotting boards and fibro chips onto the tip truck.

He looked up at Hirsch and lowered the mask. 'Soon be out of your hair.'

'Where's your mate?'

'Shoulder issues,' Powick replied, his tone saying that Tetsworth had a history of shoulder issues, back issues – or simply issues.

Taking a risk, Hirsch said, 'I suppose his uncle gives him sick notes?'

Powick froze, then relaxed. 'Mate, you don't know the half of it,' he said, but left it at that, tossing another brick onto the load.

'If you've got spare gloves and a mask, I can lend a hand.'

'Can't. Against regulations. But have a cuppa with me? I'll finish in a tick.'

The tick was ten minutes, and then Hirsch sat with Powick and his cane basket containing a thermos flask and a lunchbox in the shade of the gumtrees between the oval's northern goalposts and the town paddock. He accepted a mug of tea. Brushed away flies and asked if cleaning up rubbish was a big part of Powick's working life.

'Yes and no,' the council worker said.

And that was it for a while, Powick tearing bites from a sandwich and washing it down with gulps of tea.

Then, tossing away the dregs, he said, 'Mostly cleaning. Graffiti. Blocked drains and culverts. The odd oil spill. Mowing. Filling in potholes. You name it. Not so many of us anymore, hence the range of jobs.'

'Budget cuts,' Hirsch said, swigging at his tea, which was strong enough to strip paint.

Powick gave consideration to the remark. 'Well, yeah. But no one lasts long with this bunch. High turnover.' His eyes were half-closed, expression oblique. He wanted Hirsch to follow up.

'Pay no good?'

'The pay's never been good, barely above the award, but what I'm talking about is – what would you call it – *workplace relations*.' In finger quotes.

Hirsch nodded. Said what he thought he was expected to say: 'Difficult?'

Powick picked at something in his teeth. Examined it, flicked it away. A strip of gumtree bark fluttered onto Hirsch's sleeve; he looked up uneasily, not wanting a branch to conk him on the head.

Powick said, 'Difficult: you could say that. The way they talk to us, it's like we're servants, a bad smell on their shoes.'

'I've had sergeants and inspectors treat me like that,' Hirsch said.

'Yeah, but I bet it's easier to sack a council worker than it is a cop,' Powick said.

Hirsch wasn't so sure, but he didn't want to get into the relative strengths and weaknesses of his and Powick's unions. 'Few of you been sacked, have they?'

Powick seemed to consider the question as he methodically finished his last section of sandwich and folded the ragged square of greaseproof paper in which it had been wrapped. He took so long that Hirsch opened his mouth to rephrase the question. Then Powick said, 'A few – but it's more a case of good people quitting. High turnover.'

'Okay.'

'Not exactly bullying, not after what happened a few

years ago. More like ... disrespect, these days. It's not a happy place.'

'What bullying a few years ago?'

'Before your time. Back when Mitch Stanyer was the Tiverton councillor. He made life a misery for the women in the office. Arrogant, always shouting at 'em. Put-downs, you know ...'

'Never heard that.'

'Like I said, before your time. He had to step down.'

A car came along the town paddock's access road and paused. A rubbish-dumping chancer, thought Hirsch, climbing to his feet and strolling to the fence. He gave a little grin and wave. The car, a pink Hyundai, took off again. He didn't recognise it and it was too far away to get a plate number.

He returned to Powick, who gave him a cockeyed grin. Unspoken between them was the fact that they were talking about a man whose wife was now Powick's boss. 'Mitch had to step down?'

'Different mayor back then: a decent bloke. He referred the matter to the local government minister and Mitch was told to do a personal development course and avoid interacting with the staff.' Pause. 'That didn't sit too well, so he quit.'

Hirsch said, 'I've only met him a couple of times.'

'A grin and slap you on the back kind of guy – when he's not shouting at clerical-grade women,' Powick said sourly.

Hirsch knew he should tread carefully, but Powick seemed keen to talk, so he asked, 'What's his wife like?'

Powick was pleased to be asked. 'You mean, what's she like as mayor, or as my boss?'

'Either. Both.'

'Like I said, not a happy place, local government.'

Cagey, hinting at more. Hirsch tried to find it. 'So what about Mitch? A bully because he enjoys it, or only when things go wrong?'

'I'd say both. He treated the clerks like shit anyway, but he was really pissed off when he couldn't get the miners' dugouts rezoned for larger-scale tourism.'

Hirsch nodded. There was a walking trail along Redruth Creek with the better-preserved dugouts marked by simple plaques. That seemed sufficient. Maybe Mitchell Stanyer dreamed of boutique hotels with expansive lawns.

'One of the clerks found out he had a financial stake in developing the creek,' Powick continued.

Hirsch thought of the End Point Park road project. Mitch's days of wielding influence as a councillor might be over, but his wife's were not. 'A busy boy,' he said.

Powick cocked his head. 'You're wondering why I'm telling you all this.'

'Crossed my mind.'

'When my boss assigned me this job yesterday, the mayor happened to be there. She's always there. Turn a corner, and there she is. Anyway, she said you were quote, unquote, inadequate to the task of small-town policing. She told me you were lazy and inefficient and I shouldn't let you interfere today. Her exact words.'

'Well, yeah, that's me in a nutshell,' Hirsch said, betting

that Clarissa was the type to polish a grievance as if it were a brass name-plate.

Powick grinned and changed the subject. Gesturing at the council's tip truck he said, 'You mentioned asbestos. Sore point. Last year a mate of mine was sacked when he wouldn't take a load of fibro to the tip. Decades old and riddled with asbestos.'

Hirsch understood that Powick was saying he'd rather take asbestos to the tip than complain and lose his job. Not that he'd be happy about it.

'At least keep your mask on,' Hirsch said.

Powick was saying, 'Will do,' when they heard the approach of another vehicle. Hirsch stood and showed himself – but it was a Mercedes van marked *SiteSecurity Inc.* Watching it park, he said, 'The CCTV crew.'

'And my work here is done,' Powick said.

The rest of the day passed slowly, then it was time to freshen up and drive to Wendy's for the night.

Early Saturday morning, Hirsch kissed her, returned to Tiverton and had barely made a start on his fucking emails when Annika Nordrum called.

A tremor in her voice: 'I just found Mum's chair and shade cloth.'

26

'Near where you saved my neck the other day.'

The nature reserve. 'Can you be sure they were hers?'

'Who else?'

Could be anyone else, Hirsch thought, but he should check before reporting it, and even if he agreed with her, senior officers in Adelaide or Port Pirie would demand more information before mounting a search operation.

Unless Annika also stumbled upon human remains in the next hour.

He told her to stay put, let Sergeant Brandl know where he was going, and by mid-morning was driving slowly past the nature reserve named for the old Mischance Creek merino stud, one eye on the potholes, the other on the long scar that was Pattenden's Fissure. When he finally spotted the Mazda, it was further east than he'd expected, parked in the shade of a few wattles growing beside some boulders in a shallow depression. A spring? he wondered. Some kind of water-retaining shelf underneath? He parked on the verge of the road, got out, swung one leg and then the other over the top fence wire, and walked down the slope until Bella barked and Nordrum emerged from behind one of the boulders and waved a spatula at him. Eggs and bacon, he thought. And he doubted she'd sought permission to camp.

When he was directly opposite her, she pointed, said, 'There's a spot further along where you can cross,' and began to pace it with him on the opposite bank in a strangely non-companionable way: the gulf that was the fissure; the need to project their voices a little.

Until she stopped, pointed and said, 'There.'

A cluster of rocks in a bed of flood-borne soil and debris. Hirsch edged down onto the highest point and, testing each step, crossed the provisional bridge and clambered up onto the other bank.

She grinned. 'Have you had breakfast?'

'A coffee wouldn't go amiss.'

'Coming up.'

He followed her back to the wattle grove. One of the perimeter rocks was flat-topped, the size of a card table, cluttered now with a small gas stove, a greasy plate and cutlery, salt and pepper shakers, an egg carton and a cutting board. A bucket of water sat nearby – he guessed for extinguishing flames – together with water and food bowls for Bella.

'A very special place,' Annika said, pointing to one of the other rocks. 'I probably shouldn't even camp here, but I didn't notice anything until this morning.'

Hirsch crossed the little clearing to the designated rock.

A simple petroglyph had been carved into one smooth flank, telling the story of a kangaroo hunt. He wondered if Steph Ingram knew it existed. It was somewhere to bring her schoolkids.

'Maybe not stay here tonight,' he said, joining Nordrum again.

Adjusting the flame under a stove-top espresso maker, she paused to fork-scoop scrambled eggs into her mouth, then said, 'While this gurgles away, let me show you something.'

She took him around behind a third boulder and pointed to a patch of sparse, lumpen undergrowth: dirt, bark, struggling grass. 'It helps if you squat,' she said. Shrugged shyly and added: 'I needed to pee at the time.'

Hirsch obliged, focusing until he was able to distinguish a couple of regular shapes from the irregular. A half-metre strip of weathered metal. Next to it, a fold of material.

'I see it.'

'I didn't touch anything.'

Hirsch got to his feet. Maybe she'd seen too many cop shows but, for all he knew, this *was* a crime scene, and a good thing she'd not compromised it – apart from camping here to begin with. On the other hand, would a lab be able to lift prints or DNA after all this time?

He drew closer and squatted again. Using a twig to nudge aside some of the plant litter, he revealed a folded aluminium camping chair upholstered with strips of coarsely woven nylon, and a fold of shade cloth with lengths of faded blue rope tied to metal eyelets along one border. All of it ravaged by time and weather.

He rejoined Annika, who handed him a coffee. 'I mean,' she said, 'other people have probably camped here at times, but it all speaks of my mother: the best spot for cooking and eating; the chair; the shade cloth.'

Hirsch didn't say that it was too soon to tell. 'It's possible this place is the question mark on your father's map, the dotted line is the fissure and the little squares represent the Mischance Creek ruins.'

'I think so.'

'Did they ever talk to you about it?'

'No. Or ... they might have, but it would've gone in one ear and out the other because I'd never been here.'

Hirsch glanced around at the boulders, the wattles, the hillslopes and the fissure itself. He'd heard visiting geologists use terms like igneous, alluvial, sedimentary and metamorphic – he even had dim memories of learning these terms at school – but knew he wouldn't be able to tell a topaz from a gold nugget to save himself. 'Is this particular area conducive to gemstones?'

'No idea,' Annika Nordrum said.

And grinned at him.

Then she grew serious. 'But it makes sense, I suppose. They used to talk about sifting through stream gravel, and here we have a readymade channel for floodwater.'

'True.'

'But if Mum camped here, was she alone? Was she with Dad but he went off to Breadbox Plain by himself? Or did she go with him? Or is she here somewhere? We come back to the same old questions.'

'Good questions,' Hirsch said.

But still not good enough to bring in a forensic crew or even a search party. Not until he had evidence of another scenario, one not considered by Annika – or not aloud. What if her mother – or her father, too – had been attacked? Attacked right here, just as Heather Nordrum was about to set up her customary cooking and eating spot. He glanced again around the little grove. The recess behind the table rock was invisible from the clearing. You'd not bother to check behind it if you were a killer cleaning up in a panic.

Annika finished her coffee. 'Sorry if I've brought you here on a wild-goose chase, and I know you're busy, but can you spare an hour?'

They agreed to spend that time searching in opposite directions, using the rock crossing as the mid-point. Bella trotted with Hirsch for a few minutes, until, with a whimper of distress, she charged back the way they'd come. He kept one eye on the break in the ground as he walked, the other open for snakes. No wildlife, just rocks, gravel and sand drifts, ever repeating.

Even a bit of shaped polystyrene. He stopped, peered in. The lid of an Esky? Been there a long time. Blown there? Tumbled there on a flood?

He was about to continue when he heard the blast of a horn.

He trotted back along the fissure and caught up with her at the Mazda. Tightly wound, she was treading in one spot. 'Hard to describe, but you'll see.'

And she was off again, Hirsch following her for three hundred metres to a wider than normal section of the fissure. 'I'm too scared to look closer.'

Indicating a section of the opposite bank, she added, 'Bella started acting strange.'

Hirsch saw that a slab of soil had fallen in, possibly months or years earlier, revealing a natural cleft in the crumbling wall, the floor of which was a slab of rock. Resting in the hollow was a pair of what she'd thought might be calcified tree roots. 'Or megafauna remains ... or stone pipes. Some kind of strange formation, anyway.'

She paused. And her voice was threaded with dread when she said, 'Then I realised they were human leg bones.'

Hirsch felt his heart unfold, and put an arm around her. At the same time, he tried to fashion a story from what he was looking at over her shoulder. The hollow looked natural, not carved into the fissure wall – perhaps originally a small cave? Deep rather than high, with a partly concealing overhang – a casual gaze would pass over it. But Annika Nordrum's gaze hadn't been casual. She'd spotted what were clearly shin bones bracketed between the tops of weathered walking shoes and the cuffs of rotting cargo shorts.

'I'm going to check, okay?' Hirsch said.

'Be careful. It doesn't look very stable.'

He stepped in gingerly, feeling and hearing disturbances under his feet as he teetered over stones and sand and tested footholds when he reached the opposite bank. Dirt and pebbles spilled, his feet slipped, until finally he was able to haul his head level with the hollow. He could see a skull and torso now. The remains of a shirt. Skeletal hands outstretched with a loose wristwatch. Loose rings on two fingers.

Eye sockets stared at him.

Another spill of dirt had him scrabbling, sliding, twisting for balance and spilling onto his hands and knees at the bottom.

'You all right? Is it her?'

He got to his feet.

'Is it her?' Annika persisted.

Hirsch didn't know. Knew only that it was a smallish figure with thin, corroded metal strips tangled in the ribcage – the remnants of a bra? – and the expulsive shattering of a possible exit wound above one eye.

27

Hirsch photographed the body from several angles – in case of a cataclysmic flash flood or earthquake in the next thirty seconds – then clambered out to rejoin Annika on the bank.

Again she said, 'Is it her?'

A reasonable question in the circumstances, even as she must have known that he couldn't confirm or deny. 'Time will tell.'

She was still agitated. 'I know, I know – teeth and DNA.'

He showed a photo of a skeletal hand. 'Do you recognise the rings?'

Annika seemed to grimace and roll her shoulders. Eventually said, 'I *think* so. I wish I could remember; I wish I could be sure.'

'Not to worry, we'll know soon enough,' Hirsch said. He paused. 'I have to tell you, a lot's going to happen now – if slowly at first.'

He glanced upslope at the police HiLux baking in the sun. It should stay there: no point in driving it in and disturbing the scene further. Then he glanced along the fissure to what had probably been the murder scene: the little oasis of wattles and boulders, three hundred metres away and barely visible. Annika's Mazda ute should stay where it was, too. The fact that six years of weather extremes had passed was irrelevant: the crime scene officers would be looking for a projectile and a cartridge case at the very least, and it was bad enough that the area had been disturbed by Annika's tyres and hiking boots, let alone Bella's paws and his own clodhopper shoes. The Mazda would be allowed to move once the greater area had been searched, but that could be hours, days, from now.

'Can you tell what happened?'

Hirsch couldn't see the point of hiding anything from her. 'There's a head wound. There may be others, but I couldn't tell without moving the remains, and I need to leave that to the forensic team.' He paused. 'Sorry.'

She opened and closed her mouth in little gulps. 'All this time I've been thinking she got lost, or hurt herself, anything like that, but seeing *where* she's been all this time – and now you say there's a head wound – I'm seeing someone putting her there.'

Hirsch nodded. The hole in her head didn't necessarily mean she'd been murdered – she might've accidentally impaled herself on a metal spike of some kind – but she had been moved and hidden by someone.

Like her husband.

But he didn't say any of this.

'I have to get on the radio now,' he said. 'My boss, Port

Pirie CIB and probably the Homicide Squad. It's going to take a while.'

'I'll wait by my ute.'

'Sorry, you can't,' Hirsch said, going on to explain why.

Nordrum looked around wildly at the heat-struck distant hills and the dirt under her feet. The sun burning overhead. 'But it's so hot.'

Hirsch clasped her shoulders briefly, calmingly. It worked. The tension eased and then she was shaking her head, tears forming. 'I half thought I'd find her stretched out under a tree or at the base of some cliff – you know, tragic but somehow dignified. Now I can't help thinking she was scared at the end; someone was hurting her.' A violent head shake. 'But not Dad. He adored her. What happens now?'

Hirsch told her: a long wait as local experts arrived one by one. A search of both scenes. The remains taken to the city for analysis. She'd be questioned, he'd be questioned. A doorknock campaign along all of the neighbouring backroads.

She was frustrated. 'That will take forever.'

Hirsch made a ham-fisted attempt to explain, knowing from his experience on the job how urgent, agitated and frustrated crime victims or their friends and family could get. But the police had procedures and protocols to follow, especially if a matter was likely to end up in court.

'Okay, okay,' she said, capitulating finally, swiping at a limp tendril of hair with the edge of her hand. 'I get it. If that's Mum' – she pointed – 'she's been there a long time.'

'Yes.'

'No urgency.'

'Sorry about that.'

'But meanwhile do I hang around here all day, getting sunstroke?'

The answer popped into Hirsch's head. 'A woman named Trina Gould lives half an hour from here – with her husband, Pete. They're nice, I'm sure you can spend the day with them.'

And she'd be nearby, he thought, for questioning and eventually for the Mazda. 'Shall I give Trina a call?'

Annika nodded wordlessly.

Two minutes later it was settled and Hirsch was making a U-turn, aircon on high, Annika in the passenger seat.

She rode in silence as he made his radio calls, then asked, 'Will they want a DNA sample from me?'

'Probably.'

'Because I was here and to see if there's a familial match to the body?'

'Yes.'

She mused on that as the HiLux shuddered over corrugations and potholes. 'Will they reopen Dad's case now?'

Hirsch couldn't tell her that it wasn't a case. Not yet. 'They may decide to do that.'

'Obviously they will,' Annika Nordrum said with satisfaction. 'If it's Mum we found – and I have no doubt it is – and she was murdered, then they'd have to think he was, too.'

'Maybe,' Hirsch said, thinking: Or they might think he

inflicted a fatal wound on his wife and couldn't live with himself.

'What sort of questions will they ask me?'

Some hard ones if they think you're involved, Hirsch thought, but he said, 'Just tell them everything. What happened six years ago, from your point of view – they'll have read the files beforehand – and why you're here now. How I got involved. What we talked about. The map and diary you found tucked away in the glovebox. Everything.'

'They'll look closely at me, won't they?'

'At everyone.'

'I have the perfect alibi.'

Hirsch was on the final stretch. He could see the Goulds' roof and fledgling garden trees in the distance. 'You do?'

'I was in my final year of teacher training. I spent the whole of that week at Salisbury High, being assessed.'

'Be sure to tell them that.'

'I could've hired a killer, I suppose.'

And don't think they won't consider that, too, thought Hirsch. Meanwhile Annika was twitchy, as if she had things to say, or ask, and couldn't find the words. He waited.

'Can they find evidence after so long?'

'Depends. If a gun was used and left behind, then possibly. If you mean prints or DNA, then a doubtful maybe. Anything organic degrades over time.' Hirsch paused. 'That reminds me, I'll need your boots. I'm sure Trina can find some sandals or slippers for you.'

She understood immediately. 'Shoe prints. My feet are hot in these things anyway.' She bent to tug at a lace, then straightened. 'Maybe I should wait until I'm in the open air?'

Hirsch grinned. 'Maybe.'

'Will this lady let me have a shower?'

'Sure, but—'

'I know, I know, water shortage, I'll be quick.'

Hirsch slowed for the entrance and rolled down the driveway to the house, where Trina was waiting on the veranda, shading her eyes. 'Before you get out: there's going to be some media attention.'

He barely heard her say, 'There was a lot of it six years ago.'

But bigger this time around, Hirsch thought.

Ten minutes later he was making the return trip, Annika's boots in a rear footwell. He'd refused Trina's offer of a cup of tea, but stayed long enough to see her gather Annika in with tender concern in her voice, eyes and plump arms.

No sign of Pete. 'Oh, he's off making a delivery.'

Sergeant Brandl called a few minutes before Hirsch reached Pattenden's Fissure. She was in her Kia, lifting her voice above the road noise: 'I have Sandy with me.'

'Good.'

Sandali Pillai was the local doctor on call in suspicious-death cases. The police only requested more specialised help – a day-long round trip from Adelaide – in difficult cases.

Hirsch was hoping that the doctor would make a confident call today, maybe even release the remains. Otherwise they'd be here forever. In which case some mug might be required to guard the remains overnight.

'We should get to you in about an hour,' Brandl went on. 'There's a regional crime scene unit coming from Port Pirie, along with CIB.'

'Homicide?'

'I've been briefing a Senior Sergeant Webb. She's seen your photos and read up on the Nordrum story. She's happy for us to start the process. The scene's cold, after all, no immediate threat to life, and they're overloaded with three active cases from the past fortnight.'

'Okay.'

'But she intends to drive up early tomorrow morning and base herself in our briefing room initially – unless several other bodies turn up this morning, all with suspicious head wounds, in which case she'll drive up immediately with a hundred officers and take over the town.'

Brandl and Dr Pillai arrived with pastries, salad rolls, flasks of tea and coffee, fold-up chairs and a beach gazebo. After the latter had been erected just inside the fence beside the Kia and the HiLux, they all settled in to eat, talk and drink until the Port Pirie team arrived.

The doctor was wearing running shoes, cargo shorts and a T-shirt, and looked incongruous to Hirsch, who'd only ever seen her wearing scrubs or office clothes. He said, 'Thanks for coming.'

'A breath of fresh air – literally. First thing this morning I patched up a kid who broke her forearm falling off a horse during the week but couldn't arouse Mum's interest until now, and yesterday it was an old man who halved his bronchitis antibiotics because he wanted the dosage to last longer – he's quite wealthy, by the way – and before that a young man who thought he'd test his new birthday chainsaw on one of his bare feet.'

'People like that keep *us* in business, too,' Hirsch said. Then with a glance at Brandl, he added, 'Would it be possible to ask your opinion about a couple of individuals, their mental health?'

The doctor grew wary. 'Who?'

'Alastair Stanyer and Trent McRae.'

'I can't, Paul, you know that.'

'I know. Sorry.'

'We're worried about them, Sandy,' Brandl put in.

'In what way?'

'Mainly,' said Hirsch, 'are they going to hurt themselves or someone else?'

The doctor wore a small frown of disappointment. 'I haven't seen either man for some time. Mr Stanyer for blood pressure sometime last year. Before that, Mr McRae needed help detoxing after his little adventure in the pharmacy. But even that's saying too much, sorry. Look,' she said, 'if they or anyone else was in immediate danger, I would tell you.'

The exchange seemed to make her faintly cross with herself and the three of them sat there talking desultorily until late morning, when a dusty white Camry arrived, followed by a Hyundai van marked Crime Scene Unit. Only one man got out of the sedan, a bulky Port Pirie CIB detective named Jeff Comyn, who'd once treated Hirsch with derision but mellowed since.

He leaned on the fence. 'All right for some.'

Sergeant Brandl toasted him with her coffee mug. 'Where's the cavalry?'

'Just me for now,' Comyn said, turning to greet the four crime-scene officers, a man and three women, who nodded as the introductions were made and began to pull on blue over-suits.

One of the women approached. Lyn Dekic on her name tag. 'This is how it'll go. Two of my team will work the body, two the campsite. The rest of you remain here, please.'

Comyn nodded. 'You're the boss.'

Dekic turned to Hirsch. 'Can you point the way please? Without actually walking there again?'

Hirsch pointed – the body; the distant campsite trees – and heard her discuss crime-scene matters with her colleagues: how best to establish common approach paths to each scene, cordon them off, shelter them.

Hirsch, Pillai, Brandl and Comyn talked after that, with half their attention on the crime-scene officers. Soon Dekic came to fetch Dr Pillai, who returned half an hour later and told Comyn that, in her opinion, the victim was female and the death suspicious. 'The wound to the head was the main clue,' she said, with a crooked grin. 'It was in all likelihood caused by a bullet or some other projectile, and in fact there's a second wound in the upper chest area, a chipped ribcage bone aligning with a chipped vertebra.'

'Shot twice.'

'I believe so, probably from behind. But a pathologist will be able to give you a clearer answer.'

'Thank you. Hold on while I call it in.'

Comyn wandered away from the gazebo, a satellite phone pressed to his ear. He gazed at the sky as he talked; wiped the toecap of one shoe against his suit pants. He seemed to make several calls. And then he was back, saying, 'I've been given the okay to remove the body. The crime-scene techs can't do much while it stays where it is. A hearse from Redruth Funerals is coming to collect it and take it down to the city. Paul, assuming this is Heather Nordrum, where's the daughter?'

Hirsch told him.

'We'll need to speak to her and get her DNA.'

'She understands.'

'We already have yours. Doc, thanks for your help. You and Sergeant Brandl can head back to Redruth now if you like.'

Brandl nodded. 'I'll leave the beach tent, if you could bring it with you on Monday, Paul?'

'Sure.'

'That's if we hold our regular briefing. The Homicide Squad might have other ideas.'

Time passed and Hirsch and Comyn talked. When the hearse arrived, two crime-scene officers monitored the removal of the body before erecting a protective shelter and beginning an intensive, hands-and-knees examination of the cavity in the fissure. More photo and video. Sifting, tweezering, labelling. The same would be happening at and around the folding chair and the shade cloth.

Hirsch knew the logic of some of the procedures and

guessed the rest – what was happening on-site and what would happen later, in labs in Adelaide.

An odontologist would examine the teeth, not only to identify the body but also to ascertain the victim's age. A pathologist would examine the pelvis and hands and feet to determine if the victim was male or female. DNA samples would be taken from the femur, jawbone and teeth. The clothing scraps would be tested for blood. Clothing labels and style and the fabric itself might indicate a certain era – though Hirsch was certain the victim hadn't been wearing 1970s flared jeans or 1960s Witches Britches. Finally, buttons and metal objects such as rings, coins and belt buckles might yield useful information.

It would all take time, starting with immediate impressions, followed by an autopsy and lab work. And every opinion, speculation and fact would be proposed in light of other factors: the elapse of time; the seasons; animal and insect activity; and the involvement of humans, with their hopes, fears and desires.

Comyn seemed to brood meanwhile, as if thinking ahead. 'Did you go to the Breadbox site recently?'

'Yes.'

'Did Ms Nordrum?'

'Yes.'

'Find anything?'

'No.'

Comyn patted his face with a handkerchief. Unfastened a shirt button. 'Even so, we'll need forensics to poke around out there, too.'

'One suggestion,' Hirsch said. 'Annika Nordrum kept some of her father's things. There's the ute itself, and some of the camping gear, but she might also have kept his watch or his wallet or belt – even his clothes.'

'You're thinking if he was murdered there might be DNA transfer?'

'Yes.'

'If so, let's hope it's not too degraded.'

Dekic came to them as the shadows were lengthening and the heat dropping. 'I think we've found all we're going to find. No bullets, no shells, no pool of blood that magically lasted all this while. But we'll be back tomorrow.'

She turned to Hirsch. 'I understand this relates to a body in a mineshaft at a place called the Breadbox?'

'Yes.'

'May or may not see you there,' she said. 'Meanwhile, I've released the campsite, the ute can leave.'

Hirsch left when Comyn did. First, he collected Annika Nordrum and quizzed her on the way back to get her Mazda. Yes, she probably did have a few of her father's old things. Wallet and watch, sitting in a drawer, untouched, ever since ... She couldn't be sure if she'd kept his belt. She'd have a look when she returned to the city.

Then he had her follow him to Tiverton and the home of Nan Washburn, who'd converted half of her sprawling old house into an Airbnb.

Finally, mid-evening, he was home, and the phone calls began – to the office landline, not his mobile, thank God.

Channel 7 news, the ABC, the *Advertiser*, the *Mid North Record* and others. He referred them to the media unit and stuffed in his earplugs before he went to bed.

28

There was a text from Sergeant Brandl on Sunday morning: *Homicide Squad briefing at eight, my office.*

Hirsch reasoned that if he had to be up and about early on a Sunday, then so could certain other people, and was knocking on Audrey McRae's door at 7.30. No Subaru SUV, no caravan.

She said, 'I haven't seen him, I don't know where he is, I keep telling you that.'

Standing foursquare in her doorway, puffy-eyed from sleep, still gaunt in the face but with more colour in her cheeks, she then backpedalled a little. 'I've tried calling but he doesn't answer.'

'And you have no idea who his friends are?'

It might have been a trick question. McRae glanced both ways along the little street, as if her son might appear with the correct answer. 'No.'

Then, as if sensing that Hirsch wanted clarification she added: 'There's really no one around anymore. All the young ones have moved away.'

'We still need to speak to him, Mrs McRae.'

She looked at her swollen feet and lower legs. 'I'll tell him.'

'Here's my card again,' Hirsch said. 'Get him to call me so we can sort everything out.'

She took it wordlessly.

Hirsch drove around the corner to Erica Woodhead's house. No vehicle of any kind, no answer when he knocked, no sign of prone legs, pooled blood or overturned chairs when he peered through the windows. Church? Visiting family?

There was a Channel 9 news van parked outside the Redruth police station. He repeated his mantra, *No comment, speak to the Media Unit* and walked in with Sergeant Brandl's beach gazebo bundled in his arms.

Through to the station's briefing room, where he was introduced to a Homicide Squad senior sergeant named Webb – 'Call me Allison' – and her senior-constable offsider, Leavitt – 'Call me Joe.' Files at their elbows; laptops open; a plate of pastries, mugs, glasses, water, tea, coffee, milk.

Webb, tall and broad, in linen pants and a loose-fitting short-sleeved shirt, eased out of her chair to greet them. Limping, Hirsch noticed. About forty-five, with fuss-free brown hair and clear lacquer on her nails. Friendly enough as the introductions were made, but the smile was no more than serviceable. She has a job to do, thought Hirsch. Not here to make friends – unlike Leavitt, who held back like someone who was always excluded, yet wanted to be in the thick of things. Late twenties, thin, with a raw-looking skin-fade haircut offset by thick-rimmed inner-city glasses.

Gesturing for Hirsch and Brandl to sit, Webb began summarising as she returned to her chair. 'A cold case, so just the two of us for now, and we'll probably ask for your assistance from time to time.' She looked at Brandl, then at Hirsch. 'For example, we'd like one of you to take us to yesterday's site and the mineshaft site at some stage today.'

'Senior Constable Hirschhausen's the one you need,' Brandl said. 'It's his patrol area and he's more familiar with it than I am.'

'Good. You okay with that, Senior Constable?'

Hirsch nodded. 'But if you're viewing both sites, are you assuming—'

'Assuming nothing,' Webb said, with a steely kind of geniality. 'But since we're going to be out and about anyway, I'd like to fix both places in my mind – especially if the body found yesterday proves to be Heather Nordrum and not some random stranger.'

'Makes sense,' Hirsch said, reaching for a croissant and regretting the flakes immediately.

'It does,' Webb said. 'For all we know, the body you found is someone who went missing last year. We'll be relying on tests to reveal how long the remains have been there, and on teeth and DNA to reveal identity. Which means that further down the track we may need help with witness statements, general background information, intelligence reports and doorknocking, that kind of thing.' She paused. 'The trail is cold, there's no suggestion of the public being at further risk, and the preliminary stages of the investigation are likely to be mainly in the forensic labs. Depending on those findings,

I'll bring in more officers and set up a major incident room somewhere.'

She had a measured, almost report-writing style of speaking. 'There's a useful room in the town hall,' Hirsch said.

Leavitt made a note.

Sergeant Brandl leaned in. 'If it is Mrs Nordrum, are you thinking Mr Nordrum was also murdered?'

Webb tilted her head. Doesn't like to be interrupted, Hirsch thought. Or considers us to be idiots.

She began slowly, but Hirsch could tell she was well prepared and had already been playing out scenarios in her head.

'It's simply too soon to tell. Perhaps Mrs Nordrum was killed accidentally and her body hidden by Mr Nordrum, who then committed suicide. We don't have his body – I understand he was cremated – so we can't re-examine his remains. I have the inquest and autopsy reports' – she tapped her files – 'which ruled that his death was accidental. That said, if we *have* found Mrs Nordrum, then it would be remiss of me not to reopen Mr Nordrum's case, even given the limited evidence at our disposal – namely, a mineshaft that's been subjected to weather extremes for the past six years, not to mention trampled on by fossickers, tourists and farmers. But we spoke with the daughter just now – she's agreed to be interviewed at her Airbnb, by the way, so that will be our first port of call today, Senior Constable Hirschhausen.'

'Sure.'

'And she informed me that she'd retained certain possessions of her father's, which we intend to—'

'She thinks a leather belt, wallet, boots and wristwatch,' Leavitt said.

'Yes, thank you, Joseph,' Webb said. 'And to keep the chain of custody intact, she has agreed to meet a squad detective at her flat in Unley when she returns to the city later today.'

Brandl said, 'Let's hope we find foreign DNA.'

'Indeed. The same foreign DNA at both sites.'

A long shot, thought Hirsch. DNA left on what? And still viable after all this time?

Meanwhile Webb was saying, 'Whether or not there is a connection between the two events, we have many unanswered questions to tackle over the next few days.'

Brandl, rocking her lean frame minutely in her chair, said, 'First and foremost, who the dead woman is.'

'Indeed,' Webb said, and Hirsch realised that you didn't want to be at the receiving end of one of Webb's 'indeed' responses. Brandl saw it, too, and flushed as Webb continued.

'We intend to obtain a sample of the daughter's DNA today, and she's agreed to hunt down the name of her mother's dentist. She also thinks she might have a box of her mother's cosmetics, lipstick, a comb and a hairbrush, that kind of thing.'

Then Webb paused to glance at each of them. 'But what other questions and scenarios should we be considering? Senior Constable? You first.'

Hirsch, surprised to be asked, had been in the act of

reaching for the remaining Danish. He was starving. He began to order his thoughts.

'For the sake of argument, let's assume the remains we found do belong to Mrs Nordrum, and her husband accidentally fell into the mineshaft or committed suicide ...'

Webb nodded. 'Go on.'

'He drove to the Breadbox site alone. Why? Because he'd argued with his wife? Or they were getting on each other's nerves and needed a break? Or they were running out of time, needed to get back to the city, and to cover more ground it made sense to separate? The thing is, it seems that soon after he arrived, still to unpack properly, he ends up dead at the bottom of a mineshaft. It's well signposted how dangerous the area is: perhaps his eyesight wasn't the best or he was dodging a snake and tripped. Or he was upset and did himself in.'

'That scenario assumes someone else came along and killed – or certainly moved – Mrs Nordrum.'

'Yes.'

'But couldn't Mr Nordrum have done that before driving to where he was found?'

'Yes. Except ...'

'Go on.'

'According to Annika Nordrum, her parents had a loving marriage, they didn't own a firearm – if that was the cause of death – and had no plans to fossick at the Breadbox. They were after gemstones in Anna Gorge, not gold at the Breadbox.'

'The firearm could've come from anywhere and was later

hidden or thrown away by Mr Nordrum,' Webb said. 'But do go on.'

Hirsch swallowed. 'Even if they *did* decide to split up, why would Mr Nordrum pack up everything – yet leave only the chair and shade cloth for his wife? If he was intending to return after a couple of days, he'd have left plenty of supplies for her – even left her the dog.'

Joe Leavitt leaned forward. 'Perhaps he only intended to be away for a few hours.'

'Perhaps, but the two sites are a long distance apart, you'd want to make it worthwhile – which explains why he had so much gear with him but doesn't explain why he'd leave his wife with nothing. And if he'd killed her and committed suicide because he felt so bad, why leave the area to do it? Pack up almost everything and drive such a long distance?'

'Fair enough.'

'Which brings me,' Hirsch said, 'to my second main scenario, two linked murders.'

He glanced around the room. They were listening.

'The possibility that they were both killed at the same time, in the same place.'

They thought about that for a while. 'Assuming,' Webb said, 'it was Mrs Nordrum we found yesterday.'

'Yes.'

'I like it,' Leavitt offered. 'Whoever did it couldn't throw both bodies down the mineshaft; it would look suspicious. But if one body is found, and it looks accidental, then everyone starts to think along those lines, that Mrs Nordrum wandered off and got lost or she fell into another shaft that perhaps collapsed in on her ...'

'He's not just a pretty face,' Webb said. 'So, what's the primary crime scene, in that case? The mine?'

'The fissure,' Hirsch said, going on to explain about the dotted line on Ben Nordrum's hand-drawn map. 'It starts not that far from Anna Gorge, where they began their fossicking trip. They even phoned their daughter from there.'

'Where is this map?'

'The daughter has the original, I have a photo,' Hirsch said.

He passed Webb his phone. She stared at the screen, grunted, slid the phone back and turned to Leavitt. 'Make a note: we need the map and the notebook.'

'Boss.'

Swinging back on Hirsch, she said: 'So they didn't stay long at Anna Gorge?'

'No.'

'Disappointed? Decided to range further afield?'

'It's possible.'

'We need to speak to gemstone experts,' Webb said, glancing at Leavitt again.

'On it,' he said.

Back to Hirsch. 'Another scenario, the husband died separately and accidentally, and the wife was killed by a stranger who stumbled upon her camp, or he spotted her on the road looking for help because her husband hadn't returned.'

'It's possible,' Hirsch said, 'but—'

'But the coincidence factor. We hate coincidences.'

Hirsch shrugged, tried to look genial. 'Among other things. It just doesn't seem likely that her husband would abandon her, taking everything with him except the chair and the shade cloth.'

'But why not bury Mrs Nordrum instead of sticking her in a cavity? If she's never found, everyone thinks she *did* die tragically and alone, whereas if she's found, everyone takes one look at the hole in her skull and thinks: murder.'

'Ground too hard? Running out of time?'

'Or better still,' Webb said, as if Hirsch hadn't spoken, 'why didn't they bury both bodies and dump the ute somewhere else – Adelaide airport, for example?'

'That would look too suspicious. I think they wanted everyone to think the whole thing was just another outback tragedy and forget about it. And everyone did think that.'

Webb slapped both hands on the briefing-room table. 'Anyway, early days. Do we know if the Nordrums were travelling with money? Expensive equipment?'

She's thinking robbery, thought Hirsch. 'I asked Annika Nordrum. She said no. There was twenty dollars in her father's wallet and sixty-five in her mother's purse.'

'Travelling with gemstones, though.'

Hirsch pictured the bag of dull, dusty pebbles in the rear of the Mazda. 'Potential value only. You'd need to cut, polish and set them first, which would be a pain for any thief.'

Webb nodded. 'Depending on how things pan out in the next couple of days, we'll get a forensic accountant to look at their financial records: loans, mortgages, bank accounts, debts ... And we need to interview everyone involved back then. Police, volunteers ...'

She looked at her watch, then Hirsch. 'Time to hit the road. Tiverton first, and I'll ask you to make yourself absent while we interview Ms Nordrum. Then the mineshaft area, and then this fissure place. A nice round trip, and we'll grill you gently along the way, starting with the day you first got involved.'

Lovely, thought Hirsch. Shunted to one side and expected to do all the driving. Hours of the senior sergeant's measured, faintly ponderous voice. And probably not allowed to listen to his CDs.

29

It was the tail end of Sunday afternoon now and Hirsch, bone weary after touring the outback, was trying to catch up. He checked in with Wendy, Annika and his mother, monitored Facebook and familiarised himself with viewing the town-paddock CCTV footage.

He soon saw that fast-forward would become his closest friend. And people had got the message. He saw only one figure stray onto the town paddock: Daryl Cobb, a slow, vacant kid in his late teens. Wearing shorts and a singlet top, he was caught by the cameras wheeling his bike in from the access road, his drone in one hand. Hadn't the sense to wear a helmet or protect his gingery skin from the sun or carry a water bottle. As Hirsch watched, he dismounted. Stood staring vacantly at the freshly raked dirt as if afraid to get too close. Stared up at one of the cameras. At the warning sign. Gaped in alarm, mounted his bike and took off again.

It should've occurred to Hirsch earlier: maybe Daryl had captured useful footage from his drone?

Making a mental note to call on the kid soon, he stared gloomily into his freezer. Took out and defrosted a leftover chicken korma; ate it in front of the TV news. Rinsed his bowl, poured another glass of wine and began watching the first episode of an iView series. But screen-buffering made it unwatchable. Maybe at that moment the whole town was playing Jedi Survivor 2.

Eventually he wandered into his bedroom and glumly regarded the to-read books piled beside the bed. Many dated from last Christmas and included a Claire Keegan novel from Wendy, a Sachin Tendulkar biography from his father – 'Dad,' he wanted to say now, into the void, 'it's a long time since I was a cricket tragic' – and a novel promising *Outback noir in the tradition of Jane Harper*, a present from Kate Street, in smart-arse mode. And from Ed Tennant's second-hand shelf, *Diamond Dove*, an Oxford poetry anthology, a Ron Rash short-story collection and the third of Helen Garner's diaries. Hirsch assumed they'd been owned by local readers. Who, though?

He was almost relieved when someone pressed the front-door buzzer. He stepped through the connecting door into his office and found Dorrie Alkawaro on his doorstep. She slipped shyly through the gap and a moment later they were facing each other across the front counter, keeping things formal.

Hirsch smiled. 'More tailgating?'

She darted her gaze from the countertop to his eyes and down again. Shook her head shyly and said, 'No. But I saw him.'

'Where?'

'Facebook.'

Hirsch understood. 'Rosie Llewellyn's video clip?'

'Yes.'

'You recognised the driver?'

'He's the one run me off the road.'

'I thought you didn't get a good look – it was night, you were trying not to hit trees ...'

'It was him.'

When she was gone, he checked Llewellyn's Facebook feed again and muttered, 'Damn.' She'd reposted the video. With two responses. A Sikh cook from the Caltex service station in Redruth reported that he'd been harried when delivering curries to a twenty-first birthday back in September, and Uncle Doug had been forced off the road in early November when visiting a friend in Penhale.

Hirsch called them. 'You're positive it was the man in Rosie Llewellyn's video?'

Both were adamant: 'Yes.'

When he checked with Auntie Steph, she was strangely cool. 'But whether or not we see action from the Redruth police is quite another matter, wouldn't you say?'

'What do you mean?'

'Talk to your boss,' she said, cutting the call.

30

Monday was marginally cooler. Rain was forecast for the settled areas, but only a few cloud shadows blessed the Mid North before rolling south, limping into Adelaide and feebly dampening the city's exhausted streets and parklands.

But Hirsch wasn't to know any of that until the evening news. Responding to an early-morning text from Sergeant Brandl – *briefing as normal* – he made the run to Redruth again, where the sergeant dispensed with ongoing bread-and-butter matters quickly and said, 'We have a problem on our hands.' She paused. 'And I need to apologise to you guys.'

They waited. She shifted in her chair. 'Trent McRae. I took my eyes off the ball ...'

'You took him under your wing, Sergeant,' Tim Medlin said loyally. 'Not your fault if he's being an idiot.'

'We're well past the idiot stage,' Brandl said. 'Yesterday I had a very intense run-in with Steph Ingram. She said she doesn't know if she can rely on us anymore. Accused me of giving Trent a free pass.'

Jean Landy scowled. 'It's not as if we haven't been looking for him.'

'After what she told me, we need to look a lot harder.'

Hirsch waited, recalling Steph Ingram's coolness on the phone. To distract himself he reached across the table for a Danish.

'What'd she say?' Landy demanded.

'It seems Trent and a few others roughed up Uncle Doug's nephew a couple of days ago,' Brandl said, looking further diminished.

'Which nephew?'

A fair question. The drop-in centre's amiable handyman came from a big family, but plenty of non-kin kids called him uncle. Naive enough to get hoodwinked by an unscrupulous used-car dealer, he nevertheless kept the Wurlie going and had good relations with all of the district's Indigenous kids.

'Lindsay,' Brandl said. 'Used to live here, but moved to Clare with his mother a few years ago and now has his own flat.'

She fired up her laptop. The wall-mounted monitor flickered into life. 'What we have here is the Facebook page of the Lone Pine Patriots, would you believe, and what they like to do is use social media, posters and flyers to name and shame car thieves, burglars and shoplifters – who, funnily enough, all seem to be black, Asian or Muslim. In the case of Lindsay – who doesn't have a record, not even a whisper – they went in mob-handed. They were banging on his doors and windows and shouting. "Come out or we'll pull you out." Things like that.'

Hirsch leaned in. 'Was he hurt?'

'Pretty shaken. Few bruises.'

'Where were the Clare police in all this?'

'They broke it up in time, but everyone scattered so they're looking at CCTV. Lindsay didn't tell them he recognised Trent – they were at Redruth High together before he moved to Clare – but he did tell Doug.'

'And Doug told Steph.'

'Yes. Who thinks because I'd been mentoring Trent, I'm giving him a free pass.' Brandl paused and added: 'I know I messed up. People have been hurt, and it's made your lives harder.' A shrug. 'Maybe mentoring's not all it's cracked up to be. Maybe hard-line from now on.'

She looked so glum that Hirsch tried to break her train of thought. 'Lindsay recognise anyone else?'

Brandl slumped. 'No. Tim, I want you to find out what you can about this Lone Pine bunch, and keep pestering Clare police about CCTV.'

'Sergeant.'

'Meanwhile I've worked out a course of action. First, serve a search warrant on Trent's mother. Paul, you're with me on that: now, before lunch. Second, a concentrated doorknocking of his friends and acquaintances. Jean, I want you on that all day tomorrow. With me in Redruth in the morning, and with Paul up around Penhale and Tiverton in the afternoon. Anything you can find out. Who he hangs out with, places he likes to go, where he drinks, hobbies, interests ...'

'Sergeant.'

Brandl focused on Hirsch. 'Jack Minack assured me McRae isn't hiding out on his place, but check again.'

'Sergeant.'

Perhaps Tim Medlin felt he was out of the loop. 'Where do you want me, sergeant?'

'You have a vital role in the station. Like I said, liaise with Clare police and do a deep dive into the Lone Pine mob. You're our IT guru,' Brandl added.

As intended, she'd pleased him. He went pink. 'Sergeant.'

Brandl's gaze was harder now. 'Whatever happens, I want all of you working in pairs. Trent's dangerous. I don't want you acting solo and getting your heads blown off.'

31

Hirsch would not be returning to Redruth, so they set out in separate vehicles, Brandl first, then Hirsch, trailed by the Channel 9 van. When Brandl pulled over soon after leaving the police station side street, Hirsch pulled in behind her, puzzled, until he saw her get out and walk past him determinedly. He watched her in his mirrors as she waved the media van down, rested both hands on the driver's door, then patted the roof and returned to her police Kia. She's told them we're not on mysterious buried remains business, he thought. When they pulled away, the Channel 9 van stayed despondently parked, and wasn't behind them when they reached Penhale fifteen minutes later.

Hirsch followed the Kia to Erica Woodhead's address first. As they pulled up Woodhead was emerging with a listless Josie, carrying a stuffed Thelma the Unicorn backpack.

He joined Brandl in the driveway, the sergeant saying, 'Just us again, Erica.'

'I haven't seen Trent,' Woodhead said, bundling Josie

into the passenger seat of her Polo. 'And we're late for the doctor.'

'Anything serious?'

'Running a temperature.'

Brandl paused before asking, 'Has Trent been with her recently?'

Woodhead froze, then flared. 'No. And he's not the kiddy-fiddling kind anyway, if that's what you're thinking.'

'I'm not,' Brandl said. 'But has there been anything from him? Calls, texts, emails? Messages forwarded by his mother? Asking after Josie, that kind of thing?'

'Not a thing.'

'It's not too late for him, Erica. I have some faith left. But he's getting deeper into trouble.'

Woodhead was exasperated. 'Sergeant Brandl, we're *divorced*.'

Brandl ploughed on. 'His involvement with the Lone Pine Patriots. What can you tell me about that?'

'Get it into your head: we're divorced. I grew up. I moved on. And I've never heard of Lone Patriots, whatever.'

'They've been posting stuff on Facebook, the names and addresses of Indigenous kids they think have been stealing cars, breaking into houses, et cetera.'

Erica Woodhead looked at her watch, rattled her car keys. 'Yes, well, if the police did their job and protected the community and actually *investigated* crimes like break-ins and car theft, there wouldn't be a *need* for ordinary people to take action.'

Hirsch heard in the grievance a faint echo of something

she'd said the day he first met her. And maybe the sergeant was deliberately poking at the beehive. In any case, it was apparent that it wasn't ideological differences that lay behind Woodhead's decision to divorce her husband.

'If you see or hear from Trent,' Brandl continued, 'please urge him to hand himself in. He's just making things worse for himself.'

'*If* I see or hear from him. Big if.'

A few minutes later the sergeant was saying, 'We have a search warrant, Mrs McRae.'

Audrey McRae peered at them through the wire screen door, her hollowed-out features registering neither outrage nor puzzlement. 'For what?'

'Everything, I'm afraid. Your car, the house, the shed, Trent's man cave ...'

McRae responded by stepping out, shutting the main door behind her as she swung open the screen door. 'Trent's not here and what he does is none of my business.'

'That pretty much sums you up, doesn't it, Audrey?' said Brandl with a curling malice Hirsch had never heard from her before. 'Out of the loop about everything. Who owns what car in the family. What your only child gets up to. The names of the really great guys he hangs around with ...'

Audrey McRae went rigid, coiled like a snake and might have thrown a punch if Brandl hadn't stepped back and if reason hadn't prevailed. 'If you must know, he belts me. All right?'

'Oh.' Brandl was abashed. 'Audrey, I'm sorry, I didn't know.'

'There's a lot you don't know. All I want is for him to settle down and find a job and live somewhere else.'

'Sorry.'

'And I *don't* know what he does or where he is. You think I want to ask questions and get bashed up for my pains?'

'Of course not, I understand.'

Audrey McRae lost her spirit again and, opening both doors as far as they would go, said, 'Search away.'

'We'll be quick as we can.'

'Will there be a mess?' she asked helplessly. 'My things ...'

'We'll put everything back neatly,' Hirsch said, not telling her that her things would be fingered, opened, unfolded. Not telling her that her rooms might well be hiding places for her son's drugs, stolen gear or printouts from the dark web.

Pulling on gloves, they started in Trent's bedroom, expecting a cesspit but finding a clean, tidy room. No unwashed jocks or socks, crusty tissues, slippery mounds of car magazines, tangled AV cables, mouldy pizza boxes, crushed beer cans or the dope fug that Hirsch usually encountered when he searched a young man's bedroom.

Audrey does everything for him, he thought, sifting through the contents of the bedside cabinet before feeling for envelopes or other flat items taped to the underside and rear of each drawer, tapping for false bottoms and checking the hollow beneath the bottom drawer.

Nothing.

The wardrobe next: same approach to the small drawer set, then squeezing the pockets of the clothes hanging from a dowel rail, before dragging in a chair from the kitchen to check the top. Lots of dust.

The bed: under it, under the mattress, inside the bedclothes. It wouldn't be the first time he'd found baggies of cocaine, stolen credit cards, child pornography or cash under mattress protectors or inside doona covers.

Behind the wall decorations: a poster of a Navaho in full headdress; a dusty Eureka flag; a football calendar.

He even tested that the room's two wall sockets were genuine by plugging in a hairdryer from the bathroom.

'Nothing here,' sighed Brandl, searching the other half of the room. 'I'll start in the kitchen.'

Hirsch heard her there, murmuring in a calm counterpoint to Audrey's shrill complaints. Stashing the hairdryer under the bathroom sink, he sorted through rolls of toilet paper, a plunger, a hot water bottle. He shook the packet of bath salts and a bottle of headlice treatment: nothing. The wall cabinet above the sink contained generic meds, an electric razor, a comb, a hairbrush, two toothbrushes in a coffee mug with no handle. The toilet: nothing taped to the underside of the cistern lid. The chipped old bath was freestanding: nothing under it. The extractor fan and the screws holding it in place were thick with fluffy grey dust.

Another fruitless search under the laundry sink and inside the wall cabinet, dryer, front-loader and basket of T-shirts, shorts and underwear waiting to be washed – nothing but a ten-cent coin caught in the washing machine's rubber seal.

Hirsch found Brandl in the corridor. 'Nothing in the kitchen,' she told him.

A search of Audrey's bedroom yielded an unfired shotgun shell behind the cornice of the old wardrobe, and there were only a few old receipts in her car. But at the bottom of a canister of tennis balls in the garden shed they found a few grams of ice in a Ziploc bag. 'Fetch her,' Brandl muttered.

As soon as Hirsch reappeared with Audrey, Brandl demonstrated. 'Tennis balls at the top, drugs at the bottom. Care to explain?'

Audrey was wringing her hands. 'I stopped playing years ago. Trent.'

'Trent hid these?'

'I don't do drugs.'

'What can you tell me about your husband's shotgun?'

She said in a small voice, 'He used to keep it on top of the wardrobe.'

'You said a few days ago that you didn't know anything about it.'

'I meant I forgot about it! Bert never used it and then he got sick and that went for years and I totally forgot about it.'

'Do you think Trent has it?'

'I don't know,' she said miserably. Adding: 'Please don't shoot him.'

Now for the man cave. 'I never go in there,' Audrey said, wringing her hands on the side path. 'I got enough to clean in the house as it is.'

'Does he keep a spare key handy?'

She looked around helplessly at a bucket on its side, a wheelbarrow with a flat tyre, a hose reel hanging from the wall of the house, a line of garden-border stones painted white. 'Maybe ...'

They didn't find it, so Brandl fetched a crowbar from the shed and waited as Hirsch, heaving his shoulder against the jerry-built weatherboard wall, opened a gap to reveal the lock tongue. The sergeant prised it open.

They found themselves in a small space taken up mainly by an older model flatscreen PC and an inkjet printer on a small table, a straight-backed wooden chair and a plastic crate of photocopied Celtic crosses. The power source was an extension lead that had been threaded through a hole drilled through a window frame on the side wall of the house. Clothing was hooked onto the far wall: a ballistic vest and a hi-vis jacket.

Brandl edged past everything to a mess of equipment dumped in the far corner. Walkie-talkie radios, gloves, a gas mask, traffic cones, GPS units, a first-aid kit, sealed syringes and random packets of the kinds of bandages and meds stocked in the rear of an ambulance. 'I think we've found the gear stolen at your fatality a few weeks back.'

'Looks like it.'

'The charges against our friend just keep mounting, don't they?'

Hirsch grunted, took photographs, fetched evidence bags from the HiLux and began stowing and labelling. Meanwhile Brandl was on her knees beside the desk, removing crumpled balls of A4 from a wastepaper basket.

Rocking back on her heels, she flattened them out on her upper right leg and began reading. 'I'm assuming his computer's password-protected,' she said eventually, handing a wodge of paper up to Hirsch, 'but this is just as good.'

Hirsch read at the table. The top sheet was a poorly worded letter full of typos and angry capitals addressed to the state premier. From the Lone Pine Patriots League, it accused her government of unlawful and unconstitutional legislation, policies, fines and levies. And of being part of a global conspiracy responsible not only for advocating the introduction of fluoride to drinking water, a cashless society and pro-trans initiatives, but also of holding kidnapped children under the White House for the purposes of ritualised killing and organ harvesting, concluding: *And here too probably, like under government house.*

The next letter was from My Place Mid North Branch – 'an alternative people's council'. Addressed to the 'illegitimate' councillors of the current 'illegitimate' council, it called for the removal of the Optus 5G tower ('radiation poisoning') and all CCTV cameras ('big brother'), the reopening of Penhale and Muncowie primary schools (*you just want our kids to be like sheep not themselves*), and an end to Dr Pillai's Covid vaccinations (*in the pay of big pharma and she didn't even study medicine in this country*). Furthermore, the current illegitimate council's rates, taxes and fines were invalid, and all monies collected should be returned to those who'd been hoodwinked into paying them.

In any case, everyone could expect *a great reset* and a *great awakening* very soon.

Getting to her feet, Brandl said, 'I think we've actually

solved that hate-mail issue I was supposed to be investigating.'

Hirsch said, 'Well done, Sarge.'

He reached down for a hi-vis jacket and folded it into an evidence bag, trying to match people like Mark and Fran Button, Pete Gould or even Jack Minack with Trent McRae and his rabid thinking. He couldn't. Maybe Trent was opportunistic, running around with like-minded dickheads like the Lone Pine group, but also elbowing his way in whenever there was a grievance against the status quo. Jack Minack's beef with the bank. Ratepayer criticism of the council. Perhaps Trent was recruiting, perhaps he was just a stirrer.

He opened a desk drawer. A bayonet, a flick knife and a slingshot. 'Sarge.'

Brandl looked. 'But no shotgun.'

32

Tuesday. Jean Landy was due at noon, so Hirsch spent the morning catching up on office work, which included fast-forwarding through hours of town-paddock CCTV footage. Nothing from the main camera. He switched to the second, which was aimed in the opposite direction and showed one corner of the blighted soil, a few parched heads of wheat and a patch of the Barrier Highway. The usual passing parade: farm vehicles, family cars on school or shopping runs, a couple of tour buses, big low-loaders hauling earth-moving equipment, and another Isuzu truck loaded with fuel drums.

Almost noon. He made a few phone calls. His mother, in a determined mood, said, 'I'm driving up to see you on Saturday.'

'Excellent. Want me to book a room somewhere?'

'Already done, the Woolman Hotel.'

Then at 11.45 Jean Landy arrived; slight, wiry, flip and wry, her dark hair in its usual battle with a scrunchie.

'Like what you've done with the place,' she said later, eschewing his offer of lunch but accepting a mug of coffee. As he made and demolished a sandwich, she wandered around his sitting room, gazing at the scuffed walls, cobwebby ceilings and threadbare carpet.

'A work in progress,' he said.

'What progress?'

She paused for a while at his print of *Christina's World* and said, 'Depressing.'

'You're not the first to say that and you probably won't be the last,' he said, dumping his plate and mug in the sink. 'Your car or mine?'

'I'm your sealed-highway kinda gal,' she said.

And so they took the HiLux rather than the Redruth police station's Camry, Hirsch saying, 'When I'm boss of the world – or just sergeant, actually – I'll make it mandatory that junior constables learn how to drive on dirt roads.'

'For your information, I've driven on plenty of dirt roads. They're everywhere. But up here it's more like driving over some great stony desert.' She grabbed the safety handle above her head as if in emphasis, snorting, 'Boss of the world. Who'd promote you?'

'Harsh. But not unfair.'

It was a form of the pointless, not-very-funny banter that Hirsch had been trading ever since his Police Academy days. It probably occurred in all workplaces – if the culture was healthy. As a police officer you instinctively knew that the colleague you joked around with was the most likely to cover your back in the event of a shootout, or anything else.

Time passed and dust leaked in. Landy said, 'You still going out with Whatshername?'

'That's Wendy Whatshername, Ms Whatshername, to you.'

'Wendy Whatshername.'

'Still going out,' Hirsch said, wondering what Landy was leading up to. She seemed glum suddenly, and he found himself frantically trying to recall what he knew of her personal life. There was a boyfriend, Justin, Jason, one of those 'J' names. A wine merchant based in Clare.

Eventually she said, 'Hypothetically speaking, if you got an official email tomorrow posting you ten hours north of the black stump, what would you do?'

'You've been posted somewhere?'

'Not me, no. Come on, what would you do?'

'I don't know. You mean in terms of my love life? I honestly don't know. There's something of the weekend romance about my relationship with Wendy to begin with,' Hirsch said. He paused. 'But we talk every day.' Now he shrugged as the HiLux ate up the shuddering kilometres. 'Adapt, I suppose.' He paused. 'Not split, just adapt.'

Landy didn't respond. She sat slumped beside him, her head against the glass, looking out but not registering.

Hirsch said, 'Your bloke's been sent somewhere?'

'Soon. Kuala Lumpur, of all places. Australian wines are booming there.'

'You don't want to go?'

'No, I don't.'

Hirsch felt useless. 'Perhaps take leave for a year and see how you like it there. Come back if it doesn't work out.'

Jean turned her head to him and said, slowly, evenly: 'I've already moved for him – from Tasmania.'

Right, thought Hirsch. 'So …'

'So the question is, do I love him enough to do it twice?'

There was a long pause. Hirsch believed she had her answer, so he didn't follow up, and she changed the subject anyway. 'Paul …'

'Yes.'

'Today's going to be a waste of time, isn't it? Knocking on doors?'

He knew what she meant. 'Did you learn anything this morning?'

'Not a thing. No one's seen McRae or had anything to do with him. We even tracked down his best friend at school.'

'Who?'

'Name of Moloney, first name Tyson.'

'The name's familiar,' Hirsch said, frowning to help himself think. 'What about Nick Sampson?'

'Same thing. The sergeant went in hard, but he played dumb, said McRae was just a client. When I said I'd seen him with McRae at the council meeting last week, he said it was coincidence. When the boss asked if he usually attended council meetings, he said it was his fucking democratic right.'

'A prince. He'll do you a deal on a car, if you're interested.'

'Sorely tempted,' Jean Landy said. 'Guys in greasy wife-beaters get me all flustered.'

They drove on, thinking of Sergeant Brandl and her slightly nervy mission to track down Trent McRae and put things right with everyone: her officers, the community, Auntie Steph.

By 1 p.m. they were sinking strong tea in Trina Gould's kitchen – but not with Trina.

'Pete took her to hospital yesterday,' Milly Gould said. 'Baby girl!'

Pete's sister was dark-haired where he was ginger; slim and quick where he was a gormless lump. But stepping in to help her little brother. 'All going well, they'll be home in a day or two.'

Unlikely that secret societies or council meetings are at the forefront of Pete's mind just now, Hirsch thought. He showed Milly a photo of Trent McRae. She didn't recognise him and had never heard of him.

Next, Mark and Fran Button. Mark said he'd met McRae for the first time at Jack Minack's farm foreclosure, thought he was 'a bit of an idiot' and had no idea where he was staying. As for council meetings: 'Never been but I'm thinking I should. They're corrupt, the bunch of them.'

'Would you be going as a member of My Place?'

Button was genuinely bewildered. 'What?'

Finally, Jack Minack.

'Wouldn't have a clue where he is. And he's a mate of Nick Sampson, not me.' Pause. 'Why? What's he done?'

'How often have you seen or talked to him over the years?'

'Like I told your sergeant, I never laid eyes on him till the other day.'

'He didn't park a caravan in your back paddock?'

'No. Go and have a look if you don't believe me.'

They were on Minack's front porch. Drifts of dust, dead plants in pots; torn, weather-stained deck chairs, a slow, panting golden retriever and a few wine cartons stuffed with towels, copies of the *Stock Journal*, framed photographs and crockery wrapped in scraps of newspaper.

'Thought you might've met him at a My Place meeting,' Jean Landy said.

Minack was bewildered. 'What?'

But Hirsch and Landy had both seen the brief shift in his expression. Wariness and anxiety under the good-old-Aussie-battler face he liked to wear. Landy followed through: 'Mr Minack, have you and your My Place friends been making threats against the mayor? The councillors? Hate mail, phone hangups ... Is there anything you can tell us about that?'

'Jesus Christ, nothing,' Minack said. 'They're a mob of drongos, wouldn't trust them as far as I could throw them. But, you know, each to his own ...'

'You're not a My Place member? Sympathiser?'

'Nup. Not me.'

'How about council meetings. Been going to those?'

'Waste of time if you ask me.'

'How about last month's meeting?'

'Didn't go.'

'In case you're *thinking* of attending, there'll be a strong police presence in future,' Jean Landy said.

Another switch was flipped in Jack Minack: here was a woman telling him what he could and couldn't do, could and couldn't think. 'So what? Nothing to do with me.' He gestured at the boxes on his veranda. 'I've been forced off my own land, in case it's escaped your notice.'

On the way back Jean Landy muttered, 'Like I said, a waste of time.'

33

Late afternoon now. Hirsch waved Landy goodbye on the street outside the police station, headed inside and bent his head into his fridge. There was a tub of tabbouli Wendy had made for him, and he stood in his miserable kitchen and forked it in. Little explosions of flavour.

Then he walked the short distance to a small, crouching house next to the highway. Stepping through the knee-high front gate, which had hung from one rusted hinge for as long as he'd been in Tiverton, he walked around to the rear – a region of dead planter boxes, arid lawn and Daryl Cobb's dumped bicycle. Normally it was his sister, Laura, or occasionally his mother, Marie, who kept everything alive in the garden, but their corner tank was dry and town water was rationed.

He knocked on the rattly screen door and presently Marie answered. Her bipolar was evidently giving her a day off: eyes not too vibrant and movements not too agitated. Like her daughter – and unlike her son – she was slight and dark-haired. Dressed today in shorts and a T-shirt. She liked Hirsch. Knew he kept an eye on her kids whenever she couldn't. 'Come in out of the heat.'

Through to the Cobbs' time-warp kitchen: worn lino, dulled chrome, scratched Formica. A fat old fridge, wall cupboards with listing doors, Daryl at the cluttered table. And Laura calling hello from the sitting-room, just visible through a chipped plaster archway.

Hirsch returned her greeting, one shoulder propped against the archway wall. 'Homework?'

She had her own little Corolla these days and was studying veterinary nursing while working part-time for the Redruth vet. Right now, she was at the dining-room table with a half-circle of textbooks, photocopied articles, pens, notepaper and a laptop under the cone of an Anglepoise lamp. 'Exams next week.'

She had brains. The tragedy was, she also had a highly developed sense of responsibility for the mother and brother who needed her, and she might never leave the town.

'Good luck.'

'Thanks.' Her head was already down again.

Hirsch returned to the kitchen, where Marie had returned to her chair and half-finished cigarette. She gestured grandly. 'Lovely to see you, Paul. Please, take a seat.'

Hirsch glanced at her more keenly. Too mannered? On her way to her next episode? He sat, said thank you and turned to Daryl. 'Hi, Daryl.'

The response was barely there: 'Hi.'

Daryl looked hot, red, damp and, not unusually for him,

stricken with guilt. He was a big, soft, floppy boy in his late teens. Now that he'd finished with school he did a bit of stable mucking-out for Nan Buchanan, helped empty bins at the primary school and kept Ed Tennant's front veranda free of dust in summer and clumps of mud in winter. He would grow old in Tiverton.

'There's something you might be able to help me with,' Hirsch said.

'I didn't do nothin'.'

'You're not in any trouble. I just need some information.'

Daryl swallowed, nodded rapidly. He was sweaty, unwashed, looking for an escape route. 'I was just ridin' me bike.'

He knows I spotted him on the CCTV footage, Hirsch thought. 'Like I said, you're not in any trouble.'

It was then that he spotted the curling edge of a photograph stuck to one side of the fridge. He stood, stepped across, peered: in the foreground was an old Kombi decorated with hippie-style swirls and, in the background, Kata Tjuta glowing red.

He returned to the table. 'Fantastic photo.'

Daryl was shrill. 'I didn't steal it!'

And now Laura was propped against the archway wall. 'He found it, Paul. Someone dumped it.' She paused. 'We were going to tell Mrs Llewellyn.'

'Keep it,' Hirsch said. 'She has copies.'

They weren't sure if Hirsch had the right to grant them that privilege. Marie swelled with largesse again. 'A bit of colour for the room. Heaven knows we need it.'

The little house with its frail mementos and stunned inhabitants. It did need a spark of life. Hirsch visualised the slow, instinctive wonder in Daryl as he'd come upon the stolen and dumped photographs and selected one to take home.

Shaking off all of that, he turned his head to take in each of them. 'I need your help. I know the rubbish has been cleaned up and maybe that will be the last of it, but I'd still like to know who dumped the nasty stuff, like the building rubble, the asbestos. Daryl, you always check the video after flying your drone: did you see anything, anyone, a strange vehicle?'

'The dumping was always at night.' Marie snatched smoke from her cigarette and jetted it to one side. She couldn't quite believe Hirsch's foolishness. 'He doesn't fly it at night.'

'There is a bit of film,' Laura said.

They watched it on her laptop. Mostly the footage was incidental to Daryl's actual purpose, which was testing the drone's aeronautics with swooping close-ups, dives, figures-of-eight and nifty slaloming down the line of gumtrees separating the oval from the town paddock. But then, thirty seconds of video gold.

Not that Hirsch could do anything about it. 'Looks like he yelled at you.'

'Yes,' Daryl whispered.

'What did he say?'

'Called me a perve.'

To accidentally film a man as he tipped a load of old bricks, boards, furniture and fibro sheeting onto the town paddock was hardly perving. Hirsch patted Daryl's bulky shoulder. 'I assume he told you not to tell anyone?'

Another whisper. 'Said he knew where I live.'

'You're safe, Daryl. He's moved on, never coming back.' Thinking about it, Hirsch realised a corner of Daryl Cobb would still be fearful. 'Actually, he was killed in an accident.'

Jerry Poulakis, DV tyrant, smeared across the Northern Expressway a couple of weeks ago.

But not before demolishing a fair portion of his ex's house.

34

Returning to the police station, Hirsch added to the Poulakis file. After dinner he sat on his sofa. The sitting room seemed more gloomy than moody in the light of the floor lamp at his shoulder. He flicked through the free-to-air channels, then tried SBS On Demand.

When the buffering defeated him again, he opened the crime novel Kate Street had given him. 'Outback noir' – just another small-town-with-a-dark-secret story. He resisted hurling it across the room and made a few landline calls.

Annika Nordrum said, 'I was just going to call you!'

'News?'

'Yes. It's Mum we found; the DNA confirmed it. I heard a little while ago.'

'I'm sorry.'

'Thank you. It feels … complicated,' Nordrum said, a catch in her voice. 'I'm glad we found her, but I feel so awful about how she died.'

She sounded so desolate that Hirsch had to swallow. He recovered and asked, 'How's the media attention?'

'Heinous.'

He confirmed it later when he checked the news on his phone. Annika outside her Unley flat, flinching away from cameras and microphones until, with some heat in her voice, she snaps: *'Closure?* There's no closure, anyone in my position will tell you that.'

Next, he called his mother, who said, 'About next weekend.'

Hirsch groaned. She'd changed her mind.

'You'd be right in thinking I said yes to please you,' she went on, 'but as it turns out, I find I'm actually looking forward to it.'

She did sound bright. 'That's great.'

'Sorry to be blunt.'

She'd always been a little blunt. His father had been slower and milder. They chatted a while and then he called Wendy. 'She told me she's looking forward to it.'

'Well, that's good. Makes it easier. Have you booked a table?'

'Yes.'

'Aitch, she does know she can stay with us?'

'She doesn't want to be—'

Hirsch had been about to say that his mother didn't want to be a nuisance, a burden, but the call dropped out abruptly. He replaced the handset, waited a few seconds and lifted it to his ear again, forefinger poised over the keypad.

There was no dial tone.

'Good old Telstra.' It was rural Australia's default reaction. Outdated, poorly maintained wires, pits, poles and exchanges, and blackspots throughout the country. But to make sure, Hirsch used his mobile to call Bob Muir, thinking it was likely the landline service in and around Tiverton was down again. 'Can you check your landline dial tone for me, please? *Jesus—*'

He flinched as a rock smashed through his sitting-room window, hurled rather than tossed through the glass, the shards in its slipstream spraying the room and showering his lap.

The rock landed beside him. His heart pounded.

Bob's voice was tinny. 'Paul?'

Hirsch clamped the mobile to his ear again. 'Someone just threw a bloody great rock through—'

This time it was the kitchen window. And now shapes flickered out there in the moonlight. Voices crooned and wailed, alternating between low, hollow moans and terrified shrieks and hoarse whispers in a parody of B-movie horror.

Then he heard glass breaking in his office. And, out on the highway, tyres screamed, motors redlined. Horns sounded in the laneway behind the old lockup.

About ten seconds had passed and Hirsch thumped his fist against his heart, rolled off the sofa, crawled around to the lamp. Thumped his fist on the floor switch. Placed his mobile to his ear again and realised that Bob was no longer on the line.

He cut the call. Made to dial triple zero. His phone rang

and it was Wendy's number on the screen. Then the lid of his barbecue came sailing in from the backyard.

First things first. Keeping low, he crawled in semi-darkness to the kitchen and had neared the back door when he was spotlit by a torch. A voice in the darkness cooed, another parody: 'I can *seeee* you.'

The torch jerked as whoever was holding it stumbled, tripping over the sunlounge. Another voice called through the kitchen window, *'Come out, come out, wherever you are.'*

Hirsch didn't recognise the voices. Pitched too high; almost falsetto. He darted along the corridor now, past his bedroom door, and stopped at the connecting door to his office. Put his ear to it. He heard nothing in the room itself but out on the highway they were still hooning. A Sunday evening; not much traffic to bother them. And who in their right minds would challenge a gang doing donuts and burnouts?

Hirsch burst in at a crouch, barely registering the house brick and broken glass, and retrieved his pistol from the locked desk drawer. Hell to pay if he shot anyone, let alone fired a warning shot, but he felt threatened – and boy, did he want to scare the shit out of someone.

Best not to do that on the highway, forced to dodge out-of-control cars and utes. He crept through to the kitchen again and, taking another moment to listen, nudged open the back door. Eased into the moonlight in stages, crouching, sweeping with the Glock in his right hand, and was smacked in the stomach with a shovel.

35

Dropping his pistol, Hirsch doubled over, placed a hand on the ground, lowered himself onto one hip. That left his other hip vulnerable and the flat of the shovel smacked again. Seeing it swing up and back for a third strike, he straightened and flipped over, first onto his screaming guts, then his back, crying out involuntarily as muscles wrenched and stretched. He rolled again as the shovel came down, whanging a spark from a paving stone, and there was a curse.

'Fucken ...'

Fucken what? Hirsch didn't know, and his attacker – bulky, masked in black – didn't say, perhaps taxed by having to speak and act simultaneously. Up and then down went the shovel and Hirsch dodged, feeling the blade clip his left shoulder and spark off the paver again.

'Fucken ...'

A woman screamed from the laneway. 'Ty, we got company!'

The man named Ty halted mid-swing; cocked his head.

Cries, grunts and shouts in the night; feet pounding; an alarming thump and the back fence rattled. A pause, then the sounds of struggle came again: thumps, grunts, meaty punches.

Ty was slow to respond, almost irresolute, so Hirsch goaded him, his voice tight with pain as he felt about for his fallen service pistol: 'As I live and breathe: Tyson Moloney.'

Hesitation. 'Who? Fuck you.'

'Bit stupid of your girlfriend to use your name.'

'Fuck you.'

'Good match, though. Dumb and dumber.'

Ty thought about it, struggling for a comeback, then said, 'We cut your landline, so who's stupid now?'

He raised the shovel again and Hirsch scuttled away on his backside, intending to roll into his kitchen, but his shoulder caught the open door and slammed it shut, closing off his escape route. Now all he had to save himself were a tattered welcome mat, an iron boot scraper and the voice of reason.

'When all else fails,' he muttered, and hurled the scraper.

It missed by a mile, sailing past Moloney and clanging against the rotary clothesline.

A glimpse of teeth signalled a grin of delight in the moonlight. 'Piss-weak.'

A series of rolling thumps against the fence and then Bob Muir was spilling through the back gate, grappling with a bulky figure in black.

A woman, shrieking, '*Ty!*'

Moloney turned, shovel raised, and lumbered across the yard to help. Stopped and did a strange little jig as he waited for a clear shot at Muir. Then he was hauling back on the shovel and Hirsch yelled, '*Bob, behind you.*'

Muir shoved the woman, ducked and weaved as the shovel blade plucked at his sleeve, then charged, catching Moloney around the waist and smacking him against the clothesline pole.

Again his woman screamed his name: '*Ty!*'

Moloney slid down the pole, winded.

'*Ty.*'

He lifted his head; tried to speak. Managed a creaky, 'Piss off, love.'

She dithered.

Clearer now, Moloney said, 'Just fucken clear out, will ya, ya dumb bitch.'

'What a gentleman,' Bob Muir said, claiming the shovel. Brandished it at the woman, who yelped and staggered out into the laneway.

Hirsch retrieved his Glock from under a deckchair, cuffed Moloney and called Sergeant Brandl, and not long after that, Wendy arrived, worried that she hadn't been able to reach him on either of his phones. She got him into her car and down to see Dr Pillai, who told him that no bones were broken but he'd be stiff, sore and impressively bruised for a few days.

Hirsch's Wednesday morning took a while. He fielded a panicky call from his mother, who'd just listened to the news, concerned calls from Jean Landy and Tim Medlin, and a follow-up from Sergeant Brandl. Meanwhile Wendy helped him in the shower, fed him eggs and bacon and drove him back to Tiverton on her way to school with Kate. Reporters following up the Heather Nordrum story were waiting for him, and some even wanted to know if the police station 'siege' was related to the discovery of her remains. Hirsch wanted to say, 'What do you think?' or 'I don't see how.' Instead he referred them stolidly to the Media Unit. Other reporters called him throughout the day. He referred them, too.

Meanwhile Nan Buchanan and Yvonne Muir delivered meals for his freezer, and other townsfolk called in to commiserate. Ed Tennant was less well-meaning. When Hirsch limped across the road to buy milk, he was asked sourly if the town could be considered safe anymore. 'Nothing to fear, Ed,' Hirsch said, returning glumly to the police station.

He could sit, but not for long. He could barely hold a tape measure to his broken windows. And the calls were a chore: finding a glazier; finding a phone-line repairer; back and forth to Sergeant Brandl.

Lunchtime, and he was experimenting for the tenth time with the lumbar-support settings on his desk chair when there was a knock on the door. Getting to it took an age.

Clare Valley Glazing was scrolled across the overalls of the two men who stood there. 'Some breakages?'

'You could say that.'

They started with his living quarters, leaving the office until last, and were working on the front window by the time Hilary Brandl and Jeff Comyn arrived. Hirsch showed them the broken windows, the tyre burnouts on the highway, and the dents – a hammer? – that pockmarked his old Nissan.

Brandl looked wretched. 'I've always worried something like this would happen. These little one-officer police stations are sitting ducks. Sorry, Paul. Sorry it happened, sorry it happened to you.'

Comyn, less concerned, shrugged and said, 'We've all been at the sticky end a few times.'

'Of course. In a pub or whatever – but to attack a police station?'

Comyn shrugged again. 'A pub, a dark alley, a police station, it all boils down to one thing: we rubbed someone up the wrong way. Just being police is usually enough. In this case' – he clapped a hand around Hirsch's shoulder – 'our friend stirred up a hornets' nest.'

Hirsch winced. 'Easy tiger.'

Comyn let him go. 'At least we have one in custody and know the identity of another.'

Brandl nodded. 'Ty Moloney and his lovely girlfriend, Penny Goldfinch. Care to hazard a guess who else?'

Hirsch shrugged – big mistake. Taking a moment to stifle a gasp of pain, he said, 'McRae. Some of his Lone Pine friends.'

'We're still waiting on Clare police for their names,' Brandl said.

Hirsch had had enough. 'Tea? Coffee?'

He took them back through to his living quarters, faintly brighter with the new windowpanes. With drinks poured and biscuits on a plate, they sat around his kitchen table, toasting him. 'Here's to a full confession.'

Hirsch nodded. 'I assume he went full no-comment?'

'Our Mr Moloney can't utter it often enough,' Brandl said. 'Any blowback on Bob?'

Brandl shook her head. 'Legitimate citizen's involvement. Pity the others got away.'

'We should be able to find the girlfriend easily enough.'

'She didn't go home; we know that much. We'll try extended family.'

Hirsch lifted his coffee mug, winced and tried again with his other hand. 'I wonder if it's worth checking if any of these clowns own property we don't know about.'

The sergeant glanced at him keenly. 'Why?'

'They're organised enough to harass the mayor and her mob. To letter-bomb parliamentarians. To post on social media. To arrange a siege of my place.' He gestured at the walls around him, then laughed, realising what he'd just said. 'My Place.'

Brandl shook her head. 'All you need is a computer and a bedroom. And who's going to notice if someone's got a few cars in their driveway now and then? There's no secret HQ with this mob.'

Comyn agreed. 'We break one of them, he or she gives us the next name, and so on until we know who they all are.' He checked his notebook, then looked at Brandl. 'You told me the Goldfinch woman's a tax expert?'

Brandl barked a laugh. 'You could say that. In fact, she's only had a bit of bookkeeping experience, but she's set herself up as a tax expert and her main advice to her clients is they don't have to pay tax. Any kind of tax. Taxes are illegitimate because the government's illegitimate. She charges three hundred dollars for this advice. It's going to bite her on the bum eventually, when her clients get audited and charged with evasion.'

Comyn shook his head. 'The country's going down the gurgler.' He turned to Hirsch. 'What about vehicles last night?'

Hirsch shook his head. 'Heard them, didn't see them. Ask Bob.'

'We did,' Brandl said. 'A Holden ute, a Falcon station wagon, a Nissan Patrol – which we think is the one Sandy Pillai tooted at.' She paused. 'Be nice to get Penny Goldfinch charged with stealing from her mother, on top of assault police, criminal damage, everything else ...'

'And Moloney?'

'Assault police. Affray. Unlawful assault. Also, he had ice in his system and in his glovebox, so possession and DUI.'

'So they're as thick as pig-shit,' Comyn said, 'and prepared to use violence. I think you both need to watch your backs.'

Well, they knew that. Silence reigned for a while as they sipped tea and Hirsch shifted to get comfortable and the glaziers in the front room made a racket.

Eventually Brandl turned to Hirsch and said, 'Don't feel you need to work today.'

Hirsch shifted uncomfortably. 'I'm okay. So long as I don't have to chase anyone.'

36

Thursday. A vivid mix of blue-black bruises starting to yellow across Hirsch's chest, hip and shoulder. Still tender, but mostly when he knocked against something now. He counted that as an improvement.

Then an early call from Sergeant Brandl. 'Webb wants a briefing. You up for it?'

'Like I said, so long as I don't have to chase anyone.'

A slow, careful drive south, avoiding the worst of the dips, potholes and asphalt patches, saw him decelerating past the Redruth town hall just before 8 a.m. Media vehicles were parked up and down the street and he spotted Allison Webb on the forecourt, directing the unloading of desks, computers and landline phones. Something's happened, he thought. She's ramping up the investigation. He saw her stop to shade her eyes as he rumbled by – probably drawn to the police markings on the HiLux. Finally recognising him, she tapped her watch meaningfully and then he was past, slowing to swing around the town square. He parked outside the police station, went in, and found Brandl and the others already gathered, a plate of pastries and a thermos of coffee on the briefing table.

He endured some good-natured ribbing and then at 8.30 Webb limped in, trailed by Leavitt. Hirsch had googled both. Nothing of note on Leavitt, but Webb's limp dated from her uniform days – a fall from a police horse spooked during a clash between MeToo demonstrators and MRAs.

'I'll be brief,' she said. 'As you know, yesterday we confirmed that the remains found at Mischance Creek Reserve belong to Heather Nordrum.'

Then she stared around at them with an air of satisfaction. 'What we didn't release yesterday: we found a reasonably preserved print on her watch glass.'

Everyone stirred.

'And,' Webb said, lifting one eyebrow, 'it matches to a Northern Territory cold case.'

In June 2016, she said, twenty-four-year-old Rodney Culleton of Newcastle, north of Sydney, failed to return from a six-week wild-pig hunting venture in inhospitable scrubland east of Daly Waters and two hundred kilometres from the Gulf of Carpentaria. He'd been outback hunting since he was twenty, the father said. Living off the land, trekking, shooting pigs for the pet-food market. Having fun, basically, thought Hirsch, reading between the lines. Or he was an unsettled kid.

'Apparently things weren't great at home,' Webb continued, 'but he had a satellite phone and when he didn't answer a birthday call, his parents contacted the police.'

A fruitless search. Then, seven months later, a stockman found his putrefied remains wrapped in a sleeping bag – which had also been wrapped in petrol-soaked rags and set alight – and buried in a shallow grave. He'd been shot twice in the head. 'The sleeping bag didn't burn well, for some reason, leaving us with a DNA trace and a set of prints, as yet unidentified.'

'His belongings?' asked Hirsch.

'The expensive stuff was gone,' Webb said. 'Phone, wallet, firearms.' She checked her folder. 'Weatherby rifle, Beretta shotgun and Browning twenty-two target pistol. Not cheap.'

On a sour note, she added, 'If you want to know more, the case featured in a recent episode of *Nowhere to Hide* on Channel Nine.' She scratched her forehead. 'If you stream it, take it with a grain of salt.'

Hirsch knew the show. Controlled hysteria, unsupported speculation and waffle.

'Naturally we're upgrading the investigation,' Webb continued. 'A murder, with links to another. Too soon to fold Ben Nordrum's death into the same investigation – as speculated, he might have died accidentally or offed himself. But my unwavering dislike of coincidences means we'll be looking more closely at his death, too.'

She paused. 'However, the inquest ruled it accidental, which means any evidence potentially pointing to violence or third-party involvement was overlooked, destroyed or compromised. One good thing: the Nordrums' daughter, Annika, called me last night to say that when she went through her parents' belongings again, she found a dog collar.'

Hirsch saw suppressed excitement as she added: 'The original collar; it hadn't been thrown out.'

Joe Leavitt swung his head around smilingly. 'Blood.'

'Yes, thank you, Joseph,' Webb said. 'The collar is badly frayed around the buckle and a miracle it had still been on the dog, but the main thing is it's made of some kind of absorbent fabric and shows traces of human blood, according to preliminary tests.'

'DNA?' asked Hirsch.

'Waiting on that. If either of the Nordrums left that blood, then we're no closer to an answer. Let's hope it was deposited by a third party, hurt in a scuffle or bitten by the dog.'

'Lucky it wasn't thrown out.'

'Indeed. Ms Nordrum was very apologetic: she remembers buying a new collar and intending to throw the old one out after she'd removed the tags, but hadn't got around to it.' She paused, adding: 'The thumbprint on Mrs Nordrum's watch is our only useful piece of evidence at the moment. Her remains are pretty much skeletal, but there's no scavenger activity. They're intact enough to tell us that she was probably shot in the back as she was running away, then in the head where she fell. So far, no bullets, fragments or shells have been found, but we've still to finish sweeping the wider area.'

Hirsch visualised the Mischance Creek Reserve, the slope up to the road on one side of the fissure, a longer, gentler slope leading to a distant hilltop on the other. Grass; loose and embedded rocks; stone reefs; ant holes

– even rabbit burrows and stubble quail nests.

'How good's the print?' he asked, visualising environmental wear and tear.

'Not too degraded. Dry conditions, out of direct sun and wind,' Webb said. 'As for the prints and DNA found in the Northern Territory case, we don't know if we're looking at one person or two. One theory worth consideration is that we have an itinerant killer or killers. Seasonal workers, perhaps. Possibly still active. Possibly active for years.'

Brandl frowned. 'Just stumbled on the Nordrums?'

'Possibly,' Webb said. 'Fellow fossickers, for example. Or itinerant shearers or farmhands driving past their campsite.' She paused. 'Or it wasn't random at all.'

'You're suggesting a local connection?'

'Not suggesting anything,' Webb said.

She sighed. 'But I can see a lot of digging into unexplained remote-area deaths and disappearances in my immediate future. Meanwhile, there are ways in which your team can ease some of the workload, Sergeant Brandl.'

'Happy to help.'

Webb nodded her thanks. 'Obviously, we need to interview all those who live or lived in the general area of both scenes, and the original Breadbox search party. And we really need to track down the farmer who found the dog and Mr Nordrum's body. The blood on the collar could be his, with some innocent explanation – the dog was distressed and bit him, for example. But he could be our killer, and he's not named in the paperwork. We need to rule him in or out.'

Hirsch raised a tormented arm. 'I can probably help with that.'

Kropp, his old sergeant.

37

But his calls to Kropp kept going to voicemail, the old sergeant's suspicious, forbidding growl saying, *Leave a message.*

Hirsch complied, twice, received no response, and put it aside for the remainder of the work day, washing down ibuprofen every few hours. He checked for updates on McRae and his cohorts – no news – and then, mid-afternoon, a call came in: the theft of twenty bales of hay.

A welcome reminder that he was just an everyday beat cop, really: that his job was to deal with the humdrum. He set out immediately, reaching Peta Renshaw half an hour later. She lived on a 500-acre mixed farm – legumes and merino sheep – south-west of the highway, where the average rainfall was slightly higher than in the areas Hirsch had been ranging over recently. More grass, even if it was dying, and healthier-looking stock.

He found her seated on her veranda steps, picking grass seeds out of a pair of old khaki army socks. About sixty, with the kind of pale skin that should never see the sun, she wore shorts, a sleeveless work shirt and fraying white sandshoes. A solid figure, concentrating hard, tugging at and flicking away the seeds with a terrible fixedness, sometimes peering at them through her glasses, sometimes over them, as if the seeds swam in her vision either way.

'Damn things,' she said, barely glancing at Hirsch but shuffling sideways to give him room. 'Be with you in a tick.'

Hirsch had had his own experiences with grass seeds, the two most memorable being when he'd helped Nan Buchanan chase after a bolting pony, and when he'd trudged across a paddock to a farmer killed under a rolled all-terrain vehicle. He said, 'Take your time,' and settled alongside her, moving stiffly.

'You all right?'

'Getting old,' Hirsch said.

She looked him up and down. 'If you're getting old, I'm ancient. I heard what happened the other night.'

Everyone had. 'You should see the other guy,' Hirsch said, trying to get comfortable.

Peta Renshaw waggled a sock in his face. 'Every year I do this. I should learn my lesson and buy a pair of gaiters.'

'Ed Tennant sells them,' Hirsch said. 'About your hay ...'

'About my hay. I bought a hundred bales a year ago, when prices were reasonable. Stored in that shed.' She gestured across her yard to a cluster of outbuildings: barn, hayshed, implement shed. 'But prices have skyrocketed since and some moron's pinched at least twenty of them. He'd need a small truck.'

Hirsch had taken out his notebook. 'When?'

'Yeah, well, that's it, isn't it? Last night, when I was visiting my daughter in Clare.' She lifted her head from her work to peer at him with squinting humour. 'Saw you at the council meeting last week.'

Hirsch grinned. 'Saw you, too.'

'*Why* were you there, though, that's the question.'

Hirsch shrugged. He wasn't about to get into a police-state conversation with her. 'Seems things got rowdy last month and the councillors have been receiving hate mail.'

Renshaw shrugged. She wasn't blaming him for anything. 'Fair enough.'

'Who'd know your movements? Family, friends, neighbours. Gardener, cleaner ...'

She gestured. 'Could be anyone driving along that road.'

'Have there been other thefts? Smaller items you haven't bothered reporting?'

'Not that I know of. Even if someone stole my ninety-nine cent Kmart bucket I'd report it.'

Hirsch grinned.

Renshaw picked and flicked grass seeds in silence, the seeds either arcing away to arrow into the dirt or flipping back, carried on the morning's hot northerly wind to land on the veranda and occasionally Hirsch's lap.

Now she stopped, her fist inside a sock. 'It was before your time, but did you know the mayor's husband used to be our councillor?'

Hirsch cocked an eyebrow. 'Smooth segue,' he said. 'I did know that. Why?'

'Did you know he had to step down?'

'Accused of bullying.'

'Accused, hah. He was a bully full stop.'

'Okay.'

'And my daughter, Bec, caught the worst of it.'

'The one in Clare?'

Renshaw nodded. 'She works for the district council there now.'

Hirsch absorbed this. 'What was her job here?'

'Assistant to the finance manager.'

'Tell me about the bullying.'

Renshaw flicked a last seed away and leaned down to pluck another sock from the pile in a pale blue plastic laundry basket. 'Well, she was young for a start, and female, which is usually enough for men like Mitch Stanyer.'

Hirsch sensed there was more and waited.

'But mostly she quit when she realised dodgy stuff was going on. Deals, handshakes, fake invoices, under-the-counter money going back and forth. Not only in her department but also in planning, waste management, roads, conservation, development ...'

'In an organised way?'

'Hardly. Bec did business studies at uni. She knew her stuff and she could see some of the councillors didn't have any idea about their responsibilities. They never took minutes properly, they were always breaching the Local Government Act, and there was no proper audit committee to oversee spending. When grant money came in, they'd use it however they wanted – like a couple of years ago when the Wurlie got a fifteen-thousand-dollar grant for a part-time healthcare nurse? The council hived off two thousand as a commission and spent the rest repairing the livestock pavilion for the ag show.' A shrug. 'It's like the comfort of a few cows and sheep was more important.'

'Steph Ingram raised that at the meeting.'

'Fat lot of good it did her.'

'What about actual criminal activity? Fraud and embezzlement?'

Renshaw shrugged. 'Bec's not a lawyer. But she told me about a weed-spraying contract. It went to the sister of one of the councillors. Is that the kind of thing you mean? Things like that went on all the time. A lot of it's just ignorance and greed. Power going to the heads of stupid people, kind of thing.'

'I heard Mitch Stanyer tried to have Redruth Creek zoned for tourism.'

'While Bec was working there. He'd been buying land along the creek for years. He couldn't get around the heritage overlay, so that put a stop to that – and afterwards his behaviour just got worse.'

Renshaw looked away and her voice when it came was quiet and hoarse: 'He took it out on Bec, mostly. She ended up having a nervous breakdown.'

'I'm sorry.'

'All down to that prick.'

A silence settled until Hirsch said, 'You think the mayor's trying to achieve what he couldn't?'

'Wouldn't put it past her. I mean, look at the birthing tree. You know about that?'

'Mitch wanted to cut it down so he could widen End Point Road.'

'Because it leads to a property he owns up there, except no one knew that at the time. Anyway, Bec said this man came in one day asking to see personnel files. He was a lobbyist hired by Mitch to influence the other councillors. Except we had a good mayor back then and the vote failed, but boy was Mitch Stanyer angry.'

Into the pause that followed, Hirsch said, 'And a few years later, along comes Clarissa.'

'Exactly. And the lobbying starts up again. Except then along comes Steph Ingram and at least the tree's safe for now. I don't know about the road itself.'

'Fuel trucks have been seen coming and going,' Hirsch said. 'Maybe Mitch Stanyer's using his own money.'

'Or Clarissa's. She's rich.'

'Did your daughter ever say anything about waste management?'

'Not really. Why?'

Hirsch related Adam Powick's asbestos-dumping story.

Renshaw nodded. 'Sounds about right,' she said, tossing the unfinished sock into the plastic basket. 'Meanwhile, much as I like to shoot the breeze, I suppose you want to visit the scene of the crime?'

The removal of twenty bales from a hundred had made a significant hole in the haystack. Telling himself to check Facebook Marketplace for the next few days and weeks, Hirsch took photos, promised Renshaw a case number for her insurance claim and made a mental note to interview the daughter soon.

Returning to the police station, he powered up his PC and dived more deeply into the Redruth district council. Clarissa Stanyer first. But information was patchy, with few references to her past work history and none casting doubt on her prior business actions or decisions. An on-line *Mid North Digest* story covered her marriage to Mitch, but made no reference to her first marriage. It just said Clarissa Stanyer, nee Thrupp, had grown up in the Adelaide suburb of Medindie, the only daughter of the late Clay Thrupp, a trucking magnate, and his wife, Erin. Googling these names, Hirsch learned that Clarissa was now co-owner, with her mother, of Thrupp Transport. She had law and business management qualifications from the University of Adelaide and was a silent partner in surveying, real estate and tourist development firms.

Which probably made her successful in business, with useful contacts, but not necessarily corrupt.

Then he googled the ward councillors, and again learned little. One was a wheat farmer who'd switched to growing carob trees – wouldn't that indicate he was a progressive? Another was a wealthy grazier with a mid-north name older than Mitch Stanyer's. He was elderly; he'd been mayor himself three times over a twenty-five-year period. Maybe a hint of noblesse oblige? Or he was easily swayed? Redruth ward was represented by the owner of the Woolman pub. Would she have benefited if the creek was rezoned? It ran right along the pub's rear fence. And then there was Craig Tetsworth, the owner of Coppertown Adventures, a small outfit specialising in walking tours of the old mine and full- and half-day 4WD trips out to participating sheep stations east of Redruth.

Whose nephew worked for the council and whose brother-in-law was Don Beadel, arts and tourism manager.

Ordinary men and women, ordinarily weak and greedy.

But the mayor … Clarissa already had money, nerve and influence when she arrived up here, Hirsch thought. But it helped to have a bunch of timid or like-minded people in her orbit.

What to do with all this information, though? He didn't have proof of anything. He didn't know, with any clarity, what crimes had been committed. He could approach the Fraud Squad or the minister for local government, he supposed. But tell them what?

38

Feeling restless, Hirsch asked Wendy if he could come around to stream the *Nowhere to Hide* episode devoted to the Northern Territory murder.

'Sure,' she said. 'Come for dinner. I need to tend to those bruises anyway.'

Now it was after dinner and he was leaning gingerly against her on the sofa while Kate did homework in her room.

Hirsch had sometimes watched *Nowhere to Hide* because his father would put it on, convinced that his son the cop would get a kick out of it. The format rarely varied: a cold-case murder would be outlined and the original investigation scrutinised, then theories proposed – often far-fetched – and future directions suggested. Sometimes a finger might get pointed – the brother-in-law was worth another look. Each episode amounted to about ten useful minutes padded out to sixty.

It was also one of those retired-detective-as-media-star shows. In the case of *Nowhere to Hide*, the host was a dour Sydney ex-homicide inspector who liked to claim that people called him the human magnifying glass because he spotted clues missed by others.

But the show had the budget for appearance fees. Other cops, retired and serving; witnesses, victims' friends and family, prosecutors, veteran crime reporters, crime-novel-writing criminologists and talk-show psychologists. Most of them were filmed inside what appeared to be a converted warehouse, all bare bricks and wood beams.

And the show could afford to fly the host, plus a relevant guest and a film crew, all over Australia. In this case, up into northern Australia's Gulf Country.

Hirsch learned no new facts as the story unfolded, but tucked in with the waffle was a theory that seemed to chime with something Webb had said, that Culleton might have encountered travelling killers. 'It's not beyond the realms of possibility,' said one of the talking heads, 'that a naive young man like Rodney Culleton might run into psychopaths in remote outback Australia. Away,' she continued, 'from the civilising and normative forces that keep ordinary people on the straight and narrow.'

Hirsch snorted. 'There's a lack of civilising and normative forces in every parliamentary sitting.'

'Every classroom,' Wendy said, squeezing his hand. 'Tea?' she added, getting to her feet.

'Camomile.'

She returned as *Nowhere to Hide* was winding up. A million-dollar reward had been offered. Settling against Hirsch, she said, 'Are small-town cops allowed to get rewards?'

'There's a way around that,' Hirsch said. 'I solve it, but I don't tell anyone. Then I let some time go by, quit, and break the news as a civilian.'

He grew aware that Wendy wasn't listening. She'd brought her eyes right up to the side of his face. The warmth of her breath, the warmth of her words: 'And right now?'

'I'm injured. I'm battered and bruised.'

'Uh huh.'

'Let me at least finish my tea first,' Hirsch said. He aimed the remote. The TV screen went blank. Bountiful evening crept in, softening everything.

Early the next morning as he was tiptoeing around the house, he spotted the tea on the mantelpiece and tipped it down the kitchen sink.

39

Friday was uneventful, a day at the desk until, mid-afternoon, Kropp finally answered his phone.

'Speak,' he growled.

Five minutes later, Hirsch was driving south-west, towards the sun, to an 1890s stone cottage on a sealed road near the Clare aerodrome. The sign on the front gate read Aspara Eats, and when Hirsch had parked and got out, he could smell, almost hear, spices cooking in hot oil. Hot work, he thought, ducking down the side of the house to a shiny new shed fitted with fuming roof vents.

He eased open the main door. Kropp's wife Aspara was standing at a huge industrial stovetop, quick-frying vegetables in a wok. Making spring rolls, he realised. Fridges, freezers and ovens lined one wall. Stainless-steel tables in the middle, with Hirsch's old sergeant working at one of them, grating carrots. Spotting Hirsch, he held up a finger, mouthed, 'One minute,' and walked to a steel sink to wash and dry his hands. This alerted his wife, who turned, saw Hirsch and smiled shyly before returning to her work.

Kropp came up to Hirsch, sticking out a slab of a hand. He was solid, late-fifties, with fierce, unchecked eyebrows and bristly grey hair. A slash of a mouth and a pugnaciously bent nose. 'How's tricks?'

'Good.'

'I can spare half an hour,' Kropp said. With a jerk of his head, he led Hirsch out into the dry heat and forged across to the house in his familiar old-bull style. 'Got a sixtieth birthday tonight.'

His wife's catering had been providing him with a sideline income long before Hirsch had arrived in the Mid North. In fact, rather than prioritise police work, Kropp seemed to use every opportunity to encourage and promote the business, with the result that his junior constables' bullying and harassment had gone unchecked, and many crimes were under-investigated. Eventually SA Police headquarters had separated and reposted the constables and forced Kropp to resign.

But Aspara's cooking was well-known by then and Kropp had fallen into the lap of a cushy retirement, albeit spent peeling onions and grating carrots.

He'd had the good sense not to hang around in Redruth, though, where he was still loathed.

'Come in,' he said, holding the back door open, still full of his old, quick, surging power, as if life as a citizen suited him and he hadn't left pockets of ill-will behind him.

He frowned as Hirsch stepped past. 'You're walking like ya got a kicking.'

'Spent the night ridding Tiverton of Hells Angels,' Hirsch said.

'Good on ya,' Kropp said without interest.

He took Hirsch into the kitchen, a small space typical of the era when the house was built. Too small for catering, yet furnished with top-of-the-range stove and appliances. Some light from the curtained window above the sink. A shelf of old-fashioned, pale-blue tins in descending order of size on one white wall: flour, sugar, salt, tea. A bright calendar familiar to Hirsch: the September wildflowers east of Tiverton. Not this September, though.

Kropp boiled the kettle and delivered two mugs of tea and a plate of sticky-rice cakes to the table. 'Like I said on the phone, I wasn't aware of these new developments. We've only just got back from visiting the wife's parents.' He named a village outside Phuket.

Hirsch nodded, wondering how much to reveal. Whatever his faults, Kropp had been a policeman for a long time. He decided to trust him.

'Keep this under your hat, but there's evidence linking Mrs Nordrum's murder to an unsolved shooting years earlier, way up in the Gulf Country.'

Kropp and his bristly eyebrows. Then his fierce expression relaxed and a canny old cop's glint came into his eyes. 'Roaming killers?'

'One theory.'

'You said you want to pick my brains. Pick away,' Kropp said, blowing over the surface of his tea.

'The search where Ben Nordrum was found. Anything strike you at the time?'

'About the people involved? The usual suspects: locals,

police from as far away as Georgetown and Peterborough, CFA volunteers – even a handful of Army Reservists on a survival course up near Wilpena Pound.'

Travelling killers, thought Hirsch.

'The search itself went on for days,' Kropp said. 'Every inch of the area.'

'But not Anna Gorge.'

'Not my call. I'd've searched it if I'd known early enough about the wife, what their plans were, but Adelaide got involved and I was shunted sideways.'

Hirsch hadn't known that. Maybe Kropp hadn't been inept or lazy after all – or not at the time. 'Let's go back a bit. It all started when someone found the dog.'

Kropp nodded. 'Bloke called Bob Hortle, on his way home from the pub.'

Hirsch sat back, delighted. 'You remember his name after all this time?'

Kropp looked abashed. 'He hired us for his fiftieth wedding anniversary a couple of years ago. He reminded me.'

'What can you tell me about him?'

'Well, he's old. Lives on a farm a few ks outside Muncowie, towards Breadbox.'

'You spoke to him at the time?'

'Not directly,' Kropp said, some embarrassment showing again, 'but I heard the story. He picked up the dog, looked around, found the Nordrum bloke dead and phoned it in.'

'From his home?'

'Went back to the pub. Liked a drink, apparently.'

'Was he the type to get aggressive when he'd had a few drinks?'

'What do you mean?'

Hirsch shifted in his chair, not wanting to lead too much but feeling that that was unavoidable. 'Was there any hint that Hortle had *conveniently* found the body?'

Kropp put his head on one side. 'That he already knew the dead bloke? He'd come from killing him? No.'

'Would he hurt a dog? Some of these old farmers ...'

'I know what you mean, whip sense into them right from the start. But Hortle? Couldn't tell you,' Kropp said. He cocked his head. 'You've got some evidence. Blood?'

Hirsch evaded the question. 'So he doesn't go home to phone it in, he does that from the pub. That didn't strike you as strange?'

'Far as I recall, the pub was closer, he liked a drink and he probably wanted something to calm his nerves.'

'What about the dog? He took it home with him?'

'There it gets interesting,' Kropp said, staring at the ceiling without registering it. 'I didn't even know about the dog at first. Far as I knew, this Hortle bloke spotted a ute in a paddock, went to investigate and saw a body at the bottom of a mineshaft.'

Hirsch gazed at the old cop. In the case of suspicious or unnatural deaths, the police normally take a close look at the person who found the body. Kropp and his Redruth constables had dropped the ball.

'So how *did* you learn there was a dog?'

'The daughter called a couple of days later, wanting to

know where it was. So I called Mike Farrelly, the Muncowie publican, and it turned out *he* had it. Wanted to know when someone was coming to pick up the blasted thing – his words.'

Hirsch sighed. Another DNA sample into the mix. 'How come he had it?'

'Bob Hortle more or less dumped it on him. Said his wife wouldn't want it in the house. Anyway, I drove up there, collected the bloody thing and gave it to the daughter.'

Kropp was getting impatient. 'If that's all, I need to help the wife finish up.'

40

With Webb's approval, Hirsch waited until Saturday morning before poking around in Muncowie. 'A country pub on a Friday night, I won't get a straight answer out of anyone,' he explained.

Now, mid-morning, he was taking a swing around the town. Muncowie was drab, exhausted, its layout similar to Tiverton's but, like Penhale's, on a reduced scale. One tiny all-purpose shop, one pub and a few short, broad streets in a grid pattern, four running east–west, four north–south. Small houses, some built of local stone, others of rusting corrugated iron in the old three-room settler style, with a corridor running straight from the front door to the back, a chimney against a side wall and a long-drop toilet in the yard. Everything in the town was either rusted, sun-bleached or dusty, and the primary school, now permanently closed, already looked derelict.

The pub sat long and squat behind a vine-hung veranda with a rattly West End Bitter sign beside the front door. The veranda floor, concrete worn to a glassy finish from decades of foot traffic, had once been painted red. Unless that was old blood.

Hirsch pushed through to the bar, across creaking, uneven floorboards. Decades of foot traffic had also polished the nail heads, and the atmosphere was a mix of stale beer, hopelessness and the odours of rural work: diesel, sweat, dung, lanolin.

Two drinkers, whiskery, bleary old-timers in crumpled work clothes, sat at one end of the bar. No one else, just Michael Farrelly, the publican, a man who oozed corner-cutting. Hirsch had first met him not long after being posted to the Mid North: a suspicious hit-and-run out on the highway. Now Hirsch called in every few weeks. He'd even broken up a bar fight between a geologist and the town drunk one Saturday afternoon.

'Paul.'

'Mike.'

'Heard a mob of yahoos attacked the police station.'

'Yeah, well, it was character building.'

'Good on ya.'

Farrelly was short, narrow, a beamingly efficient man with a neatly rounded belly. No personality of his own, just the banter and patter of a professional publican as he served drinks, took payment, swiped things with a rag. What he bantered about with the two old men holding up the bar was anybody's guess. They weren't drinkers, they were nursers, sitting on the same drink for hours. Yarning, complaining, sometimes sipping.

'Drink?'

'Lemon squash.'

'One day you'll order a beer.'

'One day I'll be off duty,' Hirsch said.

His drink delivered and tasted, he said, 'Remember the Nordrum case a few years ago? Body in a mineshaft?'

'Of course. And it's in the news again, now you've found the wife.'

'I was wondering if I could talk to you about the dog.'

'The dog? Lead suspect, is she?'

Hirsch gave the man a tired smile and said, 'The local who found her: Bob Hortle?'

'Not only found her but lumbered me with her for a coupla days. Till the police collected her.'

'Did she bite you at all?'

'Bite me? No. A friendly thing. Why?'

'Did she bite Mr Hortle?'

'Not that I know of.'

Then Farrelly cocked his head at Hirsch, realisation dawning. 'The collar.'

Hirsch tingled. 'What about it?'

'Practically falling off, from memory. But there were tags on it, so I took it off and popped it in an envelope.'

And a good thing you did, thought Hirsch. 'Anything else about the collar?'

'Made of cheap material. Hanging by a thread.'

'And?'

Farrelly had the look of a man playing a trump card. 'Depends. Could've been blood.'

Hirsch leaned forward and lowered his voice. 'Sorry, Mike, but we need to eliminate—'

'So it *was* blood.'

'We need to eliminate you,' murmured Hirsch. 'May I take a DNA sample from you? Right now? Quick and painless.'

'Nothing to hide. But in the back room if that's all right with you,' Farrelly said, indicating the old-timers with a subtle head jerk.

A couple of minutes later, with the sealed DNA sample in one of his pockets, Hirsch resettled on his bar stool to finish his lemon squash. Keenly aware of the old-timers' curiosity, he raised his glass. 'Gents.'

They toasted him back, a glint of curiosity in their eyes: they knew all about the Tiverton incident. 'Paul.'

One was Ted, the other Ken, and sometimes Vince was with them. Otherwise, they were interchangeable, and it might have been Ted who asked, 'How're the bruises?'

'Coming good. You remember the body in the mineshaft a few years ago? Bob Hortle bringing in the dog? Calling the police?'

'Most excitement we've had in years.'

'I know the whole thing must've seemed unusual, but did anything strike you back then? Strangers, strange vehicles …'

'Always strangers,' one of the geezers said. 'Stopping on their way to Broken Hill, that kind of thing. As for back then, all I remember is how busy the place was. Mike made his first million that week, didn't you, Mike?'

Mike, polishing a glass, said, 'And I've been watching it drain away ever since.'

Hirsch slid his empty glass across the bar and stood to go. 'If someone could give me Mr Hortle's address? Phone number?'

'Won't do you much good,' the second geezer said. 'He died, beginning of last year. His missus sold up and I heard she carked it six months later.'

Hirsch sagged. Then he thought of familial DNA. 'Kids?'

'Nup.'

A dead end. And he doubted Mike Farrelly's DNA would get him anywhere.

He stuck around for another hour, teasing out more information about the Hortles and scoping out the farm they'd owned. On his way back to Tiverton, he checked in with his mother – she told him she'd had to stop for petrol but hoped to reach the hotel by five – then Senior Sergeant Webb.

Who wanted him for a briefing in the Redruth police station, soon as he could get there.

41

Hirsch stopped in Tiverton for a shower and a change of clothes, then climbed behind the wheel again. He was tired of driving back and forth. He was sick of Redruth. His body ached.

He found Allison Webb presiding in the Redruth briefing room again with Leavitt at her left elbow, Tim Medlin and Jean Landy further along the table. He sat opposite, next to Sergeant Brandl.

'I'll keep this short,' Webb said. 'Paul, thanks for driving down again. How's the bruising?'

'Colourful.'

Webb nodded, turned to Landy. 'Jean, thanks for coming in on your day off.'

Webb's a good manager, Hirsch thought, somewhat mollified. Keeps track of who we are, our circumstances. Makes us feel we've been useful.

'An update,' Webb said now. 'DNA from the blood on the Nordrums' dog collar matches DNA on a handkerchief found at the Culleton scene. Which gives credence to the argument that Mr Nordrum's death was also probably a murder. We still don't know if the person who left the thumbprint and the person who left the DNA are one and the same, but planning and effort were involved at both sites, and I think we're looking at two or more killers.'

She paused. 'Are they itinerant? Still together? From around here and just happened to be in the Northern Territory back in 2016? Who knows?'

'We could always take DNA swabs of everyone in the area,' Leavitt said, looking amusedly around the room.

'Indeed,' Webb said, and Leavitt sank in his seat.

'Okay.' Webb nodded at Hirsch. 'Senior Constable Hirschhausen has the full story of the farmer and the Nordrums' dog.'

Hirsch coughed to begin. 'I tracked down my old sergeant. He told me a farmer named Robert Hortle found the dog walking along the road that runs past his place. It's a few kilometres from the mineshaft area. Unfortunately, Mr Hortle died a couple of years ago.'

'Unfortunately,' agreed Webb. 'Did you learn anything about this man? Could he have been one of the shooters?'

'He was in his late eighties when he died, which would have made him in his early eighties when the Nordrums were killed.' Hirsch shrugged. 'Not impossible, but he'd also have been pretty old when that kid in the Northern Territory was shot, and by all accounts he was a homebody, rarely went anywhere but to the pub and back.'

'Any possibility of obtaining his DNA, or some kind of reference sample?'

Hirsch shook his head. 'His wife has since died, they had no kids, and both were cremated. The farm was bought by a big agri-company, who cleaned the place out and remodelled it for the new manager. No convenient toothbrush left behind.'

'Still, it would be good to rule him in or out somehow. Did anyone remember seeing him with a bandaged hand or similar?' Then Webb gave a little shake, as if she'd irritated herself. 'Well. That wouldn't necessarily make him one of the killers. He could just as easily have cut himself climbing through a fence. Did you learn anything about his friends? Friends he went on remote outback tours with? Did he hate tourists, fossickers or rock climbers visiting his neck of the woods?'

'I asked around. Hortle was a drinker and a smoker and liked to escape his wife, hence he was often at the pub, but he didn't really mix. The other locals found him a bit standoffish.'

'So be it,' Webb said. 'My people have been looking more closely into the notion of travelling killers.' She shook her head. 'You'd be surprised at the number of unsolved remote-area murders and unexplained disappearances there have been in the past fifteen years.'

They all knew that an unexplained disappearance in remote country could be code for a murder and burial. 'Unless anything compelling turns up,' Webb went on, 'I may have to wind things down again. I've had detectives doorknocking the properties in each of the areas where the Nordrums were found. Doorknocking being a relative term,' she said, with a roll of her wrist that underscored eloquently the great emptiness of the world north-east of Redruth. 'So far, nothing.'

'Which leaves the original search party,' Brandl said.

It was the sign for Webb to flick stapled sheets of paper to each of them. 'This is not an exhaustive list of names. See if you can add to it. Ask your interview subjects what names are missing. Ask them who they walked alongside, how they got to the area and who they travelled with ... Anything they can remember, no matter how trifling.'

Hirsch glanced at his copy. He recognised several Tiverton-area names, including Ed Tennant, Bob Muir, Nan Buchanan and Mitchell Stanyer.

They could wait. Time to see if his mother had arrived in town.

42

Hirsch found her weeping in her room at the Woolman Hotel. He sat beside her on the high, lumpy old bed and held her. Presently Eva Hirschhausen's bony tension ebbed and she sighed into him.

'Sorry!'

'I know, it gets to you sometimes. Gets to me.'

'I shouldn't have come, dear, and you look stiff and sore.'

'I'm fine, and lovely to see you.'

'I don't feel right.'

Hirsch glanced around at the room. Flock wallpaper, dark floorboards and flowery furnishings. A photograph of a Sturt desert pea. An antique dresser. Her weekender suitcase on a luggage rack. Had she even unpacked yet? She'd checked in at 5 p.m. Hirsch had reached her from the police station by six; a table booked at the Dugout for seven.

'You could've stayed with Wendy and Kate. Or in an Airbnb.'

'Don't be dense, dear,' his mother said, not so loose in his arms now. 'I'm happy to stay in a hotel. I don't want to have to talk to anyone – except at dinner. What I'm trying to say is, people keep telling me I must move on, get out and about, don't brood or mope. But I like moping. And it's not really moping, it's just losing myself in memories of life with your dad. It's not as if I'll do that forever.'

'Sorry. I thought—'

'My mental health's fine, if that's what's worrying you.'

Hirsch thought about that. 'Not really. I just hate to think of you being lonely or—'

'How can I not feel lonely? It's natural. Your dad was in my life for forty years, and now he's not. Simple as that. Happens to everyone at some stage or other. It can't be fixed. It must be endured for a while, probably quite a while.'

A complicated kind of guilt swamped Hirsch then as he realised his mother had probably been consoling her consolers for some time now, rather than the other way around. He gave her another bolstering hug and they continued to sit bony-shoulder-to-bony-shoulder, looking into space, until 6.55. 'What a godawful carpet,' she said at one point.

The Dugout bistro represented upmarket dining in Redruth. A converted miner's cottage on Redruth Creek, its window tables overlooked a grassy picnicking slope, with the creek at the bottom – mostly dry now, the bulrushes forlorn, the ducks long gone. The décor was minimal: a couple of miner's picks and a sieve, a sluice box and a pan on the whitewashed walls. Wooden floorboards and burly dark ceiling beams.

Some locals, one crowded media table, but too many empty spots, and Hirsch feared the business might soon fold, as many local businesses had this year. He'd hate to see it go under. A favourite place, whenever he and Wendy wanted somewhere special to dine. Kind of special.

Enjoy it while he could. The food was generally good. Better than pub food – no burgers or schnitzel – and vaguely French with a nod to the Cornish miners who'd flocked to Redruth in the 1850s. On one occasion, when Hirsch had helped Barry Atkins, the owner and head chef, get rid of a light-fingered bookkeeper, he'd learned that the Dugout's famed Penzance Pie was a French Canadian tourtière, and the Truro Tart a caramelised French onion tart with gruyère.

Hirsch had cocked his head. 'Atkins, Atkins ... From the Auvergne region of France, if I'm not mistaken?'

'Fuck off,' Atkins had said cheerily that day, serving Hirsch a thank-you Cornish pasty with tomato sauce.

Cornish pasty was on the menu tonight, of course, along with the pie and the tart, but Hirsch ordered Saltash salmon, which was simply a chunk of salmon served with capers. His mother ordered Polperro pasta – a mushroom and tomato linguine. Kate had a Seaton salad and Wendy a Bodmin broth – which were green salad and leek and potato soup, respectively.

Nothing pretentious, Cornish or French about the wine, though: a good, plain Clare Valley red.

Hirsch sat back in the dim candlelight and let his tension ease, Wendy's knee and foot against his, her hand in his beneath the tablecloth. Kate, on his other side, talked animatedly with his mother, drawing her out with stories about his father.

He leaned in, his upper arm brushing Wendy's. 'Your daughter's pretty impressive.'

'Except when she's not. But yeah, she is.'

Their food arrived, and a shadow fell over the table as Nicholas Sampson said, 'How's the car going, Mrs Street?'

He wore ironed black jeans and a white business shirt and was with his wife, a woman who looked tired of life, washed out in an ill-fitting pale blue tunic dress. She bobbed her head shyly when Hirsch smiled at her. Their son was with them, shifting his feet, looking hunted. Didn't want to be there with his parents; didn't want to be in the same room as a schoolmate and her maths-teacher mother.

Sampson hadn't finished. Waiting until his wife and son were seated at a distant table, he said, 'Good car that Golf. Sorry to see it go. I reckon you got a bargain.'

Wendy said at once, 'Let's see if I've got this straight. The Golf that I didn't buy at your business address but as a result of an ad in the school newsletter? The Golf shown to me by your wife, not you, in the grounds of the school? Thank you, yes, a good car.' She paused. 'Bit too good for your yard, though? I suppose it would take longer to sell there.'

Hirsch was enjoying this. He watched Sampson flush. Strange guy, he thought. The kind who needed to discomfit people – turn even the most innocent thing they did or said into an insinuation.

But Sampson recovered quickly. Gave their table a salute and said, 'Hope you all enjoy what you've ordered.'

There it is again, Hirsch thought: sowing a tiny doubt that we might've chosen badly.

'Thank you,' Wendy said, her eyes lazily hooded.

Sampson turned to Hirsch. 'Paul.'

'Mr Sampson.'

'Let's hope you find that McRae kid eventually.'

As though I've been spinning my wheels, Hirsch thought. 'Indeed.'

With a hacked and dangerous smile, Sampson added: 'I mean, dragging a caravan up and down the Mid North. Can't be that hard to spot.'

'He does get around,' Hirsch said, wondering if it was significant that Sampson knew about the caravan. Probably not. Probably common knowledge by now. He gave Sampson the flattest and sunniest of smiles.

Hirsch spent the night at Wendy's – 'Your bruises are coming along nicely' – and returned to Redruth mid-morning on Sunday to collect his mother for a tour of the town. They started with a walk along the creek, where plaques detailed its importance to the Ngadjuri people and later the Cornish miners, before driving to the mine, these days a region of dusty hillsides dotted with old buildings: stone walls, a boiler shed, batteries, chimneys, iron frames and gantries, all of it looking down on a great excavation full of depthless blue water. From the top of the slope, they could see Redruth laid out over seven small hills named for Cornish towns. Peaceful tiled roofs, a range of eucalypts, the sun on windscreens and a hawk floating.

Finally, the museum, where they were the only visitors and dutifully wandered among the display cabinets: napkin rings, cufflinks, embroidery, christening gowns, porcelain shepherds. Old department-store mannequins dressed in 1850s trousers, dresses, bonnets and shawls. Wall-mounted shovels and brass telescopes next to spears, shields and woomeras. And photographs: colonial-era picnics; horse-drawn wagons laden precariously with hay; the 1954 Adelaide Show prize-winning merino ram; 1917 Great War volunteers; a Redex Trial Holden spinning its tyres on a gravelly bend. A pedal radio. A school desk with an inkwell and carved initials. Grinding stones and carved clap sticks.

Hirsch watched his mother, convinced – even hoping – that she might light up any minute and say, 'My mother had one just like this!' But she was sharper and less easily distracted than that. Five minutes in, she said: 'I suppose this stuff meant something to someone, back in the dim dark ages.'

Hirsch felt he was getting to know her all over again. Or for the first time.

After lunch he took her on an abbreviated tour of his back-country beat. The birthing tree first, followed by Pattenden's Fissure, the Mischance Creek ruins, Anna Gorge and the Breadbox diggings, outlining the knowns and unknowns of the Nordrum case as he drove. It was this that lit his mother up. Intrigued, lively, she said, 'Doesn't it all boil down to geography? Where things intersect, and how, and why?'

43

He waved her off late afternoon, and made three stops on his way back to Tiverton. First stationing himself on a rise four hundred metres from Nicholas Sampson's garage and vehicle lot, he scanned the place with his binoculars. No Subaru tucked away, no caravan. Next, Penhale. Audrey McRae still hadn't seen her son. Erica Woodhead was not at home.

Finally, the Stanyers. No one answered when he knocked at the front door of the big house overlooking the valley, so he went looking and found Mitch in a shed at the rear. His Range Rover was parked with the bonnet up, and he was cleaning the air filter. His expression deadened when he recognised Hirsch.

'Fat lot of good you lot were the other night. Lucky Clarissa wasn't attacked. If you're looking to apologise, she's not here, she's at work.'

'On a Sunday?'

'Council business. Never ceases.'

'Actually, I'd like to talk to you, Mr Stanyer.'

Stanyer frowned. Blew on the filter, then banged it against a workbench so hard that Hirsch wanted to say, 'Don't, you'll damage it.'

'What about?' Stanyer said eventually.

Hirsch waved the search-party list at him. 'To do with that case a few years ago, the body in the mineshaft. A long shot, but we're interviewing everyone who took part in the search.'

Stanyer wiped his hands on a rag. 'Really?'

Hirsch showed him the list of names. 'As you can see, you were there. I'd like to know if there are any names you think should be added to the list. And if you can remember anything from back then.'

'Jeez, tall order,' Stanyer said, grumbling but intrigued. 'This is years ago.'

Hirsch watched him scan the names, then shrug and return the list. 'Nothing strikes me as out of the ordinary. Obviously, there are names there I don't recognise. I mean, people came in from far and wide.'

'Your wife didn't take part?'

'My wife? I hadn't even met her then.'

'Okay. What about Alastair? His name's not on the list.'

Stanyer frowned, cast his eyes up. 'Trying to recall. I mean, I wouldn't be surprised if he took part and somehow got overlooked. At the same time, no one ever said he was civic minded.'

Lovely. 'Have you heard from him?'

'I have, in fact.'

'Oh. And?'

'He's in Tasmania. Took the car ferry, said he's sick of the heat. Wanted me to wire him some money.'

'Did you?'

'Yeah, well, he is my brother. Just a few hundred. Not enough to start a new life in the Bahamas, if that's what you're thinking.'

'If he contacts you again, please ask him to get in touch. He's not in any trouble; nothing we can't sort out.'

'Sure,' Stanyer said, turning to the air filter again to signal that he'd finished with Hirsch.

Hirsch spent Monday at his desk. After a lunch of Kropp's wife's spring rolls, he walked the Nordrum search-party list around to Ed Tennant and Nan Buchanan. Bob Muir would have to wait; he was out rewiring a heritage-listed woolshed.

Nan said she had only a vague recollection of who'd been in the search party. Ed was stacking tinned tomatoes, brand names facing out. 'I was there, but only for half a day.'

Like all police, Hirsch hated inconsistencies. 'The other day you told me you'd had the best week of trading ever. That you were here.'

'Yeah, I was here – except for that first half day,' Tennant said testily. 'I turned up, got my name put on a list and walked up and down a designated area with a dozen others. Then the wife calls me, rushed off her feet in the shop, so I came back. What – you saying I let the side down?'

Hirsch breathed in, then out. If Ed Tennant had a mantra, it'd be: *It's all about me.* 'I know it was a long time ago, but if you could check this list of names? Any missing?'

The shopkeeper took the list with ill grace; scanned the names; returned it. Then snatched it back, his face clearing. 'Wait: Al Stanyer was there. He'd been drinking, so the Redruth sergeant sent him home again. Scared he'd fall into one of the mineshafts.'

Hirsch returned to his office and called Kropp.

The growly crackle on the landline: 'Dimly remember it.'

'Dimly remember Alastair, or dimly remember sending someone home?'

'The latter.'

Then Hirsch tried Alastair Stanyer's mobile and home numbers for about the twentieth time in the past two weeks. No luck.

It was one of those things. Police work was more a waiting game than anything else. He made other calls, wrote and lodged reports, walked around to Bob Muir's at 5 p.m. Bob recalled the Alastair Stanyer incident, but nothing else. And then the waiting game was cut short when Michael Farrelly, the Muncowie publican, called to say that he needed to clarify something.

44

'It's about Bob Hortle finding that dog.'

Hirsch's heart sank. 'Okay.'

'It seems I didn't have the full story.'

'Which was?'

'Well, Bob certainly had the dog with him when he came in to use the pub phone – I remember giving the poor thing some food and water. Gave Bob a brandy too, he was so cut up about finding the body ...'

Hirsch tried to be patient. 'But?'

'But Vince Johnston told me just now that someone else found the dog on the road and took it to Bob, thinking it was his because it was running loose near his place.'

'Jesus Christ, Mick: who?'

'Bloke called Al Stanyer. The one you asked about the other day. And no, he still hasn't been in.'

Hirsch raced up to Muncowie, bought a beer for Vince Johnston, who was just as inclined as the others to idle along the byways of the past, confirmed his story in well under an hour, and now had Webb on the line as he raced back to Tiverton.

'Sounds like we have a horse and stable-door issue,' responded the senior sergeant, 'but detour out to his place anyway and seal it. I'll be there with a forensics team as soon as possible. But why are we only hearing of this now?'

'One of those no-one-asked-me situations.'

Hirsch heard Webb groan. Good cops learned to make imaginative leaps and connect disparate bits of information, but witnesses tended to misreport, misremember and fail to distinguish the relevant from the irrelevant. If someone asked why they didn't say anything at the time they'd reply, 'You didn't ask me.'

'It seems,' Hirsch went on, 'Mr Johnston has always known it was Stanyer who found the dog. He just didn't think he needed to put anyone straight. Didn't think it mattered.'

'This Stanyer person's driving along, spots the dog and takes it to the nearest house?' Webb asked, still fixing the story in her head.

'Robert Hortle's. They knew each other from the pub. He dumped the dog on him, in fact. Said he was late for an appointment.'

Hirsch tried to imagine what Hortle had done next. He's intrigued and wants to do the right thing. Or perhaps he's a bit irritated. Anyway, he loads the dog into his own car and drives up the road and finally spots the red Mazda ute. He pulls over, gets out, pokes around further and finds Ben

Nordrum's body, with a bit of help from the dog, at the bottom of a mineshaft. Drives into Muncowie to report it. By now he wants a stiff drink. And it's his story. A good one. Perhaps he doesn't actually claim to have found the dog, but people just assume it – he did find the *body*, after all. Eventually one or two locals like Vince Johnston learn the full story but by then Stanyer's role is irrelevant.

Pretty relevant now, though. Enough for a search warrant; enough to justify the collection of prints and DNA, whether or not Stanyer had returned to his shack.

Webb grunted. 'I'm looking at the map. Stanyer lives nowhere near the Breadbox area.'

How to explain to a city cop like Webb that distances mean something different in the bush? You could turn up at a pub an hour and a half from where you lived, and no one would raise an eyebrow.

Webb was still speaking. 'But the thing is, he was in the area at the relevant time. True, there could be an innocent explanation. He was taking a back way to the pub and found the dog and it bit him. Or he scratched himself on barbed wire earlier in the day. Or there was already blood on the collar. But we need to rule him in or out.'

Now it was an hour later, and Hirsch had secured Alastair Stanyer's shack and settled in to wait. He hadn't bothered with crime-scene tape or marking a defined path: there was no passing traffic, and the search focus would be the interior of the house. Even so, he parked some distance from it and didn't add to the footprints already in the dirt.

Webb and Leavitt arrived in an unmarked sedan, trailed by two technicians in a crime-scene van. Hirsch, recognising Lyn Dekic, indicated the disturbed soil. 'Mostly me.'

She glanced at his feet. 'Have you been inside?'

'Several times over the years, most recently a couple of weeks ago.'

'We'll need to eliminate you.'

'Sure. I touched a couple of doorhandles, the back of a chair – and maybe the cup I drank out of is still in the sink.'

The other technician was lifting her nose to the wind. Hirsch had seen that before; he'd done it himself: checking for decomposition. 'I've walked around the house a couple of times since, and I'm pretty sure he's not in there. He's in Tasmania, according to his brother. Just not answering his phone.'

Webb had been watching the exchange. 'We'll need to speak to this brother.'

Hirsch nodded. 'Understood.'

'I want prints and DNA samples,' Webb said, turning to the forensic technicians.

'Unless he's wiped everything,' Dekic said.

Hirsch shook his head. 'Big job, and I doubt he had the time. I think my visit panicked him. He'd been shooting a twenty-two in his backyard, but he doesn't own a twenty-two, and by the time I'd twigged to that and raced back here – half an hour later? – he'd packed up and left.'

The technician swiped at the perspiration on her neck. 'Let's hope he left a toothbrush or a comb, a snot-rag, a spoon ...'

An hour later, the technicians were preparing to leave with fingerprints on strips of tape, a comb with hair caught in the teeth, a toothbrush and two crusted tissues from the floor beside the bed.

'He's as bad as my teenage son,' Dekic said, with the air of someone who's never surprised. 'As for the gun safe, unlocked and empty.'

'Great.'

When they were gone, Webb and Hirsch searched for other types of evidence. As Webb put it, 'A diary saying, "I murdered a young man ten years ago and a husband and wife six years ago, and I was working with Joe Blow, who lives at number twenty-six High Street."'

It wasn't really funny and she hadn't meant it to be, and they found nothing that linked Stanyer to the Culleton or Nordrum cases. On the other hand, they didn't find a time-stamped photo putting him at the Eiffel Tower in June 2016 either. What they found proved only that he was lonely and beset. Some low-key pornography – DVDs and pre-internet stick mags. A fat folder of legal correspondence related to challenges to his father's will. Aggrieved letters to and from his brother. Three sharply worded letters from Clarissa, threatening an intervention order if he continued to harass her or her husband. And a separate folder of short-story fragments, draft poems, creative non-fiction. Hirsch had expected to find sentimental bush themes, but Stanyer dealt subtly with his childhood: his father; his mother; his brother; boarding-school life; his first, unreciprocated stirrings of love and desire.

Webb, removing an irate letter from the legal correspondence, said, 'If Cody Morris of Redruth Family Lawyers ever turns up with a bullet in the head, we'll know where to start looking. Otherwise, it's all down to prints and DNA.'

Assuming that Webb would be putting in official requests for Alastair Stanyer's phone and bank records, Hirsch photographed numbers pencilled on the wall above a grimy landline phone on the kitchen bench.

45

The following afternoon he was summoned to Redruth again. On the drive in he tried not to think about work as predatory birds rode the paddock thermals and long shadows striped the land. Instead, he lifted his forefinger to oncoming motorists and pondered his mother and her pluck. Their meal at the Dugout – notwithstanding Nicholas Sampson on the other side of the room. Wendy's face. Her fingers tracing his technicolour abdomen later that night.

He suddenly burst into song: '*Let me count the ways.*' Words from a song, a poem, long-forgotten pillow talk, a greeting card? He didn't know. But apt.

He blinked himself into the real world as he slowed for the outskirts of Redruth, passing the showgrounds, saleyards, pub, corner shop, tyre dealer and handful of cottages that counted as North Redruth. It seemed appropriate that Ty Moloney and Penny Goldfinch lived here. Then past the old mine and finally, the two fine old stone churches

– Protestant and Catholic – situated just before the town hall, where Webb wanted to meet.

Unable to find a parking spot, he continued down and around the town square before slotting into a space outside the IGA. A quick stop at the bakery for a latte and a Danish, which he ate as he toiled up the slope past the Commonwealth Bank. He tossed his empty cup before shouldering through the hall's heavy main doors. Into a warren of meeting rooms at the rear, and finally into a room normally reserved for the Country Women's Association. Charles III reigned here, on the main wall – with his mother on a side wall, as if reluctant to cede him the throne. And there was a quality of austere stillness in the room, despite the Homicide Squad's portable whiteboards, monitors, landline phones, laptops and printers, and the busyness of Webb and a dozen other officers ranged around the CWA's big old meeting table.

Hirsch joined Brandl and Landy who were hovering, ignored, in the far corner, next to a sticky little plastic side table loaded with sugar sachets, teabags, instant coffee, an urn and a stack of paper cups. They were the only uniformed officers in the room.

'Know why we're here, Sergeant?'

'Not yet.'

Landy said what they were thinking: 'We might as well not exist.'

'Jean,' Brandl said – not unkindly, almost tiredly. She agrees, Hirsch thought, but it's not the kind of thing you can say out loud.

*

They waited, unacknowledged, for ten minutes. Then Webb gestured for them to sit among her detectives and opened the briefing.

'Yesterday, through the efforts of Senior Constable Hirschhausen, based in Tiverton' – she gestured at Hirsch – 'we came up with a name. Alastair Stanyer. A local man. It seems he found the Nordrums' dog on a stretch of the Breadbox Plain road – or *contrived* to find it, more likely – and handed it to the farmer who lives along that same stretch of road. This man, Robert Hortle, decided to go looking for the owner, and the rest is history. The fact that neither man's name appeared in the original files owes a lot to sloppy policework.'

She glanced around the table. 'Anyway, Mr Hortle has since died, and Mr Stanyer has disappeared – ostensibly touring around Tasmania with the support of some spending money from his brother. We've searched his house, got some DNA and fingerprint samples. I put a rush on these, and learned this morning that it's not his DNA on the Nordrum dog collar or the Culleton handkerchief – but his prints place him at both scenes. When the blood got onto the dog collar, we don't know. Or who left it. But it helps confirm our theory that two or more individuals are involved.'

Murmurs, people shifting in their seats. News to everyone, Hirsch thought. She likes to keep things close to her chest.

'Senior Constable Hirschhausen has already been trying to track down this Stanyer fellow in relation to a firearms offence, but going forward we need to ramp that up. Our colleagues in each state including Tasmania have been given his photo and vehicle details, but in the meantime, we're going to be digging into who he is, who he spends time with and what he's been doing, going back ten years or more. Credit-card history. Unusual bank transactions. Holidays. Hotel and motel reservations near unexplained remote-area deaths. The hope is we'll discover who his accomplice was in both sets of murders. Is it another local? Are they in regular contact? Still operating together?'

She turned to Hirsch. 'You have a theory about his disappearance, Senior Constable Hirschhausen?'

Hirsch almost stood. He felt awkward. 'It's possible I spooked him unwittingly.'

Half the young hotshots looked on with a kind of relish. This was going to be good: country yokel stuffs up.

But Webb seemed to sense this. She raked the room with flinty eyes and said, 'Listen, don't judge. Senior Constable, carry on, please.'

'I'd been doing a firearms audit,' Hirsch said, going on to explain what had happened next, and to outline Stanyer's family history.

'I'm wondering if his reclusive personality is the result of guilt, and/or a fear of being caught. He's been living with it for years. Then the Culleton murder features on *Nowhere to Hide*, and I turn up on his doorstep a few days later. Two rifles and a twenty-two pistol were stolen from the Culleton kid, so it's possible the shells I saw came from that pistol. Anyway, it was too much for him – perhaps he even thought the firearms audit was a police trick to catch him out – and he grabbed everything and ran.'

Someone asked, 'Any reason to doubt he's in Tasmania?'

'Hard to say. There's no love lost, but the brother has bailed him out before.'

'How much money did he send?'

'A few hundred.'

'He's been spending it?'

Webb cut in. 'We're still waiting to access his card activity.'

Another detective asked, 'Is he dangerous?'

'I don't know,' Hirsch said. 'My read was: on edge and a bit sad.'

'On edge driving around with rifles and a pistol.'

'True. And his life over the past few years has been a bit of a mess. Maybe he's not the no-hoper everyone says he is, but if he's one of our killers, I don't think he's the brains of the outfit. I think he's been under the thumb of someone more powerful. The day I called in he looked as if he'd been in a fight. He said he'd fallen off a ladder, but it looked more like someone had bashed him. A warning not to panic? To keep his trap shut? I don't know.'

Webb didn't seem overly impressed by this analysis but didn't dismiss it either. 'What about Annika Nordrum? Could she have spooked him, too? Did she post about her search on social media?'

'Possibly. I'll ask her,' Hirsch said, chancing a quick glance around the table. He hadn't quite disgraced himself. One nod, two smiles, everyone else looking at Webb.

'Some clear actions now, going forward,' Webb said. 'Find Stanyer. Always go in pairs: he's armed, remember.'

'What if whoever beat him up has now killed him?' Leavitt asked.

'Because he was a liability?' pondered Webb. 'That's possible – which would make *that* person potentially armed and dangerous, too. *Go. In. Pairs.*'

Webb turned to Brandl. 'Sergeant, I'd like you and your officers to help us where you can. Anything about Stanyer you can dig up. Friends, family, enemies – even his dentist, doctor, accountant …'

'Of course.'

Then Webb closed the briefing and herded Hirsch into a corner as everyone dispersed. 'A moment.'

Hirsch waited.

'The brother. He's at home, expecting me, but I want you along, too. You know the history. You know him.'

'Not well.'

Webb went on as if he hadn't demurred. 'Several questions come to mind: does he have proof that his brother's in Tasmania? Does he like to hunt? Where was he in June 2016? Things like that.'

46

Half an hour later Mitchell Stanyer was saying, 'My brother had a few lost years back then. He's not much better now, in fact.'

They were in his kitchen, Stanyer on one side of the long table, opposite Webb and Leavitt, with Hirsch at the far end looking on, thinking that if his function was to be the familiar face that disarmed Stanyer, it wasn't working: the grazier was at ease, and also sarcastic.

'What do you mean, lost years?' Leavitt said.

Stanyer turned to Webb's offsider with exaggerated patience. 'I mean he used to drink and gamble. Lost years. I'd have thought you'd know the term. Anyway, he used to disappear for weeks at a time.'

Leavitt didn't like it. He leaned in, curling his lips. 'Hunting?'

Stanyer sat back in surprise. 'Hunting? No. On a drinking binge.'

'What about you? Do you hunt?'

'Me? Never hunted.'

'Target practice?'

Stanyer turned to Webb. 'What's he on about?'

'Travel,' persisted Leavitt. 'You like to go off-road, maybe? Drive to distant places?'

Hirsch glanced at Webb. She seemed annoyed by Leavitt's studied combativeness, and placed a warning hand on his forearm. She shouldn't have. Hirsch saw Stanyer notice it with a faint smirk.

He took the opportunity to break in. 'Mr Stanyer, we have reason to believe that for the last decade or more your brother has often spent time in northern Australia. Tennant Creek, Derby, Wilcannia ... Is there anything you can tell us about those trips?'

He asked the question knowing that Alastair could only be tied directly to the Northern Territory shooting. The other locations marked unsolved murders and unexplained disappearances going back to 2010.

'Like I said, lost years,' Stanyer said. He looked at his watch and then up at a bold, white-faced clock on the wall, the kitchen's only decoration if you didn't count the appliances, which were so clean and ultra-modern they seemed more for looking at than using.

'Who did he associate with back then?' Webb asked.

'Usual crowd, I suppose. Fellow alcoholics. He was always getting into brawls, owed money right, left and centre. He wasn't all that popular, really.'

Hirsch gave Webb a look, trying to convey that this wasn't quite the received version. The people he'd talked to had assured him that, sure, Alastair liked to drink and cadge money sometimes, but he was a docile drunk and never ran up a bar bill of more than fifty dollars.'

Leavitt said, 'You can't name anyone?'

'Are you people even listening to me? We had very little to do with one another. What's this about? Do you suspect him of something? Do you suspect *me* of something? Do I need a lawyer? He's only a phone call away. And I should point out that in addition to being the mayor, my wife has legal training.'

'To have legal representation is your right, Mr Stanyer,' Webb said, as if preparing to wrap things up. 'In which case I shall ask you to present yourself to the Redruth police station, with your lawyer, for the purposes of obtaining your fingerprints and DNA – so that everything's on the up and up, legally speaking.' She held up a warning hand as Stanyer's features tightened. 'A simple identity procedure,' she said. 'At this stage.'

'Jesus Christ. Can't believe my ears. Jumped up bloody ... Are you allowed to just swan in and ask for my DNA?'

'As I said, for purposes of identification and yes: a lawful request. I'm afraid you don't have the right to refuse, obstruct or resist.' Webb paused. 'But we can obtain it from you now, if that's more convenient.'

'You're acting like I'm a criminal,' Stanyer said. He stretched his mouth open with a finger in each corner and said, voice garbled: 'Go on, take your swab.'

Webb cocked her head. 'To be clear: you are giving permission?'

Stanyer removed his fingers. 'I am,' he said expansively.

'Nothing to hide. I'd like to know why, though. You think Al and I were in on something?'

'To eliminate you from our inquiries,' Joe Leavitt said, his hip spectacles flashing. He was enjoying himself.

'The infant speaks again,' Stanyer said. 'Eliminate me from the Nordrum enquiry, right? Everyone knows that's why you're here. You think my brother's connected, and therefore I am too.'

'Are you?'

'You have prints or DNA you can't account for, correct? You want to see if I'm a match?'

'We'd simply like to eliminate you,' Webb said patiently.

'And I simply want you off my back. Whatever Al's been up to, I wasn't part of it.'

Hirsch leaned in. 'But you have bailed him out of trouble at least twice that we know of. You bought him out of his share of the farm a few years ago, and transferred him some money the other day.'

Mitchell Stanyer lifted his hands, flopped them onto the table again. 'He's my *brother*.'

'If he asks for help again, will you?'

'Within reason.'

'Like sending him money.'

'Well, sure. But as I told you, I didn't send him much – not enough to fly first class to somewhere he can't be extradited from, if that's what you're worried about. As it stands now, he's driving around Tasmania with the help of a measly five hundred bucks.'

'How often do you speak?'

'Get it into your thick heads: we don't speak. Maybe at Christmas, birthdays, but that's about it. Then out of the blue he calls and texts from Tasmania the other day, wanting spending money.'

Stanyer tilted onto one hip and fished out a Samsung phone. Poked, prodded, said, 'Calls and texts,' and sent it scooting across the table. Webb slapped a hand on it to stop it tumbling into her lap. Half-turning the screen to Leavitt, she read the information, passed the phone to Hirsch.

Briefly confused by the unfamiliar layout, he searched recent activity. A call had come in from Alastair Stanyer two days after the firearms audit. Then, the following day, a text: *Can you transfer a bit more? Scared of running out.* A final text: *Pay you back honest.*

Hirsch returned the phone as Webb asked, 'How much did your brother originally ask for?'

'Five thousand.'

'And you sent him five hundred?'

'As I just said,' snarled Stanyer. 'Don't play games with me. I'd bet the farm that you've already checked bank and phone records.' He added: 'Do us a favour, don't tell the wife? She hates his guts.'

His tone belied the words. He was delivering a command, not a request. Hirsch said, 'Mr Stanyer, I've been stationed here six years now and I often call in on your brother. He's on my patrol schedule. And I have to say that he's never struck me as a drinker.'

Stanyer was clipped. 'He *binges*.'

'In fact, he seems a bit lost. A loner.'

'Doesn't mean he doesn't drink,' snorted Stanyer.
'If he drinks, where does he do it?'
'Everywhere. Anywhere. Check the pubs far and wide.'
'Who does he drink with, far and wide?'
'How the fuck would I know?'
'How about when he was younger.'
'I'm trying to get through to you all, we've had very little to do with each other, even less so since I got married. He had no interest in the land, lost money hand over fist, used to drink and gamble a lot and probably still does when he's got a bit of cash in his pocket. But that's as far as I know.' He thumped his chest. 'I, in the meantime, have been steadily building on my father's heritage.'

'Building on my father's heritage,' snorted Webb later, seated with Leavitt at Hirsch's kitchen table.

Hirsch blew over the surface of his coffee. 'Is he right, you checked bank and phone records?'

'We did. And he seems to be telling the truth – as far as he knows it. He did transfer five hundred dollars into his brother's account when he said he did. And his brother withdrew fifty dollars the very next day and used his credit card thereafter. Twenty dollars here, sixty there, on food, petrol and camp sites.'

She smiled bleakly. 'But not in Tasmania,' she said, waggling her iPhone at Hirsch. 'I've just received an update. His card's been used in Adelaide' – she checked the screen again – 'then Hay, Armidale … That's where he seems to have run out of money.'

Hirsch let that sink in. 'He lied to Mitch.'

'Looks like it. As for his landline history, he regularly called Doctor Pillai, the Tiverton shop, Redruth Fuel Supplies, places like that.' She paused. 'And this, an unknown mobile.'

She passed Hirsch a call list from her briefcase. 'That's your annotated copy.'

There was a mobile number highlighted in yellow that Hirsch didn't recognise. Stanyer had called it several times over a two-day period. The dates were significant: the first flurry had occurred after *Nowhere to Hide* was broadcast on Channel 9, the second after Hirsch's firearms visit.

'We think it's a burner,' Webb was saying. 'It's since been taken out of service.'

The other shooter, thought Hirsch.

47

Just before dawn, and Hirsch was dreaming. The locations kept shifting but always returned to a riverside campground crammed with caravans and motorhomes. He couldn't find Trent McRae among them; couldn't find Alastair Stanyer. Couldn't find his HiLux, either, and people were looking at him and he realised he had no pants on. 'This is *our* place,' they shouted, 'you have no jurisdiction here.' Then the campground manager said that Mr Stanyer had left the previous day – driving the HiLux. Hirsch tried calling Senior Sergeant Webb: her number was not connected. And now he couldn't get home. Couldn't find his wallet and the river was rising and the current swirled.

A shake-you-up sort of a dream. As he prowled his town in the morning, he walked off the last jittery wisps. His mind gradually cleared, and he remembered the phone numbers he'd photographed on the wall above Al Stanyer's landline phone.

After a quick shower and breakfast, he checked. Smudged

names, smudged numbers. Numbers called regularly? If so, they pertained to *shop*, *clinic*, *feral* and *diesel*.

Feral was the odd one out. Not only in name but also because it boasted two numbers, a landline and a mobile. He checked the log of calls supplied by Webb: the mobile number for *feral* matched the no-longer-in-service burner phone. He tried it anyway. Yep, out of service.

Then he tried the landline.

Now it was almost two hours later and he'd driven to the Port Pirie police station and been taken through to the CIB office, where Jeff Comyn was his usual blunt, blockish self. 'How're the bruises?'

'On the mend.'

A trademark grunt. If the stocky detective was pleased on Hirsch's behalf, he wasn't about to dwell on it. Rattling a set of car keys, he led Hirsch back to the foyer, saying, 'What's the plan?'

'Interview her about her ex.'

Comyn grunted again. 'That's what Webb told me, but I'm none the wiser.'

Hirsch explained as they stepped into a hot wind blowing in off Spencer Gulf. The *feral* landline number belonged to a house in Spalding. The woman who answered had been bewildered: she didn't know Alastair Stanyer, why he'd have written her phone number on his wall, or who or what 'feral' was. Hirsch had asked how long she'd lived there. Four years. He asked who used to live there. Dalia and Brad Ullmer.

'Ullmer's a licensed shooter,' Hirsch explained. 'Hence "feral".'

'Got it,' Comyn said, leading the way across the side yard to a white unmarked Camry.

'They had to sell because they were going through a divorce. Dalia returned to her single name, Cook, and moved here to Port Pirie. Ullmer lives just outside Tiverton.'

'Got it,' said Comyn again, aiming the keys at the Camry.

'Webb doesn't want me going in alone.'

'In case this guy is still good friends with the ex-wife, and when we arrive he's sitting at her kitchen table with a shottie in his lap.'

'Something like that,' Hirsch said, slipping into the passenger seat.

Then Comyn was beside him, turning the ignition key. 'She might not tell us anything.'

'Still have to try,' Hirsch said.

'And Ullmer?'

'Webb's probably searching his place as we speak.'

Hirsch had made a cursory pass as he left Tiverton. Ullmer's house, on Wildongoleechie Road, had looked forlorn and abandoned.

He said, 'Thanks for doing this.'

Another grunt from Comyn. 'Makes a change for me, a job in town. Usually I'm driving all over the joint. I might even get to pick my kids up after school today.'

He turned on the aircon and entered Dalia Cook's address into the GPS. 'Just up the road,' he muttered, reversing out and onto Main Road.

Port Pirie was a small, flat, smoke-stacked city on the east coast of Spencer Gulf, known mostly for its multi-metal smelter and local agriculture; also an export hub for zinc concentrates, grain and seed. From Hirsch's point of view, it was regional police HQ and the CIB hub for the Yorke Mid North Local Police Service area. 'Just up the road' took them to a dusty white fibro house in Californian bungalow style, on one of the town's broad, heat-stunned streets. A couple of slender gums in the side yard and a massive prickly pear brushing the stuccoed veranda pillars.

Dalia Cook came to her front door before they'd reached her veranda steps. In her late forties, she was stocky and tanned in shorts, a T-shirt and bare feet. She handled the screen door with fingers splayed, explaining wryly: 'Keep your distance, just done my nails.'

A fresh bold red. Hirsch caught a whiff of acetone as he stepped past her into the hallway. 'Unless we have to wrestle you to the ground.'

She laughed, then took them to a darkened sitting room. 'I'll keep the blinds down if that's all right with you. Not trying to hide my guilty expression – it's the coolest room in the house.'

Likes to joke, Hirsch thought. By nature, or because a detective and a uniformed cop were visiting. 'Fine by us.'

The house dated from the 1930s but was pure Ikea inside, as far as Hirsch could tell from the sitting room and the two rooms he'd passed on the way to it. Clean pine furniture in the sitting room; pastelly fabrics.

'Water? Juice? Tea or coffee?'

They settled on water and then, when a tray had been delivered, Cook sat opposite them, rubbing her palms up and down her upper thighs. She smiled at Comyn and said, 'Your daughter does ballet with mine.'

Comyn was surprised. 'Yeah?'

'I've seen you collect her a couple of times.'

'You mean the two times I've collected her this year.' He grimaced. 'I wish it could be more often, but, you know, the job.'

She smiled again. She turned to Hirsch. 'Tiverton, huh? Long may it slumber in the sun. What can I tell you now that I couldn't have told you on the phone earlier?'

Hirsch smiled. She wasn't charmed. He started carefully: 'May I ask, are you and Brad close?'

'You mean, am I going to ring him as soon as you leave?'

'Yeah, pretty much.'

'Not close at all.'

'He doesn't see your daughter every weekend, for example?'

'We have a son and a daughter. And no, they mostly see him on their birthdays and at Christmas and sometimes Easter. Suits everyone. Why? What's he done?'

Her story of the family's dynamics could be checked easily. But that didn't mean Hirsch was prepared to give much away. 'We'd like to speak to him about someone who's come to our attention.'

'That doesn't sound good. They in cahoots?'

Hirsch would have to be more careful. 'We'd just like to talk to him.'

'If you can find him.'

'He's away?'

'He told me the other day he had a big roo-culling job on a property north of Quorn.'

'Do you know which one?'

She shook her head. 'He didn't say, I didn't ask.'

'Do you often meet up with him?'

She was briefly irritable. 'I didn't meet up with him. I phoned him.'

'Okay.'

'Like I said, we're not close, I'm not going to tell him the police were here. It's just that he's supposed to pay child support but he's late as usual, so I called him. Sick of it. Christmas is coming up. I need the money. The kids, all that. He said he'd pay me soon as he finishes this new job.'

'Who did he go with?'

'No one, far as I know.' She watched him carefully. 'You interested in him, or his mates?'

'Both. Either.'

'Look, if he's culling roos or goats, he's probably by himself. If it's a longer trip, hunting, not work, he might go with a mate. But I haven't seen much of him for the last few years. What he does or who he sees now is none of my concern, just so long as the child support comes in and he takes his shit out on someone else. Just out of curiosity I asked if he had a girlfriend: he wouldn't say.'

Comyn leaned forward. 'What do you mean, take his shit out on someone else? Was he violent with you?'

Cook paused, as if she'd said too much. 'How can I put

this ... He was a moody bugger, couldn't sleep, short temper. Got worse over time. In fact, splitting up was his idea but I'd been thinking about it anyway.'

'Again, was he violent?'

'Not as such.'

'But a bit?'

'A bit. Short-tempered more than anything. I mean, he makes a living killing animals. Surely that sort of thing gets to you after a while.'

'Numbed him?' asked Hirsch.

She cocked her head. 'Could be right; numbed him.' She shrugged. 'He's probably better off living alone if that's the case.' She laughed without humour. 'He told me once he wished he'd joined the foreign legion. He was dead serious, got quite hostile when I kind of laughed. It hurt his feelings. He said he was frustrated with farm and town life. Too tame, he preferred the wide open spaces. No rules or regulations. No government to bother you. Where survival was all up to you.'

'Are you saying he's political?'

'Political? What do you mean?'

'Has he joined any kind of like-minded group? Anti-government?'

'I doubt it. He's a loner, really.'

Hirsch exchanged a glance with Comyn. Police everywhere had a greater fear of lone-wolf neo-Nazi mass shooters than skinny brown kids strapped into a suicide vest.

Returning to Cook, he said, 'Casting your mind back several years: did Brad go on a hunting trip into the Northern Territory?'

'He was always going up there. Or Queensland, outback New South Wales. Every couple of years.'

'With a mate?'

'Like I said.'

'Anyone in particular?'

'Al Stanyer. He lives over your way somewhere.'

Hirsch relayed everything to Webb on the drive back to Tiverton and was told to meet her at Ullmer's house. A small fibro place – in full crime-scene mode when he arrived. A cluster of marked and unmarked police vehicles and crime-scene vans, and uniformed and plain-clothed officers in the yard, including Webb.

He parked on the verge of the road and joined her.

'No one home,' she said, removing crime-scene booties and shoving them into a garbage bag. 'Hasn't been here for days, according to the neighbours. Which would tie in with what the ex-wife told you, he's away on a big job.'

'If she's telling the truth,' Hirsch said. 'If the news stories haven't spooked him.'

'Yes, thank you, Senior Constable Hirschhausen, bucket of joy that you are.'

'Sorry, boss.'

'A long day,' Webb said, heaving a sigh. 'He's shooting on a property out of Quorn, did you say? How do we find out which one?'

'Was there any paperwork?' Hirsch asked, inclining his head towards the house.

'No. All on his phone, presumably. We'll get his records.

But we do have his prints and DNA now, which I'll put a rush on. Go home. You look worn out.'

As evening drew in, Hirsch settled on his sofa with a beer and made a few calls. Redruth, first, Sergeant Brandl telling him that Penny Goldfinch had been arrested at an aunt's house in Plympton and had named every member of the Lone Pine Patriots involved in the attack on him. 'It seems,' she said, 'Tyson Moloney called her a dumb bitch once too often.' Pause. 'But that doesn't let her off the hook if the pair of them ripped off her mother.'

Investigating that would be a job for someone else. Hirsch was thinking morosely that even if Lone Pine was broken up, there were other groups just like it throughout the country. Next Trina Gould. She, baby and Pete were doing well. Pete had been like a rock, barely leaving her side since bringing her home from hospital.

'See if you can keep him away from any outfit calling themselves Lone Pine or My Place.'

'Don't worry. Me and his sister have been earbashing him about that.'

Then his mother – she sounded more cheerful – then Annika – impatient – and finally Wendy, who invited him to dinner, saying, 'I need to check those bruises again.'

If you know what I mean.

Hirsch was attending to paperwork in his office on Thursday morning when Jean Landy called.

'Is the sergeant with you?'

'No. Why?'

'I checked: she's not with CIB, either.'

'She hasn't come in yet?'

'Paul, we haven't seen her since knock-off time on Tuesday.'

48

Half an hour later, Hirsch was in Redruth, Landy showing him a scrap of paper.

'It's just one of her usual to-do lists and it was waiting on my desk when I came in yesterday. I don't know if she left it before I got in, or the previous evening.'

'She didn't say what she'd be doing?'

'No.'

'How often does she do this, leave a list?'

'Hardly ever. Only if she has a dental appointment in Clare, a departmental meeting in Port Pirie or Adelaide, that kind of thing.'

He peered at a scrawl at the bottom. '"See you both before you go home." Seems like she expected to be back in the office by knock-off time.'

'I did call her now and then, but didn't want to overdo it in case she was in the middle of something personal. Went to voicemail. Then when she didn't show this morning, either, I walked up the hill and knocked. Her car's there, but the place felt empty, and she's still not answering her phone.'

'Let's check again.'

Landy looked ready to protest, but saw the expression on Hirsch's face and said, 'Lead on, Macduff.'

They set out on foot, three hundred metres uphill, leaving Tim Medlin to man the police station. Massive trees shaded them, reaching canopy to canopy across the road. 'So she usually tells you where she's going if she leaves a list?'

'Yep. And she's always good about answering her phone when she's away.'

'Has she been obsessing about anything lately? Work-related? Personal?'

'No more than usual – but I don't know much about her personal life. I think there was a shitty boyfriend in the past ...'

'Years ago,' Hirsch said. But he'd check it out.

They kept walking, a garden sprinkler dampening their trousers briefly. Water restrictions were in force, but a hand-painted sign read *tank water in use*. A wren twitched in the spray, washing itself or simply having fun.

'Envy that bird,' Landy said.

'Me, too. Anything else about Hilary? Doesn't matter how small or unlikely.'

'Well, she hated what happened to you the other day.'

'Hardly her fault.'

'I mean she *really* hated it.'

Would she turn avenger? Hirsch visualised the sergeant stewing away, thinking she'd let Trent McRae pull the wool over her eyes. That she'd not paid enough attention to the nonsense he and his mates were spouting. That her negligence had led to one of her officers getting hurt.

Dread crept through him as they reached the departmental house permanently allocated to the Redruth sergeants. The little wrought-iron gates were open, with a silver Skoda hatch in the driveway, the patches of lawn on either side slowly burning away. Blinds down on the front and side windows.

No reply when Hirsch knocked on the front door. Landy followed him around to a struggling backyard: tomatoes on dying stems; rigid, sun-baked tea towels and knickers on the clothesline; an abandoned hose leaking water slowly from the spray attachment. He knocked on the back door; rattled the knob. 'Do you know if she keeps a spare key anywhere?'

Landy shook her head but began looking under flowerpots and pathway rocks. Hirsch, peering into the narrow gap between the hot-water service and the back wall, found dusty cobwebs and a small magnetised spare-key box.

It opened the back door, which led straight into an orderly kitchen. No dirty plates, cups or cutlery; electric jug cold to the touch. But mostly Hirsch and Landy were letting their noses lead them. Was there a body here, on the turn?

They searched every room. All had been sitting stale for hours, days.

'So she's definitely somewhere in the station Kia,' Hirsch said.

'But I'm glad we checked.'

'So am I.'

Then Landy's mobile rang. Hirsch, listening in, understood

that she was talking to Tim Medlin. She paused, holding the phone against her chest. 'Sorry, but there's a car nose-deep in the newsagency. Tim's there, but someone needs to direct traffic and get a tow organised.'

'You go,' Hirsch said. 'I'll keep looking.'

He passed the newsagency on his way to the council offices later. Tim gave him a smile and a salute. Jean had her arm around an elderly man.

The small back room marked District Clerk was crammed: filing cabinets, wall charts, subdivision maps and planning applications scattered across a table running the length of the space. A computer, printer and landline phone on a scuffed desk. A stuffy room, with a desk fan ruffling loose papers, and most of the light supplied by old-style green-shaded desk lamps.

An antediluvian cave, but suited to the clerk. Dean Hopper was in his late sixties, short, thin, balding, dressed as usual in a collar and tie. Also as usual, he'd come to work wearing a jacket and had hung it on the back of his chair before tending to business with his sleeves rolled. If his visitor had been the mayor or some other VIP, he'd have put the jacket on. Hirsch was only Hirsch.

'Constable.'

'Dean.'

'What can I do for you?'

'The usual, a property search.'

'Happy to oblige,' Hopper said, his arthritic fingers poised over his keyboard.

'First, though, has Sergeant Brandl been in recently? Similar request?'

'Yesterday morning.'

Hirsch tingled. 'Can you show me?'

Hopper went still. 'Is she all right?'

Hirsch cocked his head. 'Why do you ask?'

'She wanted to know about Nick Sampson, and ... well, he's not a very nice man.'

'Show me.'

The stubby fingers flew over the keys. 'Here we are. It took a while, Joppy Holdings.' He angled the screen to Hirsch as he explained: 'His wife's maiden name, Jacklyn Oppy.'

Hirsch peered. Joppy Holdings owned fifty acres outside Hanson, thirteen kilometres south-west of Redruth. 'Google Earth?'

'Can do,' Hopper said, switching screens.

The aerial shots showed an irregularly shaped block surrounded by empty farmland. It was heavily treed in one corner, with a dam in another and a broad open area containing two buildings and a scattering of vehicles. A dirt road in. No other houses in sight.

'I don't see power or phone lines.'

'Correct.'

Hirsch pointed. 'Those vehicles ...'

Button shrugged. 'Wrecks from his car business?'

'I'd love to have a look inside those buildings.'

'That's what Sergeant Brandl said.'

Then Hirsch updated Landy.

'If you can wait an hour or so, I'll come with you,' she said.

'Can't wait an hour. Just a drive-by,' Hirsch said.

She wasn't fooled. 'You know what she said, no more going in solo.'

'Look, she's been missing too long. If I spot anything I'll let you know immediately.'

'Text me the address.'

The trees had looked dense in the Google Earth photographs but when Hirsch reached the property, he realised they allowed glimpses of the two buildings, a shack with a nearby shed. Sparse cover for scouting, but better than nothing, and there was a gate nearby – rarely used, judging by the state of the grass and soil. Driving in as far as the trunks and low-hanging branches allowed, Hirsch covered the HiLux with the dusty old tarp he always carried. His sun shelter, rain shelter, picnic blanket and crime-scene preserver.

Then he slipped through the dappled light cast by the trees, his boots snapping and crushing fallen twigs and bark. Crouching behind a ghost gum, and blessing his dun-coloured summer uniform, he studied the open ground between the trees and the buildings. It had looked flat in the aerial photographs, but he could see shallow dips and hollows. Useful cover if he had to dash across it.

He switched his attention to the cars. All wrecks, with a patina of dust and rust; rotting tyres; weeds growing up through the bodywork.

Now the dam. To Hirsch's eye, the banks looked higher than normal, heaped with fresh-looking soil. A recent clean out with the excavator?

Finally the buildings. The shack told him nothing. But Rosie Llewellyn's caravan did, parked in the open-sided implement shed. So did the Subaru SUV last seen towing it; and a yellow excavator. And the Redruth police station's Kia.

49

Hirsch checked his phone: one bar. He tried to call Jean Landy: no connection. He texted her a precis of the situation. Time passed; the message failed to go through.

He watched for a while, expecting to hear or see something to explain what might be occurring here, but it was another sense that gave him the answer: a nasty hint of cat piss, rotten eggs and paint thinner on the shifting breeze.

Meth lab? If so, it was in the shack, and explained why Trent McRae hadn't driven off into the sunset two weeks ago: he was minding it, maybe even cooking the meth.

But what had he done with the sergeant? There was no way she'd have parked the police Kia in the shed. Meanwhile, no sign of Nicholas Sampson's old brown station wagon.

Hirsch eyed the shack, imagining Brandl tied up on the floor next to chemical drums, tubes and burners. Breathing in fumes dense and inflammable while hoping some dickhead in a polyester jacket didn't flex his muscles and set off a spark of static.

He eyed the chimney. No smoke, just that hint of fumes

from a recent cook. No generator chugging away behind the building.

He checked his SMS screen, pressed *try again*. Waited. Saw the text to Landy go through this time.

The place was silent apart from a scratchy breeze, a distant vehicle, birdcalls. Whether or not the sergeant was tied up in the shack, Hirsch couldn't sit and look at the place forever. He began to skirt along the edge of the open ground in a half-crouch, ready to duck or slip back into the tree line. He'd gone a hundred metres, aiming to reach the driveway fence which would give him a good sightline to the back wall of each building, when something, some alteration in the ground cover ahead, some oddity about its mix of colours and textures, made him freeze.

Buried landmine? Bear trap? Heart hammering, he looked behind and beside him, searching for something to prod the soil, eventually grabbing a fallen branch that looked exactly like a snake but was comfortingly knotted, brittle and sun-warmed in his hands, sensations to remind him that he was alive. Returning to the patch of ground that was bothering him, he jabbed at it with the stick.

A woven-together lid of branches, twigs, leaves and dirt simply collapsed in front of him. He tensed, stepped back in alarm until he felt safe. He inched forwards again, peering over the lip of the pit that had opened up.

A mantrap. Upright wooden stakes sharp enough to punch through your guts. That explains the excavator, Hirsch thought. The soil heaped around the dam. And if there's one trap, there's going to be others.

He edged around the pit and kept walking, staying just inside the tree line, occasionally ducking out to test the ground. Just because surface anomalies had alerted him to one trap, that didn't mean the next would be so readily spotted.

At the fence that ran beside the long driveway, he paused and listened.

What? ...

Nothing. He was starting to spook himself. Figuring that sometimes movement was better than caution, he left the shelter of the trees and followed the fence for a hundred metres.

A vehicle was slowing at the driveway entrance behind him. He went flat to the dirt, then popped his head up and down again to fix its position. He saw roiling dust and the snout of a brown station wagon. Too late to retreat to the trees, so he waddle-dashed a few metres across the uneven open ground and into what appeared to be a shallow depression. Panicky and clumsy, scuttling over turned soil with great carved clods of dirt waiting to do him in, he tripped as Nicholas Sampson's car accelerated up the driveway. Slid along on his belly, hands ploughing the soil, clods scraping the flesh from his palms and forearms. Slowing him as they loosened, crumbling, and toppled ...

Over the lip of another mantrap. This one was open. It had already been sprung.

He peered in. At first, nothing made sense. He could see straw, sticks and loose soil in the corners, and hear the plink, plunk and pitter-patter of disintegrating clods landing, but ...

He recoiled. The dirt was bouncing off Sergeant Brandl's uniform. Off Trent McRae's T-shirt and trackies. Clothing that was no longer soft but a resonating board of stiff, dry blood.

Hirsch flopped onto his back and looked up at the sky, hyperventilating, one hand over his heart as if to stop it racing. He took one deep breath, let it out, then settled into a rhythm, in slowly through his nose, out slowly through pursed lips for a couple of minutes. When he felt halfway human again, he rolled over, looked into the pit and called, 'Hilary? Trent?'

Nothing. He'd known it was useless.

Cringing at the violation, he poked experimentally with his testing stick. Just blowflies rising, buzzing. Settling again.

Hirsch bit down on his sudden nausea and chanced another couple of quick up-and-down reviews of the driveway. Sampson's station wagon hadn't altered pace as it trundled past, before slowing for the shed. Hirsch saw it stop, brake lights flaring. Next time he checked, Sampson was getting out. Hirsch flopped down again.

This time he leaned in and shot a few photos with his phone, his cop coolness returning. Better to preserve the crime scene on film before Sampson buried and disturbed it with his excavator. Because surely that was the guy's next step?

Hirsch rested briefly, trying to piece together a story from what he'd just seen.

Hilary arrives at the property some time yesterday. Is immediately bailed up by Trent McRae with his dead father's shotgun, maybe even shot at. She runs. McRae gives chase; fires again. She glances back over her shoulder – and pitches into a mantrap. One spike impales her. A bad strike, near the groin, tearing open the femoral artery. Blood saturates her lower body and the ground beneath, even lapping at the base of the other spikes.

She'd have bled out in under five minutes. But her head, arms and torso were unimpaired. Fading, she unholstered her pistol. Aimed it right where Trent McRae's head might appear.

Hirsch imagined McRae's glee as he trotted up to the edge of the pit, shotgun across his chest Hollywood style. Peering in, ready to gloat.

Perhaps the sergeant's bodycam caught the moment her shot took half his head away. Caught him toppling in, slapping down onto two spikes – stomach and shoulder – to die twitching with his shotgun at his side, his ravaged face gaping at the woman who'd tried to steer him away from all of his small-town shit.

Hirsch risked another quick scan of the pit. The sergeant was clutching her mobile, knowing she didn't have long. Five minutes, four minutes, getting weaker. Running out of time, even if her phone had been able to pick up a signal, and now Hirsch was blinking and gulping too quickly. He should be trying to anticipate Nicholas Sampson's next move. Nothing worked in him. Only grief.

A harsh, popping clatter. Sampson had fired up the excavator. Now a kind of cold, cop anger stirred in Hirsch.

50

He let a few seconds pass, listening to the engine settle into a hacking complaint as it warmed up. Another few seconds, and now he heard a low growl as the excavator began to roll out of the shed on its rubber tracks.

He visualised Sampson at the controls, lurching over the choppy ground towards the pit. Wouldn't take him long to reach it, fill it and scrape it smooth. Maybe even scatter some innocent grass stalks, bark and twigs afterwards. Then dump the sergeant's Kia somewhere far away: the airport; out in the wilds. Even here, if he had the patience to dig a large enough hole. Then he'd empty the shack and move the meth lab somewhere new. The sergeant and McRae were merely collateral damage. No reason to go out of business.

The excavator sputtered, rattled unevenly, stalled. Hirsch cocked an ear and heard Sampson turn the motor over. It didn't fire. Empty tank? Rat damage? Didn't matter – what mattered was that he'd be distracted while Hirsch dashed across to the driveway and up to the shed. Better to stop

Sampson there than out on open ground, perched at the controls of the excavator and able to spot Hirsch, even sideswipe him off his feet with the bucket arm.

Hirsch retreated from the pit, turned, raced to the fence and slipped through the wires. Sprinting up the driveway now, he had a clear side view of the shed and the shack: nothing behind either of them, and only the excavator's bucket arm visible at the front of the shed. As he drew nearer, he could hear cursing, the clang of metal against metal. Sampson's fixing the motor, he thought, or giving it a thrashing.

Ensuring that his bodycam was recording, Hirsch slowed to a rapid walk, trying to plant each footfall quietly on the hard-baked soil. Somehow – he had no memory of it – he'd drawn his pistol.

Reaching the driver's-side rear tyre of Sampson's station wagon, he knelt, unscrewed the valve stem cap and jammed in a twig. Air leaked out noisily. He scooted around to the passenger-side rear tyre and was repeating his fine bit of sabotage when Sampson came charging out of the shed, a wrench in one hand. Puzzlement shifted to rage. 'You fucken ...'

Fucken what? Why couldn't the men of the Mid North fucken name whatever he was? Hirsch aimed the Glock and with a twist of loathing said, 'Put it down, you prick. Nicholas Sampson, I'm arresting you on suspicion of—'

Sampson threw the wrench overarm and pivoted away in one motion; Hirsch felt a painful blow on his shoulder as he ducked, twisted and fell onto one hip. Then he was up again but he'd lost vital seconds. Sampson was far ahead, streaking past the shed, then the shack. Hirsch powered after him, meth odours searing his nostrils, tacking left and right behind the shack, trying to keep to Sampson's path and hoping like hell he remembered where he'd dug the mantraps.

Sampson veered suddenly, racing at an angle towards the tree plantation. Hirsch chanced a quick halt to draw breath and bellow: *'Don't be an idiot.'*

Sampson ignored him, continuing a straight run across the open ground to the beckoning trees. Hirsch pistoned after him, again not straying from Sampson's path, when Sampson shrieked suddenly and backpedalled, throwing himself sideways. He thudded onto one hip, momentum flipping him onto his back, his outflung hand slapping the ground.

Which opened up beneath it.

Dirt was still rattling down onto a clutch of stakes when Hirsch trotted up, panting, his anger beginning to dissipate. '*Keep still*. Now, start wriggling backwards. Slowly, slowly ...'

Sampson panted. Turned his head wildly, trying to find Hirsch's voice, visibly relaxing as he realised he was safe. 'God.'

'Roll onto your stomach.'

Sampson didn't move. Instead he said, 'So what happens now?'

Hirsch realised with astonishment that Sampson wanted to negotiate. He said, '*Roll onto your stomach, Mr Sampson,*' his tone like gravel on a shovel.

'Yeah, yeah.'

Heaving his stocky hips and torso, Sampson flopped over and rested one cheek on the ground. 'Do what you have to do.'

Hirsch straddled him, wrenching his hands behind his back and ratcheting on the cuffs. Turned him over again and recited the arrest warning before hauling him to his feet. Assault police would do for now. Plenty of other charges to follow.

'You up for a few questions?'

'No comment.'

'Sergeant Brandl got here yesterday?'

'No comment.'

'Trent was here and got the drop on her?'

'If you know so much, why are you asking me?'

'And he even fucked that up. Or were you part of it?'

'No comment.'

'From the state of the bodies, I'd say it happened yesterday, not this morning. Were you here yesterday?'

'No comment.'

'Did you find them yesterday or this morning?'

'No comment.'

'Was it you who drove the Kia into the shed?'

'No comment.'

'Why wait so long to bury them? Not very bright.'

Some tension in Sampson's jawline when he said, 'No comment.'

Sometimes the old appellations were best. 'What a fucked-up operation – putting a sponging, workshy layabout in charge. Says a lot about you, really.'

Sampson wrenched at the handcuffs. 'His fucking mother and my wife are cousins, all right?'

'Ah, family,' Hirsch said. 'So what happened?'

'No comment.'

'Come on, Nick.'

Still disgusted, Sampson said, 'I wasn't here yesterday. I don't know what happened.'

'But you had a good guess.'

'Nothing to do with me. Trent asked a few days ago if he could set up camp out here, couldn't stand being with his mother, and I said yes.' A shrug. 'I popped in this morning to see how he was getting on.'

'Goodness of your heart.'

'Look, it's not my fault, what happened here. It shocked me. I panicked.'

'Of course you did,' said Hirsch blithely. 'So, you find them dead ... What next? Clean out the lab first? Go home, destroy paperwork, warn your idiot distributors? Then back here again to finish off?'

A smouldering silence before Sampson said, 'I want a lawyer.'

'Fuck yeah,' Hirsch said. 'You are in *deep* shit.'

Someone bawled, '*Paul*.'

Jean Landy, standing beside the Redruth patrol car in front of the shed. He waved; she waved back before setting out towards him in her determined way.

Hirsch waved frantically, screaming, '*Stop. Boobytraps.*'

The terror in his voice ... Landy froze, stared down at her feet, began to retreat. Her thighs hit the grille of the patrol car. And she remained perched there uneasily as Hirsch propelled Sampson back the way they'd come. His HiLux was closer, just through the trees, but this path, straight ahead, was the only safe one he knew.

51

At the end of a day in which other police wanted to know everything and told him nothing, Hirsch was invited to a sit-down with Senior Sergeant Webb in the Redruth briefing room. Fatigue had tightened her features, but she was also fired up. The Nordrum killings were cold; these new killings were red-hot.

'Sorry about Hilary.'

Hirsch nodded.

'You did well.'

Hirsch said nothing.

'First,' Webb said, 'Mitchell Stanyer is in the clear. Brad Ullmer, on the other hand, is not. DNA results show that not only is it his blood on the dog collar, he was also present at the Rodney Culleton shooting. So we have Ullmer and Alastair Stanyer at both scenes, but there are still many unknowns. For example, who did what, are others involved and are they responsible for other murders? In any case, the main thing that concerns us right now is nabbing them before they kill someone else.'

Hirsch made an effort to shake off the blues. 'For what it's worth, I think Ullmer led and Stanyer followed, but yes, let's get them behind bars.'

Webb regarded him now with faint regret. 'Meanwhile, the Redruth police station. I've received word that you're to be in charge until it's been decided who'll replace Sergeant Brandl. You might be in the hot seat for a day, a week, all summer, who knows.'

That didn't gladden Hirsch's heart. His head dropped to his chest.

'Sorry. She was your friend.'

'Yeah, she was.'

But Hirsch's feelings were complicated. He wouldn't be in this fraught new position if his boss had heeded her own advice. She'd followed a lead without a backup partner and died a needless death. He knew *why* she'd done it – to atone for the messy fallout of her softly-softly approach to McRae's rehabilitation – but the knowing brought him no comfort.

On the other hand, he'd done exactly the same thing. And the evidence – the two dead bodies – might have been buried, or at least compromised, if he'd waited in town until Jean Landy could accompany him, as he should have.

His voice sounding hollow, even to himself, he asked, 'Is Sampson saying anything?'

'Now that he's got a lawyer, yes. He feels bad that he threw a spanner at you – but claims it wasn't an assault. You startled him. He shouldn't even have been arrested.'

'Uh huh.'

'And he realises it was a mistake to have let anyone, especially an in-law, camp out on his wife's property.'

'I bet.'

'He's mortified that this in-law would stretch the relationship to the extent of digging boobytraps and cooking methamphetamine on the place.'

'Yep,' said Hirsch, 'and he had no idea there were two bodies in one of these traps.'

'Exactly. That's what he's saying now, but I understand he made certain admissions to you, after the official warning?'

Hirsch patted his chest. 'Bodycam. Did he have an explanation for a police vehicle in his shed?'

'Again, he rarely visited the property, otherwise he would've known about the meth lab. And when he arrived today, he didn't see Sergeant Brandl's Kia because it was obscured by the caravan.'

'And the excavator?'

'He'd bought that to clean out the dam. It doesn't hold water very well, apparently.'

'What about his phone, computer, call history, bank and business records ...'

'Fine-tooth comb, Paul, don't you worry,' Webb said. She almost leaned forward to pat his hand.

'It's not only the meth lab,' said Hirsch, tensing. 'He's been ripping off the locals for years. Dodgy cars, rebirthing, selling second-hand parts as new. Undeclared income. And I think he might be active in a local My Place group.'

'That may be,' Webb said, 'but there are clearer indications that he'd been using Trent McRae's connections to recruit cooks and dealers.'

Hirsch shook his head. He'd been trying to see a rational pattern behind all of this, and saw only accumulating chaos and disarray. Grief and tiredness washed through him again so heavily that, when he was finally allowed to quit for the day, he snarled at the reporters permanently camped outside the police station and barely made it to the solace of the little house on Bitter Wash Road.

There was a swift reaction the next morning when he said one mental-health day would be enough.

'Aitch, you need *several*.'

'Life as we know it will collapse if I take more than one.'

Wendy flared at him, and it was bad. 'Why the jokes all the time? It's not funny. Honour your fucking friend's death, all right? Honour yourself.'

Hirsch rolled his shoulders and sought help from the top of her kitchen table. Tried to speak.

'You need a *week*. Fucking martyr complex.'

She was dressed for work. Kate, dressed for school, scraped her spoon under a last wodge of muesli and said, 'Listen to her, Aitch.'

'Listen to me, Aitch.'

He lifted and dropped his hands. 'I *am* listening. It's just—'

'It's just that you really do think things will fall apart if you take time off.'

He shook his head lamely, 'It's just that they've put me in charge of the whole area, mine and Hilary's.'

The name silenced them. Wendy swallowed. 'She was my friend too, you know.'

Hirsch gripped her hand tightly. 'I know.'

Dinners, picnics, the occasional film in Blyth. Not weekly, not in each other's pockets, but they'd seen Hilary Brandl socially several times a year.

Wendy said, 'How about I take a personal day? I'll drive Kate to school and come right back.'

Hirsch was about to baulk and they read that in him and glared. So he thought: why not? He was teary when he said, 'That'd be great.'

A few things unlocked inside him when he was alone. People cared. He could repay that. He should. And empty his head for a day.

It wouldn't stay empty, of course, but for just one day. After that, he wasn't expecting plain sailing. He'd have to 'train' Sergeant Brandl's replacement, for example. And would he ever feel quite safe in the Tiverton police station? There was his mother to think about. And the people who lived in his beat: their ongoing anxiety, watching a rain cloud that didn't exist.

But could he keep dealing with the shit? Babies mauled by dogs; friends impaled on stakes ...

He could switch careers. But to do what? Or serve out another twenty-five or thirty years in the police – and then what?

Would Wendy still be in his life in another twenty-five or thirty years? What if he was alone at the end? What if he went the way of his father?

Kropp came into his mind. A dinosaur, but a lucky one. Keeping active; doing something that gave him pleasure and earned money. Many male police weren't so lucky. After years of hard grind, danger and being overlooked, they were given a plaque at an awkward, boozy goodbye and that was it. They were on their own. Mentally and physically diminished suddenly. Left exposed without the authority of the uniform, the badge, the gun, the cuffs – the role they'd had all through their working lives. And if they were with a wife or partner, was the love still there? Did she live in daily fear of coming home one day to find him swinging from a rope? Spread out on the carpet next to a throw-down pistol pocketed during a raid one day and kept hidden ever since, just in case?

More likely the drinking, the need to control, the flashbacks and the hair-trigger moods would have driven her away years earlier.

Hirsch didn't want to be the cop who couldn't put up his hand and say, 'I don't feel right.' The one who cracked one day and punched some dickhead too hard. The lonely single guy who comforted himself with a trauma dog.

Trauma cat? Hirsch tried to cast Cynthia in that role – if she outlived his mother. That damn cat did seem to like him. He laughed harshly. It was good to laugh, even if it was black all the way through.

When Wendy returned from the school run, they hugged, swapped Hilary Brandl stories over coffee, tried to read, pottered about with chores and sought the comfort of each other's arms again. Said plenty. Left plenty unsaid, but acknowledged. The tenderness and intimacy they'd always shared was less carefree this time, as if they both realised you needed to hold on to the things that mattered in a life ruled by chance and accident.

Hirsch remarked at one point, 'I need to see how Jean and Tim are doing.'

'Sure.'

He called them one by one. They'd each taken a mental-health day, too, leaving the Redruth station in the hands of a pair of junior detectives from Webb's squad. Both were tearful, still in shock, with an overlay of anger in Landy and bewildered distress in Medlin.

'But what about you?' Landy said.

'Still reeling,' Hirsch said. He paused. 'Take as much time as you need.'

Meanwhile Kate would have to be picked up from after-school tennis practice, and Hirsch and Wendy felt cooped-up anyway, so they drove aimlessly for a couple of hours after lunch, through a landscape strange to their eyes. No less drought-stricken, but drought-stricken after the death of an indomitable someone they'd both loved. Over to the Clare valley, where the vines, the little old towns and Martindale Hall baked in the sun, and finally back around to the tennis courts in Redruth.

Hirsch stayed another night. And in his office late the next morning, with memories of the past two days surging through him as he tried to clear his desk before taking over in Redruth, a call came in on the station's landline.

Rosie Llewellyn, out and about with one of her old cameras, had just found a burnt-out Land Rover half-buried near the top of End Point Road.

52

When she told him where she was calling from, he was astonished. 'You've got a signal?'

'Sat phone.'

Hirsch said sourly, 'Been trying to get one of those for years.'

'I'd be lost without mine.'

'Rosie, that's Stanyer land. Don't trespass.'

'I'm not. I'm across from them, in the nature reserve.'

Hirsch reached down to get his Glock from the bottom drawer. 'It'll take me an hour to reach you.'

'I'll be here.' She paused. 'I'm betting you know whose Land Rover it is?'

'An older model? Two doors, canopy top, dent in the rear bumper?'

'The canopy's all burnt up; otherwise yes, sounds like the one.'

She waited; he wasn't forthcoming. 'I checked for a body,' she said. 'Couldn't see inside it very well – full of dirt.'

'Okay.'

'Went for a walk around and found where it probably came in, but I didn't see anyone or anything.'

'Be careful, Rosie.'

She was silent. He let it build until she said, 'Thanks again for finding the caravan.'

'I'm sorry it's still in evidence.'

'What about the stuff inside it? You said my cameras and laptop are still there? I'm using an old Nikon today.'

'Sorry,' Hirsch repeated.

She was silent again. A fits-and-starts person who'd lose her temper, catch herself, calm down. 'Could've been worse, I guess,' she said now. 'They could've sold or wrecked everything.'

'True.'

Another silence before she said, 'Sorry about your boss. She was good people.'

Hirsch hated that expression. For just a moment, he hated Rosie Llewellyn.

An hour later he was turning uphill at the birthing tree, which was glowing as the sun caught it. Not the finest gumtree in the Mid North, but significant given that the area was better suited to mallee scrub – and for how long it had escaped the axe.

Engaging four-wheel drive, Hirsch began a bumpy, slewing climb up End Point Road. It was easy to understand why Mitchell Stanyer wanted it graded and widened, less easy to understand why the council would endorse that level of improvement for what was essentially a rarely used track. It wasn't as if Stanyer or his farmhands were likely to use it more than once a week. And it didn't really give access to the nature reserve either: everyone used the main entrance, back on Mischance Creek Road.

Hirsch wondered if the Stanyers were building a tourist mecca on End Point Park station. That would be right up their alley. Cabins, swimming pools. Eco-tourism. In which case they might agitate for a new entry to the Mischance Creek Nature Reserve, directly opposite their gate.

That was his sour mood speaking. There were more important and immediate questions. Assuming that Alastair Stanyer owned the Land Rover Rosie had found, he must've driven it into the creek, torched it and walked across the road to End Point Park Station. His brother's property, but had he known Mitch would be there? And what had he been after? Refuge? Money? Another set of wheels?

And when? The day of the firearms audit?

Hirsch recalled the afternoon he'd come upon Brad Ullmer helping the truckie with the puncture. Not so far from here. Ullmer said he'd been on the way home from culling feral animals. On End Point Park Station? So maybe Alastair had been seeking help from Ullmer, not his brother?

Powering up the last incline, Hirsch came to the end of the road, expecting to find graders. Instead, on his left was Rosie Llewellyn's LandCruiser; on his right, massive new padlocked gates, with a large *Warning keep out* sign for those who hadn't noticed that this was also *Private property* and that *trespassers* would be *prosecuted*.

But plenty of churned dirt on each side of the gates: an indication of heavy vehicles coming and going. He tilted his gaze, following the driveway up its slight incline to the horizon. The hint of a rooftop beyond the brow. Maybe a fine new homestead, a big new tourist development. An airline terminal, he thought sourly.

He pulled in behind the LandCruiser. The air was still and soundless, hot, a breeze carrying the odours of sun-blasted things: dirt, dead leaves, gravel, creosoted fenceposts. And a hint of something else. Diesel fuel? Too rancid for that. Sheep dip, weed spray? The wind shifted and the elusive odour was gone ... then back again.

Rosie had said he'd find her in the nature reserve, a couple of hundred metres downhill. Hirsch was approaching the fence when he caught the glint of bright new metal. He squatted. Someone had cut each of the fence wires, top to bottom, and made a rough job of reattaching. He peered at the dirt. Mostly baked hard; a hint of old tyre marks with an overlay of crawler tracks. He stood again, removed his hat, resettled it after climbing through the fence, and headed downslope, dust on his boots and grass seeds in his socks as he made for a distant patch of scrub and dead grass. Stone reefs; the tips of a couple of boulders. Soon he was side-stepping as the slope got steeper, slipping occasionally on a scree of pebbles, dirt and dead grass.

Then, skirting the scrub, he stumbled upon Rosie Llewellyn aiming a telephoto lens at the sky, a camera bag at her feet and her .22 rifle over one shoulder. Hearing him, she swung around, nodded, returned to what she was doing. Hirsch looked up: an eagle sailing on a thermal.

He was about to speak when they heard the labouring motor of a heavy vehicle. Hirsch checked uphill automatically but the road was out of view. He heard a down-shift of gears, a hiss of airbrakes. A door slamming. Arriving, not leaving, whoever it was. Another fuel-drum delivery? God knows what the driver would make of a police vehicle parked at the side of the road.

'Sorry to drag you all the way out here,' Rosie said, hoisting the camera bag over her other shoulder.

To Hirsch she looked ready for anything: the rifle, the camera with its big telephoto barrel, the equipment bag, the satellite phone in a pouch on her belt. He cocked his head, listening. The truck was on the move again, presumably driving through the gates onto End Point Park Station.

He nodded at the rifle. 'Expecting tigers?'

'Expecting tiger *snakes*, and it wouldn't be the first time.'

'Where's this creek?'

She pointed, saying, 'I followed the tracks.'

He peered at the ground. The crawler tracks again. He trailed them to a distant scar in the ground. It resolved as a short overflow channel running from a ragged, stone-lined hole about five metres wide and eight deep. It wasn't until he reached the rim that he could see the shape of a Land Rover.

It had gone in nose first, then presumably been set alight – or caught fire. At some later time, it seemed, dirt had been scraped over it. That would explain the crawler tracks: a grader blade. If it was an attempt to conceal the Land Rover, it had failed: the dirt had been settling ever since, flowing into the footwells and cabin of the Land Rover itself and down into the hidden corners of the hole, leaving the rear third of the old vehicle visible again. Scorch marks; burnt soft-top scraps. And the rear plate had been removed. No residual smoke or heat; no odour: it had been there a while.

Hirsch had no idea where to find the VIN on an old Land Rover, but three facts about this vehicle were compelling: very few examples like it existed in the Mid North, the dented bumper was familiar, and Mitchell Stanyer owned the property on the other side of the road.

There seemed no point being coy with Rosie. 'I think it belongs to Al Stanyer.'

'I think so, too,' she said, giving him a nothing-gets-past-me look.

'You know him?'

'Met him a couple of times over the years. Sad bugger. But his brother, God. He bought two photos from last year's exhibition and had the nerve to haggle over the price. At the opening. In front of everyone.' She looked back up to the top of the slope, then at the Land Rover. 'This is how the gentry get rid of their rubbish, is it? Just dump it? In a nature reserve?'

Hirsch recalled what his mother had said: it's all about geography. The fact that Alastair Stanyer had come here. The fact that the Nordrums had been killed nearby. This wasn't a case of dumping an unwanted vehicle. Why would Alastair remove the plates? Why seek help from a brother who'd scorned him to begin with? Like Rosie Llewellyn, he glanced back up the hill and then down at the wreck again. Calculating, eyeing the stones and rocks that might provide him with footholds when he searched the old wreck, and had just turned to say, 'I'll have a closer look, just in case,' when he saw that she'd aimed her camera at him.

He placed a hand over his face. 'Jesus, Rosie, please don't.'

She shrugged and laughed. 'You looked very outback-cop just then.'

'Rosie ...'

'Okay, okay. We're after a body, right? I did look. I suppose he could be right at the bottom, under the grille ...' She was looking into the little chasm again.

And searching it will be someone else's responsibility, Hirsch thought. 'He could also be in a shallow grave.'

Rosie opened her mouth. Shut it with a click. Opened it again to say, 'Oh.'

'Fresh, mounded dirt,' Hirsch said, just as a rifle shot cracked somewhere above them.

Then again, and twice more: four evenly spaced shots.

53

Hirsch ducked, grabbed Llewellyn by the wrist and began tugging her upslope to the patch of mallee scrub. She didn't resist, and when they were crouched behind gnarled trunks and a sparse mesh of twigs and leaves, she whispered, 'Was he shooting at us?'

'Our tyres, I think.'

Two on each vehicle, rendering the spare tyres pointless.

Hirsch, squatting with his service pistol, was pretty sure what had happened. The truckie had told someone on End Point Park about the police vehicle at the front gate.

Rosie was panting hoarsely beside him. Thumping her chest, she said, 'Asthma.' He saw her twist awkwardly, lower one shoulder, shrug herself free of the rifle strap and pat a pocket for her inhaler. Then that done, she settled the butt of the rifle into her shoulder and aimed uphill.

'Rosie ...'

'You want to die out here?'

'Let's just ... Give me your phone.'

She frowned: she'd forgotten it. 'Call backup?' she

wheezed, unclipping it from her belt pouch. 'Always wanted to say that.'

Hirsch plucked it neatly out of her hands. 'Let me.'

He called Webb, keeping it brief, his voice low, all of his other senses concentrating on the road above, listening for the twanging of fence wires, the thud of boots, the ratcheting of a rifle bolt. He gave their location, Rosie's presence, the burnt-out Land Rover, the fact of the fissure's proximity to the Stanyer property.

The senior sergeant seemed to absorb everything quickly. 'I'll get a Star team organised and head up there myself. Could be a couple of hours.'

Hirsch didn't say that he and Rosie didn't have a couple of hours, maybe not even a couple of minutes, and he needed to apprise and direct Webb, just in case. Speaking rapidly, he said, 'I think Alastair Stanyer's dead because he was a weak link. I think Brad Ullmer's the one hunting us. And I think the Nordrums were killed because they stumbled across something Mitchell Stanyer's up to.'

'Keep your heads down. I'll see if I can rustle up a helicopter. *What was that?*'

A rifle shot, snapped off a metre from Hirsch's right ear. Leaves whipped about; a severed twig flicked away.

'*Jesus, Rosie.*'

She ignored him and removed the butt from her shoulder. 'Got him.'

'Call you back,' Hirsch told Webb. Brushing against Llewellyn's shoulder, he said, 'Where?'

She parted a couple of scraggly branches. 'There.'

A man lay in the dirt uphill of the mallee clump. On one hip, chin sagging onto his chest. One hand propping himself upright, the other wrapped across his stomach. Then he tilted his head as if to howl at the sky.

Brad Ullmer.

He drooped again. Rosie made to get to her feet. Hirsch grabbed her. 'Keep low. Watch and listen. Come in on his blind side.'

'But he dropped his rifle.' She pointed to a spot behind Ullmer.

'He could have a handgun. He could be faking it. He could have friends.'

They approached quietly, one eye on Ullmer, the other on the road above, but Ullmer heard them. He started hunting around frantically for his rifle and even reached for it, before the struggle for breath overcame him. He sagged, stretching out along the ground in an exhausted slide.

Hirsch came in behind him. Stopped with his foot on the rifle. 'Brad?'

A weak, creaky voice. 'What?'

'Any other weapons?'

Ullmer lifted his head again. Fixed on Rosie Llewellyn. 'You shot me.'

'Sure did,' she said, lifting her .22 back up to her shoulder.

Hirsch said warningly, 'Rosie.'

Her face was defiant. 'Don't trust him.'

Ullmer flopped again. 'You gut-shot me.'

Hirsch scooped up the rifle. '*Brad*. Any other weapons?'

A long wait. 'Pocket knife.'

'Toss it away.'

Ullmer tried to prop himself upright again; reached blindly for a back pocket but the action defeated him. 'Can't.'

Hirsch watching him, called Webb again and explained. 'We need an air ambulance.'

'How bad?'

'Stomach. With a twenty-two.'

Webb would know the significance. Better a little .22 slug in your guts than close-range shotgun pellets or a rampaging heavy-calibre bullet. Even so, Ullmer might still die – just not so quickly. The .22 was probably still inside him and, if he was lucky, it hadn't torn his insides apart. Worst-case scenario: internal bleeding if the aorta or vena cava had been hit. Or bladder leakage, leading to peritonitis. And no medical assistance before it was too late.

'Is he alone?' Webb asked.

Hirsch glanced uphill again. 'There's at least one other,' he said, explaining about the truck.

'Stay where you are. We'll be there as soon as we can.'

And then Webb was gone. Hirsch pocketed the phone and stepped closer to Ullmer, who lifted his head, flopped again and curled up in the dirt, saying, 'It's a bad one.'

'I've asked for an air ambulance.'

'Won't do any good,' panted Ullmer. 'I've been shooting all my life. You get to know how it goes.'

'Save your breath,' Hirsch said, ready to run uphill and grab the first-aid kit from the HiLux. Then remembered: Trent McRae had nicked it. He edged around so that his body shaded Ullmer's face.

Then when Ullmer said, 'If I die, I'm not going down for everything,' Hirsch felt the old familiar shift to cool professionalism. Forget grief, sadness, pity, hope, doubt and all the other messy emotions of everyday life: he was a cop. He made sure his bodycam was working and, for good measure, set his phone to record.

Time, date, location, the names of those present, then the first question. 'Did you and Al Stanyer shoot Rodney Culleton in the Northern Territory ten years ago?'

A blurred, 'Yes.'

'Steal his firearms?'

'Yes.'

'Did Al keep Mr Culleton's twenty-two target pistol?'

'Yes.'

'Did you both murder Mr and Mrs Nordrum?'

'Yes.'

'Staged everything?'

'Yes.'

'Why not bury Mrs Nordrum?'

'No time,' panted Ullmer. 'Ground too hard and Al knew of this cave thing in the creek.'

'We found your blood on the collar of their dog ...'

Ullmer frowned, as if trying to remember. 'It had a go at me when I shot the woman. It was okay with Alastair.'

'Did you hide and burn his Land Rover?'

'No. He did that. Fucked it up, no surprise.' A moment of weak panting. 'I tried towing it out but it's wedged in so I bulldozed dirt over it.'

'Half-arsed job,' Hirsch said. 'Where is he?'

Ullmer rolled onto his back and flung an arm over his head, effectively pointing uphill to End Point Park Station. Hacking a phlegmy laugh, he said, 'You'll need hazmat gear.'

'What do you mean?'

Ullmer hacked again but it might not have been laughter.

'Did you kill him?'

The words emerged full of effort. 'Mitch.'

'Who went up through New South Wales using his phone and credit card?'

'Mitch asked me to do that.'

'Did detectives come doorknocking recently?'

A faint nod. 'The boss fobbed them off.'

'How involved was Mrs Stanyer?'

'Don't know what she knew or did,' Ullmer said and it brought on weak coughing.

Hirsch waited; switched gears. 'Why did you shoot Mr Culleton?'

'His guns. Plus, he was a dickhead.'

'Why the Nordrums?'

'Poked their noses in.'

'Into what?'

But Ullmer closed his eyes, rolled onto his side again and jack-knifed weakly a couple of times as if to ease his burning stomach. Blood seeped and he said, 'God it hurts.' He lifted his head to Rosie Llewellyn. 'Only a twenty-two?' he added, as if impressed.

'Yes,' she said, but there was no conceit in her now.

'Did the job,' Ullmer told her, and he fell into unconsciousness.

54

Whether or not Ullmer should be moved was a moot point: he was being scorched by the sun, they all were, so Hirsch and Llewellyn carried him gingerly back into the patchy shelter of the scrub and Rosie rigged up further shade using a snap-open reflector and a small tarp from her camera gear.

As she worked, distress started to well up in her. What had she done? Why hadn't she fired a warning shot? What would happen to her?

Hirsch clasped each of her hands for emphasis, then stroked her thumbs with his. 'He was going to kill us.'

'You don't know that.'

'You heard him confess to other murders.'

'Yes, but—'

'He shot out our tyres. So we couldn't get away.'

'What if he was just going to take us prisoner?'

'Rosie, he's a hunter by profession. He shoots to kill. Look, you saved our lives. I'll make sure everyone knows that. You won't get into any trouble from the law.'

She was halfway convinced.

He squeezed her hands a final time. 'And there could be others up there, waiting. Asking themselves where he is. Wondering about that last shot.' He put his face close to hers. 'Do you understand?'

She jerked away in alarm. 'We just wait for them to come?'

'I go to *them*, Rosie – do you understand?'

He saw her work it out. She slumped, all of her energy evaporating as she said, 'Be quick.'

'I will.'

Waving irritably at a fly she said, 'Leave me my rifle.'

'Of course.'

She shuffled closer to Ullmer, who was conscious again, sweaty, pale, his eyes flickering. Reaching into her camera bag for a water bottle, she dribbled a tiny stream into his mouth. 'I used to be a nurse, believe it or not. Probably shouldn't give him water, but just a little, in the circumstances …'

'I know. Enough to keep him comfortable. I'll need your phone.'

She was about to quibble when Hirsch said, 'My mobile won't work here and the police radio's probably been wrecked. I need to keep in touch with my boss.'

She looked downhill, as if planning a way out.

'But here's my mobile,' he said. 'You might be able to hold on to one or two bars, even send a text. And if he starts talking, even babbling, I need you to record it.'

Rosie took the phone from his hand as if it were unclean. 'I could never do your job.'

Hirsch grabbed Ullmer's hunting rifle and trotted uphill to the HiLux and the LandCruiser. Sure enough, two tyres had been shot out on each vehicle and the police comms smashed. He swigged from the water bottle stowed in the HiLux's centre console then started to run at a half-crouch through the End Point Park gates, which now stood open. Up the driveway to the top of the low rise, intending to drop to his belly and survey whatever lay on the other side.

But there stood Mitchell Stanyer. In the middle of the track, clutching his pump-action shotgun. Swivelling his eyes ahead, then behind, as if wondering where Ullmer might be, wondering if he should go look, wondering what that last rifle shot had meant. He recovered when he spotted Hirsch. Gaped and brought the barrel up, but fired too soon. The recoil smacked into his shoulder. He staggered; a stray pellet plucked Hirsch's arm. He lifted the barrel again, saw that Hirsch had a bead on him and simply turned and ran clumsily downhill in his grazier's boots.

Hirsch sprinted after him. Skidded and ducked when Stanyer swung the shotgun around and fired. This time the pellets kicked up dust at Hirsch's feet, driving him off the track and into the shelter of a couple of empty fuel drums.

He chanced a look. Stanyer had reached a camouflage-painted implement shed and was grabbing at the driver's door of his Range Rover, which was parked there with Ullmer's twin-cab and a few mustering bikes. Hirsch fired the rifle; couldn't tell if he'd hit anything. Stanyer fired back, a raucous clatter of pellets against the drums.

Hirsch hugged the dirt. What next? Shoot out the tyres Ullmer-style?

He'd lost his chance. Stanyer accelerated violently out of

the shed, the Range Rover clipping a support pole before wheeling away, bumping over the uneven ground, deeper onto the property.

A fairly big place, forty thousand hectares, plenty of back ways out.

But the truck he'd heard earlier must still be around – along with its driver. Hirsch waited for several long minutes, scanning, fixing everything in his mind.

First, no freshly erected homestead buildings, tennis courts, swimming pools, tourist cabins or airstrips here. Just a churned-up yard and an implement shed with an attached lean-to in the foreground. Living quarters?

Beyond the yard and the shed was a rutted track leading to a row of long, low dirt humps, too regular in shape to be natural. At the far end of them, a few hundred metres away, was a cluster of camouflage-painted shapes: grader, excavator and bobcat. Closer to, a huge mound of tyres on a broad acre of charred earth. Another dozen or so empty fuel drums scattered here and there, all of them too bent or buckled for reuse.

But Hirsch was more interested in a white Isuzu truck, and the man who was sliding the tines of a forklift into its tray to pick up a heap of bundled tyres.

He was wearing earmuffs and facing away from Hirsch, who now made a fast, crouching run towards the shed, first pausing at a Portaloo next to an almost depleted pile of last winter's firewood. Setting Ullmer's rifle down – it was too awkward – he seized a small mallee log and tossed it onto the lean-to roof. Waited.

No one came charging out, guns blazing.

He slipped across to the door of the lean-to, turned the handle, and went in at a hard, fast crouch, leading with his Glock. It was empty. Only a slow roil of sweaty, overheated air.

He began a quick search, one ear open for a change of engine beat at the tyre dump, the tip of his pistol continuing its jerky probe of the interior. Eventually he relaxed. The monastic army cot was no source of danger. The narrow, chipped wood-veneer wardrobe, the armchair aimed at a small TV/DVD combo sitting on a milk crate, the sink and tap in one corner. An ashtray swimming in pinched roll-your-owns.

Business letters and hunting magazines addressed to Ullmer at his Tiverton address.

He checked the wardrobe. Two shirts, two pairs of jeans, a full hazmat suit and respirator. A few drawers for underwear, T-shirts and shorts.

But two rifles stood upright in one corner, behind the hanging clothes. And in a shoebox on the bottom, weighed down by a pair of steel-toed boots, was a .22 Browning target pistol and shells.

Hirsch cursed. He'd left his phone with Rosie and the satellite phone didn't have a camera.

Executive decision: wrapping his hands in two of Ullmer's T-shirts, he bundled the firearms together and hid them in the woodheap.

Too much time had passed. He called Webb and filled her in.

'Ullmer's dead?'

'Close to it.'

'Calling up Stanyer's details now ...'

Hirsch heard a keyboard rattle and then Webb was back. 'Black Range Rover, got it. We'll put out a bulletin.'

'He's got a shotgun.'

'Noted. Is he likely to go home?'

Hirsch tried to find an answer. He didn't know if Mitch, or his wife, or both of them were the brains behind everything. 'Couldn't hurt to look.'

'These guns you found ...'

'I hid them, just in case. I think the pistol could be the one stolen from the Culleton kid.'

'Leave your prints?'

'No.'

'Photographed in situ?'

'Couldn't, sorry.'

'Not to worry. This truck driver ... Is he a threat?'

'Remains to be seen, and there could be others working here who I haven't spotted yet.'

'Go carefully, for God's sake – but preserve what you can.'

'Boss.'

Hirsch rested his cheek against the door jamb and scanned the yard. Still empty. He ducked out and around into the shed. Ullmer's ute was unlocked. No keys; probably in Ullmer's pocket. Hirsch opened the bonnet and yanked out a few wires anyway.

Now for the man with the forklift.

Hirsch watched him from the corner of the shed briefly,

waiting for an opportunity. When he saw the driver dismount, shake his head and start tugging at a jammed tyre bale on the tray of the Isuzu, he streaked across the yard, grabbed the man by one arm, spun him around and clapped one cuff around a grimy wrist, the other onto the tie-down rail running the length of the tray.

'What the fuck?'

It was Shane Arnold, the truckie with the flat tyre. 'What'd I do?' he asked, yanking off the earmuffs with his free hand.

'I am arresting you on suspicion of the illegal dumping of rubbish,' Hirsch said, going on to recite the official caution.

'What? *What?* Me?'

'Tyres this time?'

Arnold was still trying to make sense of the situation. 'What?'

'Tyres, industrial waste ...' Hirsch said.

Arnold began to recover. 'Look,' he said, the voice of reason. 'All I do is deliver. Sometimes here, sometimes other places. Depends. Not my concern what's on board, I just go where I'm told. I deliver.'

'You're babbling, Mr Arnold,' Hirsch said. 'Last time I saw you, you were carrying empty drums. What was in them?'

'Like I said—'

'It's the same every time? You empty them here, then drive them back to be refilled?'

Arnold said nothing.

'I assumed you were delivering diesel fuel,' Hirsch said. 'More fool me.'

Arnold looked as if he wanted to snigger. 'Yeah.'

Hirsch eyed the heaped tyres. They ranged in size from wheelbarrow to tractor, and all were worn, some shredded down to the steel bands. They were bundled together and bound with heavy-duty nylon rope. In his old life, Hirsch had worked on an investigation into tyre-dumping cowboys in Adelaide. He knew that a bale of old tyres could weigh up to a tonne, and he estimated that he was looking at several thousand tyres in this heap.

'When are you going to set light to it? After a few more trips?'

A shrug. 'I just deliver.'

'You drive for Thrupp Transport?'

'Yeah, so?'

'Do you know Clarissa Stanyer?'

'Nup.'

'She's a Thrupp. You've never seen her here?'

'No place for women.'

'How about Alastair Stanyer? Ever seen him here?'

'Who's that?'

'What about Brad Ullmer?'

Arnold shuffled his feet. 'He's here whenever there's a delivery. Look, it's not like it's every day. Maybe once or twice a month.'

'The drums, Shane. What do they contain?'

'I just drive.'

Hirsch glanced at the long line of dirt heaps. 'You tip everything into a pit and when it's full, the dirt gets bulldozed over it?'

'Well, sure. This is a certified dump.'

'Yes mate, you tell yourself that,' Hirsch said, wandering across for a closer look at the piled tyres. Probably sourced from tyre dealers who wanted to avoid the high cost of an accredited recycler. Better to pay a man like Mitchell Stanyer three bucks per tyre than a recycler ten, or whatever the price was now.

Stanyer didn't recycle, of course. He stockpiled, and when the pile grew large enough, he put a match to it. Hirsch could see small clumps of unburnt rubber in the scorched area. Steel bands. Brass inflation valves.

He returned to Arnold. 'I'm going to have a squiz at the rest of the place. Are you alone?'

'Boss's around somewhere. And Brad.'

'Brad's dead, I think – and the boss just took off when your back was turned.'

Arnold screwed up his face. This had got beyond him. 'What's going on?'

'A big criminal enterprise, that's what, so when the time comes, and they drag you into an interview room, I suggest you don't hold back.'

Arnold struggled, looked at the sky. 'I'm boiling out here.'

Hirsch took him into the shade of the shed, manacled him to a post, gave him water from Brad Ullmer's lean-to, then went searching.

He checked a handful of empty drums first. Fuel drums, originally, but liquid-waste containers by the time Shane Arnold and his fellow drivers were carting them to End Point Park. Grease-trap waste, chemicals, pesticides, used cooking oil from take-away shops ... Legal dumping at legitimate waste-disposal sites was expensive, and Hirsch knew it was getting harder for the cowboys to dump industrial waste down drains and sewers.

Meaning that one way to get rich quickly was to set up a business, charge companies large sums for the 'environmentally safe' disposal of their waste, then bury or burn it in some out-of-the-way place – such as a disused, isolated sheep station three hours north of Adelaide.

He walked a long distance past the line of dirt-capped dumps and came to an open trench at the end. He peered in; a rising stink seared his nasal membranes. Acetylene gas cylinders and pesticide drums bobbed around in a pool of greasy liquid, mostly black; swirling with reds and purples. A toxic soup. And tumbled here and there around the rim, still waiting for the grader to tidy up, airbag detonators, chips of asbestos and split bags of hospital waste, spilling syringes, tissue samples and bloodied gauze.

His breath caught; his eyes watered. He stepped back and shaded his eyes to gaze deeper onto the property. More dirt heaps in the distance, grass struggling to grow on them. Clearly the dumping had been going on for years. He began coughing; he had to get out. He ran back to the lean-to shelter, where he washed out his eyes and mouth, spat, gargled and tried to rid his lungs of every bit of foetid air.

Then, taking a cleansing breath – which brought on another burst of coughing – he called Webb.

'You'll need hazmat suits and respirators. You'll need months. Years.'

*

Finally, he joined Rosie Llewellyn. She'd covered Ullmer's face.

She got to her feet immediately. Looking hollowed out, she waved her telephoto lens at him. 'I need to be alone for a while.'

'Okay.'

'Just for a while.'

'I'll be here.'

'It's safe?'

'It's safe.'

When she was gone, trudging forlornly downhill, Hirsch put a forefinger to Ullmer's neck. Nothing. Placed his ear to his mouth. Nothing.

He moved a few metres away and sat looking out, trying to put the bits and pieces together. Ullmer changing Arnold's tyre that day: he hadn't been passing through after a culling session, he'd been working his other job, accepting deliveries at the toxic dump. Only natural that Arnold would call him when he punctured a tyre on his way out. And Rosie Llewellyn's photo of the Isuzu delivery truck: taken a couple of years ago, she said; but it looked like the dumping had been going on for much longer than that. And Clarissa Stanyer's family history: her transport-magnate father. Either Mitch had wooed her for her contacts and fleet of trucks, or she'd always known what he was up to and was happy to oblige.

But one day a couple of gemstone fossickers had appeared, setting up camp next door on Mischance Creek Nature Reserve. Perhaps they'd strolled along the fissure and wondered what lay beyond it. Perhaps they'd strayed up End Point Road and grown curious about the stink, or the coming and going of trucks. Walked in on Brad Ullmer and Mitchell Stanyer.

Had they been caught and forcibly taken back to their camp, or followed back after being seen? Were they interrogated? That might explain Ben Nordrum's head injuries, and Heather, running for her life, being shot in the back.

Why not simply sink their bodies in the foetid sludge – that, presumably, was Alastair Stanyer's last resting place. They probably figured it would be better to present a plausible accident narrative than one with too many suspicious elements. If both Nordrums had disappeared off the face of the earth, police interest would have been more intense.

And so, according to this narrative, one Nordrum died tragically in a fall and the other, deeply distressed, not thinking straight, had expired somewhere out in country where few people ever trod.

Except that the daughter hadn't been satisfied with the search effort and had come looking. Had found her mother's bones. And those bones had told another story.

Bella, the dog, had also led the way to a story that didn't fit the cover-up narrative.

When had Alastair Stanyer been roped in? Hirsch tried to reconcile this new scenario with what he knew about the guy. Overlooked, derided, short on friends and luck. More confident in his younger days, though – even a champion shooter. He'd become friends with another shooter;

they'd gone on hunting trips together. And Ullmer was a much harder man. Hirsch visualised that 2016 hunting trip, Ullmer and Alastair stumbling across another shooter – a kid, maybe a bit cocky, bragging about his expensive guns. Perhaps they were drinking around a campfire and the kid's attitude had got too much and Ullmer had snapped. No one around …

The years passed and that murder weighed on Alastair. Depression, insomnia. Drinking, gambling losses, bailed out by his brother. Unloved, unreliable, a liability.

Then, a few years later, he's caught up in murder again. No random impulse this time – the Nordrums could have put them all in jail – and Alastair was enlisted to help dispose of the bodies, and maybe even in the killings. But he can't bear to get rid of the dog.

More years go by and Alastair might have remained sad, reclusive and self-effacing, a man whose presence went discounted by everyone, if not for the Rodney Culleton case being highlighted on Channel 9's *Nowhere to Hide*. It set him off: guilt, fear. Perhaps he'd been following the show for a while anyway, waiting for them to cover 'his' murder.

And shortly afterwards, the local plod paid a visit. An innocent visit, except that Alastair had carelessly left .22 cartridges in the dirt. Fired from a gun he stole from a man he'd helped murder.

He'd gone running to Ullmer – or his brother – hiding his Land Rover first. Hadn't got much of a welcome. A bullet instead, probably. Then his phone and credit card had gone travelling. That last bit had involved two layers of deception:

a sleight of hand that appeared to show Mitchell had been duped, even as the police were duped.

Had Mitchell Stanyer deceived his wife, too?

Now blades were chopping at the sky above Hirsch and Rosie was joining him and they stepped out, semaphoring the air ambulance – and the police chopper, hard on its heels.

55

'If I were sergeant,' said Hirsch that Sunday, 'I'd get my underlings to do this.'

Wendy Street patted his knee. 'You've got me.'

Then she glanced into her rear-view mirror. 'You okay back there?'

From his seat next to Wendy, Hirsch also checked on the passenger in the back, craning around to peer between the seats. If Rosie Llewellyn felt as tossed about in the little Golf as he did, she wasn't showing it. Head down, she was absorbed in scrolling through the photos stored in her old Nikon. He saw her reach out a hand and absent-mindedly shove a second-hand tyre away from her shoulder.

Hirsch turned to face the front again. 'She's fine.'

It was mid-afternoon and Wendy was transporting them to retrieve his HiLux and Rosie's LandCruiser. Most of Friday and Saturday had been taken up with interviews and debriefs, but Hirsch had found time to phone around and secure a tyre and rim for the HiLux from Redruth Tyre

Service and one for the LandCruiser from Sammo's Motors.

With the help of Mrs Sampson, who'd asked him anxiously, 'Will he ... Is he ...?'

'No parole,' Hirsch assured her. 'Your husband's going away for a good few years.'

The car shuddered. Wendy slowed, clutching the steering wheel for dear life. 'Godfather, as my old dad used to say.'

They'd struck a patch of heavy corrugations and the little car protested and Hirsch placed his hands on the dash. Welcome to my world, he thought.

'Much further?'

'Not long now,' he told her. They'd passed the Mischance Creek ruins and the birthing tree was in the distance. Dust seeped through the door seals.

Wendy shot him a look. 'Maybe the illustrious Mr Sampson didn't sell me such a good car after all.'

'Designed for autobahns,' Hirsch said.

She decelerated: Auntie Steph, Uncle Doug and half-a-dozen other elders were working at the base of the birthing tree. 'Want to say hello?'

'Sure,' Hirsch said.

Waiting for Wendy to pull into a patch of shade cast by the old tree, Hirsch got out, stepping into the hot day. He ambled past a couple of sedans parked at the side of the road, slipped through the fence and raised an arm in greeting. 'Come on, put your backs into it!'

Steph Ingram said, 'Yeah, well, some people get to ride around in air-conditioned luxury while others work for the greater good.'

She peered past him, recognised Wendy and Rosie, waved. Returning to Hirsch, she asked, 'Where you off to?' Jerked her head at End Point Road. 'Up there?'

'You heard what happened on Friday?'

'All over the news.'

'My car's still there,' Hirsch said. 'So's Rosie's.'

'Word of warning: just saw a TV van turn in.'

'Okay, thanks,' Hirsch said, glancing at a scattering of pine posts, boards, shovels, fencing wire and strainers in the dirt. 'Putting up an enclosure?'

'We are, plus a bloody great sign explaining the significance.'

Hirsch grinned. 'With the mayor's approval, and funding from the council?'

She grinned back at him. 'What'll happen to her?'

He shrugged. 'In terms of the toxic dump or council mismanagement?'

'Both.'

It wouldn't hurt to tell her. 'She's claiming she knew nothing about any rubbish dumping. Her husband had been fooling her for years, using her transport company, getting council approval to improve the road, so on and so forth.'

'Uh huh.'

'Exactly. And she knew nothing about the deaths of the Nordrums, or Alastair – shocked that we'd think she was involved. Didn't think her husband was involved either. Might be a rogue, but not a killer.'

Auntie Steph swiped the sweat from her forehead, removed her hat, combed her fingers through damp hair, replaced the hat. Behind her, some desultory digging continued and Wendy gave a polite little toot of her horn. Hirsch turned to go.

Steph said, 'You might want to check every dam, old gold digging and industrial incinerator her highness has access to.'

He stopped, interested. 'You think she did away with Mitch?'

'Wouldn't put it past her.'

'I'll consider it,' Hirsch said, as Uncle Doug ambled up to say hello.

'Just the man,' Hirsch said. He took out his phone, swiped through his stored photos and showed Doug the screen. 'Recognise him?'

Doug glanced down, said, 'Yeah,' and with a quick, shy, apologetic look at Ingram, added, 'The one who put the hard word on me to get Steph to change her mind about this here tree.'

Brad Ullmer.

When Hirsch was back in the Golf, Rosie said, 'Think they'd let me take a few snaps?'

A woman who recovers quickly, he thought. 'Ask them when you leave.'

The little car laboured up End Point Road and, halfway along, came to a Channel 9 outside-broadcast van canted at an angle and spinning its tyres in powdery dirt.

Hirsch got out. 'You guys get around,' he said, recognising the driver, reporter and videographer.

'So do you. Why are you here today?'

Hirsch raised a forestalling hand. 'Retrieving my wheels, nothing more. No statement at this time.'

'That's what you've been saying all along.'

'Don't make it worse,' Hirsch said, pointing at their tyres, axle-deep in dirt. 'I'll be back to tow you out.'

'Buy you a drink after?'

'Busy,' Hirsch said.

He got into the Golf again and they continued to flog it to the end of End Point Road where the LandCruiser and HiLux stood abandoned. After Friday's hectic activity, the place simply looked bleak and deserted, an effect reinforced by crime-scene tape flapping in the hot wind and two big signs, one hammered into the ground, the other wired to one of the gates: *Hazardous Chemicals Do Not Enter.*

Meanwhile, the opposite fence had been peeled back again to give access to the last resting place of Alastair Stanyer's Land Rover. Another sign: *Crime Scene Do Not Enter.*

They jacked up Rosie's LandCruiser. Knocking on wood for luck, they manoeuvred the Sammo's Motors replacement wheel into position. It fitted. The original spare to follow, then it was the HiLux's turn. Hot, sweaty work. The sun reached higher above them; eagles floated; the wind shifted and Wendy gagged. 'Gah! What a stink.'

Hirsch had described it to her on Friday night: the tyre dump, the buried waste, the still-open trench. 'Pity the people who have to clean it up,' he said now. 'They reckon it could take months.'

Rosie was listening. Hirsch could almost hear her thinking: rural life in all of its aspects.

And then a buzzing sound above their heads: the Channel 9 van had sent up a drone. Hirsch was dressed in off-duty gear, dammit: no Glock strapped to his waist. Rosie, on his wavelength, said, 'Wish I had my twenty-two with me.'

Time passed, Hirsch splitting his time and responsibilities between Tiverton and Redruth, the latter without a mayor or a council after the local government minister appointed an administrator and mounted a commission of inquiry.

Then it was Christmas and Hirsch was persuaded to be the Tiverton Santa again, and he came riding up to the general store one moonlit evening on the back of a draught horse supplied by Nan Washburn. Leaned down in the saddle – almost pitching headfirst onto the asphalt – and distributed toys and lollies to the local kids: fewer kids every year. Complained of a sore backside for days afterwards.

That was his first Christmas of the year. His second was the very next day, a turkey dinner insisted upon by Kate before she and her mother headed off to spend Christmas Day with relatives, and his third was on 25 December, with his mother. The sensation of absence hit them harder than they'd expected.

Summer rolled by and, crime waves permitting, Hirsch visited his mother every couple of weeks, driving his newish personal car, a Forester better suited than his old Nissan to the treacheries of unsealed roads. They talked, ate at the pub, sometimes watched the news together, and one weekend learned that through the efforts of drone-mounted ground-penetrating radar, metal detectors and test excavations, thirty-two distinct waste burial sites had been found on End Point Park Station. Learned, on another occasion, that forty-four thousand acetylene cylinders had been dug up.

Later still they learned that Alastair Stanyer and his dog had been found, their remains strained out of the gunk in the open trench. A two-part story: it was also revealed that Thrupp Transport had been placed into receivership and Clarissa Stanyer – nee Thrupp – was facing criminal charges and heavy fines in regard to the illegal transportation and burial of toxic waste, and the creation of an environmental hazard.

In one clip, TV cameras had caught her, flanked by lawyers, on the courthouse steps. She looked frightened and flustered, and wept a little wretchedly. Hirsch had met plenty of liars in his career. He didn't think she was lying when she said she'd not known a thing about her husband's dump, her husband's murders.

But she'd known enough not to ask too many questions. And perhaps what distressed her most had been learning that Mitchell Stanyer had been almost broke when he met her. An illegitimate waste-disposal site had been his ticket out of having to sell the acreage he'd inherited from his father.

Justice, the law and police work plodded on. Early in February, the Department of Public Prosecutions informed Hirsch that although Ty Moloney and Penny Goldfinch had pleaded guilty and would not face court, he would be called as a witness in the trials of the remaining Lone Pine members, who'd claimed sovereign citizen status. That was all he needed. As the prosecutor muttered, 'Expect a complete circus.'

Hirsch was with his mother, watching the TV news in her sitting room – recently remodelled, all of the heavy old sombre stuff donated to the Salvos – when the screen showed vision from the Philippines of a balding, bearded man trying to hide his face with a wing of his Hawaiian shirt. Mitchell Stanyer being paraded for the cameras.

Hirsch's hand floated to Cynthia's spine as he watched and listened. He stroked her and her claws dug in and, if she was ecstatic, then he was pretty happy too.

That was a Sunday evening. Not wanting to be late for the Monday briefing, Paul Hirschhausen was up at four-thirty – too early for scrambled eggs, really, but his mother insisted. His parents had never understood coffee, either. Battling sluggishness, he stopped at a strip of shops for a large double-shot latte before winding down and out of the hills.

The sun, when it appeared, rode with him all the way back to the Mid North – low, but coming in hard through the windscreen or his side window, according to the directional vagaries of the road. Down onto the plains and through the Barossa Valley and across to the Barrier Highway, listening to Emmylou Harris and Gillian Welch as the dawn shadows receded.

Finally, Redruth, where he slowed for the little hospital, the Toyota dealership and the old ANZ bank, now a closing-down-sale craft gallery, eyeing a cloud that hovered above the district. Nothing new: he'd been watching that cloud all year.

What *was* new – after he'd parked in the backyard of the police station, greeted Mr Pickett behind the front desk, entered the keycode and stepped into a greater number of rooms than he'd ever administered before, was the sign on a door.

Brevet Sergeant Paul Hirschhausen.

The time was 7.46.

About the Author

Garry Disher has published over sixty titles across multiple genres and is best known as Australia's King of Crime. He has won the Deutscher Krimi Preis four times and the Ned Kelly Award three times. In 2018 he received the Ned Kelly Lifetime Achievement Award.

garrydisher.com